WHITE NIGHTS

A VAMPIRES OF MANHATTAN NOVEL

WHITE NIGHTS

A VAMPIRES OF MANHATTAN NOVEL

A NEW BLUE BLOODS COVEN

BY MELISSA DE LA CRUZ

PART ONE | BROKEN

At the door of life, by the gate of breath,
There are worse things waiting for men than death.
— ALGERNON SWINBURNE, THE TRIUMPH OF TIME

1 | KING OF THE CASTLE

Someone was following Oliver Hazard-Perry. He knew it without needing to turn around, or even to shoot a wary glance over his shoulder. After eight months on the run, a universe away from his former life of order and luxury, his instincts had grown razor-sharp. Even at this time of the evening, close to midnight, when the sky had turned an inky velvet and the streetlights dotted sickly yellow pools on the sidewalks, Oliver had a sixth sense for menace lurking in the shadows.

Today was Tuesday, so he must be in Budapest. He'd flown in this morning, and spent a long afternoon wandering the streets on the Pest side of the river and dodging clanging trams, too wound up to pause for coffee at one of the grand old Viennese cafés. He was just trying to kill time until the arranged meeting with his contact at Fisherman's Bastion, high on Castle Hill.

The day had been warm for this early in the summer, and Oliver approached the Gothic-looking terrace out of breath and sour with sweat. His pampered old self, body swathed in linen and silk and the finest of wool, wouldn't recognize this new Oliver, gaunt and disheveled, his shirt yellow under the armpits. He hadn't taken the funicular up steep Castle Hill in case someone was on his trail. In a small, confined space like that, he would be way too easy to corner. So Oliver had chosen a hike over the three-minute ride – but all that had achieved was to freak himself out even more. There were too many looming trees and dark paths, his own footsteps echoing through the quiet evening. He'd lost so much in his life, but maybe this was the worst thing of all: Oliver realized that he'd lost his nerve.

The person he was just eight months ago, strong and confident and arrogant, had disappeared. Somewhere along the way, between the swampy stillness of the Amazon basin and the long, bleak stretches of Australia's Great Sandy Desert, between the dusty squalor of the back streets of Guatemala City and the clamor and crowds of a market in Senegal, Oliver had lost his strut and his certainty – even his health.

Now he was pretty much the textbook definition of a broken man. He was lean to the point of being haggard, and never felt rested or clean. When he caught sight of himself in a shop window, like the Prada store he'd passed today, Oliver barely recognized himself. His shoulders were hunched; his eyes looked sunken and haunted. These days, he had more in common with the down-and-outs slumped in Wenceslas Square than his former New York neighbors, the denizens of the "Power Tower," 13 Central Park West. He would never make it past the doorman.

When night fell, the spires of Fisherman's Bastion looked like an eerie miniature castle, tree branches casting spidery shadows onto its pale stone. Through the arches, Oliver could glimpse the cathedral on the other side of the river, lit up and sparkling. The old Oliver would have paused to take it all in. The new Oliver had to keep moving, looping back around the Church of St Matthias. Past the late-night lovers, the rowdy stag party, the tourists taking pictures of the Chain Bridge, far, far below. Wherever he went, he knew that someone was following, someone was looking for him. Someone who wanted to kill him, or at least stop him in his tracks.

Because he was looking for someone as well, and something told him he was getting close.

Once upon a time, Oliver had been the most powerful vampire in the world. Last summer, he was Regent of the Coven in New York City, on top of the world – almost literally, living the high life in his sprawling luxury penthouse. He'd had a valet to dress him, a chef to cook for him, a chauffeur to drive him. Back then nothing was too expensive or too exclusive for Oliver. It made him laugh now, just thinking of it – a bitter laugh, all he could manage these days. In New York he'd had to go to the gym and swim laps in the Power Tower's pool to keep in shape. Now he was clambering up hills and trekking across deserts, dirty and hungry, with nobody there to hand him a plush robe or massage his aching shoulders.

How art the mighty fallen.

In that old life, Oliver had overseen ten years of peace and prosperity for the Coven, and his reward, he used to think, was the view he awoke to every morning. Not just the grand stretch of park far below his floor-to-ceiling windows, but the beautiful woman in his bed. Seraphina Chase, the love of his life, his human familiar, his mortal beloved.

Finn, lost and gone forever.

After eight long months apart, the thought of her still made him ache. In his heart and, even now, his groin. His fangs responded as well, sharp with desire for the soft white skin of her neck, and he bent his head, avoiding the gaze of a middle-aged couple strolling by the golden walls of the church. Not that they could see anything; his fangs were as well-hidden as ever. He just didn't want them gawping at him, and seeing how desperate he was. How mad he was with desire, and longing, and fear, and regret.

Oliver wove through a drunken group of young men, shouting and singing their way to another bar, and merged into a straggly tour of Haunted Budapest, gazing up at the giant bronze statue of King Stephen: anything to throw off whoever was following him. The drunk guys weren't that much younger than him – maybe five years? They acted as though they didn't have a care in the world. Oliver envied them.

One of the drunk guys had no pants on, and was dressed in a pink apron, cartoonish lipstick kisses smeared on his cheeks. The prospective groom, Oliver thought, getting tormented and toasted by his buddies before the big day. He and Finn had never had a big day. He'd thought they were happy enough as they were, and that a wedding wasn't necessary. Not for a vampire and his human familiar: that wasn't the way things were done in their world. They had a deeper bond, a blood bond. She was much closer to him than a wife could ever be.

But that was the problem. While he thought that their ten years together were physical and emotional bliss, Finn was thinking something else. He'd discovered, dangerously late, that she wasn't content with being his consort. Finn had grown tired of living life in a gilded cage, tired of being Oliver's *possession*. That was the accusation she'd flung at him, that last terrible night. She'd felt owned and used. She wanted much, much more than Oliver could give her.

She knew that Oliver was a mortal who'd become a vampire. Why couldn't Finn do the same thing? She wanted her own shot at immortality, whatever the price.

Too high a price, Oliver thought, bile rising in his throat. Their perfect life destroyed and god knows what manner of hell unleashed in the world.

The church bells began to chime, startling everyone on the tour so much they burst out laughing. Oliver didn't laugh. At long last it was midnight, and the person he was here to meet should be in place. Third arch from the left, smoking. Of course, it could be a trap, like the meeting in Senegal where Oliver had to run for his life. He'd only managed to escape by clinging to the back of a moving truck loaded with squawking chickens, obscured by a choking cloud of dust.

So now he'd play it safe, hanging around with the tour group, who were all gazing up at King Stephen's spindly green horse. Even bronze statues looked sinister at this time of night. But maybe everything looked sinister to Oliver now that he knew that Finn was one of Lucifer's army, her pure soul tainted. The sweetest girl in the world had been corrupted by Lucifer's silver poison. The fate she'd chosen. No longer a beautiful mortal but a beautiful demon.

If you come after me, I will destroy you.

That was the threat she'd made. Oliver thought of it every day. It wasn't that he didn't believe her, but surely she realized that he *had* to come after her. She was the love of his life. He had to find her and win her back, before she was lost forever in the dark world of demons.

And what did a threat like that mean, anyway, when Oliver was already destroyed? He'd lost everything: his stewardship of the Coven, his reputation, the woman he loved. At this very moment Venators, the Coven's own secret police, were on his trail, with orders to bring him back to New York. Oliver still had enough contacts to know what was said about him, that he was a loose cannon, in way over his head. He needed to leave this job to the professionals, because he was just a pampered rich boy, a has-been figurehead who should be drowning his sorrows with cocktails at the Four Seasons, while the Venators got on with the down-and-dirty business of tracking and capturing the wild beast Finn had become.

It wasn't only Venators Oliver had to worry about. To the Nephilim, those half-human demons unleashed like mercenaries by the Silver Bloods to fight their dirty wars, Oliver Hazard-Perry was still the Most Wanted vampire in the whole world – even in this pathetic, ragged state. Not only was he the fallen Regis of the Coven: Oliver was the one-time familiar to no less than Schuyler Van Alen – daughter of Gabrielle, The Uncorrupted, the Virtuous, the Messenger, Archangel of the Light. He knew exactly what the Silver Bloods must be thinking. Capture Oliver, and his old friend Schuyler would be forced to come to his rescue, along with her husband, Jack Force – better known in the vampire world as Abbadon, Angel of Destruction. The Silver Bloods and their sadistic Nephalim flunkeys were itching for another violent show-down. After more than ten years of peace, it turned out that the order of the world was only an illusion. Oliver and his allies had only won the battle, not the war.

That was the talk now, and Oliver heard it everywhere he went –

every continent, every city, every dive bar, every train station. His old
status, and his allegiance with Schuyler and Jack, meant he still had
contacts willing to pass on information. The sympathetic ones told him
to keep his head down, to keep moving and running and hiding. The
more hard-boiled told him to hand himself over to the Venators for his
own safety. Go back to New York and lick your wounds, they said. Let
Mimi Force – Azrael, Angel of Death, and the Coven's all-powerful
new Regent – find a way to suppress this latest resurgence of Nephalim
activity. Let Mimi and her husband Kingsley Martin, the new Venator
chief, locate Finn and reel her in.

Yeah, right.

Mimi and Kingsley were thousands of miles away in New York, as
out of touch as he used to be himself. Oliver was on the ground in
Europe, getting closer and closer: he knew it instinctively, felt it in his
gut and in his fangs. He and Finn had spent ten years together, bonded by blood and sex and love. Dazed by the seductive poison running
through her veins, he'd drunk her dry. He was the one who'd killed her,
only to see her reborn as a vampire herself.

Oliver was the one who'd driven her to the dark side, so he was the
one who needed to win her back. Nobody else could do this. He and
Finn had way too much unfinished business for him to just step away,
hands in the air, and admit defeat. This was his fault, and his problem
to fix.

His Finn to save.

The tour group was moving on. Oliver dawdled at its fringes, casting
furtive glances at the elegant arches of the Bastion. A man leaned in
the third arch, the amber glow of his lit cigarette like a tiny beacon.

Oliver took a few steps towards him. The wind wafting up from the
river brought with it the smells of an over-heated city: grease from
vending carts, the fumes of cars down below on the bridge. The metallic tang of blood spilled in a street fight, a bar brawl, a traffic collision.

Another few steps and he could make out the face of the man waiting for him. He wore jeans and a dark T-shirt, and his narrow face was

shaded with stubble. Oliver didn't recognize him, but something about the man's posture and expression reminded him of a wolf. The wolves had been good to him, especially when he was out of money and needed to get out of Africa in a hurry.

He took another step closer, and the wolf backed into the shadows, until he was leaning against the stone balustrade. Behind him, on the other side of the river, the city glittered, its yellow lights reflected in the calm waters of the Danube.

"Is she here?" Oliver asked, his voice croaky. He hadn't said a word to anyone all day.

"Too late." The wolf stubbed out his cigarette on the pale stone. "We tracked her to Vienna. Tomorrow, at the café in the Hotel Sacher … Uh!"

The wolf's mouth hung open and he stared with grim surprise at Oliver for one strange, terrifying moment. Then he slumped to the ground, a glinting blade embedded in his back.

Oliver's breath stuck in his throat. He started running, his heart pounding so hard he couldn't hear anything, not even the sound of his own footsteps hitting the cobbled streets of Castle Hill. He ran as fast as he could, trying to disappear into the darkness of the old city, his body braced for the sharp hit of a blade.

2 | HAPPY HOLIDAYS

*T*uesday was the quiet day of the week for bars and restaurants in New York, and it seemed to be the quiet day of the week for Venators as well. Every day was a quiet day for Venators at the moment.

Holiday, the Venators' dive of choice in the East Village, was no exception.

Edon Marrok signaled the barman: he wanted another frothy stein of beer. Why not? It was a warm night, and there was nothing going on that required him to be super-alert. May as well slump on a bar stool, nibble on chips and some sloppy salsa, and try not to obsess over the news coming out of Europe. His brother Mac, based in Vienna, was pretty jumpy at the moment. Come to New York, Edon liked to tell him. We got a new Venator chief, and a new Regent, and everything's just as peaceful as can be.

Edon closed his eyes, trying to block out the flashing Christmas lights strung across the ceiling. The peace and quiet in the New York vampire world should be a good thing, pure and simple. It meant the Nephilim hive they destroyed wasn't re-forming elsewhere in the city. In fact, nobody had heard a peep from the Nephilim for a long, long time. The War had been won more than a decade ago, and the Coven was still officially in its post-War state, somewhere between order and paranoia.

That crazy stuff with the dead girls and the pentagrams from last year was over and done with. The even crazier stuff with Sam Lennox, the traitorous old Venator boss, was over as well. Sam was dead and he, Edon, lone wolf in this particular pack, was still alive.

Edon Marrok and Araminta Scott, the A Team. Out on the town from midnight every day of the week, keeping the streets safe from renegade vampires and demons with the wrong ideas. The fiercest wolf and the most kick-ass Venator, together forever. Well, together as long as Ara put up with him. She was the most dedicated and hardworking Venator he'd ever met, but she was possibly the most halfhearted girl-friend. She wouldn't let him even say the word.

Lover – maybe that was the term Ara would prefer, although love wasn't really her thing. Too scared, too wary, too hurt in the past. Sam Lennox had really done a number on Ara. Used her, betrayed her – betrayed them all. But Ara was the one who felt it the most, and Ara was the one who killed him. When you had personal demons like that, you didn't need real demons stalking the streets to mess up your life. Work might be quiet, but Ara had a lot of dark stuff to work through. Every day might feel like Tuesday to Edon right now, but he knew that for Ara it was New Year's Eve and July 4th all rolled up together, every single night of the week. She was on a knife-edge, and there wasn't a damn thing he could do about it.

"Hey, wolf." It was Ara, back from the bathroom, sliding onto the stool next to his. She looked spikier and grubbier than usual, as though it was already the end of a long week rather than eight PM on a Tuesday. "Buy a girl a beer, why don't you?"

"One more, then we'll go home, OK?" By home Edon meant his place. It wasn't much, but at least he didn't live in squalor. Quiet times at work might mean a Venator had some time to spend more time at home, do some housework, get around to some chores. But Edon suspected that Ara wasn't spending her downtime laundering sheets or defrosting the fridge in her own apartment. She certainly wasn't spending time washing her clothes, because he'd seen the same crusty sauce smears on her droopy black sweater last week, and the week before. The only thing she seemed able to take care of was her short white-blonde hair, shaved to fluff like a baby bird at the back.

"I should go back to my place tonight," she told him, avoiding his gaze. "I need some sleep."

"You'll have about three hours to sleep," he pointed out. Their next shift started at midnight. They should have left Holiday already.

"This'll help," Ara said, raising her beer stein.

"Maybe." Sitting here drinking would just make tonight's shift a long one, as well as a dull one. Sometimes Edon longed for a whiff of a Nephilim, just to break up the monotony of the night. Why Kinsgley, the new Venator chief, insisted on him sticking around in New York when Europe was about to kick off, Edon didn't know. He'd rather be back in the Underworld than kicking his heels around here.

"Buy me another beer and that'll help even more," said Ara, and there was something tight and dangerous in her voice, something that made Edon wary. He leaned close to her, one hand on her thigh, and felt her tense up.

"What's up?" he murmured, so close to her that his lips brushed her soft skin.

"Nothing. Go home. You don't need to babysit me."

"I didn't think I was babysitting you. I thought I was taking my girl out for a drink ..."

"Your *girl*? How about your colleague, your partner, your fellow fighter?" Ara sounded indignant. Angry, even. Edon sighed. It was going to be one of those nights.

"OK – my respected co-worker and demon slayer. My *angel*."

"Too late." Ara glugged down the last of her beer. She wasn't looking angelic tonight, trying to scowl away her beauty. "Wow. I thought you were a wolf, but really you're a caveman."

"Nice." Edon raised his glass to hers, but Ara wasn't in the mood for toasts. "OK. I guess I'll be going. See you at mid–"

"Hey!" Ara had swiveled in her seat. She was glaring out into the bar, and Edon followed her gaze. Two booths of Venators, off-duty but pretty low-key, chatting and drinking. Trading work gossip from Orpheus Tower, their soaring HQ downtown, probably, unwinding after the day shift. Too many vampires for his liking, but nothing to get worked up about.

But Ara was definitely worked up.

"If you want to stare at him so badly, why don't you come over here?" It took Edon a second to grasp that Ara wasn't talking to him. She was addressing another Venator, sitting in a nearby booth. Deming Chen, the sexiest demon chaser of them all. Damn. Nothing good happened with Ming and Ara got in the same room together.

"What is your problem?" Deming asked, screwing up her beautiful face as though she'd just smelled something really bad. "I have no designs on your wolf, sister."

Ara was off the stool and striding towards Deming before Edon could grab her. There was way too much bad blood between these two.

"I see the way you look at him." Ara was looming over Deming now, hands on hips. "I know your game. *Sister*."

Deming spluttered with laughter. The bar was getting quiet now, everyone listening. Holiday was run by a witch, and at any given time the place felt like the Coven's common room. A lot of the customers in here tonight knew Ming and Ara, and they knew all that Ara once slept with their disgraced boss Sam Lennox – twin brother of Ted Lennox, Ming's lost bondmate. However bad a guy Sam turned out to be, Ming always saw him as the bondmate of her own twin sister, Dehua, another war casualty. Ara was the Venator who screwed Sam – and killed him.

"Ara!" Edon was off his stool now as well. This was not a fight she needed to pick. Some wounds would never heal with time.

"Hey," Deming said, the picture of poise, gazing up at lanky Ara with narrowed almond eyes. "Let's not fight over guys, OK? Even hot wolves."

"Who you slept with once." Ara was fuming. The room was practically silent, everyone intent on the office melodrama unfolding before them.

"Sure," said Deming with the most nonchalant of shrugs. "We had a fling, during the War. When we were fighting the War – oh, but I guess you wouldn't understand. You weren't fighting."

Edon grabbed one of Ara's lean, muscular arms and pulled her close.

"Come on, angel," he whispered in her ear. "Time to hustle."

Ara may have been too young to fight in the war, but he'd seen with his own eyes the way she could fight now. He'd been trying to handcuff Sam Lennox when Ara had leapt in, slicing Sam's head off with her crescent blades.

"Just keep your distance, bitch," Ara told Deming, squirming in Edon's grip. Deming smirked.

"Don't worry," she said, her voice low and measured. "I have no designs on your wolf – anymore. Unlike you, I'd never sleep with one of the team – or my boss."

With her free arm Ara swung for Deming, smashing the entire booth's beer steins to the floor. Edon had to brace himself on the bar's sticky floor to keep hold of her; Ara was flailing and jolting like a wildcat. Ming was standing up on the table now, ready to kick her would-be assailant in the face with a very small pointy boot. Some of the Venators scattered, but others were trying to help, from what Edon could work out, pulling Ara away. He managed to get her outside onto the warm street at last – everything intact except her dignity.

"Get off me," she spat at him, shaking his hand free at last.

"Ara," he pleaded. "You have to get a grip. Since you …"

"Since I what? Too scared to say it?"

"OK. Since you killed Lennox, you've been – let's say difficult. You did the right thing – everyone thinks so. So why act as though the world's against you? You have to get your act together. Stop picking fights and trying to sabotage your career. Your *life*."

Our life, he wanted to say, but that kind of personal talk was too hard, especially with Ara glaring at him.

"Lecture over?" she demanded, but he didn't reply. His phone was buzzing. Kingsley.

News traveled fast in the vampire world. They were both summoned to an urgent meeting with the chief, at midnight on the dot.

Kingsley Martin – the Angel Araquiel, Duke of Hell – did not appear happy. Dressed in the Venator's head-to-toe black, his thick hair the color of black ink, unsmiling, Kingsley looked like a dark storm waiting to crash on their heads.

Ara and Edon sat in the hounds-tooth upholstered chairs Kingsley had introduced as part of the re-fit of the chief's office when he took over the job. He'd said he wanted it to look more less like a call center in New Jersey and more like a gentleman's club on Gramercy Park.

Right now, as far as Edon could tell, all it looked like was bad news.

"Araminta," Kingsley said, his voice weary. "Picking a fight with another Venator in a public place. Really?"

Ara said nothing. She hung her head, though Edon could see the look on her face was sullen, not repentant.

"Chief, it won't happen again," Edon told him, and Kingsley managed a grim smile.

"Exactly what you said last time."

"It's just – we're not busy enough, I guess. We're like soldiers sitting around base camp, waiting for orders to go into battle."

"You have a job to do," Kingsley said, dry and unsmiling again. "You're working for the Coven, not the army. You're supposed to be out there on the streets neutralizing demons and sniffing out Silverbloods. Not drinking and scrapping with each other about your … sex lives."

Kingsley raised an eyebrow and Edon felt as though he was a teenager dragged into the principal's office. This was no life for a wolf. He nudged Ara and her head jerked up.

"Sorry, Chief, it won't happen again," she said in one breathless rush. Kingsley sighed and picked up a red folder on the desk in front of him.

"It certainly won't," he said. "You're not wrong, Marrok – there's not enough happening here right now to justify keeping you on our team. You're needed elsewhere, urgently. I have details of your new commission here."

Edon felt a mixture of relief and excitement – and then the anxiety hit. What about Ara? They were a team in more ways than one. And on good days, they were a very good team indeed.

"Who's my new partner?" Ara sounded suspicious, just the way she had when her last partner, Rowena, got a promotion and she was saddled with Edon. She'd looked at him with utter disdain. Back then, to her he was just a battle-scarred wolf well past his prime. Maybe he was.

Kingsley frowned at her and dropped the red folder on the desk.

"Ara, I'm sorry, but until I can trust you to keep your temper in check and focus your mind on the job, you need to step aside."

"What do you mean, step aside?" Ara looked aghast. Edon's stomach thudded.

"You're on forced leave," Kingsley told her. "Take a vacation. Clean your place, clean your clothes, go to the movies. Go to the beach. It's summer, or so I hear. Let's talk again in a month and see how you're feeling. How *we're* feeling."

"But Chief ..." Ara began, reeling out excuses and promises, desperate to keep her job. Edon knew none of it would persuade Kingsley. This was the lord of the underworld sitting on the other side of the desk: he'd heard it all. Whatever bleating Ara and Edon did would have no effect on his decision whatsoever.

"I'm afraid I'll need your gun," Kingsley said, and Ara blanched. Edon felt the crude punch of the statement, and knew how hard Ara would take it. She said nothing – just stood to unbuckle her holster, slapping it onto the Chief's desk. Her gun and its silver bullets, known as demon killers for obvious reasons, lay there, but Kingsley had the courtesy and sense not to grab it away.

"The blades?" she asked at last in a tight, tense voice. Edon frowned. Surely Kingsley wouldn't take her crescent blades as well? The Nephilim didn't know that Ara was on "vacation" and might attack or ambush her at any time.

"You can keep them – for now." Kingsley looked stern. "For self-defense only, OK? I don't want to hear about you slashing your way through Holiday or cutting up some hipster who annoys you on the L train."

Ara nodded. She looked almost meek now. Defeated. Edon couldn't stand to see her this way.

Kingsley nodded to the door. The meeting was over. Ara was out, and Edon was being sent away somewhere else, whether they liked it or not.

Whether they loved each other or not.

3 | UP IN FLAMES

When Schuyler saw the first tendrils of smoke rising from the vines, she knew – at once and instinctively – that this was not a safe place anymore. She called for Jack, who was in the kitchen, fixing up the scuffmarks on the skirting boards. If they were going to sell this place, it needed to look pristine.

Jack dropped the paint brushes he was rinsing and walked out onto the patio, dusting his hands on his spattered overalls. The line of smoke was long now, a fuzzy gray string across their hillside, a flicker of red just visible.

"Is Mike burning off some of the dead vines?" Schuyler asked him, her voice tentative: she knew before Jack shook his head that this was too simple and answer.

Jack fumbled in his pocket for his iPhone.

"Fire department," he said in a firm, clear voice, and Schuyler's heart sank. Mike, the latest in a string of indifferent caretakers, was away this week on annual leave. This might be a wildfire, but probably not: rain had fallen for the past three days, and the valley was too lush, the ground too muddy, to serve as tinder. And this wasn't their first suspicious fire here. The storehouse had been burned to the ground a month ago.

"Mama!" Lily bounded up, her blue eyes wide with fear. "There's a circle of fire around us. Sy says it isn't, but it is! I saw it from up in the tree."

"It's just down there, Lil," Schuyler told her daughter, ruffling the shiny black hair that was a mirror-image of her own. She was trying to sound more confident than she felt. "A brushfire. Nothing to worry about. Where's Sy?"

"In the tree," Lily said, her voice suspiciously casual, and wriggled away. This meant, Schuyler suspected, that Lily had left Sy stuck in the tree. Halfway up the tree, no doubt, because he wasn't as daring or physically strong as his sister. Sy and Lily, Simiel and Lelahel, were twins, but they were nothing like Jack and his twin, Mimi Force – the current incarnations of Abbadon and Azrael, the underworld's greatest power couple. Sy had inherited some of Schuyler's all-too-human weaknesses. Lily, on her typical high-speed setting, was always leaving him behind.

"Pack up some things," Jack murmured to Schuyler, and she gripped his arm, unable to speak. They should have left here months ago, she knew.

For almost a decade she and Jack had found sanctuary here in Napa Valley, in the white stucco house with big windows that gazed out over their terraced vineyards and the twisting road that wound up their very own hillside. As a young woman Schuyler had led the Coven to Paradise, and this was her own version of it – and Jack's as well. Building their own vineyard and wine business, building their own little family.

Hiding their true natures from the world, in the hopes that the world would leave them alone.

But everything had changed eight months ago, even before Oliver turned up on a cold, starless night, an emotional wreck, telling them how he needed to clear his name and regain control of the Coven. Schuyler was only a half-blood, but her subconscious remained one of her most potent supernatural tools. For more than a week she'd dreamed of the pentagrams appearing across New York City, and the dead girls left to taunt the Venators there. Something ugly was clouding her dreams, even on the clearest and sunniest of days.

Back then, Edon Marrok had persuaded them to stay put in Napa and let the wolves sniff out the truth of the pentagram murders, and he'd been right: he and his Venator partner had done good work. But still, Schuyler and Jack had been uneasy, and even before Oliver knocked on the door with his terrible story they'd begun their preparations to return to New York – and to return to the fight. Lucifer's forces weren't defeated: they'd just been lying low.

But nothing had gone to plan. They'd sent Sy and Lily away to what they thought was safety deep in the Oregon woods, but Sy had fallen ill, dangerously ill, with pneumonia, and Jack and Schuyler brought them both home to nurse Sy through his long recuperation. The manager of the vineyard left abruptly, and disease rippled through the vines, ruining the harvest and making the place impossible to sell. Another caretaker came and went, then another and another. Nobody wanted to work for them; nobody wanted to buy the vineyard. Their haven seemed like a cursed place. This fire – which took six hours to extinguish, by which time most of the orderly ranks of vines were reduced to ashy stubble, and everything in the house reeked of smoke – was the latest blow.

That night, when the last fire trucks had pulled away, the children were asleep, and Jack and Schuyler were slumped on the sofa, surrounded by stacks of boxes and hastily packed suitcases, they agreed it was time to leave.

"We'll have to take the kids to New York," Jack told her, filling her wine glass with some of last year's vintage. Schuyler took a sip: even the wine tasted of smoke. "My sister's place. I know it sounds crazy, but they'll be safer there than anywhere in the world. Mimi's on it."

"I wish you'd talked to me before you discussed this with Mimi." Schuyler knew she sounded petulant, but sometimes it still got to her. She may be the love of Jack's life – this life, anyway – but Mimi was his bond-mate for eternity. Mimi probably hadn't mentioned a word of this new plan to Kingsley, her husband, either. The Force twins were used to running the world their way.

"We didn't need to talk," Jack said. His handsome face looked tired, smudgy with ash. Schuyler felt like a fool. Of course he and Mimi didn't need to talk on the phone like normal people: they shared a telepathic connection.

"Things are just getting worse and worse," she said, half to herself.

"Oliver's unleashed something … I don't know. Something really terrible." Jack swirled dark red wine in his glass and frowned into its garnet depths.

"It's not necessarily Ollie …" she began.

"Oliver's a wild card and you know it," Jack snapped, with a flash of his old temper. Over the past couple of months they'd had this conversation too many times. According to Jack, and probably to Mimi, Oliver was unbalanced and that made him a danger to himself and a danger to the Coven. He needed to keep out the way of the Venators, not zoom around the world getting into fights and risking kidnap – or something worse.

"You know what he's trying to do – and why," she said, trying to keep her voice even. Eight months ago, Jack had been with her, one hundred per cent, on this. He was the one who said they needed to start selling up, to start making plans.

"It's how he's doing it that's the problem." Jack was still glowering into his glass. "Acting like the king of the Coven, refusing to follow advice. I'm tired of clearing up his mess. We have enough to deal with ourselves."

"So you think we should just abandon him?" Schuyler was incredulous. "Jack, we *promised* we would help."

"I know you're sending him money," he said, giving her a long, hard look.

"Of course I am! I'm not making a secret of it." Unlike Jack's plans with Mimi, she wanted to mutter.

"What I'm saying is, maybe if you stopped financing his Lonely Planet tour, he'd be forced to come home and stop putting himself, and us, and everyone else we know and love in danger."

There was no way Schuyler could abandon Oliver, and Jack had to know that. Oliver had been her one and only human familiar, her lover as well as her closest friend. Now there was no one closer to her than Jack, of course – the love of her life, the father of her children.

But her deepest loyalties would always lie with Oliver. He'd given her up, despite his affection and loyalty to her, because he knew that she and Jack were true soul mates. Now she had to give something up for him – the peaceful, stable existence she and Jack had enjoyed for much of the past decade. Dark spirits were spreading through the world again, and putting the entire Coven and its hard-won victory at risk. Oliver was out there, trying to solve the problem he'd helped to create.

Finn. Schuyler's half-sister. The woman who chose immortality no matter how high the price.

To Schuyler, Oliver was family. Finn was family. Any mess they were in was Schuyler's mess as well. Unlike Jack, she had no past lives. She had to fix all her problems in this one.

"So, when are we taking the kids to New York?" she asked, trying to sound blithe rather than bitter. Mimi had never liked her. Never. Nothing Schuyler did would ever change Mimi's mind.

"Tomorrow," Jack said. He put down his glass on a lumpy cardboard box and reached for her hand. "We have to get out of here tomorrow, Schuyler. Before the Silver Bloods come for us in this house. You and I can fight, but the twins can't. Not yet."

"I know," she said, glad of Jack's reassuring hand. "I know."

Jack was right, damn him. The twins needed protection. And who better to offer it than Mimi Force, Regent of the Coven, and twin Angel of the Apocalypse?

4 | JUMPING SOMEONE ELSE'S TRAIN

*T*he report of a gun awoke Oliver, jerking his body into life. He was on his feet, heart thumping, before he realized the sound wasn't a gun shot after all. It was a rap on the window. A guard was striding along the platform, walking the length of the train, making sure passengers didn't miss the stop.

The first train of the day from Budapest had arrived in Vienna.

The carriage was almost empty, apart from an elderly couple packing away their breakfast things into a canvas shopping bag, and a man wrangling his bicycle by the far door. Oliver swung down onto the platform and felt the fresh hit of morning air against his face. Though his eyes were still gummy from sleep, he could make out the time on the station clock: nine AM.

He'd spent much of the night awake, walking the streets of Budapest, waiting as long as he could before going to the train station. Yesterday he'd left his battered duffel in a locker, and this morning he had just enough time to retrieve it and buy a one-way ticket to Vienna from a machine. The contents of his duffel were just as he'd left them: some dirty clothes, and a fat envelope of creased euros, traded for his dinars in a black-market currency exchange in Algiers.

Oliver was strictly a cash economy these days, reliant on Schuyler sending money, via shady intermediaries, to collection offices on various continents. It was too risky for him to use a credit card or go near an ATM, so instead he made irregular pick-ups of cash – to eat, to travel, to bribe someone. Sometimes Oliver could see the dark humor in being one mugging away from destitution. It wasn't just a world away from his old life of luxury and power: it was a surreal and dangerous parallel universe, this place he inhabited now. No wonder he was a nervous wreck.

After a night of pacing the streets, Oliver had fallen asleep on the train, his duffel clutched to his chest like a pillow and the envelope of euros wedged low under his shirt – just where his worn leather belt hit his now-sunken belly. It had been a short and fitful sleep, and Oliver felt strung-out as ever.

He walked fast, glancing around in the jittery, hyper-alert manner that had become second nature to him. Once again he stowed his bag in a locker, slipping the envelope of cash among the dusty pile of once-crisp Brooks Brothers shirts and taking just enough notes to get him through another day. Then he had a quick coffee, standing up at a high table outside a station kiosk, pigeons pecking around his feet. He needed a caffeine boost, or some kind of quick hit to give him energy and resolve. Every day was a fresh hell.

Like so many times these past few months, Oliver had only the vaguest idea of what was facing him in this new place. He'd come to Vienna, as instructed by the wolf who now lay dead – maybe in a Budapest morgue, maybe still on the ground of the Fisherman's Bastion, where he'd been felled. Whoever threw the blade had been stationed below them, on Castle Hill. Maybe they were on their way up and decided not to wait a moment longer, determined to stop the wolf before he passed on too much information. Nephalim or Venator? It didn't matter much to Oliver anymore. Everyone was after him. Everyone was against him.

The sight of the wolf's stricken face – animated when the blade hit him, stunned and frozen a moment later – was the clearest thing in Oliver's mind right now. He tipped two sachets of sugar into his bitter coffee, trying to get rid of the tang in his mouth. He'd seen plenty of deaths and plenty of killings, but every week they grew harder to deal with, harder to forget. It was sickening, physically and emotionally. Death followed him around, or maybe it wasn't following: he was the one ushering it in, bringing havoc and loss and unhappiness wherever he turned up. Because of his own hubris, Oliver had turned Finn into a monster. One way or another, she had to be found and stopped, and this endless trail of blood and betrayal had to end.

Wednesday. Vienna. The café at the Hotel Sacher. This was all Oliver knew. It was all his informant had managed to utter before he'd been dispatched with that lethal blade. No other word on what was going to happen, exactly, at this place.

An enclosed space like a café wasn't a typical location for a rendez-vous with an informant. So maybe the wolf wasn't directing Oliver there, where he could be spotted, captured, or worse. Perhaps he was about to tell Oliver that Finn would be there, if he wanted to lurk somewhere close by and follow her. That blade in the wolf's back must mean that Oliver was getting close – didn't it?

It was a fine morning, the sky blue and cloudless. Oliver slipped off his jacket and carried it, grateful for the warm breeze ruffling his hair. These were his only pleasures in life now – small, simple things like a warm breeze, a comfortable chair, a sip of cold water. His old life of champagne and caviar seemed decadent and dream-like, a mirage. The old Oliver would have strolled the streets of Vienna admiring its handsome buildings, its stiff grandeur, its gorgeous store windows; the old Oliver would have gazed approvingly at its elegant citizens, driving past in their BMWs or Audis, or walking by in designer sunglasses and chic outfits. Vienna was a Blue Blood town, he knew, sophisticated and moneyed. Once upon a time, he would have felt completely at home there.

Now Oliver was a ghost haunting its streets, immune to its charms.

He followed the path he'd memorized from the city map in the station. The Hotel Sacher was opposite the Opera House, he'd learned, one of the city's most famous baroque landmarks, and he didn't need a tour guide to find it. Halfway down the avenue he could see its dark red awnings shading the sidewalk seats, and when he slowed his steps to pass it, he could glimpse a plush red-and-gilt interior with marble-topped tables, its waitresses in white frilled aprons. Stately, picturesque, old-fashioned – just like the city itself. A tourist attraction. Definitely not the place a gaunt scruff like Oliver would blend into the background, and definitely not the place to meet an otherworldly informant.

Oliver stepped into the hotel's wood-paneled lobby, similarly over-decorated with red and gold, looking for any potential suspects: Venator, wolf, demon. Some businessmen, speaking loud German, were checking in; an elderly lady, pristine in a white Chanel suit, sat reading a newspaper. A concierge caught his eye and nodded, smiling, though Oliver could see the wariness in his eyes. In his current scruffy state, someone like Oliver didn't belong here.

Waiting outside under the portico of the opera house seemed his best bet, but the road was too broad and busy. All Oliver could see was the blur of passing trams and taxis, not people leaving and entering Café Sacher, and he felt too exposed, blinking in the sunlight and stifling yawns. Better to be inside and in danger than out of the way, oblivious to whatever was going down there today. Whatever the wolf had tried to tell him – or warn him – about.

In the café Oliver took a seat near the door, sitting at a high-backed red banquette against the wall. He could see people coming and going, and had a pretty good view of everyone in the long, narrow room.

"Your order, please?" asked the waitress, who seemed to be able to tell at a glance that Oliver wasn't a German speaker. Is that what he looked like now – a gauche, untidy tourist, with no idea of how to dress in polite society?

"Goulash, please," he said, keeping his voice low. "And bread. I'll have coffee later."

The waitress looked surprised, probably because he wasn't ordering a slice of rich chocolate cake doused in cream, like all the other tourists in here, busily taking pictures of their plates and muttering to each other about the cost. But however foreign he appeared to the waitress, in her starched cap and apron, Oliver wasn't here for the tourist experience. In the past twenty-four hours, he'd had nothing but a gobbled-down hot dog in the street in Budapest, and too many cups of strong, sweet coffee. Right now he needed sustenance.

After he'd mopped up the last dark, succulent streaks of goulash in his bowl with a hunk torn from a crisp roll, Oliver decided he felt almost human again. The phrase made him laugh: almost human. That's what he was, after all. Not an actual human, not anymore, and a pariah in the vampire world. The tourists in the next table would drop their camera and guidebook and run screaming from the café if they had the slightest idea that the young man sitting near them preferred the rich, intoxicating taste of blood to their over-priced hot chocolate.

The waitress cleared his plate and took his coffee order, returning a few minutes later with a copy of that day's *New York Times International*. Oliver smiled his thanks and flicked it open – not to read, but to obscure most of his face from other patrons. The café was busier now, the waitresses whizzing between tables. He peered over the top of the paper, careful to keep an eye on new arrivals, ignoring his cooling coffee. Maybe he'd have to sit here all day. Maybe the wolf's information was bad, or Oliver was already too late.

A gruff voice – male, American – asked for a table for two, and Oliver froze. The couple he could glimpse, just above his wall of paper, were not ordinary American tourists. A man and woman, young and athletic, both dressed in black jeans and T-shirts. Neither of them carrying cameras, or iPads, or backpacks. Neither of them smiling. That was the real giveaway, Oliver thought. American tourists usually smiled, hoping to win over the brusque waitress and get an outside table.

These weren't tourists. They were Venators.

Oliver didn't recognize either of them, but that wasn't so surprising. When he was Regis of the Coven, he used to have regular meetings with the Chief Venator, but Oliver took scant notice of the ranks of skilled fighters at his disposal. They were beneath him, those foot soldiers of the Coven, slipping about New York under cover of darkness to do his dirty work. He should have been more attentive, more observant. It would have saved him a lot of trouble now.

Another of the waitresses gestured to a small table in the middle of the room, and Oliver spied on the pair walking, in what seemed like slow motion, towards it. They were in no hurry to sit down, he noticed; they were looking around the room in a deliberate way. He raised his newspaper, aware of the now-familiar twist in his stomach when danger was near. These Venators might be here looking for him; they might be here to accost someone else. One thing was certain: they weren't here to eat cake.

There was a crash, then the sound of glasses shattering as they hit the floor. The tourists at the next table gasped, and somewhere close by a woman shrieked. Finn? Could that really be Finn? Was she sitting here in the café the whole time?

Oliver leapt to his feet, dropping the newspaper. He couldn't see Finn. All he could see was an overturned table, and people standing up, crying out in protest or flinching as chairs flew through the air. The shrieking woman appeared to be an hysterical middle-aged redhead, clutching at her children. Oliver tried to push his way through the crowd to find out what was going on. Protecting himself was all well and good, but he was here for information, not to skulk in the corner until all possible informants lay dead on the ground.

One of the hotel's security guards shoved past him, bellowing in German. Then Oliver felt a hand clamp his shoulder and he braced himself for what was coming: a punch, a blade in his back, a gun pressed into his ribs. Maybe this whole fight was a diversion, just to draw him out of his hiding place.

"Follow me," murmured a guttural voice close by, and Oliver recognized the smell rather than the sound of the voice. The earthy, feral smell of an animal, its breath like peat. A wolf.

Following wasn't easy in the crowded café, especially as Oliver wasn't the only one making for the door. Patrons were bustling out, and armed police were charging in. In the surging crowd – some of them scared, some of them clearly excited about skipping out without paying – he couldn't pick out the man who'd spoken to him. On the sidewalk outside, the sun high overhead, Oliver paused and looked around.

And there he was, inches away – a familiar face. Mac, Edon Marrok's brother. It was years since Oliver had seen him last, but there was a strong family resemblance. Green eyes, angular face, low forehead.

"Bad business," Mac said to him, gesturing with a sharp nod of the head for Oliver to follow him down the street.

"Who were the Venators after in there?" Oliver asked. He kept his head low, and matched his pace to Mac's swift steps.

"Venators? Nephilim, I expect," said Mac. "But I was talking about what happened last night."

The murdered wolf in Budapest, thought Oliver. Of course.

"He only had time to tell me to come here," said Oliver. Police cars, sirens screaming, raced by. Shopkeepers came out to see what was going on. Tourists held their phones aloft, filming the action, or at least the tops of other people's heads.

"Well, you're too late." Clearly Mac was as gruff and abrupt as his brother. "She's already moved on. North, for the summer solstice. That's what I hear."

"Finn?" Oliver couldn't say her name without his voice catching.

"Here," said Mac, not looking at Oliver. He pressed a folded piece of paper into Oliver's hand. "You'll be safe there – for a while. If any of us are safe anywhere. Get there today, if you can."

One of the police cars slowed and a door opened, though the car was still crawling along the curb.

"Today," Mac repeated, and dived into the moving police car. The door slammed behind him. Oliver stood clutching the piece of paper, watching the car speed away; it had to swerve to avoid a tram.

On the paper was an address scrawled in black ink, Oliver's next destination on his round-the-world wild demon chase. Sweden.

5 | CLEANING HOUSE

*E*don had to pack and go, right away – orders of the new Chief. It wasn't going to take him long, because wolves traveled light. In his office the desk was bare of anything but a sleek platinum computer, and that was Coven property. Edon had never felt comfortable sitting at that shiny black desk, squinting into the blue square of a screen. He was too scruffy, too feral, for a place like this.

"What have you done with all your case files?" Ben Denham, a young Venator who couldn't keep his nose out of other people's business, leaned in the door.

"Filed them," Edon replied. Most Venators got on his nerves, especially eager beavers like Denham who asked too many stupid questions. *What was it like, the final battle? What's it like to be a guardian of Time?* Wherever Edon was headed next, he hoped vampires would be thin on the ground.

He snorted at his blank screen. Fat chance. His next assignment was certain to involve supporting a Venator squad somewhere, sniffing out Nephalim. The Fallen sure needed a lot of help.

"Well, it's been great working with you," Denham prattled on. "Great to get to know – you know, a golden wolf."

Edon slouched in his seat, wondering if it would be bad form to leave some incisor-shaped puncture marks in Denham's baby face. A sort of going-away gift for his number-one fan.

"And the chief wants to see you." Denham sounded nervous. Maybe he could mind-read. "When you're ready."

Edon stood up, flashing Denham a fake grin. Nothing showed off those incisors like a smile. Denham scuttled away and Edon headed in the other direction, to Kinsgley's office. The night shift was almost over, and Edon had spent most of it taking care of paperwork, trying not to think about Ara – no doubt fuming amid the debris of her apartment, angry and hurt that she was on forced leave. Ara didn't like being forced to do anything – especially take a mental-health vacation, while Edon got to zoom off somewhere dangerous and exciting.

Kinsgley was standing at the window, watching the sun rise over the East River. For someone so important and powerful in the Coven's world, Kingsley was hardly an imposing figure: he was tall and thin rather than broad and muscular. Maybe, Edon thought, the anxieties of this job were starting to take their toll on him.

"OK to come in, Chief?"

"Sure. Shut the door." Whatever Kingsley had been dreaming about, he was all business now. "I just got confirmation on where you're going. You fly out in six hours' time. Not too short notice, I hope."

Edon shook his head. His office was emptied of unfinished business. If only he could say the same of his personal life.

"Where am I going?"

"Scandinavia. Sweden, to be precise. Intelligence says there's been Nephilim action in the club scene and a possible sighting of Finn Chase."

Edon's eyebrows shot up. So the notorious Finn Chase was in Sweden, was she? Up to no good in those long white nights up there. Their whole world disrupted by one snooty, ambitious girl who didn't even know how to fight. The opposite of Ara. Ara was worth a hundred Finn Chases, any day.

"Chief, about Ara …" he began, but Kingsley held up a hand. His eyes looked sad rather than angry, Edon realized. Kinsgley wasn't mad with Ara, just disappointed. Worried, maybe. Someone as astute as Kingsley knew the true value of a dedicated Venator like Ara.

"Ara needs a break." Kingsley leaned back in his black leather chair. "She's been too highly strung for a while now. You know it and I know it. After a month's vacation – who knows? She'll be ready for a fresh start with a new partner. I hope so, anyway."

Edon suppressed the low growl forming in his throat. A new partner. He and Ara would be separated forever. Maybe he'd been kidding himself, thinking that somehow they could keep working together, traveling the world, getting into trouble. Together.

Kingsley stood up, signaling that the meeting was over. He pulled a black leather jacket from the sleek platinum coat stand behind his desk and shrugged it on, preparing to head home to Mimi, Edon guessed. Outside a benign June morning was forming, the moon already a faded ivory circle in the haze. The traffic on the Brooklyn Bridge was heavy. Edon wondered when he'd be back at Orpheus Tower again. When he'd see Ara again.

"I trust you to take care of this nasty business in Sweden." Kinsgley flashed something between a grimace and a grin at Edon. "The Nephilim are buzzing over there, and I have a bad feeling that Finn Chase, for some messed-up and dangerous reason, may be their queen bee. And don't worry – you'll have an outstanding Venator partner to help you over there."

I had an outstanding partner here, Edon wanted to say, but he knew there was no point. There was no talking sense with the Fallen, in his experience. Give him a feral pack of wolves, acting on instinct, any day. Wolves might not look as slick as these wealthy, over-groomed vampires, with their designer clothes, glossy hair and buffed skin. But wolves were born knowing how to hunt with a pack, and how to work alone. Edon would rather work alone than get stuck with some eco-everything, bike-riding Swedish Venator. Shame that nobody ever asked him what *he* wanted.

There wasn't much to pack up at home, or the place Edon had called home, in the loosest sense of the word, since he'd been assigned here last September. It was just a dingy room in Chinatown that another wolf had recommended, much more his style than the Midtown apartment block the Coven had arranged for him. All he needed was an efficiency – a bed and a basin. He kept his stash of worn jeans, t-shirts and flannel shirts folded in an open duffel. Boots he wore summer and winter, so he had an extra pair, and getting them re-soled and stitched every year was his sole extravagance. Not a real extravagance either, not for a foot soldier like him. A necessity.

Unlike Ara in her Williamsburg pit, he liked things clean and tidy in his den. Nothing rotting in the fridge, nothing festering under the bed. He was almost obsessive about cleaning the shower and the countertop, but that was because wolves didn't like to leave traces of themselves anywhere. Ara liked to tease him about his regular Monday drop-offs at the drycleaners, where he got his bed linen, towels and clothes washed and folded. So domestic, she said. Like a well-trained office worker, she said. Really, she was the feral one, stewing in her mess of take-out boxes, rumpled sheets and greying clothes. Nobody who knew her in her past life as Minty Scott, private-school priss in a plaid skirt and embossed blazer, would even recognize her these days.

No wonder he found her so attractive.

Someone was knocking at his door. Three soft taps, as regular as code. He'd know those taps anywhere.

He opened the door to Ara, her eyes wild with exhaustion and anxiety, her short platinum hair on end. Normally she stood straight and tall, legs firmly planted in her heavy boots, a determined look on her face as though she were about to charge into battle. This Ara was a shadow of her usual self, though even off-duty she still wore the all-black uniform of the Venator.

"Angel," he said, smiling even though she looked so wrung out. "I was planning on coming over to see you on my way to the airport."

She looked so distraught, he pulled her into his arms and rocked her over the threshold. The feeling of her lean, angular body was both familiar and a thrill, like the curve of her cheekbone sawing into his face, the regular beat of her heart. How could he leave her behind? How?

"I knew they'd send you somewhere right away," she murmured, her breath hot in his ear. "They can't keep you penned up here forever, looking after me."

"You may need a housekeeper," he tried to joke, though clearly neither of them felt like laughing. Kingsley might mean well, but what did he really think Ara was going to do if she couldn't work? Sit around drinking coffee at the scruffy little bodega she liked? Summer in the Hamptons like she used to do in the old days when she was a rich East Side girl?

Retreat to her cave and sit there, in her own muck, sulking and fuming and losing all the heart and strength she needed to be a great Venator. No way was Edon going to let that happen. Something flashed into his mind: an image of a blue passport, and he pushed her away, still gripping her arms and gazing at her pale tear-stained face.

"You got a passport, right?" he asked her. He didn't know why he hadn't thought of this before.

"Of course." Ara looked confused. "I hope you're not going to tell me to go to Bermuda for a beach vacation."

"Nope." He grinned. "I was thinking of somewhere further north. Sweden."

Ara still looked confused. She narrowed her eyes at him.

"Sweden?" she said, as though it was the craziest place in the world.

"I have a … let's call it a little clean-up assignment there. So I'll be working. But you – you could have a little mental-health vacation. Why not?"

"Kingsley would go nuts," she told him, but her eyes were bright with excitement.

"Kinsgley never said you had to stay in New York," said Edon. "He never said we couldn't live together. He never said you weren't free to travel wherever you ..."

"Shut up and finish packing," Ara said. "I've got to go home and shower and do some laundry. How much time do I have?"

Edon felt like howling with delight.

"You'll just have to go dirty to Sweden, angel," he said. "You better get those blades of yours into a bank vault for safekeeping. Can't see you getting those past the TSA."

Ara sprinted out without even pausing to kiss him. Just the mention of Sweden was good for her mental health. Clearly, Dr Edon knew just the cure for her woes.

Kingsley didn't need to know a thing about this. True, keeping a secret like this from the Duke of Hell made Edon a little nervous. But right now Kingsley Martin was night-jobbing as Venator Chief in New York, rather than ruling hell as lord of the underworld. Once Edon was in Scandinavia, he was out of the Chief's jurisdiction. And Ara – well, she was just on vacation.

6 | ALL CHANGE

Whatever Mimi thought, this place was completely un-suitable for children. First, the neighborhood. In Schuyler's opinion, there were too many clubs – and their demi-monde denizens – close by. It wouldn't take long for Sy and Lily to discover the delights of dodging traffic on the West Side Highway. They'd grown up on an idyllic hillside surrounded by rows of vines and rose bushes: they weren't used to police sirens, screeching taxis and horn battles at every intersection, or to leather-studded S&M club-goers striding by, like motorcycle gangs on their way to a fashion show.

Second, the apartment was a penthouse, its only outside space a narrow terrace with a glass barrier. Sure, the view of the Hudson was spectacular, but it wasn't somewhere the kids could play, and Schuyler had nightmare visions of them scaling the barricade and free-falling over the side.

Last, and worst of all, everything in Mimi and Kinsgley's place was white. Everything. The walls, the carpet, the furniture. Only peo-ple who'd never had children themselves would think a white leath-er couch was a good idea. They didn't know the damage fluorescent marker pens, clutched by sticky chocolate fingers, could do on pristine surfaces. The glass-topped coffee table would be smudged, or possibly broken, the first week, and its sharp corners looked dangerous. Since she'd moved back to New York, Mimi had collected some beautiful pieces of art glass: these were arranged like luminous coral along a low stone ledge near the chic contemporary fireplace. One nudge from Lily, and Schuyler could just see Sy toppling into that perilous, expensive reef, shattering every piece. The whole apartment was a child-related accident waiting to happen.

"I guess the underworld was too dark for her," Schuyler murmured to Jack, who coughed to cover up his laugh. "This place is like heaven on steroids."

"What was that?" Mimi sashayed over, her mane of blonde hair thick, straight and immaculate as ever. Clearly, serving as Regent of the Coven wasn't getting in the way of her expensive grooming routine.

"We were just wondering," said Schuyler, nudging Jack to remind him to support her and not side with his twin sister, "if the twins will wreak too much havoc on this place. It's so beautiful and ... um, white."

"We can have their rooms painted any color they want," Mimi said, beaming at her. The penthouse had six bedrooms, even though Mimi and Kinsgley – when they weren't fighting – only inhabited one. Old Upper East Side habits died hard, Schuyler thought. With Mimi Force, more would always be more.

"We're just worried they'll break things and smear things," Jack said. They could hear squeals from the other end of the penthouse, where Sy and Lily were investigating bedroom options and no doubt illicitly bouncing on beds. "You might have to put some kind of throw over your couch."

Mimi made a face.

"I'll just buy new furniture. It's time for a change anyway," she said, scooping up the spikiest piece of glass from the stone ledge. "I was thinking duck-egg blue. Or maybe Tiffany blue with gold accents. A Turkish rug or two, and one of those gorgeous low sectional couches – you know, those Italian ones from Ligne Roset."

Harem chic, Schuyler wanted to mutter to Jack, but she held her tongue. Lily was shouting for Jack, no doubt to resolve some dispute over room occupation, and he wandered off to arbitrate. Something about being alone with Mimi made Schuyler feel anxious, as though she was being judged by her sister-in-law and found wanting.

In the year since Mimi's return from the underworld, she'd obviously embraced the city life of spiky heels, salon appointments and Hermes bags. Schuyler was still only a recent – and reluctant – refugee from their Napa Valley idyll. She'd loved her days spent running the twins to kindergarten, buying fresh produce at farm stands, pruning the rose bushes that studded the terraces of vines, and meeting with their architect, graphic artist, web developer, and glass supplier. She and Jack had built their own business and their own citadel, high on a perfect hill. From that peak, she now realized, the only way was down.

Mimi was bustling around in the open-plan kitchen, moving a cut-glass fruit bowl to a high shelf, apparently oblivious to the set of Japanese knives lying on an easily reached stretch of marble countertop.

"Child-proofing as we speak," she said, with a fake enthusiasm Schuyler could see right through. There'd always been tension between them, and even now they were in their 30s, teenage passions and rivalries long behind them, something still bristled in the air. Schuyler knew that to Mimi she'd always be the Half Blood who lured the Jack Force away from his true bond mate and dragged him into some dull, granola-munching, Birkenstock-wearing farm life in dreary northern California. Mimi and Jack shared exciting, dangerous past lives from which Schuyler was completely excluded. All Schuyler knew with Jack was this life, and it was a life they both loved.

A low chime sounded and Mimi peered into a small screen on the wall, then reached for a discreet silver buzzer.

"The nanny," she told Schuyler. "She'll be taking the children to school every day and picking them up. She's a Venator's sister and fully trained to defend them from any danger – human or demon."

"So I heard," said Schuyler. Really, did Mimi think that Jack told his own wife nothing?

"Ben Denham's younger sister – do you know him?" Mimi straightened the sleek folds of her form-fitting wrap dress. "Kingsley thinks he's very promising. A little too keen, maybe, but that's better than being a slacker, I suppose."

"I've never met a Venator who was a slacker," Schuyler said, but Mimi didn't reply. The elevator that opened into the living room dinged, and out stepped a young woman who looked anything but ready to defend Sy and Lily from all danger. She was slim to the point of fragility, her dark hair soft and wispy, and her brown eyes wide and staring from a pale face. One leap from Lily would bowl her over, thought Schuyler. Of all the vampire nannies in the world, this was the one Mimi and Kingsley found? Schuyler had been expecting someone tougher, sturdier and possibly not dressed in a floaty floral top and white capri pants.

"Hi, I'm Catherine Denham," the young woman said, smiling at Schuyler.

"Schuyler Van Alen." She held out her hand, and Catherine giggled.

"Oh, I know who you are! It's such an honor to meet you. When I was growing up, me and my friends all wanted to be Schuyler Van Alen."

"Really?" Schuyler wasn't buying this. Sure, she'd proven herself as a fighter and leader during the war. But Blue Bloods tended to stick with their own.

"Don't be fooled by her sweet demeanor," Mimi called from the kitchen, where she was peering into the stainless steel fridge. Probably discovering she only had French champagne rather than the Tropicana orange juice Schuyler had mentioned the twins liked. "Catherine knows how to fight with blades."

"Fists, swords, blades, guns." Catherine smiled at Schuyler and gave a little shrug, maybe intended to be charming or reassuring. "Only if necessary, of course. A specialist in Nephilim. The Venators taught me everything I know."

"Great." Schuyler tried to smile back. This was the woman to whom she had to entrust the safety of her children, every morning and every afternoon. The woman who had to be utterly vigilant and prepared, ready for demons leaping out of the shadows, ready for silver bullets flying through the air. Was it wrong to wish for, say, someone a little taller and sturdier?

"Jack! Catherine Denham is here!" Mimi shouted in a theatrically loud voice. This penthouse was large, but you would have thought, Schuyler mused, Mimi was calling across the West Side Highway. "Remember? The nanny."

Lily and Sy came running out ahead of Jack, tumbling like puppies. Schuyler's heart skipped a beat seeing their happy faces. They had no idea that this stay in New York was anything more than a fun adventure. She'd miss them so much – their dark heads, nestled together when they cuddled up to her; their eyes as blue and deep as the ocean; their silly stories and songs.

Sy was the smaller of the two, still skinny and often out of breath since his dangerous encounter with pneumonia. He was so loving and trusting, a mini-Jack in looks but without Jack's fiery edge. Lily had inherited every piece of that, with some to spare. She might look demure in her gray Agnes B dress – a gift from chic, extravagant Aunt Mimi – but she was feisty and adventurous, a born leader. A born ringleader, Schuyler thought, always up for trouble. As much as Schuyler hated to admit it, staying for a while with strong personalities like Mimi and Kingsley might be good for Lily. Neither of them would put up with nonsense. They were, after all, the Regent of the Coven and the Venator Chief. They had reputations to maintain, not to mention order in this world and the one beneath. If the King and Queen of Hell couldn't keep Lily safe, who could?

Jack came striding into the room, his green eyes almost feline, with the same high cheek bones as Mimi and the same fair hair, though his was cropped and tousled, the way Schuyler liked it. Her heart still skipped a beat whenever he walked in. She wanted to grow old with this man, the guy she'd fallen for as a teenager. Bondmate was a good word for their relationship, something much deeper than 'husband and wife' could ever mean.

"The nanny's here," Schuyler told him, hoping he'd read her diffident expression and either overrule Mimi or reassure Schuyler that this Catherine Denham was a good choice.

"Yes, the NANNY," Mimi practically shouted, dropping one of her Japanese knives onto the counter with a terrific clatter.

"Does everyone in Hell shout all the time?" Jack teased her. "You know you're back in the city now, right?"

He swung towards Catherine Denham, who was still standing near the door with that simpering look on her face. Schuyler really didn't get this girl. Usually Venators – and anyone who'd endured their training – looked emotionless, ready for action, almost hard-faced. Maybe this was Catherine's "nanny" face, designed to be child-friendly, but Schuyler couldn't help see it as insipid and annoying.

"Lily, Sy – this is Catherine," she said, gathering the small whirling dervishes to her. They stared at their new nanny with wide eyes. "She'll be helping to look after you here. Taking you to school, and looking after you whenever Aunt Mimi and Uncle Kingsley can't be around."

"Sleeping in a room right next to you," Mimi added. She'd stopped messing about in the kitchen and joined everyone else. As usual, Schuyler couldn't help noting, she was standing right next to Jack. Old habits died hard, especially when the habits went back centuries … to the beginning of time.

"Say hello," Schuyler prompted the twins, and they both shook hands with Catherine, so solemn that it was funny. Catherine gave them that too-sweet smile, and leaned over, so she was at eye-level with the children.

"I'm very pleased to meet you both. We're going to have some fun, right?" The words were fine, but somehow they sounded forced, as though the nanny role didn't come naturally to Catherine.

Schuyler glanced at Jack to see how he was responding. She expected a frown, really – Catherine was not his kind of girl. But there was a faraway look in his eyes. Mimi was clutching his arm, and her eyes appeared glazed, like opaque green glass. Those two were such a matching set, physically and psychically. They were probably having some silent intuitive conversation.

When Catherine stood up, she looked straight at Jack and for the first time something like life flickered in her brown eyes. Nothing was said, but still – there it was. Schuyler might be going crazy, but she thought she saw something in Jack's eyes as well, almost a of recognition. It was as though a secret message was passed, in a flash, between Jack and Catherine. Schuyler felt unsettled rather than jealous: Jack had always been the most loyal and content of husbands, not heading out – like Kingsley sometimes did – on benders to clubs and casinos.

Maybe she was imagining this: it was easy to be paranoid these days, with Finn Chase spinning out of control around the world and demons seeping through fissures in the earth, trying to resurrect the darkness. Oliver on the run and in danger every single day. Silver Bloods rallying again, looking for a way back in.

Suddenly Mimi was by her side, linking arms as though Schuyler was her sister or best buddy.

"Don't worry, Schuyler," she murmured. "There's no safer place in the country for the children. No safer place in the world."

Schuyler wanted to believe her, but something sizzled in her brain like an electric current, telling her that no place was safe – not now, not anymore.

7 | SLEEPLESS IN STOCKHOLM

*I*t was already light that morning when Edon and Ara flew into Stockholm, and it was going to be light, by all accounts, until late in the evening. The northern summer day was long, and they were approaching the longest day of the year. Midsummer, a time for festivities, drinking, dancing and going wild in the country.

Not Edon's kind of thing at all. He was wild at heart all the time: he didn't need to dance around a maypole to show it.

He and Ara caught the fast train into the city, so fast he barely had time to use his tourist map to work out – and memorize – the route to the apartment Kingsley had set up. Ara had slept most of the way on the plane, slumped against him, slobbering on his shoulder. Edon thought that was pretty cute, but he didn't dare mention that to Ara. She was still groggy on the train, her feet up on her black duffel, barely conscious enough to look out the window. True, it was daylight, and that wasn't Ara's best time: she really was a creature of the night. How she was going to manage Sweden in midsummer, when it was light more than it was dark, he wasn't sure.

He nudged her awake when the train pulled into the station.

"We're here, angel," he said, laughing when her yawn turned into a scowl. "Taxi, subway or walk to the apartment? It'll take us about thirty minutes to walk. How heavy's your bag?"

"Light as a feather," Ara retorted, though Edon suspected she would have said that even if she were packing anvils. "Let's walk."

At this time on a sunny summer morning, the waterways he'd spied from the plane formed a sparkling web, drawing together the islands of the city. Passing old men fishing and street vendors setting up for the day, Edon and Ara crossed the pedestrian bridge into the old-town island, Gamla Stan, and made their way through its narrow cobbled streets. Cafes and souvenir shops were opening, metal gates whirring up, chairs and tables scraped onto sidewalks. Already a tour group clogged one of the steep intersections, selfie-sticks waving above their heads like aluminum antennae.

At first glance this wasn't Edon's kind of city – way too claustrophobic and touristy, in his opinion. The church spires and candy-colored old townhouses were pretty enough, but – unlike Ara – he wasn't here on vacation. He didn't need to gawp at the palace where the Royal Family lived or line up to see where the Nobel Prizes got handed out. If he wanted to eat Swedish meatballs, he could have gone to Ikea. It was a relief to cross a much busier bridge on the other side, noisy and stinky with traffic, and wend through a mess of roadworks that fed pedestrians around a crowded bike lane and into an underpass. Inconvenient, scruffy, reeking of urine and beer – now that was a real city. Even if underpasses made his hackles rise.

They were on a big island now, Sodermalm, heading west to the apartment. Too many hipsters around for his liking, with their man-buns and bikes. Apparently the words "gluten-free," emblazoned on a bakery window, didn't need translation into Swedish.

"Hungry?" he asked Ara and she shook her head. She was blinking in the sunshine like a nocturnal animal.

"Let's get to this place first," she said to him, and she was right. Edon was watchful and alert as ever, sniffing for potential danger, wary of anyone who walked too close to them. To most people he and

Ara probably looked like travelers who needed to unpack, shower and change their clothes, but still, Edon didn't want to draw unwanted attention. Not when he didn't know the level of threat here in Stockholm.

Or what he was doing here, when all the intelligence seemed so vague and based on hear-say. Why would Lucifer and the forces of darkness choose such a light, sun-dappled place for their re-emergence? Why opt for summer in a country where the sun barely set? Iceland in winter maybe, with steaming volcanos, long hours of darkness, and an eerie blue glint on its stark glaciers. But not Sweden in midsummer, with everyone riding around on bicycles wearing clogs, cut-off shorts and smiley faces. This place was one giant toothpaste commercial. The Nephilim would stand out a mile here.

Mariatorget was a rectangular small park, orderly and green and rimmed with tall swishing trees. Edon and Ara scuffed along its central pathway, past park benches and around a long pool studded with spraying fountains. Bicycles were chained to railings and lampposts, and small dogs bounded along its gravel paths, monitored by well-heeled elderly owners. The buildings on either side of the park formed two unblemished rows of townhouses, the sites of small luxury hotels and the kind of expensive café Edon generally avoided.

"You're not in Chinatown anymore," Ara said to him, the beginnings of a grin twitching her mouth.

"You're right," he said. "This is Williamsburg in two years' time."

"Aw, don't say that!" Ara protested. At least she wasn't tired or sullen anymore.

"This whole island used to be the working-class district of Stockholm," he told her. "Then the gentrifiers moved in. Then the hipsters. Then the Venators."

"There goes the neighborhood," Ara said, smirking at him. "Well, at least we're here to lower the tone. Which place is yours?"

"Ours," he corrected, and she didn't protest. "At the end. Third floor. Just close enough so that fountain can keep us awake."

The main set of double doors was tall, probably big enough to admit carriages when the house was built in the eighteenth century. Edon had the keys: they'd been waiting for him in a locker at the airport. No address – Kinsgley had given him that, and told him to memorize and destroy it. Just the keys and a hunting knife. Just the sort of a welcome gift Edon appreciated.

Inside the former driveway was a shadowy lobby, leading to a small courtyard of bike racks, a communal recycling center and a raised vegetable garden, tomato plants growing up pyramids of roped twigs. Edon glanced around the courtyard, taking in the fire escapes and back balconies, all the means of entry and escape. Ara lingered a few steps back, unwilling to leave the shadows. She wasn't smiling anymore.

Edon looked at her, raising his eyebrows rather than speaking: had she seen or heard something? Ara gave an almost imperceptible shake of the head. Nothing to fight here – not yet, anyway.

A door on the right led to large sweeping stairs, curving around an old cage elevator. Edon hated those things. They reminded him of the kennels in hell, and whenever he was faced with one he always took the stairs. Ara didn't even consider it: she loped up the stairs two at a time, casting suspicious looks up and down the stairwell. They were quiet movers, he noticed, despite the fact they were both wearing heavy boots. Always hunting, always hunted.

Their third floor apartment was at the front of the building, its wooden door heavy and dark. It creaked open, and Edon and Ara dropped their bags in the long, empty hallway. He pulled the hunting knife from the side pocket and sniffed. The air was close and dusty; the place smelled disused. The only other scent he could pick up was Ara's. But better to check each room. The Nephilim had their ways.

Ara was right when she said they weren't in Chinatown anymore. Compared with his bare-bones efficiency there, this Stockholm apartment was palatial in size. High ceilings, square rooms and tall windows that were swagged with heavy linen curtains. Some curtains in the ballroom-sized main room were drawn, casting much of the golden wood floor into dusty twilight. One corner of the room was consumed by a built-in porcelain-white tiled stove, its twin on the other side of the wall in the dining room. They wouldn't be needing that in this weather, and Edon was relieved: it looked breakable and delicate, not to mention ludicrously old-fashioned.

Once they were sure the apartment was empty, Ara and Edon wandered the linked rooms in stunned silence. There was a grandeur to it but also a starkness. It looked even larger than it was because there was so little furniture – a long, low sofa in the living room, and in the dining room a mahogany table with elaborately carved legs and four gilt chairs. The gray painted dresser in the kitchen was entirely empty – no plates or glasses of any kind. And in the bedroom, just one bed made up with soft white sheets. A small double, Edon would call it. But right now it looked like a cloud from heaven. He wanted to get his boots off and flop onto that billowing bed.

"So, this is the only place to sleep?" Ara sounded hostile. Edon really didn't get her. One minute she was dozing on his shoulder, like a loving, docile girlfriend; the next she was stomping around this fairy-tale apartment looking petulant because she didn't get her own room. Didn't she want to sleep with him? Weren't they an item?

Not a very appealing item right now, he had to admit, after so many hours traveling, and trudging across the city in sweaty boots.

Edon walked towards her, one hand extended.

"Come on, angel," he crooned. "Let's get some rest while we can. I might have to start working at any moment …"

"I thought you said we were *always* working," Ara said. But she reached down to unlace her boots, which had to be a good sign. He wanted her to fall into bed with him, the way she did when she let her guard down for five minutes and admitted that she and Edon were a team – not just patrolling the streets, but in the privacy of an apartment like this one. However big its rooms, it felt silent and intimate just now. The perfect place for them to re-connect, emotionally and physically. Ara made things so difficult for herself. For someone who could enter and investigate people's minds, she wasn't too hot on knowing her own.

Ara kicked her boots away and wriggled her black jeans down from her hips. Her legs were white and all lean muscle. Even without her Venator blades, Edon knew she could fight anything – well, almost anything. Nephilim played dirty.

He pulled his shirt off and flung it onto the floor. Ara took a step closer, looking away, refusing to admit that she was as into this as he was. With the tip of one foot she picked up his shirt, crumpled on the ground, and kicked it further out of reach.

Now this was a game he liked. Edon swung for his dusty boots, lying on the ground between them, and kicked them towards the wall. The smallest of smiled played over Ara's chiseled face. Suddenly she was the one reaching out, pulling Edon into her arms. Their faces were close together, breath hot, cheekbones knocking. He ran his fingers down the hard curve of her back and she arched under his touch, like a cat. A cat that was more feral than domestic, but she was letting him touch her. Was that a moan escaping her lips? Maybe Sweden wasn't so bad after all.

Noise at the front door. A key turning in the lock. Edon staggered back from Ara. His knife. He had to get his knife out of his bag. Maybe if he'd traveled through time to get here rather than on a stupid commercial flight, he could have brought Ara's Venator blades with them ...

Wolf. Whoever was creaking open the heavy front door was another wolf. He could smell her.

"It's OK," he whispered to Ara. "It's a wolf."

Ara frowned at him. He knew what she was thinking – what if it was a wolf working for the other side? What if it was a hellhound?

But Edon would know that smell anywhere. It was embedded in his brain, his senses, his body.

It was Ahramin. Fierce and dangerous, the kind of wolf you wanted next to you in battle. And in bed.

Ahramin, his one-time lover.

"Hey!" a husky voice shouted down the hallway. "I can smell you from here, Marrok. In fact, I could smell you all the way up the stairs. Way to go masking your scent, idiot."

Ara shot him a dark look – curious, alarmed, suspicious.

"So quit hiding from me," the husky voice rasped. And there she was in the bedroom doorway, dressed in body-con yoga gear, her chestnut hair in a bouncing ponytail. Still a sleek beauty, tense and ready to pounce, after all these years. Something churned deep inside Edon. Of all the wolves in the world – and the underworld – he had to meet Ahramin again.

Her gray wolf-eyes narrowed.

"I'm Mina," she told Ara, who stood speechless in her underwear and black tank. "Marrok's new partner-in-crime. I'm guessing you're a non-approved house guest. Vampire, maybe? Am I right?"

"Mina?" That was all Edon could manage. She was never "Mina" in the old days.

"Yeah. Get used to it. Don't be all nostalgic for the past, Marrok." Mina flashed her teeth at him. They looked dangerous – as dangerous as her smile. "Though I see you've moved on to the fallen now. A lovely little vampire girlfriend. Nice."

"Before you talk any more shit, you should know that this is Ara Scott, and she's a Venator," Edon began, heat creeping up his neck. Ahramin – Mina – could always do this to him. Wind him up until he exploded.

Mina whistled, feigning surprise.

"Well, well. The famous Araminta Scott." She gave Ara an ostentatious bow. "You are *definitely* not supposed to be here."

"I'm on vacation," Ara said, her voice flat. Her face was so closed-up that Edon couldn't read her at all.

"Well, we're not. And this bedroom seems kinda small for three."

"You're staying here as well?" Edon's heart sank, or maybe it was in free-fall, dropping through his body so hard it was about to hit the floor.

"I doubt we'll be in Stockholm long, Mr. Wolf." Mina's eyes glinted. She was enjoying this, the power over him, her surprise entry. Always a power game with Mina. "But yes, in the short term, it's three's company in this place. I guess there's a sofa somewhere? For you, I mean. Us girls can bunk up together. Like a supernatural sorority."

"I don't think …" Ara began, her eyes flashing with anger. Ara wasn't used to being spoken to like this, not even by someone important like Kingsley Martin. Certainly not a wolf.

"Hey! You're not supposed to be here, remember?" Mina crossed her arms and leaned against the door jamb. "I think the old king of the underworld, or whoever he is, would love to find out you're here. You'd be on Venator crosswalk duty for the rest of this lifetime, and maybe the next. So if I were you, I would be happy to get half a bed. Especially as the wolf you'll get to share it with isn't stinky and over-the-hill."

Mina stared hard at Edon, and he couldn't find anything to say. Everything had just got a whole lot more complicated, and part of him, if he had to admit it, found that very exciting indeed.

8 | PAST LIVES

He'd recognized her the moment he saw her in Mimi's apartment. Catherine Denham – so that was her name in this life. Mimi had managed to keep the information from him, though he wasn't sure how: usually he could see into his twin's mind with ease, even when they were thousands of miles apart. But Mimi wasn't Regent of the Coven for no reason: she was wily and mentally strong, able to block unwanted psychic intrusions. So she'd hatched this little plan alone, for reasons he didn't yet understand. Maybe she thought "Catherine Denham" wouldn't set anything ticking in his brain. Luckily, Jack had a long memory.

He walked through the south churchyard of Trinity Church, picking his way past stone graves dark with age, their inscriptions no longer legible. It was sentimental of him to come here, a vampire's joke, in a way. He could just remember the first, much smaller Trinity Church, built on this spot at the very end of the seventeenth century. His incarnation then was as William White, and he was a very old man at the time. The New York Coven was in its formative years. Things didn't seem any simpler then, but they were, he now understood. One thing was certain: New York City was much simpler then. Broadway was just a dirt road running to the harbor, and the towering banks of Wall Street didn't cast a shadow on the churchyard.

Trinity was his mother's name as well. Poor Trinity Force, never really loved by their father, Charles, after his bondmate rejected him. Theirs was a marriage of convenience – or for Trinity's money, as all the Blue Bloods liked to whisper. She wasn't much of a mother to Jack and Mimi, that was true: for too many years of their childhood, she was away on vacation or shopping trips. Mimi couldn't forgive her, but maybe now, as Jack got a little older, and had children of his own, he saw things differently.

Charles had believed, to the core of his soul, that he and his bondmate were bound by blood for eternity – but he was wrong. Wrong about Gabrielle, the Uncorrupted. Known in this life as Allegra Van Alen, Schuyler's mother.

After Allegra fell in love and eloped with her human familiar, Charles changed his name from Van Alen to Force. He wanted nothing more to do with that family name, so it was ironic, Jack mused, that now the Force and Van Alen clans were united again through his own marriage to Schuyler. Ironic, too, that Jack had broken with Mimi, his own bondmate, to be with someone else. Love kept getting in the way of history, disrupting the path of the fallen. It made things messy, and maybe for Trinity Force it had meant a life of always being second-best in her own family.

Allegra Van Alen's human familiar was Stephen Chase. Schuyler's father. Finn's father as well. Without him, Jack wouldn't have Schuyler. But the world wouldn't have to put up with Finn Chase either, Schuyler's long-lost half-sister. A mortal who'd ended up, thanks to Oliver, as First lady of the Coven, the first time a human familiar had ever reached such lofty heights in the vampire world.

And what had Oliver's brand-new-world dreams got them? Finn wanting much, much more than ceremonial power. Much, much more than Oliver's besotted devotion. Finn wasn't content to spend a life as first-lady arm candy, trying to ignore the sneers of the Blue Bloods, knowing she would always be seen as human and therefore second-rate. She wanted to be immortal too, even if it meant drinking silver poison and defecting to Lucifer's army.

What a mess, Jack thought, resisting the urge to kick a gravestone. Now he and Schuyler had to give up everything they'd worked for over the past ten years, see their vineyard smolder, move their children to a city far from everything they knew.

And as if that wasn't enough, Mimi hadn't exactly hired the Mary Poppins they were hoping for.

Trinity's doors were open, and inside it felt several degrees cooler. There was something about the stone arches and the ranks of wooden pews that always made Jack feel calm, as though the world was really an orderly and serene place. Sunlight filtered through the stained-glass windows at the western end, dappling the aisle. A few people, alone or in pairs, sat praying or in silent contemplation. Near the altar, one scruffy backpacker, his bag propped next to him on the seat, was reading a book, the sun picking out his fair curly hair like a spotlight.

In the back row she was waiting. To anyone else Catherine Denham might look like an ordinary young woman, neither tall nor short, neither stocky nor slight, who dressed in what Jack thought of as "girly" clothes, floaty and floral, with too much baby pink. Pretty, but too earnest in expression, like some kind of born-again vegan, or someone who spent her evenings at choir practice or knitting class.

But Jack wasn't just anyone. When he saw someone he knew from a previous incarnation, he could place them instantly. Jack Force never forgot a face. And Catherine Denham's face was identical to that of Marie Anne de Bourbon

He slipped into the pew next to her and Catherine remained gazing towards the altar, the bland expression on her face unchanged.

"Why here?" Jack asked, his voice low. The other people in the church were sitting far away, but he wanted to be careful.

"I've always liked this church," Catherine said, still not looking at him. "It's so out of place around here now, with the Stock Exchange and all the banks. It reminds me of the way things used to be. Though it's not that old, really. This is the third church on this spot. It's third life, I guess – right?"

"I didn't mean the church." Jack felt a surge of impatience. "I meant why New York? Why now?"

Catherine turned to face him, her dark eyes unreadable.

"We're family, aren't we?" she asked. "I'm here to look after your children."

"And that's all there is to it? Come on, Marie …"

"Catherine. It's Catherine now, Jack. Unless you want me to refer to you as Louis D'Orleans?"

Jack didn't reply. The demure exterior was just a façade, as Jack had suspected. There was an archness to her tone now that was much more familiar to him. Catherine Denham was the reincarnation of Marie Anne de Bourbon, the young woman who married Louis, Duke of Joyeuse, back in the early eighteenth-century. Jack was reincarnated as Louis D'Orleans, Mimi as his wife Elisabeth de Lorraine-Lillebonne. Louis of Joyeuse was their beloved son, as brave and adventurous as Lily, as kind and thoughtful as Sy. He'd grown into an athletic young man, an expert archer and rider, an accomplished swordsman. The Paris coven had high hopes for him.

Louis and Marie Anne were deeply in love – Jack had no doubt about that.

"I think about him every day," Catherine said, as though she could read his thoughts. "Do you think that's how it is for everyone who loses a bondmate? Your mother lost hers, didn't she?"

Catherine was right. Trinity had lost her bondmate, Salgiel, in ancient Rome. No wonder Jack's mother had felt adrift thought the centuries. No wonder she settled for what seemed like a loveless marriage with the Prince of the Angels, the man who would never get over the betrayal of his own bondmate. Their grief – both Trinity and Charles – for the love they'd lost had tainted Jack's childhood.

He hung his head, his own grief for Louis swirling back.

"Five years. That's all we had together." Catherine's voice had a hard edge now – anger that the centuries hadn't soothed. Louis had been murdered by a Silver Blood. Lucifer couldn't destroy Azrael and Abbadon, but he could send his agents to kill their son.

"I know," Jack told her. "But this is a new life, and we can't wallow in the past."

He only half-believed this, but it felt like the only thing to say.

"I wish I could be as forgiving as you." Catherine leaned forward, her slender wrists resting on the next pew. "I want revenge – in this life, any life. I don't care. But Louis must be avenged, and I'm ready and able to do it."

"I don't understand," said Jack, a chilly doubt seeping through him. Suddenly it felt very cold indeed inside the church. He wanted to be outside among the lush green trees, among the bustling, sweaty people thronging lower Broadway.

"I just wanted to reassure you that I'm ready this time in a way that I wasn't when … when they killed Louis. I've been training for this since I was the same age as the twins', pretty much. No one would think it to look at me, but I'm a much deadlier assassin than my brother."

"Well, good." At last something about Mimi's nanny-hiring was beginning to make sense. "We're trusting you completely to guard the twins. I can't lose a child again. It was devastating for us as well."

Jack could barely bring himself to think of Louis' blood-drenched body, disemboweled and lifeless, lying in a forest glade. It was an early summer's day, just like this, sunny and breezy. Louis' horse had stayed with him, reins jangling as he picked at long blades of grass. Not content with leaving a snaking trail of intestines, the Silver Bloods who'd killed him had etched a blood-rusted pentagram into Louis' pale forehead. And, as the ultimate desecration of his body, they'd yanked out his incisors, taking those emblems of his vampire status as ghoulish souvenirs. Vampires who hunted other vampires disgusted Jack. Their only end was evil. Their means were grotesque and violent.

He and Catherine sat in silence. It was impossible to keep the past away, especially when the Silver Bloods were back, refusing to accept defeat.

Catherine glanced at her narrow silver wristwatch.

"I have to go," she told Jack, gathering up her tote bag. "I'm glad we had a chance to talk. You haven't said anything to Schuyler, have you?"

It was more of a statement than a question.

"Not yet," he said. Catherine stood up.

"Not ever, please. Mimi thinks it's better if we keep this between ourselves."

Typical Mimi, Jack thought. To her, Schuyler would always be an outsider.

"We don't need her to worry about the past. More than anyone, she needs to focus on the crisis now. She has powers of recovery that we don't, and those may be very important with the battles coming up."

"But she's the twins' mother," Jack argued. "I don't know how it hurts to let her know about you and your … past life. Your relationship to me and Mimi."

Catherine bent over Jack in a way that suggested, to any tourist wandering in with a guide book and camera, that she was kissing him goodbye.

"Schuyler's never had a past life," Catherine whispered. "This world is all she knows. Don't make things more complicated than they need to be."

Jack grabbed her arm to stop her from walking away.

"Remember your job," he muttered, trying to keep his voice down and his temper in check. "Guarding the twins. That's the most important thing. When this operation is over, I'll help you get revenge. I promise."

"Promise?" Catherine leaned close again. She looked skeptical, almost disdainful. "What do promises mean when Lucifer is on the march again? This is much more than an 'operation,' Jack. If it was as simple as that, the Venators would be taking care of it, and you and Schuyler would still be hiding away in California, pretending to be human."

When Catherine shouldered her bag, it looked incongruously large for her narrow shoulders. She strolled to the center aisle where a cluster of tourists in long shorts and fluorescent sun visors were reading aloud from a guidebook. Jack watched her go. Was she right? Was it better for Schuyler to keep focus on the battle-at-hand rather than worry about everyone's pasts and the wrongs that happened?

"George Washington worshipped here when he was president," one gray-haired woman announced to the group. Catherine paused, and placed a gentle hand on the woman's arm.

"He worshipped at a church on this spot, but not this exact church," she told them, in her sweetest choir-girl voice. "The church Washington knew was demolished so this one could be built. This is a reincarnation, you might say."

The tourist group murmured their thanks and Catherine wafted out the door, without a backward glance at Jack.

9 | SIC TRANSIT GLORIA MUNDI

Squinting because of the glare, Oliver checked the piece of paper in his hand, and peered up at the building looming over them.

"This is Tensta?" he asked the cab driver.

"This is Tensta," replied the driver, in a clipped perfect English. "Are you sure this is where you want to go? Tensta is not a nice part of Stockholm."

That was an understatement, in Oliver's opinion. He'd felt more at home in the transit lounges of Frankfurt airport, where he'd spent half the night after his connection was canceled. When he'd flown into Stockholm this morning, spying the glinting blue waters and lush green islands of the city, Oliver had assumed he was headed for somewhere clean, pristine and Scandinavian. Not housing projects on the northern fringe of the city – rank after rank of soulless, interchangeable tower blocks encircled by multi-lane ring roads.

Though maybe a soulless area was the perfect place for him right now. The perfect place to find someone like Finn, who'd sold her soul to Lucifer. Mac, Edon's brother, had seemed adamant that Oliver should go to this address in Stockholm as soon as possible, so here he was.

Once again, doing what a wolf told him to do – for better or worse.

"Thanks," he told the driver, handing over a sheaf of Swedish krona. At this rate he'd need to get more money from Schuyler soon – the taxi ride practically cleaned him out.

Oliver knew nothing about Tensta, but he suspected the suburb wasn't covered in most Swedish guidebooks. It looked like Eastern Europe during the Cold War, the kind of place Oliver had seen on depressing documentaries The apartment towers had that gray, unloved look to– all tower blocks and graffiti, with surly immigrant kids hanging around on corners. The moment Oliver stepped onto the sidewalk and closed the door, the cab performed a wild U-turn and zoomed away, as though the driver was eager to get out of Dodge before he got ambushed.

He checked the paper in his hand again. A police car sped by, chased by dark-haired kids on bikes. One of the kids, wearing a baggy Real Madrid T-shirt, squealed to a halt and hurled a rock at the police car's back window. His aim was good, but the rock just bounced off the glass. The car didn't stop, and the kids all howled and shouted at it, in either triumph or rage.

The stone-thrower glared at Oliver. He couldn't be more than ten or eleven, Oliver thought, but he had the hardened face of a cynical criminal. His voice – when he asked Oliver a question in lilting Swedish – was still high and squeaky.

"Sorry," Oliver said, shrugging. "I don't understand."

"English? OK," said the kid. "I was asking if you are here to buy drugs. But I don't think so."

"You don't think so?" Oliver couldn't help being amused. The kid shook his head.

"People like you who want drugs, they drive up in their car and keep the engine running. You come here in a taxi. So you must be a social worker. Or a journalist. Do you want to interview me?"

Now it was Oliver's turn to shake his head.

"I'm not a social worker or a journalist, and I'm not here to buy drugs. I'm just here to stay for a while. In the Jarva building. Am I saying that right?"

"No, but it's OK," said the kid. Two girls in hijabs scuttled by, heads down, darting puzzled glances in Oliver's direction. "Follow me."

Maybe he was stupid to trust this kid, but not even the Nephilim relied on such young recruits. And without his help, Oliver would never have found his way through the concrete maze of walkways and dingy stairwells.

"Why were you chasing the police car?" he asked the kid, who looked surprised at the question.

"Nobody likes the police here. They took away my brother for nothing. No reason, man."

Oliver nodded but didn't ask any more questions. He shouldn't have asked anything at all. The last thing he wanted to do was raise suspicion. He didn't need to hear this kid's life story, and he didn't need to answer any questions himself.

"There were riots here a couple of years ago," the kid told him, wheeling his bike around a graffiti-splashed corner that smelled like urine. "Things are getting bad again. You picked a bad time to come."

"I guess so," said Oliver. This kid had no idea what a bad time it was, not just for this crumbling project, but for the whole world.

An older teenage boy, darker skinned and frowning, leaned over the railings two flight up. He shouted down to the kid, gesturing at Oliver. The kid shouted back up at him and pointed to the next walkway.

"He thought you were a journalist, but I told him no."

The teenage boy glowered down at Oliver.

"Go home, American tourist!" he shouted, and Oliver decided it was time to get moving. Dodging Venators and Nephilim was bad enough; he didn't want to have to contend with disaffected youth as well. They knew how to fight dirty.

"Jarva is this building over here?" he asked the kid. He wished he had money to give the boy, but he only had a few krona notes left, and no idea what they were worth. "I can find my way from here. Thanks."

"Watch out for the cops!" the kid called after him, and Oliver grinned. The cops were the least of his problems. Right now he needed to get to this safe house – or safe apartment, at least – without attracting any more attention. The elevator doors were sashed with bright police tape, but Oliver wasn't planning on getting into such a confined space anyway. The apartment scribbled on his piece of paper was on the third floor, and he could take the litter-strewn stairs up.

He had the address but no key. Oliver could smell a lot of things right now, including baked-on dog excrement, meat frying in dirty grease, and the astringent scent of spray paint, but he couldn't smell wolves at all. What if this wasn't a safe place to stay? What if it was just another trap?

The third-floor corridor must have been white once upon a time, but now it was gray and smudged, an empty beer bottle lying on its side outside one door. Inside one apartment people were arguing, and something hard thunked against a wall. Oliver picked up the pace, headed for number eighteen. Not a lucky number, or an unlucky one either, he hoped. And not the kind of place someone like Oliver Hazard-Perry – in his past life – would ever have frequented.

The door to apartment eighteen was as featureless as all the others along this dingy corridor. Oliver flattened himself against the wall and sniffed. Nothing. No aroma of wolf, at any rate. He reached out a hand, appalled to see it trembling. What was he going to do – cower in this hallway for the rest of his life? He was a wreck. This life of running and hiding couldn't go on for much longer. Physically and emotionally, he was shot.

When Oliver turned the handle, the door clicked open. Unlocked – that could be good or bad. He remained standing to the side, letting the door swing, waiting for something or someone to pounce, listening for the click of a gun or the slightest hint of a footstep. All he could hear was the muffled shouting further down the corridor, and the clattering of pans in another apartment. Someone was calling out a window, shouting in Arabic, and children's voices shouted back in reply. There were footsteps too, and laughter. Young men coming up the stairs.

Oliver darted into the apartment and closed the door behind him. A short hallway led to the living room, small and square, ashy black curtains closed; one hung askew on its plastic rail. The only furniture was a low sofa, a faded red, pockmarked with cigarette burns. The room had the faintest smell of fake lavender, the lingering aroma of a now-dead air-freshener. An open doorway to his left led to a bedroom; the bed, only partly visible, was a single, the mattress bare. The other doorway, to his right, led to the kitchen: what Oliver could see was similarly spartan. Depressing but functional, just like his life right now.

The bathroom was off the stunted hallway, windowless and grimy. The remains of a cabinet clung to the peeling wall above the sink, but the mirror was gone. The faucets were working, so Oliver splashed cold water on his face, trying to steady his breathing. He was here. He was alone. He'd stay here until he got another message – from a Marrok brother, hopefully – to move on. He might even be in the same country as Finn, though why she was here, and what she was up to, he didn't know. The thought of seeing again thrilled and terrified him at the same time. His fangs tingled, and deep within him he felt a surge of desire.

Oliver smelled the intruder before he heard him, and his reaction was visceral and instinctive. He swung around, mouth open in a roar, fists clenched. He saw golden hair and wide blue eyes, as blue as the waterways he'd spotted from the plane.

Then something hit him hard, swiping the back of his head, and the world turned black.

10 | ONLY DREAMING

*T*hese last moments of the night, before they softened into dawn, were some of Schuyler's favorites. Usually she didn't mind waking up early if she got to watch the sky turning from charcoal to pink. In New York it was always especially beautiful, she'd always thought, because of the way the rising sun glinted off the skyscrapers, and the city seemed to glimmer. Like a crystal ball, maybe, or a snow globe. Something that suggested a whirl of promise and excitement for the coming day.

But this morning she was wide awake, Jack slumbering next to her, and Schuyler felt anything but happy.

This was their last night in the city, staying in Kingsley and Mimi's apartment, before they flew out. Kingsley wanted them in Stockholm. He couldn't tell them much yet – just that the New York Coven was bankrolling a covert operation in Sweden. Kingsley could barely bring himself to say it, but it looked as though one of the gates of hell was opening up again, somewhere deep in the Swedish forests. The intelligence from wolves suggested that was the next trouble spot.

And Sweden was where Oliver was. Schuyler knew that, even if Jack didn't. She had intelligence sources of her own, and from them she knew that the last currency Oliver bought was Swedish krona.

All roads led to Stockholm, apparently.

Schuyler was troubled about what they were getting into – of course she was. But that wasn't the reason she'd woken up early feeling so unsettled and unhappy. It was the dream she'd been having. Not a nightmare, exactly, though it had been disturbing enough to wake her. It was as vivid as a nightmare.

OK – who was she fooling? It was a nightmare.

In the dream, or the fragments of it she could remember, Schuyler had seen Lily surrounded by green – maybe Central Park or some generic meadow. Lily was smiling and laughing, that cheeky laugh she had that made it impossible to be mad with her, even if she was misbehaving. Around Lily's face something was fluttering, and at first Schuyler couldn't make out what this thing was – maybe butterflies, maybe flags. But then she realized the fluttering things were ribbons, long ribbons of different colors, whipping in the wind and lashing in front of Lily's face, like strands of hair.

And then Lily wasn't smiling anymore. She was screaming, her face contorted. In the dream, Schuyler was powerless to help her. She wasn't even there, perhaps – she was just looking on from afar, unable to reach Lily, or to comfort her. The ribbons kept waving, bright and benign, but Lily wouldn't stop screaming. When Schuyler woke up, her heart was thudding and she was reaching out with both hands, trying to grab at something – Lily, probably, or the flapping ribbons. Anything to stop her daughter screaming.

No one was screaming in real life. Jack was murmuring the small animal noises he made when his sleep was deep and untroubled, and he lay still, his breathing even. His hair looked like burnished gold in this early morning light, his lashes long and dark on his smooth skin. In the distance the traffic on the West Side Highway rumbled and droned: for all Mimi and Kingsley's money, and the excess of this penthouse, they couldn't quite shut out all the traffic noise.

Or the noise in Schuyler's head.

No harm in checking the children, Schuyler decided. She rolled out of bed, doing her best not to disturb Jack. There was no reason for both of them to be stumbling around at dawn. She slipped on a silky kimono, feather-light and embroidered with different shades of blue, and padded out of the room. The carpet in this penthouse was as lush as a lawn.

Sy's room was closest, his door ajar. Schuyler poked her head in and repressed a smile. Sy was lying on his back in his usual starfish position, looking as though someone had flung him there. The sunlight filtering through the blind didn't seem to disturb him, though he sniffed and twitched a little while Schuyler stood watching, wriggling in his sheets until he was comfortable again.

Sy was sleeping much better these days, she was relieved to see, and seemed happy enough in this strange new world of New York City. Mimi had promised him a space travel theme for his room, complete with a desk housed inside a rocket, and for the moment, at least, that was all he could talk about. He didn't seem to miss the house in Napa at all, and when Jack told the children that he and Schuyler were going away "on vacation" for a while, Sy shrugged it off without a whimper. That was good as well: he'd been super-clingy when he was recovering from pneumonia. But still – Schuyler's heart tugged when she thought of leaving her little boy here while she and Jack charged off to face god-knows-what in Sweden.

Lily was fast asleep as well, curled up, strands of dark hair plastered on her pale, damp face. Schuyler couldn't remember what Lily had decided on for her room – something to do with the ocean, probably, because her latest passion was for the creatures of the deep and ship-wrecks. She was obsessed with watching nature shows on TV, especially ones that involved whales, dolphins, squid, sharks or anyone in a wetsuit diving into the ocean. She loved swimming, and had spent the last six months nagging for a pool at the Napa property. When Mimi told her there was a swimming pool in the building's basement, Lily was beside herself with excitement.

"We can reserve it," Mimi had whispered to Schuyler, "so nobody else will be there. The kids'll be on lockdown in this building, I promise you. And Catherine swims like a fish."

This last past sounded made-up, but Schuyler said nothing at the time. Her reservations about Catherine – which basically came down to a creepy vibe – fell on deaf ears. Even Jack wouldn't discuss them with her. He just got short-tempered in a way that he hadn't for years. Maybe being back in New York wasn't good for him. Or maybe he was more worried about what they'd find in Sweden than he was prepared to let on just yet. In Napa they played at being happy regular people, but their true natures – their destiny – couldn't be hidden forever.

Schuyler crept close, just to reassure herself that Lily was sleeping soundly. Her beautiful daughter, so spirited and brimming with energy. What did the future have in store for Sy and Lily – Simiel and Lela-hel, children of Abbadon, the Angel of Destruction? Nothing ordinary, that was for sure. This was the gift of their inheritance, and the curse. Whatever happened to them, whatever passion they chose to pursue, the children would not lead ordinary lives.

Lily stirred, and Schuyler leaned over her to pull up a thrown-off sheet. At this point in her life, Lily wanted to explore the ocean. But what about all the countries of the world? Would she have the same ravenous curiosity for travel and adventure on dry land? Schuyler remembered traveling the world with Oliver, back when he was her human Conduit. They thought they'd always be together, always roaming and exploring new places. Now he was traveling the world alone, on the run from Venators. A broken man who'd almost destroyed the Coven they'd spent centuries building, the Coven they defended from Lucifer and his demons a decade ago.

It was impossible to resist brushing the stray strands of hair away from Lily's face. Her skin was so soft, untouched by worries, unmarred by battle wounds. Schuyler swallowed back the guilt she felt, the guilt she couldn't lose. She would never say it out loud, but if she hadn't abandoned Oliver for Jack, none of this would have happened. None of the good things, like having the twins, but none of the bad, either. Not Ollie's precipitous decline and fall. She wouldn't have left him exposed, vulnerable to the charms of Finn, her beautiful half-sister. Finn, who seemed so passive and so good, so pure of soul. She'd tried to destroy the Coven in order to make herself immortal, turning to the dark side because Oliver's devotion, it seemed, simply wasn't enough.

Because Lily's room led to the terrace, Schuyler decided to check that the tall glass door, hidden behind its gray blind, was locked. More paranoia, Jack would say, but he wasn't awake. Schuyler tiptoed to the door and turned the handle. Locked. It needed a key, Mimi had taken pains to emphasize, so Lily wouldn't be able to let herself in or out on a whim. The door would remain locked at all times, though Mimi had a key stashed in the kitchen in case of emergencies.

"Like fires," Mimi had said, with a dismissive wave of one mani-cured hand.

Like demons, Schuyler wanted to respond.

Someone must have a radio or TV on nearby, Schuyler thought, still standing with her hand grasping the terrace door handle. She could hear talking. A woman's voice, but not a quiet drone, like the news readers on NPR, say. This woman sounded agitated. Her voice rose and fell, and Schuyler couldn't make what she was saying. Surely nobody else was up – though maybe Kingsley was back from work already, and listening to something in the kitchen.

"I told you, no!" said the woman's voice, and Schuyler realized who-ever was talking was out on the terrace. She pulled back the gray blind and peered out, blocking the light with her head so Lily wouldn't be disturbed.

Catherine Denham was pacing up and down outside, close to the glass balustrade, phone clamped to her ear. Whoever she was talking to at this very early hour, they were arguing.

Curiosity sizzled through Schuyler, along with a kind of righteous indignation. She was right about this girl – she knew it! Something was not quite straight-and-narrow about her; nobody could be that insipid, that demure, not in the kick-ass, high-stakes vampire world. Catherine might simper in public all she liked, but clearly in real life – in secret, at any rate – she had a darker side.

And finally Schuyler was getting to see it. She felt like rushing through to the bedroom to shake Jack awake, and tell him that she was right to have reservations about this particular nanny. Sweet-smiled nannies didn't get out of bed at dawn to have secret phone arguments on their employers' terraces. What was really going on?

After she tugged the door handle a couple of times, Schuyler remembered that it wasn't going to open for her: she didn't have a key. She scampered out of Lily's room and down the hallway to the expansive living area. One of the glass doors to the terrace had to be unlocked: Catherine had managed to get out there, after all. Sure enough, one of the doors was propped open with a chair, the morning breeze wafting in and making the sheer white curtains billow and dance.

There was no turning back now. Schuyler pulled her robe tight and stepped out onto the terrace, its white tiles cold under her bare feet. Catherine didn't see or hear her. The girl stood, in an ugly toweling robe, facing the Hudson and the glinting jumble of buildings beyond it on the New Jersey shoreline.

"No," she was saying as Schuyler approached. "I've told you, and you have to accept it."

Schuyler focused on Catherine's slight form, determined to read what was on her mind. But nothing came back – absolutely nothing. She must have thrown up some powerful walls around her own psyche, the kind that could keep other vampires out.

So Schuyler decided to resort to good old-fashioned throat-clearing. Catherine heard her polite cough and swung around. The alarm on her face when she saw Schuyler was so exaggerated it looked like horror. Or maybe anger. Certainly not innocent surprise.

Without saying goodbye to whoever it was on the other end, Catherine stabbed her phone off and dropped it into one of the toweling robe's big pockets.

"Sorry to interrupt," Schuyler said, faking a concerned smile. Two could play Catherine's disingenuous game. "I heard someone talking out here and was worried."

"No need," replied Catherine, her tone sharp. She took a deep breath and her face settled into its usual bland expression. Butter wouldn't melt in her mouth, thought Schuyler. Catherine's face was a placid mask again.

"Is everything OK?" Schuyler asked. She wasn't letting Catherine get away with that rude tone.

"Private business. I'm sorry if I disturbed you."

She didn't sound sorry at all, Schuyler thought. Just annoyed about being interrupted.

"Anything I can help with?" Schuyler persisted.

"It's just something personal, to do with my family," said Catherine, her voice softening. All the tension of a few moments ago had disappeared from her face and her tone. Now she just looked young and sad. She was either a very good actress or she was telling the truth – something personal was going on, and she didn't want to divulge it to a semi-stranger. Or to anyone connected to Mimi and Kingsley, rulers of the New York Coven. If she was squabbling with her brother, say, she didn't want his boss to know all about it.

"As long as you're OK," Schuyler told Catherine, trying once again to smile, though it wasn't easy. It was hard to warm to Catherine Denham. There was something brittle about the girl, and something fake as well. Catherine wasn't a natural nanny candidate, whatever Mimi insisted.

When she'd voiced her objections to Jack, he'd waved them away, his voice impatient. Catherine had been picked for a reason: she could fight like a demon, and that's what they needed if the real demons attacked. So she wasn't Schuyler's kind of person – that was fine. They didn't have to be buddies with her. She was an employee, not a family member.

Then he'd gone red in the face and said he didn't want to talk about it anymore. Schuyler was obsessing, and it was natural, but it had to stop. They needed to trust Mimi's judgment, Jack said.

Catherine turned her gaze to the highway and river again, to the cars and trucks already forming a steady stream north and south.

"Well, I'll leave you," Schuyler said, annoyed that she was the one who felt apologetic, the one who felt the need to scuttle back indoors. There was something a little surreal about this encounter on the terrace. Maybe, Schuyler wondered, she was still dreaming.

11 | SLAYING SERPENTS

"Glad you're settling in," the local Venator chief said with a grin. "Nice place we have for you two, right?"

Edon managed a grin, though he imagined it looked more like a grimace. Mina shot him a knowing look, which he was pretending to ignore. Instead of "you two" it was really "we three" in the Stockholm apartment. Ara was up there right now, having a shower – or so she said – before she headed out sightseeing alone. For the life of him, Edon couldn't imagine someone as wound-up as Ara was right now wandering the streets of Stockholm to look at churches and boutiques. But he didn't have time for squabbles with his blonde angel. Not with a job to do, and Mina – of all the wolves in the world – there to make sure he did it.

The Venator chief here was named Axel Andersson, and – as the fallen went – he didn't seem like a bad guy. He was very tall and his fair hair was fluffy like a newborn bird's. Everything about him was pale – hair, skin, blue eyes. He was dressed in the usual all-black Venator garb, but it was much more informal than Edon had come to expect after his year with the New York Coven. The black shirt was linen and worn untucked. The jeans were the standard black but the shoes? Edon had never seen a Venator in espadrilles before.

Axel had texted Mina arranging to meet them in the square. It wasn't a park at all, as Mina had informed Edon that morning.

"Something you'd know if you had the slightest grasp of the Swedish language," she'd said to him, lips curled in a sneer. "Mariatorget means Maria Square. Try to keep up."

Axel clearly wasn't a man for sitting still. He was waiting for them by the big fountain, and gestured to them to walk with him.

"This statue is *Tors fiske*," he told them. "Thor slaying a sea serpent. This particular serpent is from Norse mythology. It grew so large that it could encircle the entire world with its body, and bite the end of its own tail. That's why the local Venators had to summon Thor to help them."

Edon was bemused for a moment, and Axel slapped him on the shoulder, a broad smile lighting up his fair face.

"Just a little Swedish Venator humor," he said. "I forgot what you wolves are like. No joking around, right?"

Neither Edon nor Mina replied. Axel shook his head in mock despair, and started telling them about what he liked to call the Situation.

"Much as we love hosting wolves in our historic buildings here in the city, I'm not happy that we've had to call you in. We haven't seen any serious Nephilim action here for years. Almost ten years, to be precise. Maybe we got too complacent."

"So they're back?" Mina prompted him. She was in her yoga clothes again. Edon wondered when she'd adopted this new look. There was something very wholesome about it, and therefore completely misleading.

"You two know where Dalarna is?" Axel asked, and Edon shook his head.

"Not exactly, though the chief – I mean, Kingsley – mentioned it."

"Very beautiful part of Sweden, not far from here. Further inland, towards the border with Norway. Usually it's very sparsely populated, but a lot of Swedes visit at this time of year, to celebrate midsummer, because there are mountains, lakes, pine forests. I have a holiday cabin there myself."

"The word 'Dalarna' means vale or valley, doesn't it?" Mina asked and Edon rolled his eyes.

"That's right. It's the classic image of Sweden, really." Axel darted a look over his shoulder, as though the seagulls dipping in and out of the fountain might be listening. "The red cottages, the blue lakes. You'll like it, I think."

"So why are we going there?" Edon asked. Unlike Ara, he wasn't on vacation.

"To the south there are old copper mines, and recently the local Venators became aware of some … activity. Nephilim, showing their ugly faces, causing trouble by murdering Red Bloods and leaving pentagrams as calling cards. We had to scramble to contain it, getting rid of the evidence before local police started asking too many questions. I can't stand that kind of business. It's against the Code. We shouldn't be interfering in human investigations in that way, getting in the way of their own laws and prosecutions."

"Sometimes you have to," Edon told him, thinking of the events in New York last year – dead girls, pentagrams, trying to stay one step ahead of the police before the story broke and put the whole Coven at risk."

"And, of course," Axel continued, "it made us curious. Anxious. Why here of all places? Why Dalarna?"

Edon glanced at Mina. In all his time hunting Silver Bloods, he'd never heard anything about some green patch of central Sweden. Mina was frowning in concentration, her green eyes hazy as frosted glass.

"It seems incredible," Axel continued, "but from everything we see and hear, we suspect there's a breakout, or at least the beginnings of one."

"A breakout – from hell?" Mina asked, and Axel nodded.

"Almost as though a new Gate of Hell is opening in Dalarna, but not one created by the Order of Seven. One somehow created in the underworld by – well, you know."

This was grim news, Edon thought, slowing his paces around the long fountain and its blithely splashing waters. If Lucifer and the Silver Bloods had found a way to pierce hell's defenses, a new war could be looming.

"Earlier you asked 'why there in Dalarna'", Mina reminded Axel. "Any theories?"

Axel let out a long sigh.

"Theories. Rumors. Hunches. Some revelations when our Venators go dreamwalking. But nothing concrete, I have to tell you. I mean, it's not like we've seen one of the paths of the dead emerging from a copper mine. But still. When one one of our local team there in Dalarna saw Finn Chase, I knew something real was happening."

"So that's why she's in Sweden?" Parts of the puzzle were starting to swim into place for Edon.

"Why else?" said Axel. "And that's why we have Schuyler Van Alen arriving in two days. If we have Silver Bloods to deal with, not just Nephilim, then we need her here. If Silver Bloods rise up here …"

Axel shook his head. He didn't need to finish the sentence. Sweden was one of the smaller countries governed by the European Conclave, Edon knew; the big Venator forces were concentrated elsewhere. A sudden explosion of Silver Bloods through this new Gate of Hell, constructed while Kingsley – their one-time conquest and current overlord – was busy in New York … That would overpower the local Venators and cause mass panic. All three of the Scandinavian Covens could be wiped out in days, and Lucifer would have a mountainous power base in northern Europe to launch a brand new war against the Blue Bloods and whoever else stood in his way.

"But one thing, Axel," Mina said, her powerful jaw set in an obstinate frown. "Why is Finn Chase so important to this? She was poisoned through a Sacred Kiss and defected to Lucifer. She's corrupted like all the Silver Bloods but she has no power by herself. All she's done is sell her soul."

"This is what we're picking up," Axel said, lowering his voice so much that Edon and Mina were forced to draw near. He waited while a blonde young woman jogged by, pushing a baby carriage and trailing a terrier on a long lead. "In Dalarna there's talk of a White Queen, a new Silver Blood leader. Someone like Finn Chase, who was at the heart of the New York Coven, privy to all its secrets, closer than anyone to its Regent – she seems like a good candidate. I know it's a flimsy case right now, but I don't like the fact that she's here, of all places in the world, and I want her found and neutralized as soon as possible."

"So you want us in Dalarna," Edon said, and Mina nodded. They were both tensing their muscles and flexing their hands, Edon knew; it was a wolf's natural reaction when he or she prepared for the hunt. Wolves weren't supposed to languish in half-empty eighteenth-century apartments with views of a pretty park – sorry, *square*. Wolves like Edon and Mina needed to be out in the field, tracking and pursuing. They might not be able to play the mind games of a Venator, but in a war the Blue Bloods needed the wolves if they wanted victory over Lucifer and his zombie-like ranks of Silver Bloods.

"Before you go, you need to know something." Axel looked stern for the first time, his pale blue eyes glinting like steel. "We have obstacles in our way. Lukas, the Regis of our local Coven, does not support this investigation. And because he has a house in Dalarna, you will need to tread very carefully there."

"He doesn't know we're on the job?" Mina asked, incredulous. It was extremely unorthodox for the Regis to be kept out of the loop by a Venator chief. Edon didn't like the sound of this at all.

"Lukas says that the White Queen is a local legend in that area. When I tell you he has a house there, please don't imagine my little cabin – Lukas' family have long been the most important in our Coven, and he has something like a palace there –a chateau, maybe you'd call it. Every midsummer in his particular village, a beautiful young woman plays the role of the White Queen. She's lifted to the top of a giant maypole in the forest."

"So he's saying that all this talk of the Silver Bloods having a White Queen is just confusion?" asked Mina.

"Yes. He says it's a muddle of local lore with paranoia, and any operation to track Silver Bloods, or Finn Chase, is a waste of Venator time. Midsummer madness, he likes to call it." The look on Axel's face suggested how much he disagreed. Edon understood. It sounded very casual an approach for a Regis faced with rising Nephilim activity in his own back yard.

"I hope he's right," Axel told them. "But my instinct tells me he isn't, and as Venator chief I can't sit around waiting for the Silver Bloods to walk out of hell dusting off their hands – and their fangs. At Midsummer we Swedes do go a little crazy, it's true. If Lucifer is planning some mayhem of his own, this is the time to do it."

"Your Regis doesn't know about this, but the New York Regent must." Edon needed to work out the chain of command. If he and Mina were going rogue, they didn't want to end up caged in hell themselves, on the wrong side of the Conclave. "She's married to Kingsley Martin, and he was the one who sent me here."

"Oh, she knows." Axel stopped again to roll up his long sleeves. The day was getting hot. "It's the New York Coven bankrolling this operation. It was Kingsley's idea to send in you wolves. Don't forget, he's still on the hunt for Oliver Hazard-Perry, as well as Finn Chase."

"He still wants to catch Oliver?" Edon was skeptical. Oliver, it seemed to him, was the least of their problems. Axel didn't seem particularly interested in Oliver either.

"The main priority is finding Finn Chase," he said. "Whether she's just another Silver Blood or this White Queen we've been hearing about from the Nephilim, we need her dead."

Dead. At least the brief was clear.

"You got it, chief," said Mina, all business as usual. "We have our orders and we won't let you down. Finn Chase – dead."

12 | SAFETY DANCE

Oliver woke up alone. That he was used to these days. But to-day –whatever day it was, Saturday? – he was relieved to find himself still alive.

His head was throbbing, worse than any hangover. He could barely open his eyes because they were so gummy with sleep. Maybe he'd been unconscious rather than asleep. The last thing he remembered was walking through some squalid apartment high in a tower block. Washing his hands, perhaps. He remembered running water and then – nothing.

Oliver's fingers crept to his aching head. It wasn't damp with blood, at least. But the crown of his head pounded as though someone was using it as a drum kit. Someone had hit him. Smashed him on the head while he was washing his hands. And now he was coming to on a lumpy mattress, sun pouring in the windows. Fully dressed apart from his shoes, which lay nearby on the floor. He couldn't hear anyone walking around in the apartment, and he wasn't restrained in any way. The door to the room where he was lying was wide open.

So someone had attacked him and then helped into bed – even tak-ing his shoes off? Oliver tried lifting his head off the mattress and groaned aloud without meaning to. He could feel a lump forming, tender and rounded. Of all the weapons he feared – crescent blades, guns with silver bullets – Oliver appeared to have been hit with something as pedestrian as a piece of wood.

Gingerly he raised himself up from the sagging mattress and swung his legs free of the tangled sheet that covered him. Whoever had hit him didn't want to kill him, or tie him up. And whoever it was had clearly left the scene of the crime. Oliver felt his way to the decrepit kitchen, head thudding, nerves jangling. Maybe Stockholm would be the end of the road for him and his desperate quest to find Finn before it was too late. Maybe he didn't have the energy left, or the street smarts. He'd stood oblivious – in the bathroom, was it? – while someone crept in and smacked him in the head. From now on, Oliver needed to be much more vigilant or just to accept the game was up. These months on the road had taken it out of him, and he was no longer the glossy, fit commander-in-chief of the New York Coven. He was a wreck with a lump on his head, stuck in a depressing apartment in some Stockholm project.

"Hello!" The front door popped open and a friendly voice, with just a hint of an accent, was calling out to him. Oliver glanced around for a weapon, flicking open a cupboard door, tugging a stuck wooden drawer off its bearings. Nothing. Not a single cup, plate or knife. If necessary, he was going to bare-hand fight his way out of this one. Oliver stood tensed and ready, trying to steady his aching head. He didn't have the heart, or the energy, to run anymore.

A short guy with gold-rimmed glasses and messy ginger hair appeared in the kitchen doorway, brandishing plastic grocery bags. He wore baggy long shorts and a messenger bag strapped across his chest.

"Hello!" he said again. "I am Christian Dahl. I bring you food."

Christian dumped the bags on a counter and started tipping their contents out.

"I have brought you some medication as well. For your head."

"What happened to me?" Oliver wasn't ready for pleasantries.

"I thought you were an intruder. The door was open, and you know, this place is quite rough. So I hit you on the head. Sorry! My bad."

All this was delivered in a cheery tone while Christian rustled about with the bags. He pulled out a pack of Aspirin and held it out to Oliver. When Oliver didn't take it, Christian laid the pack on the counter.

"I have some juice here," he said, opening and banging shut a cupboard door, "but I think there are no cups. You must drink straight from the bottle. OK, Oliver?"

So this wasn't an issue of mistaken identity. This guy knew who Oliver was. Unfortunately, the name "Christian Dahl" meant nothing to Oliver at all.

"Who are you?" demanded Oliver. This guy's breezy attitude was obnoxious. It would take more than a "my bad" to explain away that blow to the head.

"Didn't Axel tell you?"

"Who's Axel? I don't know anyone here. All I knew was to come to this place. Where, frankly, I wasn't expecting to get attacked."

"Ah." Christian put down a plastic-wrapped loaf of bread. "I thought Axel had briefed you. Axel Andersson. He's the Venator Chief here in Sweden. Actually, he oversees all of Scandinavia – that's Sweden, Norway and Denmark. Not Finland. Sometimes Americans get confused."

"I'm not confused," Oliver said sharply, though he was – not about Scandinavia. He attended high school at Duchesne, where world geography was a compulsory subject. The dark cloud of realization was descending: this wasn't a safe place after all. He'd just handed himself over to the Venators.

"Do you want something to eat?" Christian asked him, as though this was a social visit.

"No," Oliver replied, even though his stomach was rumbling with hunger. "I'd like to know what you're planning to do with me, now you have me."

"Oh, I don't know anything about plans." Christian looked stumped. "I only know what Axel told me."

"He wants you to hold me here, I expect." If Christian had crescent blades in his back pocket, it was all over, Oliver knew. Even if he managed to run, he'd be lost in an instant in this maze-like project. Central Stockholm was a distant place, and he had almost no money left. This wasn't a city where he could disappear. It was a trap.

"I don't think it's safe for you to go out, if that's what you mean." Christian still seemed confused. "That's why you're here, isn't it? You need to re-gain your strength."

Now Oliver was the confused one.

"You're a Venator?" he asked. Christian laughed, and he sounded like a barking seal. It was a startling noise coming from someone so short.

"I'm Axel's human Conduit," he told Oliver. That was good news. It meant he wouldn't be carrying blades or a gun. Oliver must have looked visibly relieved, because Christian gave him a friendly tap on the arm.

"Hey, man, don't worry. I'm really sorry about the head-injury thing. Must have given you a bad impression, yes? You're safe here. Axel keeps this apartment as a safe house. Even though the building it's in …"

He didn't need to finish his sentence. Oliver had seen enough of the neighborhood to know it wasn't exactly the Paris of the North.

"Strange place for a safe house," he said, one eyebrow arched. He leaned back against the counter, almost relaxed – almost. His head was still thumping like a bass drum. Maybe he should glug down some pills with the OJ after all.

"I know." Christian leaned back as well and folded his arms. "It's only used by Axel and some of the most senior Venators here. Most of the Coven don't know about it. Today I had to get here using three trains, because I thought someone was following me. Believe me, it's not easy making quick changes between trains when you're carrying all this."

He gestured with his head at the shopping bags. "But I don't like bringing my bike out here. Don't want it to get stolen."

"Who's following you? Silver Bloods?

"Maybe. Or other Venators."

"Really?"

"Axel can tell you more," Christian said, "but you should know right away that things are not all sunshine here in sunny Sweden. It is not the usual happy Midsummer festivities. Not this year. Axel and some others don't trust the – how do you say it? The high-up people in the Coven."

"That's how we would say it." Oliver nodded, eager to hear more. "The upper echelons of the Coven."

"Ah – echelons! Such a good English word. Though it's a French word in origins, I guess. Old French. Maybe Latin?"

"Tell me more about the Coven here," Oliver prompted, trying not to sound as impatient as he felt.

"I'm sure it's like the one in New York. Very rich, very exclusive. Old money. That's what you would call it, I think. They would never come to an area like this, or enter a building like this. Someone would rob them on the way in! This is why I carry my little plank of wood in my bag."

Christian shot a rueful look at Oliver's head.

"And why doesn't your ... why doesn't Axel trust them?" Oliver demanded. He needed to work out who to trust himself.

"You will have to talk about that with the boss," Christian told him. "But for now, you must rest and eat. Tomorrow I will bring you fresh clothes. And then you will go to Dalarna."

"Dalarna?" Oliver wasn't sure if this was a person or a place, and all Christian did was nod.

"Tomorrow or the next day," Christian said. "Your search must wait a day or two, until we have more news, and you are not tired and achy in the head."

At least he knew that Oliver was searching for something.

"Have there been any sightings?" he asked warily, unsure of how much Christian knew. He didn't want to say the words "Finn Chase" aloud. She felt like a dream, as though she'd never existed in real life.

Through the kitchen window he could see smoke rising in dark clouds. Christian frowned. Even this high up, Oliver could smell burning rubber. Men were shouting, though he couldn't make out what they were saying, or even what language they were speaking.

"I should go now," Christian said. "There's unrest here, in this area. Many protests and anger about the government and the police. Sometimes they burn tires, sometimes cars. Last week it was a police car. Stay away from the windows. I'll see you tomorrow, my friend. I left my number on the back of the receipt, in case you need to call."

Oliver didn't know why staying away from windows was so crucial when he was several floors up. After Christian scuttled out, he peeked through the drawn curtains of the living room. A gang of kids – maybe the one who greeted him – were throwing bottles at a departing Coke truck. Most of the kids were on bikes and wearing bandanas around their mouths, maybe as a disguise, maybe because smoke from the fire on the other side of the building was spreading in the breeze.

Christian had been friendly, and at least he had some information – not to mention food, and the promise of clean clothes. But still, Oliver had a bad feeling about this place. Why would a Venator chief, of all people, want to take him in, when other Venators had been chasing him around the world? Would an apartment *really* be a safe house, so far from the city, and so close to what looked like a brewing riot? And why would a human conduit know both so much and so little?

Airing the Coven's dirty laundry … Oliver wasn't sure if he could believe a word Christian said. Leaving his phone number seemed like a kind gesture, but when Oliver rummaged through his bag for his own phone, it was gone. Had Christian taken it?

He walked down the hallway to the front door to make sure it was locked: he'd had enough surprise visitors for one day. The door wouldn't budge. The good news: it was obviously locked. But the bad news was however much he messed about with it, the lock remained in clamped position, unresponsive to any attempts to open it.

Christian had locked him in.

13 | UNDER THE BRIDGE

*A*ra wasn't used to spending her days wandering the streets: usually this was her sleeping time, the hours when she huddled in her little Williamsburg pit, shutting the Red Blood world out. She'd never been a day-shift Venator and she didn't want to start now. But there was only so much sitting around in that apartment on Mariatorget that she could stand. This morning Edon and Mina had been holed up in the kitchen, alternately sniping at each other or gossiping about wolves Ara didn't know and incidents she didn't care about. Then they swanned off, brimming with self-importance, to meet the local Venator chief.

Strange that Edon had never mentioned Mina once in however many months he and Ara had been working together – let alone sleeping together. Now it seemed they were long-lost somethings; Ara wasn't quite sure what. They seemed to dislike each other, but they also seemed very comfortable with each other. Very intimate.

Of course. They were former lovers. Ara was an idiot not to have sensed it immediately. Not for the first time, Ara deeply regretted coming to Sweden with Edon. Getting out of New York City for a while wasn't a bad thing, but she didn't need to fly all the way here to feel excluded from her past life – her real life – as a Venator. She certainly didn't need to be an onlooker while Edon and Mina played out whatever sexual psychodrama they had going on.

Once those two intensely annoying wolves had stomped off down the stairs, Ara had a brief shower in the expansive tiled bathroom. A blast under the hot water, a quick scrub of her cropped hair, a speedy rub-down with a big, soft towel. She never allowed herself to relax or luxuriate, Ara observed, as though she was floating outside her body, seeing everything from a distance. Maybe that was because she didn't want to go back to the old Minty days, when she was a spoiled princess who only knew the finer things in life. These days she was a Neph fighter, heart and soul, and everything else just seemed frivolous. The old Minty would have been gushing over the lavender soap, the shampoo that smelled like pine forests, the marshmallow towel of Egyptian cotton. Ara didn't want to become that person again. Just because she was "on vacation" didn't mean she could let her guard down.

She was dressed and out of the apartment before the wolves returned. They were talking with a tall guy by the fountain, so she gave them a wide berth and re-traced the walk from the day before. Edon had teased her that the island of Södermalm, where they were staying, was a kind of Swedish Williamsburg, and he wasn't completely wrong. Everyone here looked like a runway model, tanned and leggy, with clear skin and bright eyes. This place was way too wholesome for Ara.

Today was Saturday, she realized, and this meant the city was busy with shoppers and sightseers. Boats plied the waterways between the city's islands. Double-decker tourist buses lumbered by, blasting out the tour guide's commentary; ferries crammed with people taking photographs or basking in the sun headed out along the harbor towards attractions elsewhere.

The old town was a lattice-work of cobbled lanes and cramped old townhouses, some streets so narrow they were permanently in shade. In the old town's main square, the buildings were painted in ice cream tones, pastel and summery. If Ara had been a person who liked flowers, her spirits might have been lifted by the hanging baskets brimming with color, or the lush plantings in the window boxes of boutiques and cafés.

But she wasn't a flower person. She was a kick-some-demon's-ass vampire. Wandering around here, getting bumped by guides holding umbrellas aloft, or blocked by lines of people waiting to buy pastries or secure a table outside a café, Ara remembered why she'd opted for the night shift.

At least there were plenty of interconnecting paths to follow – streets, bridges, squares. The bigger island where they'd arrived by train had more of a familiar downtown, with big stores and food trucks selling hot dogs or kebabs. There wasn't the pace of New York City here, but near the main station and the various subway stops people looked a little less well-fed, more edgy and scruffy. There was even a homeless person pushing a shopping cart, muttering expletives in English. Home sweet home, Ara thought. Anything was better than sitting idle in that apartment, watching Mina do her yoga stretches.

Something about the vibe between Mina and Edon grated on her, and it wouldn't leave Ara alone, even after she'd been walking for hours. Of course she wasn't jealous. Of course not. Absolutely not. Edon was sexy, but he was just a mangy old wolf these days; his glory golden-wolf days were long behind him.

Anyway, Ara wasn't the kind to get hung up on a guy. Sometimes she almost envied those great Blue Bloods love stories, like Schuyler Van Alen and Jack Force, or Mimi Force and Kingsley Martin. They were so glamorous, so perfect. Save the world, get married, kiss kiss. All of the fallen were supposed to aspire to their lives, and once upon a time Ara would have been no exception. In her Minty days, dressed in her private-school uniform, she would have thought nabbing herself a hero-wolf boyfriend would have been the ultimate in cool.

Boyfriend. What a stupid word. A wolf could never be a boy, especially when he was as long in the tooth – ha! – as Edon Marrok.

As for Mina the she-wolf: Ara saw just another version of Deming

Chen. Beautiful, aloof, stuck-up. Just another cool girl who preferred the company of guys. She'd actually made a lengthwise barrier of pillows in the bed last night, slicing the space in half so Ara wouldn't "intrude," as Mina called it.

"Wolves need their space," she'd said, her tone brusque, looking at Ara with barely veiled contempt. "And sister, you need a shower."

Ara hadn't even bothered to reply.

At some point in the afternoon she gobbled down a hotdog and two tall glasses of beer in the diviest, darkest little bar she could find. It wasn't exactly the Lower East Side, and she couldn't believe the prices – it was maybe three times as expensive here as it was in New York. Then she lay out in the sun for a while, sweatshirt balled up as a pillow, arms sheltering her face, by a stretch of water that flickered with reflected sunlight. She wasn't the only sunbather on the stone ledges and park benches of this part of the city.

She must have dozed off – not the wisest thing for a Venator to do, not in public, and not in the daytime. The beer must have been strong, Ara thought, creaking into an upright position. The sun was lower in the sky now, but she knew there were still endless hours of daylight ahead. Damn this endless day. Damn this vacation. Venators didn't take vacations. How could this possibly be good for her mental health?

Back in the dark bar, which would have been perfect if it had air conditioning, Ara sat at the counter and ordered another beer.

"You visiting Stockholm for long?" the barman asked her. He reminded her of the barman at the Holiday – beefy, bearded, his skin swirling with tattoos. "Here for Midsummer?"

"I don't know. Maybe." Ara glugged back half her beer. She liked the look of it as well as the taste – liquid gold. "Here tonight, anyway. In Södermalm."

She hoped she was saying the name of the island properly.

The barman grinned, swabbing at the counter, but their conversation was interrupted by another customer, a tourist in an *I Heart Stockholm* t-shirt who wanted every Swedish beer ever explained.

In an instant Ara knew she couldn't stick around. Not in Sweden, not for Midsummer, and definitely not with Edon Marrok. This whole thing was stupid. He had work to do, and she wasn't allowed to work, so what was she, exactly? A useless appendage. Excess baggage, especially now Mina was here. She needed to go back to New York City where she belonged. She could lie low in her place, drink coffee in the bodega on the corner, maybe tidy things up a little. Kingsley would relent before long – surely he would have to relent when he saw how quiet and compliant Ara was acting.

Because it would be an act, a performance. Inside Ara would be seething with rage and resentment, just the way she was now. But Kingsley didn't need to know that.

So: mind made up. Tomorrow, when Edon and Mina headed out – as they were sure to do, claiming "wolf business" and acting as though they were singlehandedly saving the world – Ara would pack her things, hop on a train and head back to the airport. What was the time difference – five hours, six? She'd be going back in time. Fly out Sunday, arrive Sunday. Home in New York in time to watch the baseball. Not that she liked baseball.

The barman was back, gesturing to see if she wanted another beer.

"If you're staying in Södermalm," he said, "you should check out Trädgården."

He wrote the name, and its perplexing Swedish symbols, down on a bar napkin for her.

"It's like a big outside bar that turns into a club on weekends over the summer. It's under a bridge, and pretty cool. I think you'd like it."

"Thanks," Ara said, toasting him with her empty glass. He was sketching her a little map.

"It's here," he said and pointed to his scrawl. "Under the Skanstull bridge. Far side of Södermalm. You might want to catch the subway from here."

"I don't mind walking," Ara said. She needed to walk off some of that beer anyway. Maybe by the time she got there the sun might be thinking about setting.

"It'll be crowded," the barman warned her, but Ara was on her way out and didn't bother to reply. She had a buzz from the beer, and outside the evening was growing cloudy and cooler, the fading sun increasingly obscured. She crossed the long bridge that led to Södermalm and trudged south, enjoying the thwack of her boots against the sidewalk and the feeling of the breeze dancing on her bare arms. Tomorrow night she'd be back in New York. The vacation she didn't want would be over. And Edon? They'd be over as well, she guessed.

That was something Ara didn't want to think about right now.

It was easy to follow the crowds to the club under the Skanstull bridge. Everyone under 30 seemed to be headed there. Once she got over the weirdness of the giant concrete bridge pilings, Ara liked the strange set-up – as though everyone had dragged their grandmother's living-room furniture outside, and set up a whole lot of makeshift bars. It didn't bother her that everyone else was in a group, drinking and talking and laughing, or that she seemed to be the only person around wearing all black. She pushed her way up to one of the bars, handed over a wad of krona, and received a slippery plastic glass of beer. No talking, no messing around. This was her kind of place.

Perhaps she'd been hanging out too much with wolves, but tonight Ara felt like ranging about the space, keeping moving rather than squeezing onto the end of a picnic bench or perching on the arm of a sofa. Drink and walk, drink and walk. She could survey the crowd and keep an eye out for Nephs. Venators couldn't go on vacation, she kept telling herself. And club scenes like this one, where the DJ was setting up on the stage and the strung lights were already twinkling, were the kind of places the Nephilim liked to show up – selling drugs, maybe, spiking drinks or picking pockets. Taking advantage of drunk people. That half-demon blood couldn't help revealing itself, making the lives of the Red Bloods miserable. Ara hoped some Venators were here, to keep a lid on things. Maybe in Sweden Venators didn't wear black – or maybe they were here in disguise.

The music was getting louder and the sun was setting at last. The lights flashed, changing colors, and more people were crowding the stage. This was going to be one big dance party later on. Ara could sense the energy waiting to explode. A summer weekend, lots of young people, throbbing music, too much sun and drinking … this was the place to be, and a recipe for trouble. Just the kind of recipe Ara liked.

The next beer would be her last, Ara told herself. Then the next beer, and the next beer. She found herself talking to random guys, having those meaningless shouty conversations that went on in clubs all over the world. Where are you from, how long are you here, do you like it … wow, New York City, how cool, I'd love to go there, I've already been there, I want to live there some day …. On and on it went. Some guy bought her a drink, and then he'd wandered away and Ara found herself drinking with a group of people, all toasting their plastic glasses. She joined in, beer splashing onto the concrete when their glasses clashed.

"I'm going home tomorrow," she shouted in the ear of the person next to her, and wondered if she'd even be able to find her way home to the apartment on Mariatorget tonight.

"Too bad," said the girl – or was it a guy she was talking to? Things were getting blurry. "You should stay in Sweden for Midsummer. It's the best night of the year, I promise you."

"I wish I could," Ara lied. She knocked back some beer and gazed around the crowd. So many blondes here in Sweden. It was a cliché but it was true. That's why she fit in, with her platinum crop of hair. Ara started giggling at the thought of herself as a blonde Swede. A Viking, she told herself. A Viking Venator.

So many blondes, dancing in front of the stage, drinking with friends, making out with lovers. Weaving through the crowd … wearing a white dress, long hair billowing as though they were in a music video, looking beautiful and serene and somehow above it all ….

Looking exactly like Finn Chase.

PART TWO | AFTER THE BALL

And pomp, and feast, and revelry
With mask, and antique pageantry,
Such sights as youthful poets dream
On summer eves by haunted stream.
—JOHN MILTON, *L'ALLEGRO*

14 | IT'S GETTING HOT IN HERE

*T*he car would arrive for them at seven, Schuyler was told by the handsome young guy at hotel reception. This hotel in Stockholm was a mirror image of Mimi and Kingsley's apartment, she thought the moment they walked in through the sliding glass doors. Everything white, with giant light features that looked fragile and expensive. Shiny surfaces that would show every fingerprint. Just as well they were here without the twins. Lily would be spinning in one of those retro Egg chairs by now, or spinning Sy in it to make him sick.

"What car?" she asked, and the receptionist flashed a dazzling smile.

"To take you to your welcome party," he said, with a slight bow of the head. "Welcome to Stockholm."

"Welcome party?" Jack was next to her now, standing over their suitcases, his face looking strained. He hadn't slept at all on the plane: Schuyler knew that because she hadn't slept either.

Their hotel suite had been booked by the local Venator chief, someone who Kingsley lauded as one of the best in the world – but that was typical Kingsley. He was drawn and worried these days, but he still had some of the old swagger about him. Schuyler guessed this would be some kind of Venator welcome.

"I can't imagine it'll be fancy," she told Jack, yawning as she un-packed. "I brought this one dress with me – do you think it's OK?"

She held up a navy-blue summer dress with thin shoulder straps. A thin sash gathered the straps in the back, but it wasn't too girly or fancy. Schuyler liked to wear it in Napa with silver jewelry and strappy sandals, her hair loose. A glass of their own wine in her hand.

That life was gone now, she thought. Gone for the foreseeable future, anyway.

"How fancy can some Venator welcome be?" Jack was barely intel-ligible through his own yawns. "It'll probably be at some bar like the Holiday, with beer on tap and nachos. If we're lucky."

They slept for a few hours that afternoon, curled up together on the white bed like puppies. Clinging to each other, Schuyler thought, and waiting for the storm.

The car was a black Audi, with a driver who smiled and bowed but said nothing at all. His livery was impeccable. Not very Venator-style at all.

"I already feel underdressed," Jack muttered to her. He was wearing a linen shirt over jeans.

When pressed, the driver told them, in perfect English, that they were driving to the exclusive Ostermalm area, to a neighborhood called Diplomatstaden. All the embassies were located there.

"A very nice area," he said, and then fell silent again. "Nice" was an understatement, Schuyler soon realized. This had to be one of the most expensive parts of the city. The car passed grand brick villas, red or golden in the evening sun, that looked at least a century old. It was like Newport on a smaller scale, maybe – or like Southampton with better taste.

"We're going to meet the Regis," Jack murmured to her, as though the obvious had finally sunk in. Of course they were.

The car pulled up to a contemporary wooden gate, slatted and opaque, that slid open when he pressed numbers into the iPad rest-ing on the front passenger seat. Beyond a towering thicket of trees, the gravel driveway swooped in an elegant half-circle. A number of cars – Audis, BMWs, Volvos, Mercedes – were parked in an orderly line, attended by young valets dressed all in white. The house itself was white, three stories high with dormer windows and roof tiles the color of salmon. It had two tall white chimneys, and a matching white stable block, which probably served as a garage these days. Schuyler had seen versions of this house before, usually in the Hamptons, but this smacked of genuine old money and nineteenth-century elegance. In the distance, beyond the villa, a lawn stretched to sparkling water.

"We may be underdressed," Schuyler whispered to Jack, who flashed back a conspiratorial smile. The young valet opening their car doors and ushering them up the broad front steps looked more expensively dressed than Jack.

"I've never seen white suede espadrilles before," he muttered, one protective hand on the small of Schuyler's back.

"Probably reindeer skin," she said, and they both laughed. They were still laughing when the double doors swung open to admit them, and they found themselves in an elegant foyer, a staircase swirling to the upper floors, and a model-like waiter on hand with a tray of Aquavit cocktails.

"Infused with lemongrass and lingonberries," the handsome young server told them, and Schuyler had to suppress more nervous laughter. They'd imagined a glass of beer with local Venators. This was the other end – the far end – of the scale. Thank god she'd remembered to pack one dress.

"What an honor!" called a confident male voice, and a man – tall, round-bellied, his silver hair floppy and glossy – appeared before them, like an ocean liner gliding into port. "I am Lukas Stromberg, and this is my wife ... where is she? Pernilla! Our guests of honor are here!"

Pernilla instantly materialized: she was a beautiful, willowy blonde who was at least twenty years younger than her husband, dressed in a silver 20s cocktail dress, her slender arms rattling with bangles.

"So happy you could join us," Pernilla said with a nervous smile.

Schuyler felt sorry for her, though she wasn't sure why. There was something Stepford Wife about Pernilla: her trembling hands gave her away. No wonder the bangles were rattling.

So this was the local Regis and his wife, and about a hundred of their closest friends, from what Schuyler could make out, as their hosts guided them through a series of large, high-ceilinged rooms, all painted an elegant gray. So these were the Scandinavian Blue Bloods, or an even more exclusive sub-set, gathering together for "a little cocktail party," as Lukas put in, to welcome their illustrious guests from the US.

Schuyler's head began to buzz with supernatural interference. She was highly tuned to the frequencies of the vampire world, even at large social gatherings, but the messages she was getting confused her. There were secrets here, and a tension that crackled through the house and out onto the expansive green lawn. She felt as though she and Jack were being steered through a planned course, shown off to everybody but never allowed to pause or talk.

The path led, inexorably, to Lukas' wood-paneled study, its walls painted a washed gray, all the furniture expensive and faux-rustic in a pared-back Nordic way. The paintings on the wall were all landscapes of green meadows and blue skies. It was all a little too perfect, Schuyler thought, as Lukas closed the door behind her and Jack – with Pernilla firmly on the other side.

"Another drink?" he offered, and Jack glanced at Schuyler. They both shook their heads. The noise of the party hummed in the distance.

"It's very kind of you to invite us," Schuyler said, wishing they'd never come. This whole evening was a set-up. The hospitality was as fake as half the faces and breasts at the party.

"I know you're here on business rather than pleasure." Lukas' smile had frozen on his face. "Perhaps you could explain why?"

"Surely you don't need an explanation." Jack looked bemused. "Surely you've received word from the European Conclave."

"Ah yes!" Lukas chuckled. "I hear what they're saying. That the hard-fought peace we won ten years ago is under threat."

We won. Schuyler liked that. She didn't remember Lukas taking part in any of the battles.

"You don't believe it?" Jack was incredulous. He was trying to keep his voice down, Schuyler knew, but anyone standing nearby was all-too-obviously eavesdropping.

"What to believe, what not to believe," said Lukas. His golden tan glowed, as fake as his smile. He turned to face Schuyler, staring at her hard. "For example, is it true that your own half-sister is implicated in a plot to revive Lucifer's power on earth?"

"You know as much as we do," Schuyler said. Two could play his disingenuous game. "Clearly you think that something is worthy of investigation."

"There's nothing to link any of this to the coven in Sweden," Lukas said. He looked around the room for support, his expression theatrical, as though he'd forgotten the assembled Blue Bloods were locked out of the room. "Not a shred of evidence. Just some wolves howling about nothing, from what I hear."

"Let's discuss this at another time," Jack said. "When we all have more facts at our disposal."

He sat his glass on the desk and looked at Schuyler, one eyebrow arched. *Time to go.* It was fine with her. Their own Blue Bloods in New York could be snobby, but they wouldn't behave so badly to visitors. Especially not someone like Jack Force. *Do you know who you're talking to?* she wanted to shout. This is Abbadon, twin Angel of the Apocalypse, not some roaming wolf!

"Here in Sweden," Lukas was saying, strolling about the room like an actor wandering the stage, always conscious of the spotlight, "our Coven members enjoy the highest standard of living of any Coven in the world. We have an enviable position, Mr. Force. Every other Coven in Europe aspires to our lifestyle, and to the peace we've enjoyed for the past decade."

"Well," said Jack, tight-lipped, "we all want that to continue, don't we?"

Lukas wasn't smiling now.

"Your arrival here, with your beautiful wife," he said, nodding in Schuyler's direction, "is over-doing it, wouldn't you say? Scaring people. Sending the wrong message."

"We receive messages," Schuyler told him, aware of the iciness of her tone. The slickness of Lukas, and the way he'd hijacked this so-called welcome party, enraged her. "We don't send them."

His smile returned, patronizing this time.

"And who is sending these messages, my dear? Could it be the New York Regis, who is, after all, your husband's twin and former bond-mate?"

Schuyler felt her face glowing red. She'd been away from the Blue Bloods too long. She'd forgotten about the games some of them liked to play, the jockeying for social position and influence.

"Could this be, perhaps, a political ploy on the part of your Regis," Lukas continued, "to draw attention away from the ongoing misman-agement in New York? I'm referring, of course, to the thoughtless and criminal actions of your last Regent, Oliver Hazard-Perry. I believe he was your former human Conduit, Mrs. Force, was he not?"

"This is ridiculous." Schuyler didn't have time to reply, because a furious Jack had stepped forward. He had a much shorter fuse these days, and Lukas was just provoking him. "You can't blame any of what's happened – and what's happening now – on Schuyler. Or even on Ol-iver, for that matter. Finn Chase drank Silver Blood poison, willingly and knowingly. She was using Oliver, trying to destroy the whole Co-ven. We know all this for a fact. We have the confession of our former Venator chief, Sam Lennox, who was complicit in the whole thing."

"Conveniently dead now, isn't he?" Lukas smirked. Schuyler could see how his arrogance was inflaming Jack. She tugged on his arm. They needed to go back to the hotel right away. "And Finn Chase – disap-peared. Oliver Hazard-Chase – also disappeared. All your New York problems gone, just like that. Pfft!"

He wriggled his fingers as though he were sprinkling fairydust.

"And now you're trying to make them European problems, without any proof."

"Your own Venator chief here in Sweden thinks differently," Jack snapped. Lukas rolled his eyes.

"Venators report to me. I am the Regis. Your New York Venators might go rogue, but here my word is the law. And I am an actual Blue Blood, unlike Oliver Hazard-Chase." Lukas practically spat out the name. "So the Coven can trust me. Absolutely. We don't intermarry here, you'll find."

He glanced at Schuyler for the briefest moment, but she noticed, and so did Jack.

There was a tap on the door and Pernilla appeared, opening the door just wide enough to wriggle in.

"I thought our guests might like something to eat," she said. Lukas glared at her.

"I'm just explaining the way we do things here in Scandinavia," he said. "How we don't allow former Conduits to take control of our Coven, or their Human Familiars, for that matter."

The look on Lukas' face was one of utter contempt, but Pernilla seemed embarrassed. Jack reached for Schuyler's hand. She wanted to stalk out of this party, kick every piece of Gustav-the-Whatever furniture on the way out, and she knew Jack did as well.

"Well," Jack said, clear and controlled. "Your word may be law within your own Coven, but Schuyler Van Alen and I are not your subjects. And without us, your Coven would not have enjoyed any kind of peace over the last ten years. Without us, Lucifer would be dictating your *lifestyle*. In fact, you might not have lifestyle, or life, at all. He would have wiped out your Coven, one by one."

Pernilla flushed pink and even Lukas seemed lost for words.

"We'll see ourselves out," Jack said, and this seemed to prod Pernilla into action. She walked towards them, a limpid hand extended.

"Thank you so much for coming this evening," she said, beaming as though they'd all had a wonderful time. "You must visit us in the countryside. For Midsummer?"

Schuyler was so astounded that all she could do was stare. In the car home, still shaking with anger, she turned to Jack. He was holding her hand but glaring out the window, as upset and enraged as she was.

"For Midsummer!" she said, and they both burst out laughing.

15 | PROWLING

*I*t was late, so late the sun had set, and there was still no sign of Ara. Edon wasn't surprised, not entirely, but he wasn't happy either. At least she hadn't run off back to New York, because her stuff was still here, black tanks and jeans strewn around the bedroom in her usual manner.

"She'll come back," Mina predicted, slurping instant Pot Noodles at the dining room table. She'd added raw mince to it. And people said *he* was uncivilized. "She's in love with you, she doesn't know anyone else in the city, and all her stinky gear is still here."

"She might not come home tonight, though." Edon paced the floor, aware of the boards creaking with every step.

"She might get lucky, you mean?" Mina snorted and rattled her take-out chopsticks in the plastic pot. "Not unless she had a shower before she went out. Really, she smelled ripe. And in a country with so many real blondes, is anyone buying her platinum schtick?"

"Be quiet," growled Edon. "You don't know her. She's a great Venator."

"A great Venator ... on forced leave." Mina gazed up at him, disbelief in her eyes. "That sounds like a vampire who's messed up to me.

Though I know, I know. They're all mess-ups, the fallen. Trying to get back into Paradise, if only God will have them. Atoning for their sins! Poor little Blue Bloods!"

Mina gave an exaggerated sigh then returned her attention to the mound of raw mince. Edon felt even more agitated now. Ara didn't have any Venator weapons with her, which made her vulnerable. He wasn't sure how she felt about Mina showing up; he wasn't sure how she felt about anything right now. He and Mina had their marching orders: they were leaving for Dalarna in the morning, and he needed to talk to Ara before they left. She had decisions to make: was she going to find somewhere to stay in Stockholm? Because she couldn't stay in this Venator apartment without him, given that she wasn't supposed to be here at all.

Or – his preference – would she come with him to the countryside? He'd make sure that wherever they were staying had two bedrooms. That Mina/Ara roommate arrangement was going to cause major trouble, if he knew Mina – and if he knew Ara.

"You gonna prowl around this apartment all night pining for your angel?" Mina mocked him.

"I told you to be quiet."

"Come on, softie." Mina dropped her chopsticks. She sprang to her feet, still as lithe and supple as she was ten years ago. He wished he could say the same for himself. "There's no point in waiting here for her. You know what the fallen are like – always getting into trouble. Let's go track her down."

"Really?" Edon was surprised.

"Sure. I'm not completely heartless, whatever you might think." She threw him an arch look. "And I know we can't leave for the countryside tomorrow with her stuff still here. I'm not dragging all those stinky black clothes around Sweden with me. And I know your bags are full of hair product and designer underwear."

"Thanks," he said softly.

"My money's on her being somewhere in Södermalm," Mina said, retying her sleek ponytail. "You said she lives in Williamsburg, right? She won't be able to resist the hipster vibe."

Ara would have been disgusted by the hipster branding, but Edon thought Mina was right: Södermalm was a good base for their search. Trouble was, it was also a good base for dozens of the clubs and bars in Stockholm. Mina was an expert at skipping lines and befriending bouncers: there was something about wolves that made Red Bloods wary and respectful, some innate authority or aggression, maybe. Edon had a photo of Ara on his phone to flash at bouncers and barmen, hoping she had distinctive enough a look –blunt cheekbones, searing eyes and platinum crop – to have made an impression.

One bearded, tattooed bouncer shook his head when he looked at the picture.

"Haven't seen her in here tonight," he said. "But maybe she's already left for Dalarna."

"Why Dalarna?" Mina practically jumped on him, breathing fire. "Why would you say that?"

"Everyone goes there about now. All the club kids. Dalarna is where the best midsummer raves happen, in the forests. You know, the sun never really sets at this time of year. The night is one long twilight. Everyone goes kinda crazy."

"Anywhere in particular?" Edon asked. He hoped Ara hadn't taken off on a hunch – or worse, in the back of some stranger's car. The bouncer shrugged.

"The forest," he said, with a vague wave of one hand. The word "galen" was tattooed across his right knuckles. Edon tapped it into his phone, just in case there was something significant about it, but all "galen" meant was crazy.

"Ask some of the kids in here," he told them. "Or in any club. They'll know the best places, or the ones with a lot of buzz this year. Maybe checkout some of the clubs off Stureplan? You might find your friend there. And someone will tell you the place to be in Dalarna this midsummer, for sure."

Stureplan, they discovered was a square in **Östermalm, a more upmarket area** of the city on the far side of the old town. Edon and Mina jumped into a cab and named the neighborhood.

"Where do you want to go?" the driver asked, a Sikh in a green turban who spoke good English, like everyone else they'd encountered in Stockholm. "Spy Bar? Sturecompagniet? Or that new place – the Bank?"

Something about the Bank sounded familiar to Edon. He thought there might have been a club in New York with that name once upon a time, the kind of place young Blue Bloods flocked to make themselves seem cool.

"Yeah, take us there. The new place."

"It may be a little… ah, too young for you," the driver advised, and Mina rolled her eyes.

"Thanks," she said. "Thanks a lot."

"It's only been open a few weeks and they say it's closing after Midsummer. Like a pop-up club – is that what you call it?"

"It is indeed," Mina said, sounding sniffy. She was still annoyed about the age comment.

Stureplan felt more like an intersection than a square, big avenues merging, taxis veering, and people spilling out of street-side restaurants and bars, dressed – Edon thought – like wealthy drunk people everywhere: flimsy clothes, heels too high, iPhones and cigarettes waving around, a lot of shrieking and laughing. The driver sped past a weird giant mushroom sculpture and down one of the big streets that fed the square, the lurched to a halt outside a tall stone building. A meandering line of would-be clubbers stretched down the street, only the first fifty or so contained by the red velvet rope.

"Good luck getting in!" he said, Mina slamming the door extra hard to let him know what she thought of his advice.

"We'll just talk to the bouncers and move on," she muttered to Edon.

"We should take a look inside," he said. "This may be a Blue Bloods club. We may get some other intel in there."

The wolves marched straight up to one of the bouncers, dressed in black with a giant diamond-stud earring. Mina flicked him the fake Swedish police ID they'd been provided, very thoughtfully, by Axel.

"Anyone seen this woman?" he asked all the bouncers, showing them Ara's picture. Nobody had. "We need to go in."

The bouncer with the diamond stuf swung open the rope without saying a word, though the people waiting were vocal in their complaints.

"Hey! We've been waiting for over an hour," moaned one guy with a man bun and a snake tattooed on his neck. Edon had to resist the urge to elbow him in the gut. He hated man buns.

Like its New York counterpart, the club was housed in what looked like an old bank, though it was hard to make sense of its architecture and layout with the pulsating lights and throng of people on the massive dance floor or pressing up to one of the bars. The DJ was shouting something in Swedish about Dalarna, and Edon grabbed a passing waif, her blonde hair longer than her leather skirt, to ask her what the guy was saying.

"He's saying, see you in Dalarna!" she shouted. "Woo! Midsummer!"

She wriggled out of Eden's grip and disappeared into the writhing crowd on the dance floor. If Ara *was* in here, she'd be impossible to spot. Mina might be annoyed by age comments, but Edon knew this was not his scene. The throb of the music, its electronic chirrups, was giving him a headache. Why did they think they could find her anywhere in this strange city? And why the hell hadn't she come back to the apartment?

Mina was breathing into his ear, dragging some poor blond guy by his t-shirt.

"Hey, old man!" she shouted. "This kid says he knows the best place to go in Dalarna."

"Yeah, for sure," the guy said, and Edon leaned closer to catch everything he was saying. "This year, it's the White Queen's rave. That's what everyone is saying."

"Who's everyone?" Mina looked skeptical, but she flashed Edon a significant look. *The White Queen.*

"Oh, you know," said their informer, tugging his t-shirt free of Mina's grasp. "Everyone. It's going to be massive, you know? Massive."

"Where in Dalarna?"

"Hey, you should …" The blond guy glanced around, scratching his head. "One of the organizers is here. You should talk to him."

"What's his name?" Mina demanded.

"I don't know." The blond guy sounded agitated now, Edon noticed. Maybe he was afraid he'd said too much. "But I just saw him up at the rooftop bar. He's wearing a purple shirt. You can't miss him." The guy jabbed at a staircase Edon hadn't even noticed yet, and then slithered away before Mina could grab him again.

They had to tread on people lolling on the stairs, and push past groups blocking the way up in chattering clusters. A bouncer on the third floor landing held out a hand to stop them, but Mina flashed her ID again and he let them pass. There were fewer people standing around on the stairs now, and Edon got a strong Blue Bloods vibe from them, a faint scent of recognition. Mina bounded ahead, sleek ponytail swinging, still looking as good in her jeans as she always had. Damn, Edon thought: he needed to keep his mind on the job. Ara was enough of a handful without adding Mina, and all their old wild times, into the mix.

The door to the rooftop bar was ajar, but the sprawling terrace was empty. Lights twinkled along the deserted bar counter, and glasses and bottles were crowded on low tables next to more than a dozen empty sofas. There was something eerie about it, as though the place had just been evacuated and everything – drinks, conversations, work – had been abruptly abandoned. No guy in a purple shirt emerged from the gloom. There was no one anywhere. Just the evening breeze, and the sounds of busy traffic, and club-goers whooping in the street below.

Mina looked at Edon, eyes narrowed.

"What the …?" she said.

Edon didn't reply. He pulled out his knife and moved left, Mina instinctively moving right to case the terrace. But their eyes weren't deceiving them. There was no one hiding, no one in the shadows. The rooftop bar was empty. Why it was empty, and so suddenly, and where everyone had gone, was another matter.

On the far side of the bar, by the balustrade overlooking the street, they met up.

"Looks like we came to the right place," said Mina. "If we were looking for something weird, that is."

The door to the stairway clicked shut, startling them both.

"Let's get out of here," Edon said and they strode to the door; he was bracing himself to find it locked, to find themselves in a rooftop trap. But the door wasn't locked. When Mina turned the handle, the door pulled towards them, though it was heavy and opened slowly.

Before it was fully open, they could see why it was heavy. Hanging on the other side of the door was the blond kid they'd been talking with downstairs. His head was slumped and his t-shirt was bright with blood. He'd been impaled through the stomach and left dangling there. Dead, Edon could see at a glance. The weapon sticking him to the door was a crescent blade.

16 | THE SILVER TRAIL

*A*ra had lost Finn's trail – if it really was Finn. The girl she'd seen, beautiful and blonde, had climbed into a silver car and soared away. Ara had managed to hail a cab and follow, all the way across this island, and the next and then the next. So many islands, so much confusion. She didn't know where the hell she was going.

They passed high-end designer stores like Chanel and Hermes, chic department stores, restaurants with looping velvet ropes outside. This made some kind of sense to Ara: if the woman she was following was Finn Chase, then she'd head for what she knew – luxury and wealth. Finn Chase wasn't the kind to be hanging out under a bridge, drinking from a plastic cup. She would seek out some ritzy club in an expensive neighborhood, finding some Swedish version of her Uptown life. Ara had grown out of all that. Some girls never did.

The traffic snarled on one busy street, and the silver car slipped away like an eel, zipping between other cars while all Ara's cab driver could manage was a crawl.

"Hurry – we're losing the other car!" she shouted, but all he did was gesture at the police cars along the side of the road, and a man in uniform waving traffic into another lane. Drivers behind them were honking. The sidewalk was packed with people, most of them standing around rather than walking. The driver buzzed his window down and leaned out to chat to another driver, standing smoking next to his parked cab.

"There's a new nightclub there," her driver reported. "The Bank. Very popular with – you know, rich people. Just up the street. There's been a murder in there tonight. Maybe a terrorist attack – nobody knows. Everyone's had to leave the club. The police are closing the road."

The silver car was gone. Ara slammed her hand on the seat with frustration.

Four slender figures in black stalked by, and the back of Ara's neck prickled: she knew instinctively that they were Venators. Her fingers twitched, longing for her own blades. She desperately wanted to leap out of the taxi and follow those long black shadows into the club.

"So, where now?" her driver asked.

"Mariatorget," Ara said, her heart heavy. She still wanted to leap out of the car: all her instincts were screaming at her to get back to that club and work alongside the local Venators. But she was no use to them without weapons and without authorization. Something bad was going on here, even if it wasn't really Finn Chase in the silver car, even if Ara had just been hallucinating that particular sighting. Here in a club on this street, someone was dead, and Venators were piling in to investigate.

The taxi made a U-turn, like practically every other car in the street, and snaked down one side street after another. At an intersection, waiting at an interminable light, Ara watched a sleek black Audi drive past.

In the back seat of the Audi sat Jack Force and Schuyler Van Alen.

Oh my god. Ara rubbed her eyes, but she wasn't drunk. Not *that* drunk, anyway. She'd recognize those two anywhere. What were they doing in Stockholm? She thought they'd retired to life on their vineyard after the war, and were lying low until their children were old enough for the Blood Manifest. This was no coincidence. Whatever Edon's mission involved, it was much, much bigger than Ara had imagined. So big and so bad that Schuyler Van Alen had risen from her retirement.

As big and bad as Finn Chase? As Oliver Hazard-Perry? As Lucifer himself?

"Hurry please," Ara told the driver. She wanted to get back to the apartment as soon as possible and confront Edon. He had to tell her what was going on.

He had to let her help him.

With central traffic in chaos, it took what felt like an eternity to get back to the apartment. Ara had Edon's key, figuring he wouldn't need it: he was glued to that she-wolf Mina, and anyway, he could always pick the lock with his knife. He'd be sure to know something about what was happening in the city tonight, and she'd coax it out of him. Ara felt the thrill of the chase surge through her, the adrenalin rush of her Venator vocation winding her up, ready for action. Maybe Kingsley had been right: a break was all she needed. Ara was eager to get back to work.

Someone was waiting for her in the apartment, lights on, dining chairs pushed back – but it wasn't Edon, and it wasn't even Mina. Ara recognized the tall figure lolling on a chair at once, her heart sinking. It was Axel, the local Venator chief; she'd seen him with the wolves earlier in the park. He seemed unsurprised to see her. All her belongings – bag, clothes, a toothbrush – piled on top of the table in a random pile.

"So, Araminta Scott," he said. "The famous chief-slayer. I hope you're not planning to pull the same stunt here."

It wasn't a question. Ara didn't reply.

"So," he continued, sighing in a way that suggested this conversation was very boring, "are you going to tell me what, exactly, you're doing in Stockholm?"

"Um … I'm," Ara stuttered. It sounded so stupid to say it out loud. "I'm on vacation."

"Forced leave is what I heard." Axel looked unimpressed.

"Yes, but, I'm just really here to hang out. Have a change of pace. I'm about to find somewhere else to stay – really!"

Ara felt like Minty again, being chastised for muddy hockey boots by an old teacher.

"You certainly are. There's no way Marrok should have brought you here. It's a violation of professional ethics."

"It's not his fault, really." No way was Edon getting into trouble over this. Ara was tired of always being the bad-luck bear in their partnership. "I insisted. He was worried about me. But it was always going to be temporary. I'll go right now if you want!"

Ara gestured towards her mess of clothes on the table. The deodorant bottle, she realized, had rolled out of her duffel and was poised on the table's rim, ready to plop to the floor.

Axel shook his head.

"You're not going anywhere alone, OK? First you have to tell me what's really been going on tonight. You were identified in the Stureplan neighborhood tonight. What were you doing there?"

"I was at a bar on Sodermalm, just hanging out," Ara hurried to explain, her words tumbling over each other. "Then I thought I saw Finn Chase leaving the club and I caught a cab to follow her."

"Finn Chase? Really?" Axel wasn't buying it. Ara wasn't sure if she was buying it any longer either: earlier this evening just seemed like a dream. "And you followed her to …?"

"I lost her somewhere around Stureplan," Ara conceded. "Because of all the streets being blocked. There was an attack in some club."

"So you admit you know about the murder?"

"Well, I mean, the cab driver told me."

"Really?" Axel folded his arms.

"Yes, really," Ara said, her face prickling. She hated it when her neck flushed – usually because she was annoyed – and the burn crept up into her cheeks. "That's why we lost the car we were following."

"Details of the car?"

"Silver. No plate that I could see." Ara couldn't even look at Axel. This was lame Venator work, even by Noov standards.

"So, you may or may not have seen Finn Chase in a car you couldn't identify, and you say that's why you were in the very street where a murder took place less than ten minutes after it happened, speeding away in a taxi. Where a mortal's been killed, and where the police managed to arrive before the Venators could shut the story down. Now the internet is screaming about someone impaled with a crescent blade and it'll be in every newspaper front page in the world tomorrow."

"Nothing to do with me, I swear," Ara said, shaking her head. Police arriving before Venators was always a mistake – and a nightmare.

"One of my Venators recognized you from the New York team. Luckily – well, not for you."

"I had nothing to do with it," Ara insisted, really angry now. "Why would I turn up here and kill a mortal?"

"Maybe you thought she was Finn Chase?"

"I know what Finn Chase looks like, and I can tell the difference between mortal and not. I'm not an idiot, and I wouldn't kill another young woman by mistake. Anyway, I don't have my blades with me. Ask Edon."

"There's a lot I need to ask Edon, believe me." Axel stood up. She'd never seen such a tall Venator. "Grab your stuff. Let's go. Venator HQ now. Don't think of putting up a fight, or I'll be forced to report your presence here in Sweden to Kingsley Martin."

One word to Kingsley and Ara knew her vacation would be over. She'd be on permanent leave.

17 | AFTER TWILIGHT

*I*t took more than a locked door to keep Oliver stuck in no-man's-land. He hadn't been on the run for months just to get caged like a guinea pig in some godforsaken Swedish tower block. That perky little familiar Christian wasn't his keeper. And the feral kids he'd seen on the way in were more than happy to answer his bellows for help. "I need you to break in and get me out of here", screamed from his window, was like an offer of ice cream to milquetoast suburban kids. Within ten minutes the door had burst open and the kid in the Real Madrid T-shirt, along with five members of his scruffy gang, were celebrating their forced entry in the apartment's living room.

"Smash it up," Oliver told them. "Break whatever you like. And there's food in the kitchen if you want it."

He was downstairs just in time to see the mattress pushed out the bedroom window and land with an almighty thwack on the ground near the tire fire, followed by uproarious cheering from the kids. He'd made someone happy today, at least. And that little twerp Christian would get into huge trouble. A double score.

Walking with his head down, hands in pockets, Oliver made it to the local train station without anything worse than some general abuse. He didn't look rich enough to rob these days, he realized, not sure whether to be glad or bitter. He had just enough money to buy a ticket for the hour-long trip back into central Stockholm, stopping at every small station with an unintelligible name along the way. He stood with his head leaning against a dirty window, rocking with the train, the rhythm of the tracks buzzing through his brain. Gotta find Finn, gotta find Finn, gotta find Finn. He'd start in the city, the place he'd been sent, and see where any leads took him.

Back in central Stockholm at last, all Oliver knew how to do was roam. Even though it was late, it still felt like twilight still. His entire life was twilight these days, a netherworld between sun and moon, between being alive and being dead – and which of these was preferable, Oliver didn't know. Sometimes he found himself wishing for the sharp bite of a Silver Blood's fangs, the draining of his life force.

These long white nights of the Swedish summer just added to his disorientation, though at least now he was outside, moving around, able to hunt his prey in the open air. Another problem was that in Stockholm there were so many girls with heads of long, glossy blonde hair. Everywhere he looked, on a busy Saturday evening like this, there were many girls who might be Finn, sashaying along in summer dresses, long hair swaying, laughs tinkling in the evening hair. But none of them were Finn. None of them had precisely her elegant loping walk or her effortless good posture or her light way of stepping that had seemed to him, once upon a time, to look as though she was floating across a room. Oliver was still convinced that he'd recognize Finn anywhere, even from a distance, and even if everything about her character had changed – or been deformed and debased – because of the company she kept these days. He'd performed the Sacred Kiss on her hundreds of times, after all. They were bonded for life. Just the thought of it made him heady with longing and a profound sadness about everything that was lost.

Maybe he should have eaten more of the food Christian left, because Oliver was starting to feel distinctly light-headed. With every step he grew more exhausted, his feet dragging. Eventually it would be dark; eventually he'd need to sleep. and wonders where he'll sleep that night. The moon, a perfect white, climbed in the sky and Oliver's eyes flickered, struggling to stay open. On and on he walked, observing drunk and happy groups wandering home from bars, a band of girls with linked arms singing and laughing, tourists pausing to take their final selfies of the night. One cluster of young people were jumping into the water at the end of a cobbled street, shrieking on their way down, splashing about in the silver-dappled harbor. He didn't have that energy anymore, that zest for life. Oliver just felt old and spent. One way or another, he thought, Sweden was the end of the road for him. If he didn't find Finn here, and win her back, that was it. He may as well let the Nephilim take him, let the Silver Bloods drain him dry. He sank down, back sliding against a rough stone wall, and sat with his head in his hands. He couldn't move another step.

"Hey, are you OK?" It was a young woman's voice, lilting and soft. Hair brushed his face – long, silky hair – and for a heart-pounding moment Oliver thought the woman leaning over him might be Finn. But when he opened his eyes he saw a different blonde there, shorter than Finn, more white-blonde, pretty rather than beautiful, in denim shorts and a pristine white t-shirt. Her pale blue eyes were wide with concern.

"OK?" she asked again, and Oliver wondered why he'd ever thought this could have been Finn. The young woman leaning over him had a Swedish accent. Sweden, he was in Sweden.

The girl's name was Karin, and she was with the group frolicking in the water. They were calling her name and waving at her to join them. She hadn't jumped in, she told Oliver, because she was tired and wanted to go home. She needed to save her energy for Midsummer.

"Big parties," she said, shimmying down the wall to sit next to him. "What will you do?"

"I don't know," Oliver said. It was true: he didn't know what to do next. The "safe" place he'd been sent by the wolf didn't feel safe at all to him. He didn't appreciate getting locked in by an over-eager Human

Conduit. He wasn't sure where his next message, or meal, or place to stay, would come from.

"You're American?" she asked, and Oliver tensed. If Karin was a Nephilim, her black heart wouldn't take too long to reveal itself. True, he got no vibe from her, but maybe he was losing his instincts. Karin seemed nothing but sweet to him.

"Yes," he said, unwilling to venture anything else.

"I've never been," Karin said, and launched into a long story about her sister being an exchange student in Ohio, and how far it was from the ocean. Her sister had stayed in a house with a big front porch and a swing-seat, just like the ones in the movies. In the summer lightning bugs danced on the lawn. The television was big, the fridge was big, the cars were big. Everyone was friendly.

"Just like the movies," Karen said, her smile so winsome Oliver had to smile back. Her view of the U.S. was romantic, maybe, and nothing like the life he'd led in New York, but just hearing about it made him really want to go home. He was so tired of being on the run.

Karin said she lived nearby with another girl who'd already traveled north for the holiday; her parents had a place on the very edge of Swedish Lapland.

"At this time of year they go fishing. There's nothing else to do up there. It barely gets dark. Not my kind of scene."

"Do you stay in the city?" Oliver asked. His empty stomach gnawed at him, and he ached everywhere from sitting on the ground.

"No!" Karin seemed to think that was ridiculous. "I'm going to Dalarna. You should come. All the best things happen there. The craziest things. It's pretty pagan, so I hope you're not one of those American fundamentalists."

She fake-punched his arm, and he shook his head. If only she knew.

"What are you doing out here?" she asked him. "Are you staying at the hostel down there?"

Karin pointed in a vague direction. Oliver's eyes felt burned from too much sun; he couldn't even see straight anymore.

"No – but maybe. Maybe if you show me where it is …" He trailed off, realizing how walking to the hostel would be a bad idea. A hostel packed with people wouldn't be safe. Better to find somewhere in the shadows, under a bridge or tucked away in some deserted doorway.

"Hey," Karin said, gazing into his eyes. "Do you need somewhere to crash tonight?"

Despite himself, Oliver laughed. She sounded so earnest and the Americanism seemed strange in her lilting accent.

"Is that wrong? Did I say it wrong?" She was blushing.

"No, it was right," Oliver reassured her. "It's just, for someone who's never been to America, you know how to speak it."

"Movies," said Karin, clambering to her feet. She held out a soft, small hand and Oliver took it. "You can sleep in Anna's room."

"I could do with somewhere to crash," he admitted. "Just for tonight, I promise."

It was a risk, Oliver knew, but everything was a risk for him. Staying out in the street. Staying in the apartment the Venators kept. Just being Oliver Hazard-Perry and at large in the world, alternately hunted and hunting, hidden and exposed. Karin was waving goodbye to her friends and already pulling a jangling bunch of keys from a capacious patchwork bag. Maybe she had a blade in there as well, or a gun. Well, if she killed him, she killed him. Oliver had already decided this place was the end of the road.

"You're not going to turn all crazy on me, are you?" Karin asked, suddenly hesitant. "You're not going to murder me or something?"

"You're safe with me," he told her. "Completely. I just need to crash."

Oliver was blurry with exhaustion now, desperate for sleep. It seemed the most vital thing in the world. He could barely drag his feet along the street.

Karin's flat, in a narrow modern block, was tiny, its only view of an inner courtyard clogged with bikes and wheelie bins. All the furniture was flat-pack or pine, the blinds on the windows lime green and the kitchen sill crammed with pots of herbs. It barely seemed big enough for two bedrooms. Oliver thought the entire place would have fitted in his walk-in closet back in New York. You could tell girls lived there – the *Amelie* poster on the wall, the pink-and-green floral pattern on the coffee mugs, the vast array of cheap products in bright plastic bottles cluttering every surface in the tiny white-tiled bathroom.

Karin led him to Anna's room, and although the bed looked narrow and he had to navigate a treacherous sea of strewn shoes and bags to get anywhere near it, Oliver had never been so glad of a safe, quiet place to sleep. Karin stood on tiptoes to kiss him goodnight, a chaste peck on the cheek.

"If you need anything, just help yourself," she said, stifling a yawn. "I have to get up around nine to catch the train to Leksand. But I don't suppose it's the end of the world if I miss it. There'll be other trains."

Karin wriggled her fingers at him and left the room, closing the door softly behind her. There'd been a rueful look on her face, as though perhaps she was disappointed that Oliver hadn't even tried to seduce her. But he'd meant what he said: she was safe with him. He had nothing dangerous or sexy or wild left inside. Just a blank, where his bond with Finn used to be.

He sat down on the bed – it *was* narrow, and way too soft – and practically fell back onto the pillow in its pale blue case. He wriggled his shoes off, but didn't bother to get undressed. Tomorrow morning, maybe he'd allow himself the luxury of a shower. All he wanted to do now was sleep.

When Oliver woke, it was light outside, but still the milky light of early in the morning. He could vaguely remember his dream, in which a tiny wolf had been gnawing at his stomach, trying to dig its tiny teeth into his insides. But now he was awake it seemed less like a dream and more like plain old hunger. Karin had said he could help himself: he'd be quiet as a mouse.

In the kitchen he decided against cereal – too loud – and opted for slices of dark, nutty bread that were only a little stale. He loaded piece after piece with jam and butter from the fridge, greedy as a child for the delicious mix of sweet and salty. He felt as though he hadn't eaten in days. Milk he glugged straight from the plastic container, too thirsty to bother looking for a glass.

Karin and Anna's fridge was a mess of magnets and flyers and photos, and Oliver managed to knock something off onto the floor when he was returning the milk to its berth inside the fridge door. A magnet in the shape of an albatross clattered to the floor, bringing down a take-out pizza menu and some other pieces of paper. Oliver stooped down to retrieve them, hoping that the noise hadn't woken Karin. The clock on the kitchen wall read just after seven, and he knew she didn't need to get up yet to make her train.

He shuffled the papers together, wondering if he should attempt to replace them or just leave them on the counter for Karin to arrange. The largest paper was a flyer with an elaborate hand-drawn illustration in black ink. It was in Swedish, but some things made sense: the words "fest" and "Dalmarna", and the date, June 20th, the summer solstice.

And the small words at the bottom of the flyer, written in English.

The White Queen awaits you.

A recognition, painful and electric, prickled Oliver's skin. Yes, of course. Yes, Finn was here in Sweden. She wasn't one of these two-bit blonde princesses thronging the streets and clubs and bars of Stockholm. She was the queen. The White Queen the Blue Bloods had feared. And at last, without the help of anyone on "his" side, Oliver had a lead.

He needed more information about the event and where it was taking place. For all he knew, going to Dalmarna could be like saying you were going to upstate New York – wildly imprecise. Where exactly was this "fest" taking place? How could he get there? Maybe that train Karin was planning to take – could he go with her?

Karin would probably be up in an hour or two. He could wait. Couldn't he? Oliver retreated to the small room where he'd slept and tried to lie quietly, but he was way too wound up. Before long he heard muffled noises from the next bedroom that sounded like Karin getting up, maybe to go to the bathroom. He didn't want to startle her, but he couldn't lie around any longer with his heart thudding and every nerve in his body twitching and alive.

He kicked some shoes out of his path and opened the bedroom door. All the other doors in the apartment were closed apart from the bathroom door. That was wide open. Oliver took a few steps to Karin's bedroom door, hesitated, then tapped.

"Karin," he said in a low voice. "Are you awake?"

No answer. That was strange, Oliver thought, given he'd just heard her moving around.

"Karin?" he tried again, and opened the door just a sliver. Still no reply. He pushed the door open to reveal a room identical in shape and size to Anna's. Even the bed was in the same position. Even the sheets and coverlet were the same pale blue.

But these sheets were black with blood.

Karin lay there, eyes and mouth wide open, her head stiff. She'd been stabbed. Oliver could find no pulse. Although her skin was still warm, she was dead.

18 | SUSPICIOUS MINDS

*T*his had been one of the worst days of Ara's life, and not just because of the smug expression on Mina's face.

After a sullen and silent ride to the Venators' HQ, she was marched through a shiny granite lobby and down the service stairs to an underground suite of dingy offices and stark interrogation rooms. Edon and Mina were waiting in one, Edon sprawled at the table, looking like a wounded animal. Mina sat with her arms folded. Ara getting snagged by the local Venators must have been the ideal outcome for her, and Ara wouldn't have been surprised if Mina had tipped them off. Now she could have this investigation, and Edon, all to herself.

"So," Axel said, gesturing at Ara to sit down. She flopped into the chair like a resentful teen. The sickly green of the walls reminded her of going into hospital to have an ingrown toenail removed when she was about 12, and she still hated the color now. "What on earth made you think it was a good idea to smuggle Araminta Scott into Sweden?"

"Nothing to do with me," said Mina, even though it was clear that Axel was talking to Edon.

"She wasn't *smuggled* in," Edon pointed out, his voice a low growl. He hadn't looked once at Ara since she entered the room. "She came here as a tourist. She's on leave from her duties as a Venator and ..."

"And you should know better than to let her get entangled in such a serious operation over here." Axel looked and sounded angry. Ara's heart sank, something she didn't think was possible – it had already dipped, she'd thought, as far as it could go. Axel was going to send her home, she knew, and worse than that: he was going to report her to Kingsley, the last man in the world she wanted to anger.

"She's not entangled in anything," Edon argued. "Look, if you don't want her in Sweden, fine. But just let her go somewhere else – I don't know. Paris? London? She's on a break. She's done nothing wrong."

"That we know of," Mina added, just to be unhelpful. Ara scowled at her.

"Well, you know what I know." Axel sat down on his side of the table and stretched out his long legs. "You two went up to the rooftop bar of Bank because a kid told you you'd find the organizer of the White Queen midsummer rave there. But nobody was in the rooftop bar."

"Not a soul," said Mina. "The place looked as though it had been abandoned."

"Then the club kid who gave you what might be a lead got murdered in the stairwell, and it looks almost certain that a Venator did it. One of my team sees Araminta Scott fleeing the scene."

"Not fleeing," Edon scoffed. "She was seen in a cab nearby, not exactly running down the stairs."

"And I've told you," said Ara, raging with the injustice of the accusations. "I don't have my blades and I didn't do it. Why would I kill some random Swedish kid?"

"You tell me. Because he pinched your butt? You're known for volatile behavior. You start brawls with other Venators just because they look at you the wrong way."

Ara said nothing. Axel clearly had no idea of all the black marks on her file back in New York, including death walks and dream intrusion. Fighting in a bar was the least of it.

"You may have convinced Marrok here that you didn't bring your blades," Axel continued, "but you can't fool a fellow Venator. We all have our ways."

Ara snuck a glance at Edon. He looked furious. Wolves hated it when vampires talked down to them. Much more of this from Axel and Edon would probably head straight off to the underworld, never to return.

"And now," Axel continued, "you're talking about spotting Finn Chase in some Stockholm bar and following her all over town. But, conveniently, losing her just near the club where the wolves are investigating, and where their informant is murdered. I don't know what to believe."

"You need to believe *me*," Ara insisted. "I was acting on instinct when I thought I saw Finn and followed her. But I swear to you I didn't kill anyone. I have no reason to lie."

"You have no reason to *be* here," said Axel. "Bringing unwanted attention to our whole operation. It's not your job to find Finn Chase in Sweden. Your job is in New York. Kingsley Martin didn't send you here, and he certainly won't be happy to find out you're implicated in any way in tonight's events. Not to mention the headlines in the papers."

"You don't need to tell him." This was Edon, speaking quickly, before Ara had a chance to open her mouth. "Please. It would be the end of Ara's career as a Venator, and she's too valuable to us all – sorry, to *you* all – to lose. If she goes back to New York tomorrow, and agrees to lie low for a while, as Kingsley Martin ordered her to do …"

He trailed off. Axel said nothing. He appeared to be thinking. Ara didn't know what to think herself, whether to be grateful to Edon for defending her or angry that he was so willing to dispatch her back to New York. Maybe he really did just want to be with Mina alone, two wolves on the hunt. Maybe Ara was just a distraction, personally and professionally.

"I have to think about this," Axel said at last. "But clearly Scott has to go home. It's midsummer on Monday, and you two need to go north to Leksand tomorrow – I mean, today. It's already morning, for god's sake. You may as well say your goodbyes now. Scott won't be returning to the apartment with you. She's not going anywhere in Sweden but the airport."

Mina bounced to her feet and held out a hand to Ara, which Ara ignored. Edon was up as well, approaching her in an embarrassed and cautious way that infuriated Ara.

"Thanks for your support," she said in her most sarcastic tone. "You couldn't wait to get rid of me, could you?"

"Come on, angel," he whispered to her, gripping her wrist. "What choice do we have? I'll do all I can to talk Axel out of reporting you to Kingsley Martin."

"Don't bother," she hissed, too upset to be grateful. "I managed plenty of years without your help. I'm not your responsibility. You're nothing to me, and I'm nothing to you."

Edon flinched, as though she'd hit him, and Ara felt a pang of something between regret and guilt. She wasn't sure what she was saying anymore. She just wanted him to hurt the way she was hurting.

Axel hustled the wolves out and left Ara alone in the bleak room for almost half an hour. She was pacing the floor by the time someone tapped outside and the door swung open.

"Are you going to keep me in here for …" she began and then stopped. The person standing in the open doorway wasn't Axel, or another of his Viking Venators. It was Jack Force, his chiseled face unsmiling. She'd seen him in the car with his wife, Schuyler Van Alen, but in person Ara's breath was taken away: it wasn't often she got to stand this close to Abbadon, the Angel of Destruction.

"OK, Scott," he said, still not smiling. "I've agreed to babysit you on behalf of the New York Coven until we can get you on a flight home."

"I can … I can just stay here," said Ara. Kingsley Martin was Jack Force's brother-in-law. This was one radar she really, really wanted to stay below.

"Apparently not." Jack's tone was wry. "The Venator Chief here doesn't want to know one thing about you and what you are doing or not doing. I've given him my word that I'll be responsible for you until you catch the afternoon flight out. Your baggage is out here, waiting for you."

Ara felt a flash of shame about how her scruffy duffel must look to the Blue Bloods' glamor king, who was no doubt staying in the fanciest of hotels, but then she kicked herself for being so groveling. She'd done nothing wrong. Not a single thing. And yet she was being sent home in shame.

"I can just go to the airport now," she said sulkily. "Wouldn't want to inconvenience you."

"Too late! And don't think I'm going to let you wander loose around an international airport for hours. God knows where you'll turn up next."

"And don't think I'm going to be grateful to be babysat like a child," Ara said, blood rushing to her head, forgetting her place in the vampire world. "Because I'm not. I've done nothing wrong, and I don't need minding."

"Scott," he said, his voice weary. "You have no idea of the bigger picture of what's going on here. You're a distraction right now. You're not helping. From what I know about you, you take your work as a Venator seriously, so you should understand following orders better than anybody. Let's go."

On the way down the fluorescent-lit hallway, Ara scooped up her bag and tried to walk with her head held high. She should never have come here. She should never have listed to Edon – and one thing was sure: she'd never listen to him again. In fact, she doubted they'd ever see each other again.

Venator escorts were waiting in the lobby like some kind of blond guard of honor, but Jack waved them away.

"It's a short walk to the hotel," he told Ara. "And I say I can out-run you if you try to get away. What do you think?"

Ara gave a terse smile that she was sure looked more like a grimace.

She wasn't in the mood for joking around. Where would Jack keep her in the hotel, she wondered? Locked in a housekeeping cupboard? Chained to the minibar in his no-doubt massive suite?

Just as they were about to open the door, a short guy with glasses hurried up. He was gazing at Jack with open admiration. A creep, Ara decided.

"Sir, I know it's not my place, but I really think you should accept the escort," he said. "Axel really doesn't want Scott on the loose again."

Jack thanked him, but said they'd be fine.

"That was Axel's human conduit, Christian something-or-other," he told Ara as they walked into the sunlight.

"I don't like him," she said. How dare he? What was so terrible about her being "on the loose"? First thing she'd do was kick his ass.

"He's very eager to please," Jack said, raising his eyebrows. "You should try it some time."

Jack seemed to know every shortcut in the neighborhood, wending down narrow lanes and back alleys, as though he'd lived in Stockholm all his life. The morning was fine and clear: Sunday, Ara told herself. It was Sunday. Tomorrow was Midsummer here in Sweden, but she'd be back in the State by then. Whatever chaos was about to happen, with Finn Chase and the White Queen and a new door to Hell breaking open, it was nothing to do with her.

A shadow in a recessed doorway appeared to twitch and Ara got a powerful whiff of decaying flesh. The stench of Nephilim ...

"To your right!" she shouted at Jack just as a dark blur whirled out in front of them, fangs glinting in the morning sun. Instinctively Ara reached for her blades, forgetting she had no weapons anymore. The Neph was a dirty cloud now, red eyes like warning signals, and Jack was disappearing into its spiraling dust. Ara leapt into the air and kicked both legs at it: the contact felt like jumping into clogged mud, and the odor was foul. The monster staggered and Ara tumbled to the ground, landing hard on concrete and cracking an elbow. She glimpsed some-thing else glinting – a silver gun. Jack fired and the Neph, its black form ashy like a bonfire, dropped.

"Broad daylight," Jack said, wincing as he turned the monster over because of the swampy smell. Its red eyes were wide open, the burn from the bullet square on its forehead. "Nephs are getting bold. Not a good sign."

Ara eased herself up. Jack was rummaging through the Neph's ragged black garments, the gun still in his hand.

"Nothing," he said. He was frowning, but otherwise seemed unfazed. He'd fought much worse than an alley Neph, Ara realized. He'd speared demons through their black hearts.

"Lucky you had the gun," she said gruffly, bending over to catch her breath. Her elbow ached, but nothing seemed broken.

"Lucky you were with me." Jack said. "Without the warning it might have had me."

Jack pulled a vial of holy water from his jeans pocket and sprinkled it over the Neph's prone form. It shriveled into nothing, emitting a noxious black smoke that made them both cough. Some tourists passing the end of the alley peered down and then hurried along. They probably thought Ara and Jack were vandals, setting a litter fire.

"Nothing to see here," Jack joked. "Come on, the hotel's just around the corner. Let's try to make it there alive."

19 | SIX THOUSAND LAKES

*A*t the hotel, Schuyler paced the suite, waiting for Jack. He seemed to have been gone a long time. Maybe she should have gone with him, to get a briefing from the Venator Chief about any new developments. The hotel suite was lovely – sparkling water and bobbing boats filling every view – but it wasn't real. What was real was the fight that was coming. She felt as though they were just marking time here, when there was almost no time left. Midsummer seemed to dangle over her like Doomsday. It sounded so benign, but Schuyler sensed a showdown looming, maybe sooner than any of them realized.

She picked up the phone to call the twins at Mimi and Kingsley's, but remembered it was the middle of the night there and replaced the receiver. She could call Kingsley at work in the Venator HQ, just to check in, but that wouldn't be wise – not with Jack about to take temporary custody of Araminta Scott, the AWOL New York Venator. Jack thought it wouldn't be fair to Scott to report her to Kingsley, when her worst crime seemed to be a romantic attachment to Edon Marrok, and Schuyler agreed. With the world about to tip into chaos again, they needed every good fighter they could muster. Getting Scott fired was pointless.

The waters wending between the islands of Stockholm looked so sparkling and inviting on a day like this. Schuyler wandered over to the corner window and gazed out. There was an uneasiness in her belly, maybe because it felt so long since she'd been able to check in with Lily and Sy. But there was something else, particular to this place, that unsettled her. She felt certain that Oliver was here – not just in Sweden, but somewhere very close by. They'd grown apart in many ways since Schuyler left with Jack, and Oliver fell – too hard and too fast, maybe, with hindsight – for Finn. Still, the old bond was impossible to break. Olly was here, on his dogged quest to track Finn down and save her. Schuyler wasn't so sure that salvation was possible anymore. Annihilation might be the only solution to the evil Finn was breathing into the world.

The phone rang, and Schuyler jumped up to answer, half-convinced it would be Oliver. But it was just one of the smooth-talking young people on the reception desk, asking permission to send Pernilla Stromberg up to the suite.

"OK, I guess," Schuyler said, agreeing before she had time to think. But really, what was Pernilla doing here? And why did they need to meet in a hotel room rather than in reception?

Moments later Pernilla was at the door, a fragrant white cloud of linen – dress, floppy hat, espadrilles. She looked more anxious than she had at the party the night before, her beautiful forehead wrinkled as though she was bracing herself for a slap from Schuyler.

"Dear, dear Schuyler," she said, pulling off her hat and then clutching it like a nervous child. "I wanted to apologize in person for … well, the things Lukas said last night. He's just terribly worried. With the way things are right now. I'm sure you understand."

"The thing he seemed most worried about was Jack and me arriving in Stockholm." Schuyler gestured to Pernilla to sit down on one of the overstuffed armchairs positioned by the largest window.

"Perhaps that's how it came across." Pernilla's English was excellent, with only the slightest hint of a Swedish lilt, and an appealing soft hissing on sibilants. "But I assure you he did not intend to offend. Things have been difficult for him and he is a proud man. He did not want to tell you, I think, that the Venators here – well, they are not very obedient or respectful."

"I thought everything here was run in the best possible way," Schuyler couldn't help replying, remembering with a still-vivid irritation Lukas' boasts about the Scandinavian Coven.

"Perhaps he had been drinking a little too much as well." Pernilla leaned forward, her expression earnest. "He says things when he has been drinking, and when he is very worried. You know how it is."

Schuyler said nothing. Jack could have a hot temper, but he didn't have a drinking problem, and he was never rude to guests.

"I have come today to plead with you to give us a second chance. To give our Coven a second chance." Pernilla sounded so plaintive, and she looked close to tears. "Things are not right with our Venators here. We cannot trust them. I don't know all the ins and outs. Politics within the Coven was never my strong point. I just want to make a beautiful home, you know? And have a family, like you. Some day soon, I hope."

"You don't have children?" Schuyler asked, softening. Pernilla shook her head. Her blue eyes were brimming with tears.

"We've been married for two years," said Pernilla. "I had hoped by now … But these things can take time. Lukas' first wife, his bond mate Ingrid – she couldn't have children. It was a source of so much unhappiness for them both. You probably heard at the time, that she … that she ended her life because of it."

"No, I didn't." Schuyler was appalled. Vampire suicides were entirely unknown to her. How could someone choose to give up eternal life? "How is that even possible?"

"She started going out by herself a lot, for long walks in Dalarna – where Lukas has his country estate. I mean, Lukas and I. Anyway, every day she walked for longer and longer in the forest, further and further away. She was maybe 15 kilometres from home when they found her body. Silver Bloods had killed her. But I think she had – how do you say it? Put herself in harm's way. It was as though she was going out looking for them. Exposing herself to danger, because we'd had the reports of Nephilim activity in the area."

"You knew her?" Schuyler leaned forward in her chair, fascinated. What a strange thing for the wife of a Regis to do.

"She was my mother's best friend," Pernilla said. She flushed and looked even more uncomfortable. "Like an aunt to me, in a way. They'd both married young, but the difference was, Ingrid married the Regis, and my mother married someone much lower-born. Still a Blue Blood, but – you know."

Schuyler knew. She understood the hierarchies of their society all too well.

"But Lukas must have been very young to be Regis," she observed.

"Very young. Twenty-four. He succeeded his father, a unanimous decision by the Coven. He and Ingrid got married that same year, and everyone expected them to have lots of children. But not a single one. My parents had me, and then my three brothers. It must have been very hard for Ingrid and Lukas, seeing that. Aware all the time of what they couldn't have. The year she turned fifty, that was the year Ingrid died. She'd kept hoping all those years, I think, but at last she knew it was too late. She would never have children, the one thing that would make Lukas happy and their family complete. They had everything else – money, power, friends, beautiful homes, everything."

"So how old are you?" Schuyler asked, embarrassed as soon as the words escaped her mouth. It was such a rude question. Pernilla didn't seem bothered at all.

"Twenty-five," she replied. "Lukas is quite a lot older than me, as you probably realized as soon as you met us. He was fifty-two when Ingrid died. Now he's fifty-four."

"You two got married the year his first wife died?" Again, Schuyler realized how blunt she was sounding. Again, Pernilla didn't seem remotely fazed.

"A few months later. I know it's not the usual thing. But a Regis needs a wife, and Lukas really wanted stability in the Coven. Because of my mother's friendship with Ingrid, he'd watched me grow up. He knew me very well, and I knew him. It was an honor for our family, in a way. It made everyone's lives much, much easier. My parents, my brothers – everyone lives in luxury now."

Schuyler could sense the strain beneath the words, beneath Pernilla's bland expression.

"But that's not to say," she continued, eyes fixed on her crumpled hat, "that my family really approve of the marriage. They won't be spending Midsummer with us, for example. None of them."

"No? I'm sorry." Schuyler was beginning to grasp how important Midsummer was to the Swedish. She was also realizing that Lukas was probably as unpleasant to Pernilla's family as he'd been to her and Jack at the party the night before.

"This is why I'm here." Pernilla seemed relieved to have her long story out the way. "Not just to say sorry, but to ask you, from the bottom of my heart, to forgive us for the … the unfortunate events of last night. Please, you must spend Midsummer with us at our country home in Dalmarna. It's the ancestral home of the Swedish coven's rulers and overlooks Lake Siljan. That's the largest of the region's six-thousand lakes, and I think the most beautiful of them all."

"I don't know …" Schuyler began, not eager to spend more time with Lukas.

"Please," said Pernilla. She gazed up at Schuyler, her eyes wide and pleading. "It would make things so much more pleasant for *me*, if you understand. And I will do everything I can, I promise, to make sure you are welcome and enjoy yourselves. We

have a small celebration starting at lunchtime tomorrow, and in the evening there's a much bigger gathering in the nearby forest. Lukas is very involved in that this year. He will be busy with last-minute details much of the time. This afternoon, for example, and tonight. And tomorrow until lunch, I'm sure."

Pernilla shot Schuyler a significant glance, looking much more knowing than she'd seemed in her Stepford guise the night before. Lukas would be out of the house, she was saying. They wouldn't have to put up with his temper and arrogance.

"Well, I suppose we could," Schuyler said. They needed to go to Dalmarna, she knew. What better way to get to the heart of the trouble there – by staying in the heart of power?

Pernilla left smiling, in a flurry of kisses and thanks, promising to arrange a driver for that afternoon. Schuyler felt sorry for her. She was the young bride of a tyrant, a man who couldn't wait to get married again when his wife died in the most terrible way, ending her eternal life. Now she was feeling the pressure her predecessor must have felt – to reproduce or get replaced with a younger model.

Only minutes after Pernilla had gone, Jack arrived – with the young woman who had to be Araminta Scott trailing behind. They were both breathless and alarmingly wild in the eyes; Scott was gripping one elbow as though she was in pain, and Jack was carrying her bag.

"Neph attack in the alley," Jack said, the terseness suggesting how serious the incident must have been. He dropped the duffel onto the floor. "Random, probably – maybe we startled it. But that close to Venator HQ, on a sunny weekend morning in the central city?"

Jack didn't need to go on.

"Did you get injured?" Schuyler asked Scott, who looked sheepish. Schuyler wasn't sure if they'd met before. She would be a pretty girl if she stopped scowling so much, and maybe got some sun once in a while.

"Just landed on my elbow," Scott muttered, and Schuyler picked up the phone to order a bucket of ice. "It'll be fine. I can get it checked out once I'm home."

Jack was pacing the room, frowning at the floor.

"The thing is," he said to Schuyler, "I don't think she should go home. Not yet. I don't know who to trust here – the Regis? The Venators? Anybody? I think we need to keep Ara around because we're going to need every fighter we can muster."

"Well, I don't know how we can keep her around without anyone knowing. Tonight we're expected at the Regis's country home for mid-summer festivities," Schuyler told him, holding up a hand when he began to protest. "I know. It'll be OK. Or it'll be bad. But we're going."

"What are we going to do with Ara?" Jack asked and they both looked at her, as though they hoped she'd have the answer.

20 | BEDTIME STORIES

*A*t last it was time for Catherine to put her plan in place. Mimi and Kingsley were on their way out to a big society event at the Met, all dressed up. They'd been rowing all afternoon – one of their volatilearguments, involving a broken perfume bottle and a lot of slamming doors – and Catherine had begun to grow nervous that they'd decide not to go. But the temptation of something involving an overpriced dinner, overpriced clothes and the upper echelons of Blue Blood society overdrinking expensive champagne was stronger than any petulant lovers' tiff. They loved the drama, she'd learned: the drama of the fight, of the making-up, and of the grand entrance they'd make together at the Met. The fighting gave their appearance together some kind of erotic charge. Hey, thought Catherine: whatever turns you on.

She had the children bathed and dressed in their PJs, ready for goodnight kisses before Aunt Mimi and Uncle Kingsley headed off in the private elevator, Catherine smiling at them and telling them to stay out as long as they liked. The main thing, the thing her smile could never give away, was how badly she needed them to leave.

It was time to put her plan in place. *Finn's* plan, actually, to be fair. As soon as they were gone, Catherine mixed Sy a special "bedtime drink" that tasted like warm milk, but had a hit of something much stronger in it. Within moments he was drooping in her arms, so floppy she had to pour him into his bed.

"Where's my milk?" Lily asked, puzzled, looking at her twin brother's prone form.

"I didn't think you'd want to go to bed just yet," Catherine told her with a conspiratorial smile. "I didn't think you were all tired, like Sy."

"I'm not tired at all," Lily hurried to reassure her.

"Well, good. Because you know what? I have something very special for you. But I had to wait until Sy was asleep to let you know."

"What?" Lily's eyes were wide with excitement. "Is it ice cream?"

"Much better than that." Catherine led Lily to her bedroom and opened the closet door. Lily's clothes – most of them brand new, courtesy of extravagant Aunt Mimi – hung in orderly rows. "How would you like to wear that new pink dress?"

"You mean try it on now?" Lily was already ripping off her PJs. She'd been desperate to wear the dress, a mini Vera Wang, ever since Mimi had brought it home for her.

"I mean wear it out somewhere now." Catherine sat on the edge of Lily's bed, folding the discarded PJs. "I had to wait until Sy was asleep to tell you, but someone else is coming over now to look after him. Your Aunt Mimi and Uncle Kingsley think you've been a really good girl, and they told me they'd like to show you off at their big party tonight. As a very special treat."

"I'm going to the party?" Lily had already wriggled into the silk folds of the dress.

"It's more of a ball, really. The kind that princesses go to. Have you ever been to a ball?"

"Never," Lily said, almost breathless with excitement. Her life in northern California had been quiet and ordinary, Catherine knew. Balls were something she saw in movies like *Cinderella*.

"Well, your Aunt Mimi told me your pink dress would be just perfect. In fact, that's why she bought it for you."

"Why didn't she tell me?" Lily looked a picture in the dress, but her hair was a wild mess, and she had no shoes or stockings on.

"She didn't want Sy to find out and get sad or jealous. She thought the ball would be too much for him. She didn't want him to get all tired."

"He's *always* tired," Lily complained. "I never am!"

"I know," Catherine said with a broad smile. "Now, we better hurry. We don't want to miss the beginning of the ball. It's way, way uptown, and guess what? We get to ride there in a limo. Your Uncle Kingsley ordered it and it's waiting downstairs."

Lily was practically jumping out of her skin with the thrill of anticipation. She didn't even stop to ask when Sy's "sitter" would be arriving. Catherine hustled her into black patent shoes and grabbed a hair brush and pink ribbon.

"I'll do your hair in the car to save time," she promised. "We don't want to be late, do we?"

The limo was waiting, though Catherine had booked it herself: Kingsley, of course, knew nothing about it. In the back seat, she buckled Lily in, and brushed her wayward dark curls as the car purred across town to the East Side Highway. Through the darkened windows, they could both see the lights of the city sparkling.

"This is my first ball," Lily confided, and Catherine laughed.

"You're going to look such a picture," she said. "But hang on – there's something smeared on your mouth. Maybe it's toothpaste. Hold still, and I'll wipe it off."

She held a handkerchief infused with chloroform to Lily's jewel-like mouth, and watched the pale eyelids close. Just enough to put her to sleep for a while – nothing too damaging, Catherine told herself. A healthy girl like Lily would be fine. And she needed to be fine, for what was in store for her.

The limo didn't turn off the highway in the 80s or the 90s or even in Harlem, the Met receding ever farther to the south. It kept driving, just as Catherine had told the driver on the phone earlier today. They drove straight through the Bronx and out of the city, beyond its ragged fringes all the way to a private air field.

Catherine was stronger than she looked, much stronger. It was no problem at all to carry the limp form of Lily into the small waiting plane. One of Lily's patent leather shoes dropped off her foot and bounced onto the tarmac, but Catherine didn't return to retrieve it. Lily wouldn't be needing shoes where they were going. She wouldn't be needing this stupid pink dress.

Lily was the bait Catherine needed, and now was no time to weaken. The plane took off into the night, Lily still fast asleep, Catherine gazing out of the window in quiet triumph. She'd outwitted the New York Coven. Not one of them had any idea of what she was planning, how it involved Lily, and what the two of them were about to do next.

PART THREE | MIDSUMMER

This is the forest primeval. The murmuring pines and the hemlocks,
Bearded with moss, and in garments green, indistinct in the twilight,
Stand like Druids of old ...
— HENRY WADSWORTH LONGFELLOW, *EVANGELINE*

21 | THE MAYPOLE

*P*ernilla had called it a country house, but to Schuyler it was more like a chateau, grand and baroque, with wings and gables and formal gardens that stretched in every direction. The main house was painted a restful shade of yellow, like a more elegant version of sunshine. The suite into which an almost gushing Pernilla had ushered them had thick silk drapes wrangled with stiff golden cords, and a satiny eiderdown on the bed that felt plump with goose feathers.

Everything was luxurious and almost magical, including their view of a fountain in which stone dolphins frolicked, and the lake beyond fringed with reeds and rustling stands of birch trees. In the distance stood a thickly wooded forest, part of the estate. Somewhere, deep among the trees, Lukas was busy with most of the staff, organizing the big Midsummer event scheduled for the next evening.

It was late on Sunday afternoon, but the only reason Schuyler knew that was by checking her watch. It still looked and felt like the middle of the day. She'd been driven here in a private car organized by Pernilla – in the same Audi, and with the same driver, in fact, that they'd had on Saturday night. Although both she and Jack were supposed to be in the car, Schuyler had arrived alone. Pernilla's face dropped when she realized that the Audi only had one passenger.

"Your husband wouldn't come?" she asked, her voice trembling, but Schuyler shook her head, taking Pernilla's outstretched hand.

"He's making his own way here a little later. Sorry about that. Some New York business – he had to stay to get it finished."

This wasn't entirely a lie. The "New York business" was Araminta Scott, who they could hardly stick in the front seat of the Audi and ask Pernilla to put up in one of the spare bedrooms. Jack had rented a car and was driving Ara up to Dalmarna separately. He would drop her off somewhere "safe" nearby, he told Schuyler, though he knew as little about this area as she did.

"Leksand," Scott had said, easing an ice bag off her injured elbow. That was the place she wanted to stay – a village nearby, as far as Schuyler understood. And what choice did they have? Venators weren't invisible, especially feisty ones with platinum-blonde cropped hair and major attitude written all over them. They couldn't smuggle her in to the Regis' house and hide her in an attic bedroom.

Pernilla was busy dealing – in a flustered and diffident way – with a battalion of caterers, and with the florists who arrived in three trucks, laden with elaborate structural arrangements. Schuyler wandered out of the house and aimlessly through the grounds. Teams of workers, sweating in the sun, were preparing for the midsummer celebration. Three men carried an ivy-decked maypole, fluttering with blue and yellow ribbons, through the garden, trying to avoid knocking the low manicured hedges.

The fluttering ribbons reminded Schuyler of her recent dream about Lily. At some point this evening, as soon as the time difference made sense, she'd call New York to check on them. She missed the excited, squeaky voices of the twins, their infectious laughs and confusing stories and foolish complaints. That was why she was here, ready to fight, Schuyler reminded herself. For her children and their future.

The air in the garden was still, the late afternoon heavy and humid. The sky seemed a vacant blue, blameless and serene. Schuyler walked towards the lake and sank onto a bench under a shady tree. Here it was hard to know what time it was, and whether she should be tired or awake. Jetlag was playing tricks with her – that and the endless sunshine. She needed to have her wits about her.

On the lake a much bigger maypole was being lifted out of a long boat and carried ashore. It took eight men to carry it, shouting to each other and clearly straining under the weight of it. She wasn't sure why a second maypole was necessary, though clearly Lukas was all about excess, a determined display of wealth. Maybe Pernilla was as well, though to Schuyler she looked lost in the midst of all this wealth and space. She could imagine Pernilla in a pretty cottage, planting sweet peas and roses, reclining in a stripy deck chair with her pale blonde hair fanned out like pieces of faded straw. This house, with all its inherited pomp and status, wasn't her at all. Pernilla was just 25-years-old, Schuyler reminded herself. Married to a man old enough to be her father. There was something both gross and depressing about it. Maybe even sinister – though she probably thought that because Lukas was so hard to like.

The men hauling the giant maypole disappeared into the forest, which Schuyler hadn't expected. Why were they carrying it into the trees when the Midsummer party was taking place here in the garden? Then Schuyler remembered about the big party in the forest, the event that Lukas was overseeing. Not organizing, surely – that would be beneath him. But it was taking place on his land, and as the feudal lord he was no doubt eager to throw his weight around and have everyone bow and scrape to him.

It couldn't be that deep in the forest, Schuyler decided: those poor men could never manage hauling the giant maypole for miles on end. How would they even maneuver it through that thick, dark stand of towering trees? Her curiosity got the better of her, and she stood up, dusting off her shorts. The maypole men might just lead her somewhere interesting. There had to be more to this placid beauty than met the eye.

But the worn path into the woods startled her: it disappeared almost immediately, and all she could see were rows of trees, their trunks silvery, their branches low and heavy. After ten minutes walking, the forest was so thick that the sun barely penetrated. It was much darker and cooler in here, Schuyler reflected, at first relieved to be out of the relentless bright sun. But there was also something sinister, almost eerie, about these woods. She felt as though she'd wandered into a fairytale, and the height of the trees, their needles soft underfoot, made her feel small and vulnerable. She was Little Red Riding Hood – no, she was Gretel, with no idea of where she was going. The breeze swished the highest branches but didn't appear to reach ground level. The children would love playing here, she thought, hiding behind giant tree trunks, tumbling through the soft ferns and bracken of the undergrowth. But something felt off to her. Her senses tingled, alive to any movement. Even the birds stayed away.

Just as she was beginning to feel disoriented and worried that she was lost, Schuyler glimpsed the big maypole in the distance. It had been loaded into place, in a clearance or glade, devoid of any life. Sunlight filtered through the trees, so the maypole looked spotlit. All the men who'd carried it from the lake were gone now: Schuyler could neither see nor hear them anymore. She took slow steps towards the distant giant maypole, imagining the ribbons that would flutter from it tomorrow. With every step memories of her dream, vivid flashbacks, overwhelmed her. In the place of the maypole she saw Lily's face, the ribbons snapping around her in a strong wind. So strange that she had that dream just before coming here, when the idea of a maypole dangling a profusion of ribbons wasn't something her conscious mind had conjured up, or even knew anything about.

A footstep crunched in the bracken, and Schuyler crouched, her instincts taking over. Someone was close – too close. But all she could see was an endless stretch of trees, their gray bark flaking and ridged, looking ancient and still.

Schuyler felt in her pocket for the blade she always carried. It wasn't a sword, but it would do if a Neph burst out of a hollow and launched at her. An attack by a Silver Blood: now, that would be a bigger problem. Jack would be furious to think she'd wandered so deep into the woods alone, so close to this alarming new fissure in the underworld. She could be surrounded right now. The quiet of the forest could be an elaborate hoax, a trap into which she'd been lured.

A footstep crackled again, more distant this time. All Schuyler's senses were on high alert, her gaze fixed on the direction of the sound.

Then someone stepped into view, over a mossy branch and close enough for Schuyler to see in every detail. Looking at her, openly and brazenly across an open stretch of the ground, was Finn.

Schuyler's breath caught in her throat. Her sister! Here in the forest, dressed in white and looking almost surreally beautiful with her flowing fair hair and slim, elegant form. A pang in Schuyler's gut made her want to cry out: she missed Finn. The old Finn. Why had it come to this, with them sworn enemies?

Her sister's white dress was long and flimsy, almost see-through. Finn wore a garland of wildflowers in her hair, balanced there like a crown. The White Queen, Schuyler thought, her heart thumping with adrenalin and despair and rage. Finn was the White Queen, the new figurehead for the dark forces Satan was amassing and sending out into the world. It was sickening that someone so beautiful – inside and outside – would allow herself to be so corrupted, so used.

Finn might be her sister, but Schuyler could show her no mercy. In one swift movement she drew the knife from her pocket and flicked it open. A shaft of sunlight caught the blade and made it glint, just as Schuyler raised her arm, knife raised to fly through the air. Her aim had always been good, even when she in fear of her life, or – as she was now – heartsick at attacking a member of her own family.

"Ha ha ha ha!" Finn was still standing dead still, gazing at her, but Schuyler could hear a child's voice laughing. It was nearby, sweet and clear as a bird call. It sounded just like Lily. Exactly like Lily, in all her innocent, exuberant joy.

Schuyler glanced to her left, where the laughter seemed to be drifting. But she could see nothing, and the laughter stopped abruptly. She looked back at Finn, confused and furious. But Finn was gone. All Schuyler could hear was the treetops rustling, speaking a secret language she couldn't understand.

22 | THE LONG WHITE NIGHT

*A*xel had arranged another place for them to stay in Dal-marna, and this time it was more to Edon's taste. He and Mina were staying in a black-painted cabin overlooking a massive lake, a wood pile out the back, and an upturned canoe on the meadow stretching down to the water. Inside there was a wood-burning stove, not necessary on a warm day like this one, and two small bedrooms were everything was wooden and basic and not pretentious in any way.

If only Ara was with him, and not Mina, Edon might allow himself a moment of happiness.

The town nearby was really a village and way too hippy-dippy and folksy for him – some people in peasant costumes, a maypole in the square flapping with ribbons, little girls looking like miniature plant pots because of the messy green wreaths on their heads. This was like a stage set for some summer outdoor theatre, and theatre had never been Edon's thing. Hunting demons: that was his thing. Something about this picture-postcard setting was off, and he could sense it. Most of the Red Bloods here – maybe all of them – were oblivious to the dark currents pulsing through the forest and rising from the lake like a hazy summer mist.

But Edon's senses were never wrong. Danger lurked here, maybe in those rolling hills swaddled in trees, maybe in the depths of the sparkling lake. Sun, in his experience, meant nothing. People thought you needed a thunderstorm or a dark night for something sinister to occur, but tonight's long white night promised danger. Dark forces didn't need darkness to emerge into the world. They just needed numbers.

Mina had unpacked her things in her usual efficient way, and was now banging cupboard doors, looking for cloths and god knows what else so she could polish her knives. They hadn't spoken much since they arrived, but Edon knew she was was bracing for a fight, just as he was. He and Mina didn't need to speak: like many wolves they fell easily into the pack mentality, the shared mind that helped them to hunt effectively. It wasn't some gimmick like the Fallen's, dreamwalking here, communicating telepathically with bondmates there. It was pure animal, ancient and sure.

Something *had* been lost between him and Mina, and that was their sexual chemistry. Edon was relieved that the sizzle that used to electrify their encounters was gone – on his part, anyway. The tension in the room now was focused on the hunt that was about to begin.

Wolves preferred to hunt as darkness was falling, but this time of year worked against that. Tomorrow was Midsummer, the longest night of the year. Kingsley had given them orders directly, and Axel had confirmed them. Tonight they should roam the forest that bordered the Regis' property, getting the lay of the land, marking trees and landmarks as they saw fit to make tomorrow's work. Don't draw attention to themselves, try to avoid fights unless under direct threat.

If they could sniff out this "White Queen," which was now the Venator code for Finn Chase, well and good – but only attack if necessary. Kingsley was convinced that keeping Finn alive would help draw out the demon forces they suspected of planning a Midsummer invasion. With Finn dead, they might retreat and regroup, and the chance to eradicate them would be missed.

"You know, I could see you living here," Mina teased, shutting the door behind them and turning the key. "Cabin by the lake, your Ve-. nator girlfriend going feral swimming in the reeds and catching fish with her teeth. She kind of reminds me of an eel, you know. Slippery and smelly."

Edon ignored her. He stood scanning the broad stretch of forest ahead of them, curving around the lake. The Regis' estate was massive. They would need to be smart about how they approached this task. One night for recon wasn't much. And the whole area would be crawling with revelers – a lot of them here from the city, young and stupid, planning to drink and carouse for the next 24 hours. They'd be getting in the way. People, in Edon's experience, always got in the way.

They set off, ambling over the lush meadow that rimmed this part of the lake. Edon thought about the kid who'd given him the tip in the club, and how he'd ended up dead and almost disemboweled, swinging from the door. A Venator had killed him: the more he thought about it, the more Edon was convinced. A Venator who'd been following Edon and Mina, and knew exactly where they were going and why. But why kill the kid and not take on the wolves, if they were the real target? That kid was just a nobody, someone who knew the tiniest piece of information and that was all.

"What do you think that kid was doing on the stairwell?" he asked Mina. "Back at the club, I mean. We talked to him downstairs. Why did he follow us all the way to the roof?"

"Maybe he had something else to tell us," Mina replied. "And someone stopped him just in time."

"Venator?"

"Almost certainly. Shape of the wound. Probable weapon. Expertise and speed of the kill." She sniffed the air. "Damn, it's fragrant here. I feel like I'm in a perfume commercial. Fresh air, wild flowers, and a hint of … what's that drink they're always drinking here? Looks like vodka but tastes like a herb garden."

"Aquavit," Edon said, looking at the orderly row of wooden piers stretching from each property out into the lake. Lots of small boats tethered to moorings, lots of boats – small and large – out on the lake. Speedboats, sailboats, ferries. Kids near the shoreline rowing dinghies or floating on inner tubes. People on jet-skis, churning up waves, or whizzing around on waterskis. Tomorrow would be chaos, he thought, in the water and in the forest. And there was nothing a demon liked better than chaos.

Where the meadow ended, the forest began. A few steps in the temperature dropped; after fifteen minutes of walking the sun was barely peeking through the dense tree tops.

"This is north," Mina told him, and marked a grizzled trunk with her claw-like nail. "The house is that way. The rave the Regis is all involved with – that's this way."

Edon turned to walk on, but Mina clutched his arm. He froze, thinking she'd seen something, or maybe scented something he hadn't caught yet. But instead of speaking she smiled, and scratched his bare wrist with her thumb nail. Her nail was so sharp she almost drew blood. Edon suppressed a yelp.

"What are you doing?" he hissed at her.

"Marking my territory." Mina feigned innocence. "Isn't that what we're supposed to be doing?"

"Cut it out." Edon whacked her hand away. This was going to be a very long night. As far as he was concerned, the time for games was over.

23 | LEAVING

*J*ack checked the map again and slid the rented Volvo into gear. He'd settled Ara into an attic room above an inn in Leksand, for which he'd had to pay five times the usual rate just to get her in: he suspected it was the bedroom of one of the innkeeper's children, shunted out the way to make room for a very deep-pocketed paying guests.

Ara had promised to stay put until he contacted her again, on a cheap phone he'd bought at a gas station and handed to her. The forest and the grounds of the Regis' country house were going to be crawling with local Venators, and Ara needed to lie low.

"Literally," Jack had told her. "Please don't even stand in the window. You have a distinctive look, you know."

"Everyone has blonde hair here," Ara said absently, picking at the Disney duvet cover. "But don't freak out. I'll just lie here, waiting for your call."

Jack drove out of town and along a winding and picturesque country road, lined with red cottages with bursting flower gardens, the Swedish flag waving on flagpoles in practically every yard. Bicycles leaned against fences and trees. A farm stand was selling strawberries and new potatoes. Shame this wasn't an actual summer vacation, he thought. Shame this beautiful spot was the place chosen to bust out of the underworld.

Nowhere beautiful in the world would be safe, though, once Lucifer's army was on the march again. Better that none of the people here to celebrate Midsummer had any idea of the danger they were in. All it would cause was panic.

Jack's phone, lying on the seat next to him, started buzzing and he pulled over onto the dusty shoulder to check. It was Mimi.

"Oh my god, Jack – I'm so relieved you picked up." She sounded utterly distraught.

"What is it? Is Sy ill again?" Jack's heart was pounding. His boy was still frail, even all this time after the sickness that nearly carried him away.

"No. Sy is fine. Well – it looks as though he was given drugs to make him sleep, but the doctor's here, and he says Sy will be fine tomorrow."

"Drugs?" Jack felt like knocking his head against the steering wheel. Mimi was talking so fast, what she was saying was garbled. She and Kingsley were out at a big event the night before, and didn't check on the children when they got home because it was so late. And probably arguing, Jack thought.

"I'm so sorry, Jack." Mimi's voice trembled. "We should have checked on them. But it was so late and I didn't want to wake them up. All the doors were closed. And then we slept late this morning, and that's why we only found out …"

"Found out what? Was Lily given drugs as well? Has Catherine *drugged* our children?" Fury swirled up within him like a dark tornado.

"Oh, Jack. It's much worse. Catherine's gone. And … and Lily's gone. All we have here is Sy, and he doesn't know anything. The last thing he remembers is drinking milk. But Catherine and Lily – we don't know where they are. Catherine must have taken her somewhere."

"Taken her?" Jack was shouting. "Taken her? At night?"

"Yes. While we were out. Kingsley's on his way to Venator HQ now.

He's going to have every single Venator in New York searching the city. He's already called, like, a dozen teams and all the night shift is coming back in to help. They'll be all over it, I promise you. I swear. Oh, Jack! I'm so sorry."

"What time did you leave the apartment last night?" he asked, amazed at how calm his voice sounded when his insides were churning.

"Around eight. We didn't get home until three, maybe. And we didn't find her missing until about twenty minutes ago. So Catherine has maybe a 12-hour start on us? Maybe more? Venators are checking the airports, of course."

"She could have driven to Canada," said Jack. "Or flown pretty much anywhere before the Venators started checking. She could be anywhere in the world right now. Russia. Argentina. Nigeria."

"With Lily." Mimi sounded sick. "Or worse ..."

She trailed off, but Jack knew what she was thinking. Catherine might have killed Lily, abandoned the body and then flown away alone to escape repercussions. But why? Why drug Sy to get him to sleep but kidnap Lily? If she wanted to destroy Schuyler and Jack, she could have killed both kids in their beds and fled alone. She was the only one in the apartment. Why remove Lily?"

"One thing," Mimi said. "We got a Venator team at once combing the neighborhood – they were nearby when Kingsley put out the call. On the sidewalk outside our building they found a child's shoe. Patent leather, brand new, dropped in the gutter. I checked in Lily's closet and that pair of shoes is missing. So is the pink party dress I just bought for her. Her pajamas are in her room – dumped on the floor. She got dressed, or Catherine got her dressed. Dressed up, in fact. She must have thought she was going out somewhere."

"Catherine's stuff?"

"She took a bag and a few things. It's hard to tell, but I think she only took summer clothes. Her coat and boots are still here. She was prepared, though. It doesn't look as though *she* was kidnapped as well. More like she was the one ... oh god. Why did I trust her? Schuyler had that bad vibe from her, but I thought it was just Schuyler being over-protective and not liking someone because it was my idea. I would have sworn on Kingsley's head that she was to be trusted. We *know* her, you and me, from another life."

"Vampires change, Mimi. Or else they don't change. They don't forgive and forget. They just harden with bitterness. She told me she wanted revenge for Louis' death."

"What? That was two lives ago. And how does kidnapping your daughter achieve anything?"

"I don't know," said Jack, and he really didn't. Maybe Catherine was trying to force his hand – to make him help her track down Louis' killer in this life. Lily was the card she had.

"That little bitch." Mimi was fuming. "I can't wait to smack sense into her when we find her."

"Where is she, Mimi." It wasn't a question. He knew Mimi didn't know the answer. It looked as though his daughter had been kidnapped by the person they'd trusted to fight to the death to protect her. His lovely little daughter was the pawn in some centuries-old game, and Catherine was using her to blackmail them, to get her own way.

"Call me as soon as you know anything," Jack told Mimi. "In fact, call every hour. We're going to be crazy."

We. That was the next thing. Jack would have to drive to the Regis' house and break the dreadful news to Schuyler.

24 | WATERBOARDING

*I*t was Monday morning. Midsummer. Another blue sky for the longest day of the year.

But Oliver didn't feel sunny at all. His mind kept flashing onto Karin's slight, prone form, her sheets splattered with blood. The dark pool in the middle where someone had stuck a knife into her gut. Her soft, pale hands limp. All she'd done was befriend Oliver and give him a place to sleep, and she'd ended up like the guy he met in Budapest. Murdered. Oliver brought bad luck with him.

He brought death and destruction.

He'd spent Sunday night in an old shed, finding himself a dark corner to sleep among rusted farm equipment, spider webs and a small boat with missing planks. It was one of half a dozen outbuildings for a house that also seemed empty, not far from the line of swishing trees that marked one of the many entries to the eternal-looking forest. He could have broken into the house itself, he guessed, but he couldn't risk anyone arriving. This shed was just a repository for junk. Nobody was going to arrive at Midsummer and start polishing up an ancient tractor.

The shed had just one cracked window, and was so smeared with grime the sun was having difficulty leaking in. Oliver had slept in worst places than this over the past year. Sometimes he wished he'd been the kind of adolescent who joined the Scouts and went camping. That would have prepared him for life on the run far better than all those years at a fancy Blue Blood school. Reading a compass, building a fire, sleeping rough, foraging in the wild: those were actual life skills. Life-or-death skills, in fact.

Yesterday, after he found Karin dead, he'd had to think and act quickly – and cynically. Whoever had killed her was gone, most likely through the open window in her bedroom. Although he despised himself for doing it, Oliver had rifled through her bag looking for money and anything else he could use. No train ticket, not much money – but a phone, to replace the one that Christian may have taken, and enough cash to keep him going for a while. He'd flung open her cupboards and stuffed his small bag with nuts and crackers and cookies. The jam he'd been eating before he found Karin dead – Oliver considered throwing the jar in his bag. But its sticky redness reminded him too much of blood. Poor Karin's blood.

He had to get out of here. Whoever killed Karin might come back for him, or might have tipped off the police – or the Venators. Oliver had already been unjustly accused of one murder. He didn't need another false charge to bring him down.

The railway station. That's where he needed to go. Oliver walked, head down, zooming past the wandering groups of tourists and visitors in town for Midsummer. He knew where the station was, and when it was in sight – just one busy intersection away – Oliver paused. He couldn't just leave Karin there, rotting in her bed, for Anna to find when she returned from visiting her family up north. Anna's number was listed in Karin's contacts, but he couldn't call her out of the blue. *Hello, you don't know me, and I didn't do it, but your roommate was murdered this morning.*

Anyway, she'd just call the police and Oliver still had a strong enough allegiance to the Vampire world to know that Venators should check the crime scene first.

The lights changed and Oliver crossed the road, trying to lose himself in the crowd on its way to the station. The ticket vending machines were easy enough to navigate, once he'd pushed the English language button and sorted out the notes taken from Karin's wallet. A train to Leksand, on the southern shore of Lake Siljan – that was the place Karin had mentioned. She was going there, and it made sense that the White Queen's rave would be nearby. At least once he was there he could ask around. Staying in Stockholm made him feel hunted and claustrophobic.

The next train was leaving in fifteen minutes, long enough for Oliver to buy a sandwich and a bottle of water, pretending to be a Midsummer traveler like everyone else. At a convenience store packed with people loading up with magazines and drinks, he bought a new SIM card, then made his way to the platform.

With exactly three minutes left before the train pulled out, Oliver felt in his pocket for the crumpled receipt he'd kept, read the rounded numbers in Christian's neat printing, and made the call.

Without identifying himself, he gave Christian Karin's address and told him to get a Venator team over there right away, before neighbors alerted the police.

"There's been a murder and it's suspicious," he said.

"Oliver!" Christian recognized his voice. "Don't worry – we'll get onto it right away. But where are you? You must tell me. Axel is very concerned."

"Have to go."

"Go back to the flat!" Christian said, and Oliver hung up without replying. He didn't want Christian to hear the familiar "ding" of closing train doors, or the guard's whistle. By "the flat" he assumed Christian meant the apartment in the bad suburb in which he'd locked Oliver. Or perhaps Christian had meant Karin's apartment, so he could brief the Venators – and then, no doubt, be taken into custody. Neither was an appealing option.

Oliver pulled Karin's SIM card from her phone and dropped it onto the tracks. It was only a few hours, really, since he'd seen her hanging out with her swimming friends, happy and excited about Midsummer. Now she was dead, and he had her phone and money.

In the crumbling shed, its atmosphere stuffy and reeking of manure and droppings, Oliver inserted the new SIM card into Karin's phone. For the hundredth time he looked at the crumpled flyer she'd had stuck to her fridge. There was no point venturing out now, in broad daylight, when nothing would be happening until much later in the day – when the daylight would be lingering still, reluctant to creep away.

Still, though the rave in the forest might be hours away, something about it – so near, so mighty – was calling to him. Perhaps it was because he sensed that Finn was somewhere close by. She was here, he knew it. He *wanted* to know it, wanted to be sure of it. But maybe he was just talking himself into it, because he was tired of being wrong, in the wrong place, at the wrong time.

In the wrong life.

The shed was getting hot. He'd got in by wriggling back a loose board and then squeezing in; this was pretty much his only ventilation now. It was just after noon. The heat of the day was too thick in here, too unbearable. The building felt as though it was baking in the sun. Oliver pushed his bag into a corner and covered it with an old towel stained with oil.

He'd heard no noise from the main house, no cars driving up. Oliver pulled the loose board back and peered out, eyes blinking as they adjusted to the bright sun. He was thin these days, too thin; it was easy to slip out through the aperture formed by the loose board, even though he was more battered and bruised these days as well. His joints had taken a battering and once he'd been beaten up in Cairo so badly that his left arm still ached in the rain.

The distance to the forest was further than he thought – his eyes playing tricks on him. And even when he reached the trees, he wasn't there. Oliver could see this was a stand of trees separating one property from the next, not the beginning of the forest. He would still need to cross the back lawn and driveway of another big house to get to what might be the forest itself; he'd also need to climb a rocky bank, steep and exposed.

"Hey!" Down by the water, two young guys were gazing up at him, barely visible through the trees. One called to him in Swedish. They sounded friendly enough – not ordering him off the property, at least.

Oliver took a few steps in their direction, cushioned by pine needles. The guys were in their 20s, both in shorts and t-shirts. One of them was loading a case of beer into a small speedboat. The other stood on the tiniest of piers, bobbing a little when the breeze ruffled the lake.

"Sorry!" he called, holding up a hand. If they were asking him what he was doing here, then hopefully an apology would do.

"English?" one of the guys said, switching languages at once. "Want a ride?"

"Where are you going?" Oliver asked, taking a few more tentative steps towards them.

"Across there." The beer guy, finished with his loading, was pointing to a distant point on the shoreline. "We need to get some petrol for the boat first, but that won't take long."

"Quicker than walking," said the other with a laugh. "We're checking out the place for the big party tonight. You going?"

"Yes," said Oliver, and jogged towards them. A shortcut: he liked the sound of that.

The guys were called Per and Nils, and they were about ten years younger than Oliver, with the breezy friendliness of young people who were popular, responsibility-free and didn't have to pay for their own boats and cars. Oliver had known lots of people like this in New York, especially when he was at school. It was easy to be hospitable and generous when your parents paid all the bills. And if you were white, good-looking and walking around in the right neighborhood, or the right part of the Hamptons – well, you must be one of the in-crowd.

Doors opened, favors were done. You could turn up anywhere in New York in a tuxedo, someone told him once, and if you'd dressed the part, nobody will turn you away, even without an invitation. The same happened here, he guessed. If you lived in one of these big houses along the lake, or were the guest of someone who lived there, people would offer you a ride in their boat. After all, you *must* be planning to attend the same party.

Oliver wasn't well-dressed today, but Per and Nils didn't seem bothered. There were different rules in summer, maybe, and different rules for foreigners. They probably thought he was a Goth.

The boys turned the boat away from the destination they'd indicated, because, they told him, the nearest gas dock was in Leksand.

"It won't take long," Per assured him, the boat tilted back so far and traveling at such speed that the wind was whipping his words away.

"Have a beer!" Nils shouted, but Oliver shook his head. Going into Leksand again made him nervous. There'd been a lot of people getting off the train there, a lot of people in the streets, a lot of traffic clogged up with holidaymakers and honking groups of revelers. It looked like a pretty lakeside town, but there were way too many chances there of running into someone. Who, Oliver wasn't sure. But the place was sure to be crawling with Venators.

At the dock Per leaped out to deal with the pump, and Nils settled back with a beer, asking Oliver genial questions to which Oliver tried his best to reply in the vaguest way. He was staying with some friends, he said, who were borrowing a house from some Swedish friends – he didn't know the Swedish people's names.

"Probably the Lunds," Nils said. "They go to their place Morocco every Midsummer. I don't know why!"

He roared with laughter and Oliver tried to join in. Laughing about nothing much – he remembered that as well from his previous life. The main thing was to not care too much about anything, to always fit in. There was something oppressive, he'd always thought, in all that forced jollity. Nobody wanted to be the one who didn't get the joke.

Per had finished pumping gas, it seemed, but was preoccupied trying to get two girls on the dock to join them. Oliver wished they could leave. He just wanted to be gone, away from Leksand and all the crowds, and near the site for tonight's party.

"This is the White Queen's rave, right?" he asked Nils. "The big party tonight."

"So I hear," Nils said, cracking open another beer. "Apparently it's going to blow our minds."

Oliver suspected that Nils' mind would be blown long before midnight if he kept drinking at this rate.

Per clambered back into the boat, unsuccessful in persuading the girls to join them.

"That's my cousin and her friend," he told Oliver, reversing slowly from the dock. "She said they're staying at the Siljarna Inn and there's some weird woman in an upstairs room who keeps looking out the window then ducking out of view. It's like she's a spy or something."

"A spy!" Nils began roaring with laughter.

"I said to them that maybe she's the White Queen." Per spun the wheel, turning the boat around. "That's why she's hiding up there – until tonight, when they carry her in. You know, for the big surprise."

"Hiding where?" Oliver asked, craning his neck to look back at the dock, and the flower-decked wooden inn standing near it.

"Right up the top – hey! There she is!"

A woman's face appeared in the attic window of the inn – dark eyes, blonde hair. For the briefest moment Oliver willed it to be Finn. To find her at last: that was why he was here. The woman looked at him, staring down at him with a sort of horrified recognition. He realized, heart thundering, that he knew her too.

It wasn't Finn. It was Araminta Scott, one of the Venators in New York. She must be part of the team here to track him down.

And now she'd seen him.

"Let's go," he said to Per. "Please, fast as you can. How fast can this boat go, anyway?"

"Man, you have no idea!" Nils hooted, and they sped away, water spraying in their wake.

25 | MISSING

*L*ukas and Pernilla's chic guests were assembled in the garden for the Midsummer lunch feast, but Schuyler wanted nothing to do with it. She wanted nothing to do with anything anymore, because she couldn't have a second's peace until there was word about Lily. She and Jack were frantic. Beyond frantic: wild with rage and fear. Schuyler wanted to kick holes in the flock-papered walls of their bedroom and snap the twig legs of the elegant side tables. How dare Catherine kidnap their daughter?

Jack was on the phone to Kingsley every few minutes, pacing their room and barking out questions and instructions.

"Check the ports as well," he shouted, his free hand clenched. "What about the heli pads on the East Side? What the hell are all those Venators *doing*?"

They couldn't say anything to Pernilla and Lukas: that had been an easy decision, taken as soon as Jack broke the terrible news.

"We don't know who we can trust," Jack told her. "We don't know if they're in league with Catherine, or helping her in some way."

"If they are, I'll burn this house down." Schuyler was livid.

The threat of arson gave Jack a useful idea: he told Pernilla that their vineyard was burning in a wildfire, and they were terribly upset and concerned. Schuyler was sobbing, he said, though this was untrue: she was too angry to weep – not yet. Jack explained to Pernilla that they didn't want to spoil the lunch party in the garden by running in and out to make calls "to the police and our lawyers," as Jack put it.

Pernilla looked crushed, as she'd probably been looking forward to showing off their distinguished guests. But she said she understood, and would have some lunch sent to their room. Lukas didn't seem to care at all. Clearly he was most concerned with having the perfect Midsummer event for all his local Blue Blood friends, some of the wealthiest and best-connected people in Sweden.

"The latest," said Jack, putting down his phone, "is that Catherine and Lily may have left the country in a private plane last night. The air field was north of the city, and the plane took off about ninety minutes after Mimi and Kingsley had left the apartment."

The timing worked out, Schuyler thought, shredding a tissue and wishing it were Catherine's head. Jack was waiting on information about where the plane was headed, and if it connected with another private flight elsewhere, to throw them off the scent.

But what about the child she'd heard laughing in the forest that morning, when she saw – or thought she saw – Finn? Could that be Lily? Could their daughter be here somewhere already?

"She knows Finn," Schuyler told Jack, the puzzle pieces swarming into place in her mind.

"They only met once, maybe twice, in all of Lily's life."

"Sure, but it's enough. Finn could have reminded Lily that she's her aunt. She could say lots of nice, fake things about us, and say how she and I are sisters. Lily wouldn't be suspicious of her. "

"But Schuyler," Jack said, his phone practically crushed in his hand. She hadn't seen him look this devastated and helpless in years. In all the years they'd been married, in fact. "It can't have been Lily. Think about it. I've been counting out the time difference with New York. How could they have reached Stockholm – let alone Dalmarna – by the time you were out in the forest?"

Schuyler's head was swimming with calculations and what-ifs, with the sound of the child laughing in the forest, with the memory of that apparition of Finn before her, in floaty white dress and flowers, looking like some pale pagan goddess from another era.

"Let me take you there," she said to Jack, her voice pleading, and eventually he agreed, after she pointed out that staying locked in their bedroom wasn't going to accomplish anything.

They took the servants' staircase down into the mansion's lowest floor, half-submerged below ground, where the kitchen and wine cellar were housed. There they slipped through the swarms of caterers, and wriggled up the back stairs where goods were delivered. Schuyler pointed the way that avoided the lunch party, set up on the other side of the formal gardens by the lake, a Swedish flag on a tall pole marking the spot. It was a long way to get to the forest, slithering through the marshy land that skirted the pond, but they were able to keep out of sight.

"No phone service, though," Jack pointed out, just as they reached the cool shadows of the woods, pine-needle softness underfoot, and no flapping geese or swampy ground to slow them down.

"Just half an hour, I promise," said Schuyler. She could hear her own heart thumping, as though the forest was ringing with a drum beat, menacing and steady. There was a thickness to the atmosphere, a palpable danger. Jack was quiet, walking a few paces away, his eyes darting everywhere – over every fallen, moss-covered log, every leafy gully, every still mound. This place could be crawling with their enemies. Finn could be here, with the Silver Blood army who wanted her installed as their demonic queen. Lily could be here, afraid and captive, some kind of pawn in this terrible game. That such a beautiful place, at the highest point of summer, should feel like a trap – it was against nature, Schuyler thought. It suggested the perversion of Lucifer and the way he wanted to corrupt the world. There would be no beauty anymore, or serenity. The rustle of these trees would be a warning sound, like the hiss of a snake, spooling from its lair, fangs bared.

They walked for much longer than half an hour, circling back and forth until Schuyler felt certain she'd found the place where she'd heard the child's laughter. This time there was no one to see or hear, and no trace of anyone's footsteps. No debris: they picked over the ground, hoping something might have been dropped or discarded. Anything, Schuyler thought: please, may there just be something, however small. She bent over a craggy boulder, feeling around its low curves for anything more than pine cones and decomposing leaves.

"We've already looked," said a woman's voice, sounding both bored and critical, and Schuyler leapt to her feet. In the distance, two people were padding towards them. Not people, actually: wolves. Edon Marrok she recognized. His face was set in a permanent frown these days, but she was relieved to see him. He was the great hunter, the Golden Wolf they'd relied on so many times. He was older now, and no longer quite so glossy and golden, maybe. But he could still sniff out demons and tear them to pieces. Schuyler's drumming heart told her that he may be doing that very thing within hours, if not sooner.

While they approached, Jack faced them, gun in hand, as on edge as she was. He only pocketed it when they were close, and Edon introduced the other wolf as Mina.

"She's an old hand at fighting," he said, to Mina's evident displeasure. "Her claws could fell this entire forest."

"That's more like it," she said with a sniff. "And, as I said, we've already picked over this entire area. We've been casing this place for hours. No clues, no scents, no sightings."

Schuyler took a deep breath. If the wolves hadn't found Lily, she wasn't here.

Unless she'd already been dragged underground, to some pit halfway between earth and hell …

Jack's arm was around her, and Schuyler realized she was crying. His face was red too, and his eyes wet. The strain of not knowing where Lily might be was unbearable. Maybe this whole Swedish misadventure was a wild goose chase, and they'd been misdirected here with false intelligence, to get them out of the way of the real invasion.

The four of them walked together through the trees to the lake, where there was a small clearing and a short pier jutting into the sparkling waters. Marrok stood pointing out the scope of the Regis's lands to them, the wide swing of his arm suggesting how much territory needed to be covered, and how vast the task that faced them. The other wolf, Mina, crouched sniffing the ground in a way that Schuyler found disconcerting. She was out of the habit of consorting with wolves. She'd thought, foolishly, that the war was over.

A jet boat fizzed into sight, roaring around a bend in the lake heading straight for their small pier.

"It's Axel," Marrok told them without even looking around. Maybe he could smell the boat, or recognize its buzz. "Not sure why he's coming here now."

The Venator chief. Schuyler hadn't met him yet, because she hadn't gone to the HQ with Jack.

"He's supposed to be at the fancy lunch today," Mina said, standing up and dusting off her hands. She did have very long and curving nails, Schuyler noticed. They looked as sharp as scalpels. "At the Regis' house."

"Maybe he's been sent to get us," Jack muttered to Schuyler. They were both paranoid, she thought, and convinced they were being followed. Maybe Pernilla had checked on them in their room, or the caterers had tattled …

"Hello!" Axel shouted. He was very tall, so tall the boat looked like a child's toy he'd commandeered. Marrok helped him tie up, and Axel strode forward to shake Jack's hand and to meet Schuyler.

"Sorry that *this* has happened," he said, his face grim. "A twist we didn't expect or want."

They stood in a huddle where the grass verge turned sandy at the edge of the lake. He told them that he'd been on his way to the Regis' house for Midsummer lunch when he got a piece of news from one of his Venators.

"I came straight here from Dalmarna, hoping to find you," he said, squinting because the sun was so bright. "A couple of hours ago, a private plane arrived at a field near Stockholm. It had flown from New York, I was told. A woman and a child were seen getting into a helicopter. We can't be entirely sure, but their descriptions match the description of Catherine Denham and … your daughter."

"And where did the helicopter go? You're tracking it?" Jack demanded. Axel looked down at the ground, hands on hips. His black clothes looked out of place in such an isolated spot in the country, on such a sunny day.

"I don't know anymore, I'm sorry. I drove to the airfield right away. But …"

"But what?" Schuyler wanted to grab him and shake him. "But what?"

"I don't know anymore because the Venator who called me stopped speaking mid-sentence. The line went dead. I drove there right away with another team, but by the time we got there the Air control room was empty."

A wave of nausea coursed through Schuyler. So Lily *was* here, still kidnapped, still untracked.

"And the Venator who'd called me," Axel continued. "She was dead. Dead and drained. Just a husk – it was disgusting. Silver Bloods."

26 | ROUND MIDNIGHT

*T*o Edon, today really did feel like the longest day of the year. It might be summer, but there was something rotting and corrupt in this forest. He could smell evil here, sense it all around. When he and Mina had come across Jack Force and Schuyler Van Alen among the trees, shafts of light picking them out, searching under every fallen branch and mound of leaves, Edon knew they could sense it as well. There was nothing to go on now but his gut, and the instincts of the Fallen, because there was no evidence of anything right now apart from a still swathe of forest with birds chirping and the lightest of summer breezes.

But clearly Axel, the Venator Chief, was suspicious too. It meant something, him coming straight to this patch of forest from Dalmarna, without calling in on the Regis or even filling him in on this latest development. Nobody in this Coven trusted each other. Nobody talked to each other. A Venator had been killed and left as a warning, body sucked dry of its blood, its eternal life destroyed. That meant Silver Bloods, ones who were bold enough to cause public havoc. All the air control staff gone, just like everyone working and drinking in the Bank's rooftop bar. Someone killed, other people disappeared. This wasn't underground activity by small bands of guerillas. These were statements. And they'd managed to get hold of the young daughter of two of the most powerful, symbolic Blue Bloods in the world. They were the ones making sure Lily's entry to Sweden, and her continued journey who-knows-where, was uninterrupted. They controlled her. Right now, they were in charge of the game.

Edon hated it when someone else picked the rules of the game.

It was evening now, and Axel's boat was still tied at the pier. They had to stay in the forest now, he said, the few of them that could be trusted. He had his twelve best Venator teams on the job, the ones he knew were utterly loyal to him. Intelligence told them that something big was going down at the rave sponsored by the Regis in the heart of his private forest. That's where they'd all converge.

For now, Edon and Mina were prowling the edge of the lake, observing the hordes arriving at a flat sandy stretch near the party site. People were arriving in boats of all sizes, some rowing, some kayaking, some sailing in and anchoring nearby, some roaring up and making waves. A group of singing young people even floated up in a raft, one guy in baggy surf shorts standing at the back clinging to a makeshift pole and guiding them into shore.

He raised his eyebrows at Mina, and she made a face.

"Lots of happy drunk people," she said in a low voice, pressing closer than was necessary. He wished it was Ara with him now. Not that Mina wasn't good at this work. But Ara, when she was at her best and not causing trouble for no reason, had the sharpest instincts and quickest reactions he'd ever seen.

People clanked by with fistfuls of bottles; some people carried baskets or shopping bags of food. Weird Swedish food, Edon decided, with a derisive sniff. The smell of pickled herrings was overwhelming him. It would be hard to pick out a Silver Blood when his senses were drowned in fish.

Every hipster in Sweden seemed to be here – no, make that every hipster in Northern Europe. He'd never seen so many men with beards, designer tattoos and trousers rolled just above the ankles. Some of the women were dressed for swimming; some were dressed for a Pagan re-enactment or Druid reunion; and others looked prepared for a night out at a club, with bottles of water, fluorescent wrist bands and tiny cut-off tops.

In the clearing nearby there was a lot of activity around a giant maypole, tall and white and decorated with dozens of dangling ribbons. New arrivals were adding ribbons, girls hoisted onto the shoulders of tall young men to tie on additional streamers. A stage loomed in the distance, colored lights already flashing, a DJ in headphones still setting up. In the strange light of endless evening, the trees looked silver and the sky's pale blue seemed chalky and surreal. The forest went on forever. The lake stretched into infinity. Tonight would never end.

"Hey!" Mina nudged him. "Look who's here."

Ara. That was Edon's first thought. Somehow she'd managed to elude her deportation order and turn up here. But he couldn't see or smell her in the latest wave of new arrivals, and Mina had to nudge him again.

A small speedboat had pulled up to the tiniest available space on one of the stretching wooden piers, and three guys were clambering off it. Edon narrowed his eyes, trying to ignore the grit in them, the dryness, the exhaustion that kept sweeping through him today. He was getting long-in-the-tooth; that's what Ara would say if she were here.

But she wasn't here. The only people getting off the speedboat Mina was all over were men.

And one of them was Oliver Hazard-Perry.

Mina's body tensed, and he had to grip her arm to hold him back.

"That's him, isn't it?" she said. Her eyes glowed yellow, the way they always did when she sensed a kill. He used to find that attractive, once upon a time. "You move right. I'll cut him off."

"No." The strength in his own voice surprised Edon. "We're not here to take him. We need to follow him."

Mina inhaled, loud and deep, as though she was trying to control her own savage instincts. She understood what he was saying, Edon knew.

Oliver Hazard-Perry was officially public enemy number one, but the orders from New York had changed. He was just another hunter, possibly with better information than they had. Following him could mean being led to a much bigger prey – Finn Chase.

It had to be close to midnight by now. The forest, so hauntingly quiet earlier in the day, echoed with the shouts and laughter of hundreds, maybe even thousands, of young revelers. The music from the makeshift stage was pounding, the lights flickering and transforming the trees into lurid pillars of color. The area leading up a gentle slope from the lake looked like a chaotic outdoor nightclub, the pagan maypole looming at its center.

Oliver didn't head for the center of things, to Edon's relief. He looped around the crowds, keeping on the edge of things and peering in. They followed, close enough to keep his scent, but not so close he could spot them. He wasn't a true member of the Fallen, not by the kind of arcane definitions the Blue Bloods seemed obsessed with, but as a human-turned-vampire he should have enough wit to know two wolves when he saw them.

He looked rough, Edon thought. He'd seen the former New York Regis at the swank events over which he'd presided, and he'd always looked so smooth and groomed – a pretty boy, Edon had always thought, who'd taken on too much responsibility too soon. He wasn't looking so pretty these days. He was gaunt and unshaven, and so thin his clothes hung on him like shapeless sacks. That Mina had recognized him at all was incredible, a tribute to her skills as a tracker. Edon wasn't sure that he would have done the same.

Edon brushed the fingers of his right hand against the axe he was carrying with him today, hidden in a pocket – though in this dippy crowd he could be brandishing it above his head and everyone would think it was some cool Viking prop. The blade was sharp and smooth. If Oliver made a break for it, Edon was ready to attack. Not kill, but wound. No way was this guy getting away – not when he could lead them to their real prey.

As well as looking a scruffy shadow of his former self, Oliver also seemed aimless. He was wandering and then pausing, wandering and pausing. Sometimes he just stood for a few moments, zoning out. Was he lost? Mina shot an enquiring glance at Edon: there seemed no urgency to Oliver's quest, no desperation. But he kept moving on at regular intervals, so it was likely he didn't have a fixed meeting point.

That's when it hit Edon. Oliver was the hunter who offered himself up as prey. He was making himself visible, waiting to be found. And not by Venators or wolves, Edon realized –by Finn Chase. He was hoping that if his crazed, corrupted beloved was somewhere in this excited crowd, she would see Oliver and seek him out. Did he really think a romantic reconciliation was on the cards? Edon couldn't believe that. It was much more likely that Finn would have one of her Silver Blood consort kill him. He was just an irritation now – a vampire without power, a man who'd lost his heart and his head.

Oliver stumbled on uneven ground and backed away from the crowd a little. People were pressing forward, drawn to the music like moths to the pulsating colored lights. Was he losing faith? Did he realize how hopeless this was, this doomed quest of his? In a throng so large, he was just another guy. Even if Finn Chase were here, he might never spot her, and she might never spot him.

Or she might just have him dispatched, Edon thought, without bothering to say one last goodbye.

Oliver was still backing away. The strange look on his face was visible even in the gloom of the forest, even this far away from the stage and its light show. Some Midsummer partiers had positioned small candles in jars, a looping trail of white light that lit up the golden pine needles and the grizzled bark of the trees. Mina paced to the side, so they were like pincers, ready to grab Oliver if they needed to. Edon was trying to work out what that look on his face meant, something between despair and serenity.

And then it came to him, just as one of the tiny candles shimmied in the breeze. Oliver knew his quest was doomed. He had no fight left in him. He was ready to die.

The last thing they needed was another dead body right now: it would cause a stampede, and god knows what would happen then, in the chaos and the dark. They had to take Oliver and secure him. Get him back to Axel, or to one of the Venator teams.

Edon glanced at Mina: her yellow eyes were like the candles, small and bright. She nodded at him, knowing instinctively what he was suggesting they do. Oliver, still trying to back away, collided with a tree and just stood there, slumped against its gray ridges. He didn't have the energy to take another step. That's the way it looked. He'd found his stake, and was waiting to be burned alive.

A whirring sound cut through the air, low and fluttering like a butterfly on fast-forward. Edon heard it before he saw it, but he knew exactly what it was: a crescent blade in flight. He leapt, swinging his axe up as though it were a shield, blocking the blade before it soared into Oliver's belly. It hit the axe with an almighty clang, the impact so great Edon was knocked to the ground, the axe flying and taking him with it. He felt every bone in his body crunch as he tumbled, just missing a stony patch that would have broken him into pieces.

He blinked, trying to get some sense back into his head. Mina was crouched over him, her face both alarmed and admiring, and she hauled him up without saying a word. Oliver was gone, but someone was running away – a Venator, on the chase?

Kind of. Edon would know that slim form and platinum crop anywhere.

It was Ara.

27 | REVENGE

*J*ack was back in the forest – this endless forest that seemed to grow with every hour and footstep. Would this day ever end? The noise of the big party taunted him, throbbing and raging, just the way he felt inside.

He had no sense of the time anymore. It was late, very late, but the flashing lights of the rave lit up the forest like fireworks. The sun would begin to rise around three AM, he'd been told, when it felt as though it had barely set. Somewhere, in the midst of this leaping and whooping crowd of oblivious party-goers, there were Venators and wolves, Nephalim and Silver Bloods, maybe even Lucifer himself.

And Lily, just seven-years-old, far from home and in mortal danger.

Even before Axel told them about the private plane taking off in New York and landing in Stockholm, Jack knew that Catherine would be bringing Lily here. Why – now that was something else altogether. He marched through the crowd as best he could, shouldering whirling dancers out of the way, the ground pulsating beneath his feet. Why had Catherine done this? They'd met and talked; he'd given her his word that he would help her get revenge on whoever murdered Louis, her husband – his son – all those centuries ago. Was she just trying to get leverage, to refuse to hand Lily back until he acted on his word? It was a stupid high-stakes game to play, one that endangered her own life, even if she didn't care about Lily's.

Catherine had to be so blind, so desperate for revenge, that she'd risk charging into a mission as important as this one and ruining it. This seemed incredible to him, nonsensical. In a past cycle she'd been his and Mimi's much loved daughter-in-law. She'd never experienced anything from them but kindness and understanding. Why would she turn on him now, when he'd promised to help her?

And what Jack really wanted to know was where Catherine had found the money for a private plane to fly to Europe. Someone had to be helping her. Someone in New York – or someone here.

The music had stopped and the DJ was shouting something, impossible to decipher given the wild cheers of the crowd. Jack kept pushing his way along, the giant garish maypole his destination. Schuyler had insisted they separate and meet there: they'd cover more ground that way, she said. He hated being apart from her now, of being alone without any of his little family with him. Sy was back in New York – safe, so Mimi insisted. Schuyler was somewhere in this forest, lost in the mob. Lily could be anywhere. He would thrust a sword through anyone who got in his way, once he found her.

If he found her.

"Mr. Force – why are you in such a hurry?" Lukas stood before him, face bright with sweat, his silver hair glinting like an animal pelt in moonlight. He placed a warm hand on Jack's shoulder and gripped it in a way that felt as though he'd never let go. "The party isn't over, you know. I am about to make the traditional speech over by the maypole. Won't you join me?"

"Yes, of course," Jack said through gritted teeth. They'd kept the news of Lily's abduction from Lukas and Pernilla, first because Schuyler insisted and then because Axel thought it wise. Like them, he didn't trust the Regis.

"This is my annual duty, you know," Lukas continued, his hand still grasping Jack's shoulder. His fingers dug into Jack's skin. "I greet the people here for Midsummer and give official permission, as the land-owner, for the use of my land."

"A little late for that, don't you think?" Jack asked. Lukas stepped closer, his smile fixed.

"It's just the way we do things here, one of our Scandinavian traditions. It's hard for an outsider to understand."

"And do you welcome the White Queen every year?" Jack demand-ed. "Is she one of your Scandinavian traditions?"

Lukas looked bemused – an act, Jack was certain.

"Every year we have a Queen. Last year it was the Summer Queen, the year before it was the Queen of the Lake. Don't read too much into a name. It's just our small way of offering something special and new to our many guests from the city. Otherwise, why would so many people come?"

He gestured at the sprawling crowd around them, and Jack was re-lieved: his shoulder was free again. Lukas nodded towards the maypole in the distance.

"Shall we? I would be honored to have you with me when I address our guests. Of course, most of them will have no idea who you are. But those in the know ..."

"I'm really not here to stand around watching ceremonies." Jack felt his temper beginning to spiral out of control. "As you well know."

"Of course." Lukas' tone was cordial, but his smile was gone. He was herding Jack towards the maypole. "But I beg you, please don't turn our traditional Midsummer celebration into some kind of violent scene. We have a position here to maintain. You're not in the US now, are you? This is Sweden. A place of green trees, blue lakes and white nights."

Sweden, thought Jack, where a new gate of hell had cracked open, admitting scores of demons into the world. And all the Regis of the Coven cared about was political jockeying for position among the Blue Bloods, and getting bad publicity at his big party. Pathetic.

Despite his aversion to Lukas, Jack kept walking with him. He needed to get to the maypole anyway, because that's where he'd see Schuyler again. They'd share information – not that he had anything to tell her, except how noxious Lukas was, and how sorry he was not to have told her earlier that he knew Catherine Denham.

He hadn't told Schuyler because he thought Catherine's revenge obsession would worry her. Well, she would have been to have fears and reservations. He should have told her. He should have said something the moment he saw Catherine in Mimi's apartment, the moment he recognized her.

He'd betrayed Schuyler's trust and she might never forgive him. The woman he'd pledged to love forever, not just in this life but until the end of time.

As though she knew he was thinking about her, Schuyler materialized close to the maypole. She hadn't seen him, he realized; she looked dreamy and pensive, unaware of the surging crowds and their chatter and racket. Like Jack and Lukas, she was obviously walking toward the maypole, but she was alone.

"Schuyler!" Jack called. She didn't seem to hear.

"Ah, your wife! Very good." Lukas sounded relieved. "You will both be there for my little speech. And for the ceremony, with the White Queen. Not a real Queen, you understand! You know, maybe if we'd known you were coming, we could have arranged for Mrs. Force to take the role of the Queen."

Schuyler didn't need to play a royal role, Jack wanted to say, but he kept walking, his eyes fixed on his beautiful wife. She still looked both delicate and strong, her dark hair the color of volcanic sand. Lukas had no idea if he thought Schuyler would opt to be carried around a maypole in some seasonal game. She was a great fighter, stronger and faster than a wolf, quick-witted and sensitive to nuances of behavior in a way he'd never be. When she met Catherine, she knew at once that there was something suspect about her. How could he have lied to her – or, at least, withheld information?

"Schuyler!" he called again, but she was walking more quickly now, pushing her way past other people, eager to reach the maypole.

There, Jack thought, they'd find out if the White Queen was Finn – and if her coronation would launch a new war.

28 | AMONG THE TREES

*T*he trees were passing in a blur, and Ara knew all she had to do was to keep running, leaping over tussocks and rocks, darting past any obstacle in her way. She'd broken every promise to Jack Force by leaving her inn when she spotted Oliver Hazard-Perry on a boat. But she couldn't break her most sacred promise, her duty, and that was to be a Venator. Members of the Coven's secret service didn't loll around in rented rooms sighing over the view and chewing over their mistakes.

They spied on criminals and then chased their asses down.

She was out of the habit of running, Ara realized. Her heart was thundering and her lungs felt as though someone had bunged them full of bales of cotton. All she could hear was the drum of her heart and the crunch of twigs and needles underfoot. But there was exhilaration in the chase, as always, and spurts of adrenalin kicking in were like bursts of power in a sports car. The trees were giant barriers for her to swerve around; this forest was a race track, and Ara was determined to win.

The noise of the party crowd was a distant roar. In the distance she glimpsed her prey, running full-tilt up a small incline, glancing back for the briefest of moments to assess how much ground Ara was gaining. He was a fast runner – Ara would give him that. But he would never outpace her. With every bend she was getting closer, trying to conserve some energy so she'd be able to tackle him when she drew close enough. She couldn't wait to leap on him and rub his face into the ground and wrench his hands up behind his back.

She couldn't wait to pull him over and see who had dared to throw a crescent blade straight at Oliver Hazard-Perry, the only one in this forest, she was sure, who could draw Finn Chase into the open.

At first, when she saw the blade whizz through the air, before Edon clunked it away with that ugly axe he liked to carry, Ara's gut had told her the would-be assassin was a Venator. Who else had that weapon – and the skill to use it? But the guy who took off like the wind when his shot was deflected couldn't be a Venator. That wasn't the way real Venators fought. If a Venator was told to take on an enemy, then they stood their ground, even if they were disarmed. You fought: you didn't run away. Too much was at stake. Running away from the scene could mean he was a rogue Venator, not acting on official orders and not wanting to be caught in the act.

Or else – he wasn't a Venator at all.

Ara was close now. Even in this soft darkness, the moon sparkling through breaks in the trees and picking out golden pools of pine needles, it was hard to make out much about the man she was chasing. He was tiring; that much she could tell. She wasn't. All this enforced sitting-around might have compromised her fitness, but not her fight. This was the work she was born to do. This guy was a coward who ran away. And she was going to take him down.

He stumbled on something – tangled weeds, a fallen branch – and Ara seized her moment. She launched herself into the air, landing on him so hard she knocked him flat to the ground. But he wasn't giving up that easily. He bucked and struggled, trying to push Ara off him. There wasn't much to this guy, but he was wriggling free of her grasp, and she was scrabbling at stones and leaves and soil, losing contact with him altogether. She had no weapons – nothing but her hands and her willpower. Upwards she reached, wild and furious at the fight he was putting up, and grabbed a handful of his T-shirt. She dragged him to the ground with such force that the fabric started ripping. Something bounced away from him – something gold and glinting in the moonlight – and he stuck out a pale hand to retrieve whatever it was, his body slackening just long enough for Ara to pounce. That was it: she had him pinned.

Her right hand was bleeding and scraped, but it was still strong enough to pull his head back and get a good look at his face. That's when she realized that the glinting object that had fallen just of his reach was a pair of glasses, and that she knew this face – not well, but she knew it.

Christian. The Venator Chief's human conduit.

"Let me go," he said, angry and squirming, and Ara tugged on his hair so hard he squealed with pain. Really – not a Venator. Just pathetic.

"First you tell me why you tried to kill someone back there," she said, digging her knees into his back.

"I don't have to tell you anything."

"You better talk, dumb ass, before the wolves get here and rip you from ear to ear. They're right behind me, and this time they'll be using their axes on *you*."

Ara didn't know if Edon and Mina were following, or if they were preoccupied with Oliver Hazard-Perry. Whatever. She could take this dweeb by herself.

"Get off!" Christian started bucking again, trying to rid himself of Ara, so she dug her boots hard into his calves: he cried out with pain, and she tightened her grip on his arms.

"Tell me what the hell you think you're doing and who told you to do it."

"Nobody!"

"I said, tell me who's pulling your strings? No way a nobody like you is acting alone." Ara dug her knees in again. Was Axel behind this?

Another double-crossing Venator chief – really? Or was Christian secretly working for the Regis, spying on the Venators and relaying information back to the Coven's leadership?

Christian lay there, twisting to no effect, refusing to say anything.

"Speak!" Ara yelled, frustrated beyond belief. This guy wasn't a Venator. Who the hell did he think he was, using Venator blades, trying to implicate someone else? She used her legs to kick him over, so he was facing her. Christian spluttered and squirmed. What a total nobody this guy was, lying there blinking at her – he probably couldn't see straight without his glasses. He was no match for her strength – though it wouldn't be the worst thing in the world if Edon turned up sometime soon.

"You're just a mortal!" she shouted into his twisting face. "You're just a conduit! You're not a Venator! That's why you couldn't kill someone with the blades. You don't have the skill. So tell me – who put you up to this?"

Christian's face was red with rage.

"You Venators," he spluttered. "You think that you're god's gift, don't you? You're so conceited and arrogant. You couldn't possibly imagine someone mortal being a better fighter than you, or a better strategist. Well, you're wrong."

"Well, I'm not," Ara snapped. "If you were so great, you wouldn't have been caught as soon as you tried to kill someone. Don't think you're fit to clean the boots of a Venator!"

"Ha!" Christian's laugh was bitter. "Really, you think that's the first time I've *tried* to kill someone? I may not be a Venator, but I'm a better fighter than most of you. A better killer."

"That's not what I just saw, buddy." Ara couldn't stand this guy.

"You don't know anything," Christian spat at her. "Who do you think killed the kid in the club who was telling too much to your stupid wolf friends?"

"You did that. Really." Ara didn't believe him.

"Who do you think was the only person in the Coven who knew

where Oliver Perry-Hazard was in Stockholm? And when he thought he'd got away, who do you think tracked him down and killed his little girlfriend?"

"Finn Chase? You're saying you killed Finn Chase?"

"No! The girl in the apartment, the one he was staying with. The Swedish girl. Just like I killed the Venator at the airfield today."

""I have no idea what you're talking about. Shut up!" Ara was getting tired of Christian's boasts. Either he was delusional or he was covering up for someone. Someone like Axel, say. "Your boss has told you to say all this, hasn't he?"

"You don't get it, do you?" Christian wasn't even struggling now, but Ara knew she had to remain vigilant. "Finn Chase isn't the only mortal to rebel against her lowly status. Why should we conduits be expected to act as indentured servants for the Coven? Aren't we children of god as well? Your precious Oliver Hazard-Perry – he was a human conduit himself, wasn't he? And not only did he become immortal, he became Regis of your Coven. So why shouldn't I transform my own fortunes? Why should I be content with my lot?"

"Be quiet!" Ara was sick of him. When would Edon arrive? He must have seen her there, chasing Christian. Surely he'd come to help soon?

"Ara!" Edon – at last. Ara glanced over her shoulder. Both Edon and Mina were approaching but tentatively, with slow and creeping steps, one padding to the left and one to the right.

"I have him here!" she shouted back. "It's Christian. The Venator chief's guy – his human conduit!"

"Let him go, Ara," said Mina. She stepped into Ara's sight line, axe in hand. Her ferocious yellow eyes glared straight at Ara. "Step away. Hands up."

"What?" Ara spun to look at Edon, just stepping out of the shadows. He said nothing but there was a strange look on his face. Hurt. Confusion. Sadness. "What – you think *I'm* the criminal here? You think *I'm* the one who tried to kill Oliver?"

"We saw you running away …" Mina began, her axe still pointed at

Ara's head.

"Chasing this guy! Oh my god. Do you actually know me?" She looked at Edon, and felt sickened with disgust. To think of how close they'd been, how much they'd shared. How much she'd exposed herself to him and let herself be soft and vulnerable. She wished she had her Venator blades with her now. These two wolves would be cut to shreds in seconds.

"Mina said … you must have been the one who hurled the blades. That it was a Venator and …"

"A Venator!" Christian spluttered. "Listen to you all. You can't help yourselves. If someone's killed with a crescent blade, it has to be a Venator. Don't you ever stop to think, for one moment, that someone else can learn the same tricks? Someone who can slip unnoticed into meetings and clubs and apartments, someone who nobody in the whole smug, dysfunctional, conceited Coven suspects of having a brain?"

Edon was staring at him open-mouthed.

"He says he killed the kid in the nightclub. And some girl who Oliver knew in Stockholm."

"And don't forget the Venator at the airfield today," Christian chimed in.

"Shut up," Mina told him. She wasn't glaring at Ara anymore, and she'd lowered her blade.

In the distance a roar arose, cheering and shrieking. Christian kicked his feet, a maniacal grin on his face.

"You can kill me if you want now," he said. "It's too late to matter! The White Queen is here! Our time has come!"

Mina and Edon exchanged looks. The crowd noises back in the party glade were growing louder and more charged. Something bad was about to go down, Ara knew. Something evil.

Midsummer. The maypole. The White Queen.

Christian gave an almighty heave and Ara, off her guard, tumbled into the leaves. He scrambled to his feet and started to run.

"All hail the White Queen!" he cried, face raised to the sky, and then disappeared into the darkness.

"Ara, I'm sorry," said Edon. He held out a hand to her, to help her up.

"Just run," Ara told him. There was no time now for apologies. "We have to get back to the maypole. Now – it's happening now!"

29 | THE WHITE QUEEN

*H*igh in the sky the moon was a serene ivory circle, beaming down on the crowded glade. This was it. The moment Catherine had been waiting for – all her life, maybe. All her many lives, her many cycles. The old order had let her down, but a new order was dawning. At last she would get revenge, and maybe – at last – some peace.

People around her were cheering and shouting, and Catherine smiled out at them, as benign as the moon. She was being carried aloft on a wooden chair decorated with vibrant ribbons and trailing ivy, her white flowing dress so long it covered her bare feet. Her hair was loose, held back by a crown of greenery and wildflowers. Below her, so many happy young people – mortals and vampires – were waving their arms and calling out: *White Queen! White Queen!* Some people threw flowers: buds landed on her lap, and she closed her eyes, so heady was the scent and the sounds of her triumphal entry.

White Queen! White Queen!

The men carrying her reached the tall maypole that was decorated with hundreds of colored ribbons, so long they touched the ground. Every year there was a Queen here at Midsummer, but usually it was just some Coven girl with a pretty face whose father was in favor with the Regis. This year word had gone out for the past two months that the Queen would be a special one, that the whole celebration would be special in grand and unexpected ways. Catherine had no intention of letting anyone down.

It was after midnight, and that was a shame. Catherine was a traditionalist in many ways, and had liked the idea of being displayed at the maypole just as Midsummer turned – the longest day signaling the end of things. The end of an old world with its hypocrisy and status. But it was OK to be carried out later, in the deepest moments of darkness on this long white night. She'd waited so long. She could relish the final minutes, and hang on just a little longer.

The moon, so high in the sky, gazed down at her, its pale face a mask. The light at that moment on her own face was so bright and clear that it felt like a sign. Everyone around her was going wild, screaming and stamping. For the first time in her life she felt truly powerful.

She thought of Finn's promise to her. Tonight, Finn swore, would be Catherine's chance to get revenge on the Silver Blood who murdered her husband – and damned him for all eternity – hundreds of years ago. Catherine didn't even know his identity until a few months ago. Finn was the one who found out – sweet Finn, who everyone hated and raged against. Finn had contacted her, out of the blue, and sworn her to secrecy. Did she want to know Louis' killer? Yes? Then Finn would reveal this to her and make the revenge she'd craved possible. Nobody else had done that for her. Nobody else had even tried to help.

White Queen! White Queen!

Catherine smiled for her adoring public, while the men holding her aloft slowly rotated her chair, allowing everyone in the crowd to see her. It wasn't hard to pick out the shocked, blood-drained face of Schuyler Van Alen, that Coven princess, her face even whiter than the moon's.

Of course there'd been a price for Finn's information. Just as Catherine longed for something, Finn did as well – and both of them were tired of other people denying them their destiny. But Finn didn't want revenge. She wanted something much more pure and innocent. Bring Schuyler and Jack's daughter to her, here in Sweden – that was what Finn requested. She wanted a child of her own, and not just any child. A little girl with angel's blood, who she could raise, love, and nurture as a princess of the Dark Side.

There was no way Finn would harm Lily: Catherine was sure of that. And what was the difference between the dark and the light these days, anyway? What was the difference at any point in history? Lily would grow up loved and valued. She was lucky, to be so wanted by so many people. Catherine had wanted children with Louis, her bondmate, but his murder had prevented that. All her dreams over, in one jab of a sword.

Back then her esteemed and powerful in-laws couldn't locate her husband's killer, and she knew that whatever Jack promised, he and Mimi were too busy and self-important to look for him now. They'd betrayed her, and now she must betray them.

White Queen! White Queen!

The chair kept spinning, and Catherine could see them all down there, looking up at her, no idea of what she was about to do. Jack had reached Schuyler, and was clutching her arm. The ruling class of this vampire world: they thought they controlled everything and everyone. But not this moment – this moment was Catherine's.

Still, seeing them there with their outraged faces, she struggled to keep the smile on her face. That day in Trinity Church, Catherine had known that Jack was lying – saying anything just to keep her doing the menial job of running after his children. He needed to pay for being such a careless father in a past life, as well as in this. He needed to feel that terrible sorrow all over again, because apparently he'd forgotten it all too quickly the last time. What did he care? He just switched one bondmate for another. Catherine was the one who had nobody.

White Queen! White Queen!

The spinning was making Catherine feel dizzy.

"Stop!" she commanded, holding up a hand. There was hushing and laughter in the crowd, a thrill of anticipation. The Queen had spoken. On the far reaches of the crowd there was still boisterous noise, but everyone who could see Catherine fell silent. The annual tradition had begun. What Catherine knew and they didn't was that the ritual was almost over.

The men grasping each leg of the decorated chair started lowering it onto a high wooden platform, pushed into place next to the giant maypole so people in the crowd could see. Lukas, the local Regent, was the man climbing its narrow steps. It was his job to take her hand and bow, the great landowner accepting the higher power of the pagan Queen. It was the same every year, she'd been told.

Catherine rose from her chair, bare feet scrunched on the rough boards of the platform. Her white gown fluttered in the night breeze. All around her expectant faces gazed, waiting to hear the traditional words.

"Every queen needs a king," she said, her voice loud and clear. Lukas grasped her right hand, and bent his silver head low before her.

Catherine reached her left hand into the bodice of her dress, and pulled from it, in one fluent movement, a thin silver dagger. Those nearest in the crowd gasped and Lukas looked up, just long enough to see the shining blade, and for Catherine to see the terror in his eyes. She plunged the dagger into his heart, all the way to the hilt – into his bloated, cushiony body, dark blood like a spreading fungus over his white shirt. His face seemed frozen with shock, though he was still alive. Catherine bent her head close to his.

"For Louis," she whispered. "I found you at last."

She pulled the knife out and Lukas fell backwards, his eyes rolling, his body thunking down the wooden stairs. Someone screamed, but Catherine knew she had to act quickly, before anyone grabbed her. This was still her moment, still her night. The White Queen on the White Night. The blood of Lukas – silver and corrupt, seeping into the forest floor.

Catherine pointed the knife at her own belly. She'd rehearsed this many times, the thrust and the jagged line. She'd achieved all she wanted to – all she could achieve after Louis' death, after she'd been damned to eternal unhappiness.

The dagger was sharp, and sticky with Lukas' blood. She plunged it deep into her flesh: the searing pain took her breath away. She thought she could see Louis' face, just out of reach, waiting for her on the other side. In her final seconds of consciousness she was falling, falling, falling, her white dress flying around her like an angel's wings.

30 | THE DREAM

*T*he two bodies lay in a crumpled heap – Lukas on his back, and Catherine collapsed onto them. Schuyler could see them clearly, now that so many people had backed away, screaming and crying, stumbling into the trees and towards the lake. Others further back pushed forward, confused or curious, then horrified. Some people had stood watching, dumbstruck, convinced this was all an elaborate pantomime and that the two star players, Queen and Lord, would jump to their feet and take a bow. But this was no game.

Amid all the chaos, Jack was on his knees, pulling Catherine's prone form off Lukas and trying to revive her.

"Lily!" he was shouting at her. "You have to tell us – where's Lily, Catherine? Where is she?"

Schuyler was fixed to the spot, unable to move. She could see, even if Jack couldn't, that Catherine was dead. She couldn't tell them anything, even if she wanted to. Why she'd brought Lily here, and where she'd hidden her – those were secrets that had died with Catherine, probably just as she intended.

People were pushing past her, falling and stumbling; a girl was shrieking hysterically, her friends dragging her away. Schuyler stood there, trying to read the night, to read the air. There was too much interference. She needed to clear her head. Jack approached, blood all over his hands and shirt. They were both dead, he said. Axel the Venator Chief had taken over.

"Why would Catherine do such a thing, and why here? Schuyler asked Jack, and he explained, eyes glued to the ground, of his and Mimi's past relationship with Catherine, and of her desperate, unhinged desire for revenge after Louis' death. The Silver Blood who killed Louis back then was apparently Lukas in this cycle, though how Catherine had learned that, and if it was even true … well.

He kept apologizing to her, but despair and helplessness was crowding in on her again. Too many secrets. Too many lies. The past never going away. The future always at stake.

"Please, Jack," she said. "Not now. Let's just find her, OK?"

"I'll go talk to the Venators," he said, still too ashamed to look her in the eye.

"Schuyler." A trembling hand on her arm. It was Pernilla, her face drawn and streaked with tears. "We should leave. Can we go? Please?"

"Don't you want to …" Schuyler nodded at Lukas' body, flat on its back. Pernilla shook her head. She clutched at Schuyler's arm again,

"I'm scared. I think we should go. I … I don't think it's over. Do you?"

"I have to find my daughter," Schuyler said. "Your … White Queen here is Catherine Denham, our children's nanny. She kidnapped our little girl and brought her here to Sweden. I don't know why, but I'm not leaving this damned forest until I find her. But you should go home, if you can get there safely. Who do you trust?"

"Nobody," said Pernilla. She sounded bitter and miserable. "I never really trusted Lukas, to be honest. All our friends are *his* friends. Even the people who work for us – I don't trust any of them. I'd rather stay with you and help you find your daughter."

"Then can you fight?" Schuyler asked her bluntly. Pernilla was right. It wasn't over, and finding Lily tonight was not going to be easy, pretty

WHITE NIGHTS | 195

or blood-free, she suspected. Pernilla blanched.

"I've never had to," she said, and swallowed away tears. "But I'd rather die fighting than get murdered in my bed."

To Schuyler's amazement Pernilla stalked over to Catherine's limp body and pulled out the silver dagger. Jack rocked back on his heels, frowning at her.

"Can I use this?" she said, looking from Jack to Schuyler. "If there's going to be a fight? It's small, but clearly it works."

This night, Schuyler thought, was getting stranger by the minute.

Still she felt stuck to the spot, as though she was growing roots and becoming a tree of the forest. Clouds floated over the moon, smutting its clear face. Schuyler closed her eyes and lifted her face up, trying to focus on nothing but the breeze lifting her hair, damp with sweat, off her clammy skin.

The hysteria of her surroundings faded into the low hum of background noise, and Schuyler saw a vision of her daughter. Lily was smiling, her own hair shivering in the breeze. She wore a wreath of green around her head, and from it thin ribbons were fluttering, blue and yellow and red. Lily was smiling. She was looking at Schuyler and smiling.

Schuyler opened her eyes, just in time to see Pernilla wiping the dagger's blade clean on the grass just feet from where her dead husband lay.

Mama! Mama!

The voice was in Schuyler's head, but it had risen unprompted, as clear as the vision of Lily in her floral crown. She was here somewhere, Schuyler knew, and the strong signals she was getting suggested that Lily wasn't that far away. Schuyler was walking as though she were in a trance, away from Jack and Pernilla and the dead bodies, through gaggles of upset and confused people, past clumps of revelers now flopped at the bases of trees, comforting each other, holding each other close. The forest called her, so deep into the forest she must go. It didn't even feel dark anymore, as though first light had begun to emerge, bringing with it the hint of a new day. The light at this time was eerie, she thought, a time for ghosts to emerge.

And for visions to mislead.

Schuyler had no idea where she was walking now. Away from the thinning crowds but towards a stretch of dark lake; she could hear the water lapping before she saw it. The grass underfoot was longer here and it slowed her paces down. She was listening for Lily's voice, or even just the hint of a cry. She would know the sound of Lily anywhere.

She climbed over a rocky pile and descended into a small clearing, surrounded b towering trees. Her breath caught in her throat, jagged and harsh, and she wasn't sure if the small form in the distance could be Lily or just some apparition. With every step Schuyler could see it was indeed Lily, just as she'd appeared in Schuyler's dream. The wildflower wreath, the white dress, the bright ribbon streamers wafting in the wind. Lily stood alone in a glade looking straight at her mother, but she didn't run or call out. Schuyler followed her lead, simply looking at her lovely little daughter's face and not saying a word. Lily was young but she was already astute. The expression on her face was a clue, and she needed Schuyler to draw close enough to see it. But not too close – her dark eyes were wide with alarm.

She looked terrified, Schuyler realized. This was not the happy smile of the dream. Lily was not smiling, calling her forward, even pleading for help. She was warning her mother not to take another step.

So this is where it would begin – not at the maypole, but deep in the forest after all the mortals had run away, terrified by the murder-suicide they'd just witnessed.

Schuyler stood still, nodding to Lily, with the slightest of smiles, to say that she understood. As quietly as she could manage, Schuyler drew her sword. It felt long and heavy in her hands, but she was strong enough to swing it, and the sword itelf seemed to tingle with readiness. Whoever was holding Lily captive over there, and whoever was lying in wait, Schuyler would fight them. She'd driven back Lucifer and his forces before, and she wasn't letting demons take her daughter – or take her daughter's life. Over her dead body.

There was only one thing left to do. Slowly and carefully Schuyler drew the blade across her own upturned left palm, exposing a thin line of blood. The pain stung when the open wound hit the night air, but the breeze meant the scent would travel further. She held her left hand high in the air, as though she was reaching for the moon, and waited.

31 | THE BLOOD OF AN ANGEL

The wolves hadn't made it back to the maypole: by the time they were getting close, the crowd had turned on its heels, and people were running away and screaming, falling over themselves to get back to the lake – or to just scatter into the woods. Some great mass hysteria had overtaken the revelers, and Edon heard garbled cries about murder and death. He grabbed someone who he overheard speaking English, and asked him what had happened.

"The White Queen stabbed the old dude, then she killed herself. We thought it was fake, but it wasn't – there are two dead bodies on the ground! Two bodies!"

Mina's head snapped towards Edon. *Only two?* He was thinking the same thing. If the White Queen was Finn Chase – then she was dead? And who was the old dude?

A local Venator sprinted up, out of breath from running so fast. The Regis was dead, he told them.

"I told you," Ara said, punching Edon's arm. "Something big is about to go down. This is just the start of it."

"She's right." Mina was sniffing the air, eyes raised to the moon. "Can you smell it?"

"What?" Ara snapped, but Edon didn't reply. He could smell something as well – a pure note, frigid and unadulterated as alpine air, with the faint sweetness of a flower. The blood of an angel.

He remembered it from the war, from the last battle. They were being summoned.

"Go find Axel," he told Ara. "Jack Force, other Venators – whoever you can find. We're being called. The fight's begun."

"Who's calling?" Ara reeled back, her eyes intense.

"You, give her a blade," Edon demanded, pointing at the local Venator. "You have a gun as well, right? She needs a weapon."

"I said, who's calling?" Ara demanded again. Mina narrowed her eyes. They glowed like yellow lanterns.

"Schuyler Van Alen," she said. "To the northwest – north northwest. Right?"

She glanced at Edon for agreement and he nodded. The scent was strong and clear to him now. Angel blood was like a golden arrow in the sky, impossible to miss, pointing the way. He turned to speak to Ara again, but she was already running towards the maypole, crescent blade in hand. Good: they needed every fighter they could find. Schuyler would only call this way if the danger was extreme and imminent.

They ran to the place the blood flowed. Edon's senses were alive, every creak and rustle and whisper as vivid to him as a shout through a megaphone, but he followed nothing but the blood scent, Mina pounding along beside him, leaping over rocks and fallen branches.

They were running so fast that they almost passed Schuyler Van Alen altogether. She was standing completely still, sword in hand, at the edge of a green clearing. Not far from where she waited was the beginning of more deep forest, huge trees that towered like dark skyscrapers. A little girl stood just before the first line of trees, dark hair loose. She wore a wreath of greenery, trailing bedraggled ribbons. She made no sound, but Edon could just make out the tears dribbling down her pale cheeks.

Mina was sniffing the air again, and Edon could smell something else as well. Something rotting and pungent, with a metallic tang. Silver Bloods. A lot of them as well, to release such an odor.

"They must be everywhere," Mina muttered to him. "Again, to the north. Just past the girl."

Edon nodded. The Silver Bloods were here in force. Just because they couldn't see them yet didn't mean they weren't assembled – demons behind the trees, or hanging in them, secreted beneath moss or behind logs and boulders. The smell might be emanating from their new gateway to hell, an open wound in the earth releasing hell's foul stench. The demons, he was certain, were poised to attack.

"They're waiting for me to rescue Lily," Schuyler said to them in a low voice. "They're waiting for us to get close."

"The girl can't run to us?" Mina asked.

"She hasn't moved since I got here," Schuyler said. "She's terrified, or they're holding her some way. We have to draw them out."

"There are three of us," said Mina, matter-of-fact as ever. "There are more than three of them."

"Ara will be here soon," Edon muttered. He was wrong, so incredibly wrong, to have doubted Ara. She would never go rogue. She would never make a unilateral decision to murder Oliver Hazard-Perry and then run away to avoid getting caught. He was stupid to have believed Mina – especially as Mina hadn't even seen the blade-thrower. He should have trusted his instinct, and trusted his love. He loved Ara, despite all the grief they gave each other. If they both went fell tonight, in this endless forest that seethed with Silver Bloods, then it would be the best way to go. Wolf and Venator, the odd couple. Fighting demons to the death.

Footsteps crunched behind them, and Edon was relieved to see Jack Force, along with Axel and more than a dozen of his Venators. A young fair-headed woman he didn't know was with them as well, clutching a silver dagger. She looked terrified. Someone from the Coven, he guessed, but why she thought she could fight Silver Bloods wasn't immediately obvious.

Ara brought up the rear, keeping her distance. Moonlight caught the edge of her crescent blade and briefly it blazed like a white warning. There were still too few of them, Edon thought. But it was too late. Sometimes in war you had to fight with the army you had. And any army led by Schuyler Van Alen had right on its side.

Schuyler was murmuring orders so their group could break into three units, and consulting with Axel about deploying the Venators.

"Pernilla, stay with me," she said to the young woman with the dagger.

One of the Venators produced a flare gun and shot it into the air. The white flare broke in the sky like fireworks and as its pieces tumbled into the forest beyond them, it lit up the trees and ground with blinding white light. They could hear screams and the thuds of people falling – of demons falling from their perches, no doubt. The white shards hissed as they hit branches, the wood dissolving instantly into ash. More screams now, and glimpses of movement behind the trunks and rocks in the distance.

"Swedish technology," Jack Force said, nodding in admiration. "Let's flush these demons out."

Three more Venators stepped forward one at a time to shoot flare guns into the sky, the white lights blazing into the dull clouds of early morning. The forest before them sizzled and shrieked, and Edon set off to the left, keeping low to the ground, with some of the Venator team. Mina moved to the right, her axe lifted. The Venators had blades and guns with silver bullets, the kind that put demons to sleep forever. But they still had no idea how many demons lay in wait, a little more exposed – at least – in the burning white woods.

In a blur of black a demon launched itself at Edon, and the fight was on. Edon slashed with his axe, knocking off heads and disemboweling anything that got in his way. When his axe got stuff in someone's spleen or heart, he dug his fangs into exposed skin to finish the demon off. The smell now was nothing but metallic – the smell of blood – and the smell of ash from the flare-razed trees.

Edon was spinning, his axe arcing through the air. He'd always been a fighter, but he hadn't taken part in combat this violent and bloody since the war. His hands were slimy with gore, and there was a mixture of blood and sweat dripping down his own face. Demons hurled themselves at him, screaming and swinging, and the sound of his axe batting away their swords and blades rang out like a bell. He backed one against a boulder and sliced its ugly head into two pieces with his axe, the blade bouncing back so hard off the stone that it almost flew out of his hand.

When he spotted a Venator in trouble, he smacked his axe into the attacking demon, but the numbers were still on their side: he had to jump over the bodies of two Venators, demons crouched over them to drain their blood. This made him so sick that he kicked one demon away with the steel-capped toe of his boot, pausing long enough to grab the felled Venator's blade. With a weapon in each hand he was a killing machine, slicing through the enemy like a thresher in the field.

Edon had lost sight of Ara and Mina, but he could see Schuyler working her way towards her daughter, fighting with the energy and skill of ten people. Her sword whirled above her head and then whooshed through three attacking Silver Bloods. The ones who stayed on their feet, staggering, were finished off by the woman with the dagger. She tailed Schuyler, piercing exposed necks with her sharp silver point, flinching every time a demon dropped to the ground before her.

Between the flares and first light, the glade seemed lit with an otherworldly white glow. Edon glimpsed Ara, still on her feet, hair streaked with dark blood, spearing a demon right through his rotten heart. She had two crescent blades now, and worked them with ferocious expertise, carving demons up with every twist and slash. Axel fought alongside her, towering above the attacking demons. He picked one up by the scruff of its neck and hurled it into a tree. Axel's roar sounded like some Viking battle cry, energizing all the Venators who were still fighting.

A smoldering demon who must have been hit by a flare spark

rolled out from behind a rock and grabbed Edon's ankles, but a sword smacked down on the outstretched arms, amputating them both at the elbow. He didn't have time to thank Jack Force, already swinging at something else, or even acknowledge him. There was another demon, and then another, to dispatch with the sharp blade of his axe, or even with the blunt thud of its heavy handle. Swarm after swarm of them came at him, smelling foul and fighting dirty, but they had no idea how vicious wolves were were cornered.

Edon realized he was getting close to Lily. He must have veered to the center at some point when he was helping out a Venator, and now he seemed to be the closest one to her. The poor little thing was trembling, but still not moving from her spot. A dead demon, its face a mask of blood and one eye dangling from its socket, lay at her feet. Her skin was the color of the ashy branches, and ash feathered her hair. She had to be terrified out of her wits.

He reached out a hand to her, but she still didn't move. That's when he realized she was tethered to a tree stump, thick vines around her ankles and wrists gripping her in place. Unlike the ribbons fluttering from the wreath on her head, those vines looked lodged like concrete. Edon kicked the demon's body out of the way and leaned forward, just close enough to her to tug on one of the twisted ivy ropes around her ankles. It wouldn't give way: he'd have to use his axe to slash her free, and it would be tricky to sever the vines without cutting her delicate skin.

"Don't worry, kid," he told her. "I'll get you out of this."

The girl gasped, looking up in the air, and Edon swung around just in time. A demon with a long blade was flying towards him, moments from contact. Edon smacked the blade away with the flat side of his axe and then swung the blade at the demon, but this time he missed. The demon ran at him, its red eyes the color of spilled guts, and if Schuyler hadn't swooped in, one arc of her sword decapitating his assailant, Edon might not have made it.

In an instant he and Schuyler were surrounded again, fighting back-to-back with nothing to focus on but red eyes, spurting blood and smeared metal blades. When he turned again to slash the ivy binding Lily to the boulder, she was gone. Schuyler was still fighting, Jack was still fighting, he was still fighting, everyone was still fighting – but finally he spotted the little girl, still bound by the hands with the twisted vines. Someone, out of sight, was pulling her away, and although Lily seemed to be resisting – being dragging rather than walking – she was being led away. Further and further away, out of reach, out of sight.

Edon struck his axe into the back of a demon about to finish off a Venator. The fight wasn't over, but the prize was disappearing. Lily was gone, and there was nothing Edon could do to stop it.

32 | THE SILVER PRINCESS

Oliver staggered through the trees with no idea of his direction. Everything was for nothing. For absolutely nothing. He'd almost been killed by a whirling Venator blade, then he'd had to run away from the White Queen's maypole ceremony to avoid getting nabbed by the wolves and Venators. By the time he was sure he'd eluded them, the ceremony was over.

He'd been convinced that Finn was the White Queen, but it turned out that she wasn't. When he finally got close to the maypole, pushing through the fleeing and screaming crowds, he saw another young woman in white robes and floral crown lying dead on the ground. Near him lay another dead body, a silver-haired man he recognized as the local Regis, though he couldn't remember his name. Someone told him that the White Queen had murdered someone and then killed herself. Whoever she was, the body lying there on the ground, a smile on her face and a deep bloody blotch across her stomach, she wasn't Finn.

So where was Finn? She had to be here – he had told himself that so many times he was convinced of it. Was she somewhere else in the forest, and if so – why? What was the point of this whole White Queen charade anyway? When would she show herself? Maybe this whole

Swedish misadventure was yet another false lead, another chance to reach Finn that slipped through Oliver's fingers.

Now he was lost in a forest that stretched as far as he could see in any direction. The crowds who'd been there for the big party had dissolved like sugar. Oliver had been walking and walking but he saw nobody – mortals, Blue Bloods, demons. All he saw were trees, battalions of them. The gnarled bark of their trunks was beginning to look like a series of faces, looming over him. Oliver picked up his pace, exhaustion the only thing holding him back. He had to get out of here – find the lake, find a boat, swim. This endless walking and seeing faces in the trees was a madness, he realized. His love for Finn, and his profound desire to make amends, had turned him into a madman. All he'd done in the last year was take one misstep after another.

In the distance white flares shot into the sky, their bright chalk-like pieces tumbling into the trees; then there were booms and shrieks, and the smell of ash. If the forest was on fire now, he really needed to get out. The water. Oliver needed to get to the water.

He could hear more flares whizzing up towards the moon but he didn't turn to gaze at their strange illuminations. Not when he could hear something else – a gentle lapping, soft but persistent. The lake. It was somewhere close by, past all these thickets and hollows, waiting for him. He'd found his way back to the lake at last.

All along Oliver had thought his story would end here in Sweden, and maybe the chilly waters of Lake Siljan would truly be his final destination. Usually the Fallen died in fire and blood, not in watery graves. But there was something appealing about the silent depths of the lake, and the peace he hoped to find there. No Silver Blood would be able to drain him and prevent his soul from rising again.

Oliver bent to feel around on the ground for some stones, then crammed them into his pockets. He didn't want to bob to the surface. He wanted to sink deep, deep, deep into those waters and never return. Let the pike and eels have their way with his decomposing body. He'd be back, though not – he hoped – for a very long time.

Oliver could see the lake, silvery in the moonlight, before he reached it. This part of the shoreline was rocky and slippery, and Oliver was looking for an inlet, the best place to walk into the water, never to return. Not far ahead of him was a sliver of meadow, long grass rippling in the breeze. The moon disappeared under a cluster of clouds and then re-appeared, its ivory beam lighting the thin tips of the grass, the silvery bark of trees, and the lacy tips of the lake's gentle waves.

That's when he saw her, by the water's edge. Finn, his once-mortal beloved. She was standing in shallow water dressed in white, her long blonde hair pulled back off her face. That ungodly beautiful face, cheekbones picked out by the moonlight. She looked like an apparition.

Oliver was scared of frightening her away. After all this time, to see her again, for her to be close enough to touch! He stood mired in the grass, watching her haul a small wooden boat from the shadows and onto the narrow ledge of sand.

"It's OK! Come here," she said to someone – to him? Had she seen him? Was she beckoning him over?

No.

Finn was bending over to lift something into the small boat. A child – a little girl. Lily! That girl had to be Lily, Schuyler and Jack's little girl. What was she doing here? Why was Finn taking her – and where? A tidal wave of sickness drenched him, because seeing this forced him to accept what Finn had become. However much he loved her, it wasn't enough. Not enough to keep her from the dark side, and not enough to keep her from delivering the worst blow of all to Schuyler, her own sister. Taking Schuyler's daughter to Lucifer's lair, to make an angel a corrupted Silver Princess.

"Finn! Stop!" Finn he could let go, but Lily he could not. Losing the little girl would destroy Schuyler and Jack. Heaven would weep. Oliver marched forwards, determined to grab Lily whatever it cost him – Finn, or his own life. Nothing of the past mattered now. Only the future.

"Oliver!" Finn's face clouded. He reached into the boat for Lily and the child keeled into his arms. She was shaking but not sobbing. That kid had always had guts.

"Let her go, Finn," he commanded, aware his own voice was shaking. This was not at all how he'd imagined their reunion. Not at all what he'd planned, all those hundreds of nights, to say to the woman he thought he loved more than the entire world. "She's done nothing wrong. She's blameless. If you want to embrace the darkness, I won't stop you. I'll stand here and watch you go. But you'll have to kill me first before I let you take Lily with you."

"Olly!" Finn hissed. Her expression softened. She almost looked like the old Finn. But Oliver had to harden his heart against her. That had been his mistake, all along –deluding himself into thinking she could be redeemed.

"Here," Oliver said to Lily, lifting her out of the boat and onto the sand her hem trailing through the water.

"No, Olly – you don't understand," said Finn. "I'm trying to rescue Lily, not trap her. Please believe me."

"I don't." Oliver clung to Lily's hand. He wasn't sure how he could get her away, or where, but this was why he was in the forest tonight. Not to reconcile with a demon, but to save an angel.

"Please," Finn pleaded. "You have to believe me. It's true that I asked for Lily to be brought here, and that I wanted to bring her up as my own."

"Your own Silver Princess," Oliver snapped at her. Finn had gone too far. She could choose her own corruption, but not impose it on a child.

"But I changed my mind. I swear, Oliver – when I saw how scared she was, and how desperately she wanted to be with Schuyler and Jack, I just couldn't do it. I couldn't drag her down with me. You have to believe me! Everything changed for me in that instant. Help me get her away from here. This is the only boat I could find. The battle's closer than you think, and I don't know – I really don't know who's winning."

"My mom and dad will win," Lily said, her voice clear and true. "Angels always triumph over Lucifer."

"That's right, Lil," said Oliver, squeezing her hand.

"And *I* know you're right, Lily," Finn said. "But for now, we need to get you out of harm's way. You and I both know what we saw there, back in the trees …"

"My mom killed a lot of demons," Lily whispered to Oliver and he smiled at her. He could imagine Schuyler slashing her way through a whole army of demons if her daughter was their captive.

"We need to take her away *now*," Finn insisted. "No Silver Blood or Neph will question anything if they see I'm with her. We'll get her to Dalmarna and take it from there, OK?"

"Oh, I don't think you're going anywhere," said a voice behind them, and Oliver turned, still clinging to Lily's hand. He'd know that voice anywhere.

Christian.

Axel's human conduit stood on the grass, a sharp blade in his hands. The goofy, benign expression was gone. In its place was a scowl.

"You!" Christian snapped, pointing the blade at Finn. "You don't think we saw you creeping away? Stealing the child."

"Please let her go," Finn pleaded. "I'll come back with you, but please let her go."

Slowly Christian shook his head. He looked at Finn with contempt.

"You chose your side," he said, "and you promised us an angel. The Silver Bloods want their princess."

"I'm their princess," Finn said, her voice desperate, and Christian scoffed. Oliver had no weapon. There was nothing remotely close to hand but the boat oars, and Christian could hurl the blade at him in a second if he made a move.

"You're the most beautiful princess in the world," Christian said, his tone dripping with sarcasm. "But this child is the daughter of Abbadon, the Angel of Destruction. Her mother is the daughter of Gabrielle, the Uncorrupted. She is a piece of heaven here on earth, isn't she?

Far more important that anyone in any Coven. And our lord wants her
– in hell. You're to come with me, now."

"But the battle was lost," Finn said quickly. Good girl, Oliver thought
– playing for time. "Wasn't it?"

Something about Christian's face told Oliver that Finn had hit a
nerve.

"Either you come with me now," he said, his voice like ice. "I'll kill
the child right here and now. And you'll have to answer to our lord for
that. After all, *I'm* just a mortal. You're the one with *eternal life*."

"No!" Finn cried, so plaintive that Oliver 's heart stirred. The past
wasn't the past. He still loved Finn. They all to get out of here alive.
There were stones in his pockets, he remembered – stones! He dropped
Lily's hand and lunged forward, hurling a fistful at Christian's snarling
face.

With a roar of pain Christian buckled and Oliver jumped onto him,
wrestling for the blade. Neither of them could get the upper hand, and
all Oliver could feel were slicing cuts, the sting of wounds all over. He
ground Christian's face into the dirt, trying to ignore the pain pulsing
up his right arm.

"Go!" he shouted to Finn. "Take Lily – save yourselves!"

He wasn't important anymore. He'd never been important, even
when he was Regis and fancied himself the most important man in the
world. For the past year he'd been looking for the chance to redeem
himself, and here it was: giving Finn the chance to step back from the
darkness, and to save Lily, their own angel.

But Finn was listening to him. She was tugging at Christian as well,
kicking and punching him, trying to loosen his grip on the blade. The
conduit roared with rage and lashed at Finn, leaving a red slash across
her stomach.

"Go!" Oliver shouted again, but she refused.

"I'm not leaving you again. This is all my fault," she said, wincing
with pain. She doubled over, and Christian kicked Oliver away, stomping so hard on his ankle that Oliver heard it crack. Then Christian,

staggering back towards the boat, lifted his blade high: he was aiming directly for Finn's head. He meant to kill them all, Oliver thought. Or at least Finn and Oliver – so he could steal poor Lily away to hell.

There was an almighty thud and Christian reeled. Lily stood above him, balanced on the end of the boat. She'd smacked him over the head with one of the oars! She was her mother's daughter, that was obvious.

Christian staggered again, and dropped the blade onto the sand. At last Oliver had the chance he'd been waiting for. He plunged the blade into Christian's rib cage and pushed: he kept pushing until Christian was impaled, gasping and flopping on the shore like a fish. Christian's eyes bulged and his hands clutched at the blade, unable to budge it. He tried to speak and a bubble of blood emerged from his mouth, like the blood gushing from his wound. Then his head dropped back and, with one last, cracked gasp, he died.

It was Oliver's turn to collapse now, sinking onto the sand where the yellow grains stuck to his blood-soaked hands and legs. The slashes Christian had inflicted on him burned – down his arms and legs, across his shoulders. He felt dizzy, and it was a huge effort to keep his head up. Vaguely he was aware of Finn lying nearby, breathing in jagged pants, her white dress black with blood.

"They're coming!" Lily shouted, blurring in and out of focus. "My Mom and Dad, and other people! They're here!"

"Sky," Oliver murmured. He could hear her voice, calling to Lily – the joy in it, the relief. "Sky …"

He dropped his head back onto the sand. He had no energy left to speak. Lily's small face loomed over his, her dark eyes warm and loving. The ribbons from her flowered garland fluttered in the breeze, brushing his face. Oliver tried to keep his eyes open, but it was almost impossible. The sun was rising, warming the sand around him. Midsummer had passed, and he was with Finn again. She was safe. Lily was safe. It was a miracle, sent from heaven, the redemption he'd hoped for. They were together at last. And they were all still alive.

ABOUT THE | AUTHOR

Melissa de la Cruz is the #1 New York Times best-selling author of over 30 novels, including Rise of the Isle of the Lost and Alex & Eliza as well as the books in the Blue Bloods and Witches of East End series. She lives in Los Angeles with her family. Find Melissa online at nelissa-delacruz. com, on Twitter @melissadelacruz, and on Facebook and Instagram @authormelissadelacruz.

ABOUT THIS | EDITION

This book is an unedited first draft of the previously unpublished sequel to Vampires of Manhattan. Proceeds from the sale of this title will benefit the YALLWEST book festival and its school outreach programming, bringing books and authors to underserved communities.

Printed in Great Britain
by Amazon

The Abolitionist
Movement

CLAUDINE L. FERRELL

Greenwood Guides to Historic Events, 1500–1900
Linda S. Frey and Marsha L. Frey, Series Editors

GREENWOOD PRESS
Westport, Connecticut • London

Library of Congress Cataloging-in-Publication Data

Ferrell, Claudine L., 1950–
    The abolitionist movement / Claudine L. Ferrell.
        p.   cm.—(Greenwood guides to historic events, 1500–1900, ISSN
1538–442X)
    Includes bibliographical references and index.
    ISBN 0–313–33180–4 (alk. paper)
    1. Antislavery movements—United States.   I. Title.   II. Series.
E441.F47   2006
    973.7'114—dc22   2005020915

British Library Cataloguing in Publication Data is available.

Library of Congress Catalog Card Number: 2005020915
ISBN: 0–313–33180–4
ISSN: 1538–442X

First published in 2006

Greenwood Press, 88 Post Road West, Westport, CT 06881
An imprint of Greenwood Publishing Group, Inc.
www.greenwood.com

Printed in the United States of America

The paper used in this book complies with the
Permanent Paper Standard issued by the National
Information Standards Organization (Z39.48–1984).

10 9 8 7 6 5 4 3 2 1

CONTENTS

Photographs follow page 86.

SERIES FOREWORD

American statesman Adlai Stevenson stated that "We can chart our future clearly and wisely only when we know the path which has led to the present." This series, Greenwood Guides to Historic Events, 1500–1900, is designed to illuminate that path by focusing on events from 1500 to 1900 that have shaped the world. The years 1500 to 1900 include what historians call the Early Modern Period (1500 to 1789, the onset of the French Revolution) and part of the modern period (1789 to 1900).

In 1500, an acceleration of key trends marked the beginnings of an interdependent world and the posing of seminal questions that changed the nature and terms of intellectual debate. The series closes with 1900, the inauguration of the twentieth century. This period witnessed profound economic, social, political, cultural, religious, and military changes. An industrial and technological revolution transformed the modes of production, marked the transition from a rural to an urban economy, and ultimately raised the standard of living. Social classes and distinctions shifted. The emergence of the territorial and later the national state altered man's relations with and view of political authority. The shattering of the religious unity of the Roman Catholic world in Europe marked the rise of a new pluralism. Military revolutions changed the nature of warfare. The books in this series emphasize the complexity and diversity of the human tapestry and include political, economic, social, intellectual, military, and cultural topics. Some of the authors focus on events in U.S. history such as the Salem Witchcraft Trials, the American Revolution, the abolitionist movement, and the Civil War. Others analyze European topics, such as the Reformation and Counter Reformation and the French Revolution. Still others bridge cultures and continents by examining the voyages of discovery, the Atlantic slave trade, and the Age of Imperialism. Some focus on intellectual questions that have shaped the modern world, such as Darwin's *Origin of Species* or on turning points such as the Age of Romanticism. Others examine defining economic, religious, or legal events or issues such as the building of the railroads, the Second Great Awakening, and abolitionism. Heroes (e.g., Lewis and Clark), scientists (e.g., Darwin), military leaders (e.g., Napoleon), poets (e.g., Byron), stride across its pages. Many of these events were seminal in that they marked profound changes or turning points. The Scientific Revolution, for example, changed the way individuals viewed themselves and their world.

The authors, acknowledged experts in their fields, synthesize key events, set developments within the larger historical context, and, most important, present a well-balanced, well-written account that integrates the most recent scholarship in the field.

The topics were chosen by an advisory board composed of historians, high school history teachers, and school librarians to support the curriculum and meet student research needs. The volumes are designed to serve as resources for student research and to provide clearly written interpretations of topics central to the secondary school and lower-level undergraduate history curriculum. Each author outlines a basic chronology to guide the reader through often confusing events and a historical overview to set those events within a narrative framework. Three to five topical chapters underscore critical aspects of the event. In the final chapter the author examines the impact and consequences of the event. Biographical sketches furnish background on the lives and contributions of the players who strut across this stage. Ten to fifteen primary documents ranging from letters to diary entries, song lyrics, proclamations, and posters, cast light on the event, provide material for student essays, and stimulate a critical engagement with the sources. Introductions identify the authors of the documents and the main issues. In some cases a glossary of selected terms is provided as a guide to the reader. Each work contains an annotated bibliography of recommended books, articles, CD-ROMs, Internet sites, videos, and films that set the materials within the historical debate.

These works will lead to a more sophisticated understanding of the events and debates that have shaped the modern world and will stimulate a more active engagement with the issues that still affect us. It has been a particularly enriching experience to work closely with such dedicated professionals. We have come to know and value even more highly the authors in this series and our editors at Greenwood, particularly Kevin Ohe. In many cases they have become more than colleagues; they have become friends. To them and to future historians we dedicate this series.

Linda S. Frey
University of Montana

Marsha L. Frey
Kansas State University

PREFACE

The abolitionists of the 1830s–1850s have been called fanatics and revolutionaries, denounced as insecure and self-interested, and labeled fomenters of an unnecessary and violent war. They have been called troublemakers and unnecessary, even irrelevant: slavery would have ended without them, and it would have done so with less disruption and less harm to the nation. They have also been called forerunners of the Civil Rights Movement and cited as men and women dedicated to the principles of liberty and equality. This last view sees them as dedicated to human progress and to a nation free of racial discrimination. They could have ignored slavery but they did not. For them, stopping slavery's expansion was insufficient; the sin and evil of slavery had to end and a restructuring of American society had to occur in order to eliminate racial injustice.

Prior to the 1830s and even during the antebellum years, most opponents of slavery supported an end to slavery because of its impact on white Americans—on whites' morality and ethics, on whites' work habits, on whites' civil liberties, and on whites' opportunities. They generally saw slaves and free blacks alike as threatening the American (white) order; they saw jobs at risk, land misused, and race war looming. They saw blacks as inferior to whites. If slavery was to end, it should happen gradually so that freed blacks could be removed from the country, so that owners could be compensated for the loss of their valuable property, and so that disruptions and adjustments would be as minimally harmful to whites as possible.

Although the early foes of slavery "created no general sentiment against slavery,"[1] black and white abolitionists of the antebellum years built on the foundation laid by Quakers, gradualists, and colonizationists and created "a sustained, many-faced biracial movement to destroy all barriers created by white prejudice."[2] Their direct, confrontational approach attacked both slavery and discrimination because, unlike their predecessors, they believed that slavery and racism would end only when the nation admitted its sin and acted against it. The longer the nation waited, the longer the sin continued, the more slave owners were allowed to think their actions were acceptable, and the longer blacks were seen as inferiors. Thus, whereas the early anti-slavery advocates stirred little opposition, the antebellum abolitionists stirred much, even amongst themselves. Unlike their predecessors, they believed that strong words and strong actions were necessary, even if they disagreed on the strategy and tactics to use in their war against the sin of slavery. As former slave and abolitionist Frederick Douglass explained, one cannot have "the ocean without the awful roar of its many waters."[3]

The abolitionist movement was a radical movement in that abolitionists saw an American society in need of reformation, but on that point alone, one can fairly argue that the abolitionists failed: a civil war, not revised white thinking, ended slavery, and American society, even without slavery, was essentially the same after slavery as before. The abolitionists failed to change their nation's—and, in many cases, their own—racism, but they did dedicate their lives to the cause of justice and to the conservation of the nation's ideals of liberty and equality.

Abolitionists might have been contentious and self-righteous and they might not have changed the nation's thinking about race, but they made a critical difference in forcing a massive change on the nation. Theirs was more than a reform movement. Theirs was the final stage of a 150-year crusade that took white Americans from concern for their souls to concern for the rights of blacks and that took black Americans from slavery to freedom. Although, as abolitionists acknowledged, it was a flawed freedom at best, it was an accomplishment largely inconceivable and unimaginable only a few years before.

This book provides an overview of the impressive if incomplete victory over slavery and discrimination. To do so, Chapter 1 begins in the 1600s and 1700s with the earliest American anti-slavery campaign, one marked by individual efforts. Chapter 2 looks at the contradictions of the revolutionary decades of the 1760s–1780s. Chapter 3 covers the hopeful but ultimately disappointing years of the early national period; they saw the end of slavery in Northern states and congressional prohibition of the foreign slave trade, but they also saw the deepening of anti-black attitudes and restrictions. Opponents of slavery were learning that the campaign against slavery needed renewal and broadening, that colonization would not achieve the goal that they sought. Their next step is covered in Chapter 4 with the appearance in the early 1830s of the American Anti-Slavery Society and the so-called immediate abolitionists. This chapter reveals the often heated disagreements among the abolitionists over the best strategy to pursue, over leadership of their effort, and even over the scope of their goals. Chapter 5 follows the abolitionists' divisive and divided campaign during the 1840s as they sought the best plan for fighting slavery's entrenched economic and social role in the South, the South's political and economic influence in the nation, Americans' general antipathy to blacks, and the widespread concern that abolitionism would lead to conflict. Chapter 6 covers the 1850s and 1860s as the nation moved closer to civil war. It ends with slavery's end and with abolitionists unsure of their and their nation's accomplishment and of the future of their cause. Chapter 7 reviews history's evaluation of the abolitionists and their contribution to their country. Following it are short biographies of fourteen abolitionists, from Quakers Anthony Benezet and John Woolman to brothers Arthur and Lewis Tappan and former slave Frederick Douglass. Documents presenting pro- and anti-slavery views, as well as writings attacking and supporting the abolitionists themselves, are mixed with excerpts from the Constitution and with the Emancipation Proclamation. A range of political cartoons and publications from the 1820s–1860s provides a visual look at the influence of abolitionism, while an annotated bibliography provides an introduction to the major works on the dedicated Americans—black and white, male and female, northern and southern—who fought against slavery.

Notes

1. Benjamin Quarles, *Black Abolitionists* (1969; reprint, New York: Oxford University Press, 1977), 13.

2. James B. Stewart, "Assessing Abolitionism: 'So What's New?'" *Reviews in American History* 27, no. 3 (1999): 400.

3. Herbert Aptheker, *Abolitionism: A Revolutionary Movement* (Boston: Twayne Publishers, 1989), 17.

ACKNOWLEDGMENTS

I wish to thank Marsha and Linda Frey for their support. Their friendship has always been important to me, and their faith that I could complete this book guaranteed that I would do so. And for his confidence in me and for his enthusiastic and encouraging stories about writing and documentation, Jack Bales deserves a special thank-you.

I will always be grateful to Carter Hudgins and John Morello for reducing my teaching load so that I had time to (almost) meet my deadline and to the staff of the Bachelor of Liberal Studies Program for their patience and understanding as my office in Tyler Hall became a wing of Simpson Library.

Finally, Hannah and the gang, as always, provided the necessary distractions and perspective.

.

CHRONOLOGY OF EVENTS

1518	First direct shipment of slaves from Africa to the Americas (by Spain).
1619	First Africans in British North America (Jamestown, Virginia).
1640–1660	African slavery develops in Virginia.
1688	Germantown Quakers protest against the slave trade.
1693	First anti-slavery tract (by George Keith).
1738	Beginning of the Great Awakening.
1739	Stono slave revolt in South Carolina.
1753	John Woolman's *Considerations on the Keeping of Negroes*.
1754–1763	French and Indian War (Seven Years' War).
1772	*Somerset* decision on status of slaves in England.
1774	First Continental Congress bans slave importations.
	Philadelphia Yearly Meeting (Quaker) forbids Quakers to buy or sell slaves and requires Quakers to prepare slaves for freedom.
1775	First American anti-slavery society formed.
1776	Second Continental Congress passes resolution against further slave importation.
	Declaration of Independence.
1777–1804	Abolition of slavery in the North.

1782	Virginia allows private manumissions.
1783	British recognition of American independence.
1787	Northwest Ordinance bans slavery in territory north of the Ohio River.
	Writing of the Constitution.
1791–1804	Haiti revolution.
1792	Kentucky admitted as the first new slave state.
1793	Fugitive Slave Act.
	Eli Whitney invents the cotton gin.
1800	Gabriel's conspiracy in Richmond, Virginia.
1803	United States purchases the Louisiana Territory from France.
1804	Haitian independence.
1808	Great Britain and United States abolish the foreign slave trade.
1816	Formation of the American Colonization Society.
1820	Missouri Compromise.
	Congress defines the slave trade as piracy.
1821	Benjamin Lundy begins publication of *Genius of Universal Emancipation*.
1822	Denmark Vesey plans slave uprising in Charleston, South Carolina.
1827–1829	First black newspaper, *Freedom's Journal*, published.
1829	David Walker publishes his *Appeal to the Coloured Citizens of the World*.
	Mexico abolishes slavery.
1830s–1850s	Negro National Convention Movement.
1831	French slave trade ends.
January 1831	William Lloyd Garrison begins publication of the *Liberator*.
August 1831	Nat Turner's slave revolt in Virginia.
1832	Virginia legislature votes against abolition of slavery.

	New England Anti-Slavery Society founded in Boston.
	Black women in Salem, Massachusetts, found anti-slavery society.
1833	American Anti-Slavery Society (AASS) founded in Philadelphia.
	Abolition of slavery in the British empire (completed in 1838).
1836	Congress adopts the Gag Rule.
	Angelina and Sarah Grimké begin speaking tour.
1837	First Anti-Slavery Convention of American Women meets in New York.
1840	American and Foreign Anti-Slavery Society founded.
	National Anti-Slavery Standard (AASS) begins publication.
	Formation of the Liberty Party.
November 1841	Supreme Court's ruling in the *Amistad* case.
1842	*Prigg v. Pennsylvania.*
1845	Publication of *Narrative of the Life of Frederick Douglass.*
	Texas admitted as a state by congressional joint resolution.
1846	Wilmot Proviso proposed.
1846–1848	Mexican War.
1847	Frederick Douglass begins publication of the *North Star* (renamed *Frederick Douglass's Paper* in 1850).
1848	Free Soil Party formed.
	First Women's Rights Convention (Seneca Falls, New York).
	France ends slavery in its Caribbean and African colonies.
1850	Compromise of 1850, including Fugitive Slave Act.
	Publication of *Narrative of Sojourner Truth.*

1851–1854	Abolition of slavery in Colombia, Ecuador, Argentina, Uruguay, Peru, and Venezuela.
1852	Publication of Harriet Beecher Stowe's *Uncle Tom's Cabin*.
1854	Kansas-Nebraska Act.
1855	Publication of Solomon Northup's *Twelve Years a Slave*.
mid–1850s	Republican Party formed.
1855–1857	"Bleeding Kansas."
1857	*Dred Scott* decision.
1859	John Brown's raid at Harpers Ferry, Virginia.
1860	Abraham Lincoln elected president.
1861–1865	Civil War.
1863	Emancipation Proclamation frees slaves in southern-controlled areas.
1865	Thirteenth Amendment ends slavery in the United States.
1865–1877	Reconstruction.
	Fourteenth Amendment defines citizenship and equal rights.
1870	Fifteenth Amendment prohibits restrictions on black male suffrage.

CHAPTER 1

HISTORICAL OVERVIEW

While slavery had roots back thousands of years into Mesopotamia and Egypt and into early Greece and Rome, the slavery of the British colonials of North America was only a few years old when the first attacks against it began. When the first Quakers and Puritans expressed opposition to slavery, the institution was still a relatively new one in the relatively new British American colonies, and the British who owned slaves in Virginia and Maryland and Massachusetts were simply doing what many before them had done—making slaves out of other human beings. Surprisingly early in the colonies' history of enslavement, opponents appeared, however few in number they were, and remained. The political and social realities of the colonies and, soon, of the United States, required a few men and women to seek the demise of a labor institution that most other Americans accepted, if not supported, as normal and even necessary and that denied the very humanity of blacks.

Slavery over the centuries had declined in Europe—replaced not by freedom but by other forms of unfree labor, such as indentureship and serfdom—but it had grown in Africa. While most Africans enslaved by other Africans lost their freedom when they lost in battle, others were enslaved because of debt, religion, or crime. Some Africans were kidnapped into slavery; some were given as tribute. They were items of trade: close to five million were sold in the trans-Saharan slave trade before the first permanent British North American colony was founded in 1607. Slaves were sold to northern Africa, southern Europe, the Middle East, India, Malaysia, Indonesia, and China. They were exchanged for silk, spices, gold, and silver.

Over such a large continent as Africa, slave life inevitably varied greatly, but much like early Greeks and Romans, Africans did not, as a rule and as did later Americans, strip their slaves of all rights. Slaves had legal protections, could own land, and worked jobs which gave them both status and rights. Some held high political posts. In West Africa, with slavery often serving as a method of assimilation, the life of a second- and third-generation slave varied little from that of free Africans.

While most European countries had more native workers than they needed, the heavy labor needs of the European sugar plantations in the Mediterranean resulted in the use of white slaves from southern and eastern Europe and black slaves from Africa. As the European demand for sugar grew, the plantation system spread to the islands northwest of Africa by the mid-1300s. A hundred years later, the Portuguese were exploring the western coast of Africa and establishing trade as they did so, with slaves soon supplanting gold as the most desired product. By the early 1500s the sugar plantations had reached the New World; in 1515 a Spanish surgeon established the first sugar mill on Hispaniola (later Haiti). Soon, Puerto Rico, Jamaica, Barbados, and Brazil were producing sugar. Diseases brought by the Europeans, and the demands of the intense labor required by sugar, led to a rapid decline in the size of indigenous population and to the rapid substitution of African slave labor. By 1560 Hispaniola's 1000 whites were easily outnumbered by the island's over 12,000 Africans; by the 1670s Barbados's population was three-quarters African; and by the 1600s Jamaica was 90 percent African. The story was the same throughout the Caribbean.

About 2000 Africans a year were transported to the New World during the sixteenth century, a trickle before the tide of the next two centuries. As the demand for African slaves increased, competition in the slave trade intensified among European rivals. With the cooperation of African leaders who wanted to obtain gunpowder, firearms, alcohol, and other goods, England, Portugal, Spain, and the Dutch carried on what historian and activist W.E.B. Du Bois called the "rape of Africa."[1]

As Brazil's economy shifted from sugar to gold to coffee, its slave imports grew to four or five million by the mid-1800s (for an eventual total of 33 percent of all Africans transported to the Americas as slaves). In comparison, the number of Africans who reached the British colonies in North America was hardly worth noting: 339,000 were imported from 1607 to 1865 (out of the 11 to 15 million brought alive to the New World). Yet it was those small numbers that grew to an American slave population of over four million by the mid-1800s and that, however small, prompted the rise of anti-slavery arguments, pamphlets, speeches, and petitions as early as the late 1600s. Although the trans-Atlantic slave trade lasted from 1502 to 1888, most Africans reached the New World during the eighteenth century, and that is when the anti-slavery effort showed its greatest strength prior to the pre–Civil War decades that spawned the abolitionists.

Slavery in the British North American Colonies

Many people today define slavery by using the antebellum American model: race-based, inherited, few if any rights, subordinate status as both property and people, and with that status largely continuing even if slaves achieved freedom. But the American slavery which developed in the mid to late 1600s was unusual in its restrictions and flexibility.

As best as historians can determine, the first twenty Africans in British North America arrived in Virginia in 1619 on a Dutch warship. Traded for supplies, these men and women were apparently used by the 2300 white Virginians in the same way that the latter used English indentured servants: the Africans worked for a period of years to pay off their debt and were freed, their status subordinate but ambiguous. Additional Africans entered the colony in small numbers—the total black population of the colony in 1640 was but 170—either as free men or as servants. While race undoubtedly affected how the English viewed Africans—they noted on various records when a person was "Negro"— race did not define a person as slave or free. Men such as Anthony Johnson went from slavery to property holding (and even slaveholding) and held the community respect reserved for property owners.

But as wages and conditions improved in England and large-scale tobacco farming spread, the supply of indentured servants failed to keep up with labor needs. The increasing availability of Africans through greater competition in the slave trade led to race-based, lifetime, and hereditary slavery by the late 1600s. Conversion to Christianity, an early route out of slavery, did not hold the same hope of freedom by the latter years of the seventeenth century. Rights held by colonials in general were steadily denied slaves in the formal slave codes that appeared near the turn of the eighteenth century. Applying to free and slave blacks alike, the codes legitimized and organized a racial labor system that had generally developed without the benefit of laws. The system made slaves chattel (property) of a master who held total dominance.

The numbers affected were small until the last two decades of the century. In 1640, there were 1600 Africans in the British colonies; in 1680, 4600 blacks lived in Virginia and Maryland and almost 7000 in all of the colonies combined (out of a total population of about 150,000). Pennsylvania, home of many of the colonies' first Quaker anti-slavery advocates, did not yet exist. Changes were fast appearing, however. By 1700, Virginia and Maryland had 13,000 blacks, and by the beginning of the colonials' fight for independence and liberty only seven decades later, there were 200,000 blacks in the two states and 440,000 in the colonies combined.

By 1690, about the time that the first Quakers protested the African slave trade, there were fewer than 2000 blacks in the northern colonies; thirty years later, those colonies held 14,000. By the 1770s, 50,000 blacks made up about 5 percent of the population of the northern and middle colonies; many lived in port cities such as Boston and Newport. New York contained about 10,000 slaves by the end of the colonial period, 10 to 15 percent of the colony's total population. Areas of heaviest concentrations of blacks included northern New Jersey, a Quaker colony; parts of the major Quaker settlement, Pennsylvania, had a workforce that was 25 percent slave.

Thus, when the first protests against the slave trade and slavery began in the late 1600s, slavery was in a formative, albeit defining, stage. The arguments of the earliest anti-slavery advocates, as a result, are particularly striking. Among them were many of the same arguments that would appear over a hundred years later as abolitionists such as William Lloyd Garrison, Lewis Tappan, Benjamin Lundy, Lydia Maria Child, and James K. Birney struck at virtually every aspect of slavery, in particular its sinfulness and its link to racial discrimination. Even though they could be vitriolic and damning, the first American opponents of slavery have been called temperate and mild in their denunciations and were therefore quite different from their later counterparts. The slavery which they attacked, while already widespread, was still taking shape, and they could hope that their logical arguments about the "Golden Rule" and fairness would bring its demise before it became an essential and unquestioned part of the American economy and society. The Enlightenment and American Revolution brought even more logical arguments and hopes for inevitable abolition.

The hopes of the abolitionists did not end slavery. By the 1830s–1850s, it was a mature system threading through virtually every aspect of American life, and black inferiority at a time when 90 percent of American blacks were slaves was "fact," not speculation or prejudice. Nevertheless, the abolitionists who attacked slavery in those decades sought individual and national salvation through elimination of both slavery and racial inequalities. A full range of economic, social, political, constitutional, religious, historical, anthropological, gendered, and biological assumptions and opinions confronted them. The result was that the abolitionists themselves were seen as the threats to the nation. In the new republic, concepts of liberty, individualism, progress, and God's will inspired slavery's opponents, but just as they guided slavery's supporters.

Compromises during the 1820s–1850s were part of a political, not abolitionist, effort to prevent conflict between a South increasingly committed to slavery, property rights, and black subjugation and a North interested initially in preserving sectional peace and then increasingly fearful of "becom[ing] the white slaves of the masters of the black slaves of the South."[2] The search for political solutions led not to common ground but successive battlegrounds. Seeking national salvation not racial, individual, or sectional gain were the abolitionists. They tried every moral argument, every political tool, and every form of organization to convert their fellow Americans into haters of slavery. They failed, but their antebellum actions—provocative and divisive but sincere—clearly played a critical role in pushing the nation to take steps that would, through force of arms, end the formal existence of slavery.

Notes

1.   W.E.B. Du Bois, *The World and Africa: An Inquiry into the Part Which Africa Has Played in World History* (New York: Viking Press, 1947), 44.

2.   Dayton *Republican*, quoted in Gerald Sorin, *Abolitionism: A New Perspective* (New York: Praeger, 1972), 131.

CHAPTER 2

"IN MATTERS OF RIGHT AND EQUITY": FROM QUAKERS TO REVOLUTION

The history of the abolitionist movement in the 1600s–1700s—if such a movement can be said to have existed—is essentially the history of the increasing use of slaves in the British North American colonies and the growing commitment of Quakers to prove that slavery was wrong, that it was a violation of human brotherhood and of the "Golden Rule." Undergoing significant changes in their view of themselves, their community, and the world around them, individual members of the Society of Friends "groped their way slowly, with heart searching, toward the conviction that slavery could not truly be reconciled with their Christian faith."[1] It was not an easy or popular path to travel in the years when slavery was becoming an integral part of colonial economic success. But their growing commitment, coupled with Enlightenment, religious, and, soon, revolutionary ideals, helped push Americans partially onto an anti-slavery path.

Quakers and Anti-Slavery

In the 1600s and 1700s, when the colonies were constantly in need of labor and the slave trade was an increasingly profitable and competitive business, a few anti-slavery voices existed. They cited a wide range of arguments against the slave trade and slavery, many of which would appear in modified form during the abolitionist movement of the 1830s–1850s.

Enlightenment theories of natural rights prompted thinking about the wrongs of slavery but had little practical impact with few colonials publicly espousing them. Some of the Philosophes argued that man was not guided or controlled by original sin and that the universe was not run by God. Rather, fixed, natural laws ran the universe, and men could discover those laws and, using reason, affect men and their society. Importantly for the long-term if not the immediate history of abolitionism, the Enlightenment emphasized the value and potential of all people, individual responsibility, and the humanity of all men, as well as man's ability to improve. For Enlightenment thinkers, slavery might be defended by appeals to property and obvious inequalities among men, but they did not see slavery as in sync with natural law or the public's welfare, and they believed that government could and should end slavery.

Montesquieu did the most to make slavery an issue of the Enlightenment. In *The Spirit of the Laws* (1748) he asserted that "as all men are born equal, slavery must be accounted unnatural." He wrote that "to sell one's freedom is repugnant to reason," that "if a man could not sell himself, much less could he sell an unborn child," and that enslaving someone because he was a heathen in effect said "that religion gives its professors a right to enslave those who dissent from it."[2]

By the 1700s, a rethinking of Christianity was supporting such views. Some Christians were abandoning the idea of man's depravity and corruption. In the colonies, the Great Awakening that began in the 1740s spread the idea that humans made choices, including to sin, and were responsible for their choices and actions, whether good or bad. Preachers of the Great Awakening emphasized God's equal view of men: *all* could be saved. And, if all could be saved, no consideration—including race—could affect a person's status. The evangelical movement looked at individual responsibility and the need to accept personal guilt and depravity; the ethic of benevolence emphasized man's inner goodness and his need to demonstrate his virtue by ending the suffering of others. The Great Awakening encouraged people to help others in order to advance their own salvation and to support God's goals; it also led to the conversion of many blacks, thus making blacks and whites even more similar to each other.

Despite the influence of these new ideas, efforts by non-Quakers were local, individual, and unsupported by public opinion. Until (and even through) the mid-1800s, appeals to Christian ideals and natural rights were trumped by perception of the black's inferiority and of the naturalness of slavery, reverence for property rights, and arguments of economic necessity. Besides, slavery was in the Bible.

A non-Quaker who attacked slavery on moral terms, although he cited numerous other reasons for his opposition, was Puritan layman Chief Justice Samuel Sewall. In *The Selling of Joseph* (1700), he argued against slavery as a moral wrong but also as an arrangement that harmed the slave owner, not the last time that the interests of whites would receive as much or more emphasis as the interest of the slaves. Sewall asserted that color was not a consideration in how God treated men and could not support enslavement of Africans. Besides, Sewall reasoned, slavery deterred immigration of white servants, Africans were too different, and, as Puritan minister Cotton Mather had indicated, slaves were "continual[ly] aspiring after their forbidden Liberty, [which] renders them Unwilling Servants."[3] Other lone non-Quaker anti-slavery voices looked to the nature of their New World, arguing that slavery led poor whites to see labor as the lot of slaves and not of free men. Because America was the land of fresh starts, rebirths, and the achievement of human potential, support of slavery as economically necessary seemed contradictory. Counterarguments won the day, including ones foreshadowing arguments made by opponents of the abolitionists over a hundred years later: slavery saved the colonies from "a plague" of free blacks because Africans were "cowardly and cruel," "Libidinous, Deceitful, False and Rude," mischievous, and murderous.[4]

Quakers

The history of the American abolitionist movement during the colonial period is, with few exceptions, the history of Quaker arguments, publications, pronouncements, and activists. Although too late to derail the establishment of slavery before economic and racial interests defined its place in the colonies, Quakers were ahead of all other colonials in denouncing the institution. But the Quakers' path to abolitionism was not preordained. In fact, it would have surprised Quakers even a century later to know that much of their fame would rest in their anti-slavery efforts. Their process of opposition to slavery was slow, inconsistent, and piecemeal. While some Quakers opposed slavery and the slave trade, others were major participants as slave owners and slave traders.

Members of the Society of Friends believed that everyone has a seed or Inward Light of Christ inside them. Cultivating this inner light leads to salvation; thus, each person has his/her salvation in his/her control. They believed it to be their duty to do the right thing regardless of opposition or unlikely success. Opposition to slavery, however, involved challenging the behavior and beliefs of Quakers themselves, including William Penn who owned slaves and saw slavery as a way of promoting economic growth in Pennsylvania. As a result, the inner battle between "right" and "greed" became the focus of a handful of individuals from the late 1600s to the late 1700s.

The Quaker attack on slavery began slowly and with limited arguments. In 1657 George Fox wrote an epistle urging Quakers to bring God's "glad tidings to every captivated creature under the whole heaven."[5] In 1676 Fox argued that Christ "died for the tawnies and for the blacks as well as for you that are called whites" and for freeing slaves after a number of years. Like Fox, William Edmundson suggested that slaves were the children of God. He argued that "perputuall Slavery is an Agrivation, & an Oppression upon the Mind."[6]

In 1688, the Rhineland artisans who founded Germantown, near Philadelphia, asked the Philadelphia Quarterly and Yearly Meetings how the "traffick of mens-body" could fit within Quaker beliefs.[7] If slavery was good, "what can we say is . . . evil?"[8] Slavery involved receiving stolen goods, contributing to adultery, and (through the buying of prizes of war) violating Quaker testimony against war. If slaves fought against their condition, which they had a right to do, would pacifist Quakers fight back? The local Monthly Meeting, the Philadelphia Quarterly Meeting, and the Yearly Meeting, many of whose members owned slaves, decided to "forbear" this appeal.[9] Five years later, however, the Philadelphia Yearly Meeting did encourage Quakers not to buy slaves unless they planned to free them.

Also five years later, George Keith and his followers published a pamphlet, *An Exhortation & Caution to Friends Concerning Buying or Keeping of Negroes*, the first anti-slavery protest published and circulated in the colonies. They argued that Jesus died for everyone regardless of race, that "Negroes [were] . . . a real part of Mankind,"[10] and that slaves were prizes of war. Slavery violated the Golden Rule, and an escaped slave should be helped, not returned to slavery. In 1715, John Hepburn, who was concerned about Quakers' general leniency on a variety of principles, called slavery "anti-christian, a vile . . . contradiction of the gospel of the blessed Messiah."[11] Slave owning was harmful for slave owners "in Eternitie," a point frequently made by Quaker activists in the early 1700s.

For a quarter century, such protests were met with "an embarrassed silence under cover of which Quaker slavery flourished."[12] Quaker leadership used disciplinary rules to quiet anti-slavery talk that was seen as threatening community unity. Because Quakers were ending a period of persecution and divisions, unity was valued above all else. Over the next half century, pro- and anti-slavery arguments covered wide ground including the protection of slave property and the impact of slavery on slave owners' ethics and their eternal life. Discussion also involved the protection of whites seeking jobs, the impact of slavery on immigration, the possibility of slave uprisings (a type of war, and Quakers opposed war), and differences between trading and owning slaves. Opponents noted slavery's threat to the Quaker belief in humility and a simple standard of living, while supporters reasoned that Africans were enslaved because they were taken in a just war and had been spared death and because they were "ignorant and wicked." ("If that plea would do, I do believe they need not go so far for slaves as now they do."[13])

The late 1720s brought the strident anti-slavery views of Ralph Sandiford and Benjamin Lay. The former, a shopkeeper, called slavery "the most arbitrary and tyrannical oppression that hell has invented on this globe." Sandiford, whose tombstone would later note that "he Bore A Testimony against Negro Trade," resisted threats of punishment if he published *A Brief Examination of the Practice of the Times* but was forced to leave both Philadelphia and the Quakers.[14] More controversial was Lay, a short, hunchbacked, white-bearded, cave-dwelling vegetarian whose views and tactics led to his expulsion in 1738. He kidnapped a Quaker's son to demonstrate how parents of a slave girl felt. He stood in the snow with one leg bare and told those who expressed concern that "you pretend compassion for me, but you do not feel for the poor slaves in your fields, who go all winter half clad."[15] When people argued that slaves lived good lives, Lay countered, "I could almost wish such hardened, unthinking, Sinful devilish Lyars were put into their Places."[16] His *All Slave-Keepers That Keep the Innocent in Bondage, Apostates Pretending to Lay Claim to the Pure & Holy Christian Religion* called slave owning "the great Sin in the World."[17] He advocated teaching slaves "Learning, Reading and Writing, and . . . the principles of truth and righteouosness, and . . . some Honest Trade or Imployment" before "set[ting] them free . . . in a very reasonable time."[18]

Such strident, unbending arguments and acts would mark the abolitionists of the 1830s–1850s and, like those antebellum words and deeds, were "sledgehammer blows [that] merely stiffened the resistance" at a time when slavery's value as a labor system was growing.[19]

John Woolman and Anthony Benezet

In the 1750s, the Quakers were facing a series of crises that they increasingly linked to their sin of slavery and that prompted a desire to purify their faith and to return to a simpler life. Giving up their political clout in their Holy Experiment of Pennsylvania, the Quakers shifted "from the realm of the possible to the realm of the ideal."[20] Quakers focused more on their principles and how slavery contradicted them, and as they eliminated public and material elements in their lives, they had fewer reasons to compromise with those who did not share their ideals. Monthly and Yearly Meetings took more definite and thorough stands against not only slave trading and buying but also slave ownership and the treatment of slaves. As members were disciplined, expelled, or denied a role in the business of the church, Meetings reflected more anti-slavery views, even if they did not admit black members and even if rules were enforced with great variation.

John Woolman's *Considerations on the Keeping of Negroes* (1753) was the most circulated of all colonial anti-slavery writings to that point. In it Woolman calmly, logically, and with a universal appeal pointed out that, although slavery was supported out of self-interest, it harmed slave and enslaver. He argued that seeing some people as inferior would "excite a Behaviour toward them unbecoming the Excellent of true Religion." The Golden Rule applied to all. No people could rightly enslave another: "Did not He that made us make them?" Looking at the conflict between slavery and Quaker humanitarianism, Woolman wondered, "For men to be thus treated from one generation to another, . . . what disagreeable thoughts must they have of the professed followers of Jesus!"[21]

Approved by church leaders, Woolman's analysis was widely quoted from, published, and circulated by Yearly Meetings:

> To live in ease and plenty by the toil of those whom violence and cruelty have put in our power is neither consistent with Christianity nor common justice, and we have good reason to believe draws down the displeasure of Heaven; . . .
>
> How then can we, who have been concerned to publish the Gospel of universal love and peace among mankind, be so inconsistent with ourselves as to purchase such who are prisoners of war, and thereby encourage this anti-Christian practice? And more especially as many of those poor creatures are stolen away, parents from children, and children from parents. . . . Let us . . . consider what we should think and how we should feel were we in their circumstances.[22]

The Philadelphia Yearly Meeting of 1755 went beyond earlier cautions against buying slaves and directed that "transgressors" who were "importing or buying slaves"—but not owning them—be reported so that they could be disciplined and potentially disowned. In 1757 slave owners, citing the need for unity, appealed. In response, Woolman cited self-interest, not the desire for unity, as their motivation. The Meeting made him one of four to "visit and treat" with slave owners in order to discourage "importing, buying, selling, or keeping slaves."[23] In 1762, Woolman, who abandoned the use of sugar, rum, and silver (largely products of slave labor that corrupted their users), published the second part of *Considerations on the Keeping of Negroes*. In it he noted that Africans' "Understandings and Morals are equal to the Generality of Men of [our] own Color" and that color was meaningless "in Matters of Right and Equity."[24]

Influencing Quakers and other colonials as much as, if not more than, Woolman was Anthony Benezet, a Quaker convert and a general reformer. He published pamphlets in the late 1750s and 1760s against the slave trade, calling it "stained with . . . [the] Dye of Injustice, Cruelty, and Oppression."[25] Seeking to convince Parliament to abolish the slave trade, in 1762 he published *A Short Account of that Part of Africa*

Inhabited by Negroes in which he described the slave trade in all of its horrors and Africans' desire to resist slavery and remain in Africa, thus countering arguments that slavery rescued Africans for a better life.

Title to a slave, Benezet added, was simply proof that one held a person stolen from Africa: owner, trader, and enslaver were little different from each other. Like most anti-slavery advocates before the 1830s, he suggested a gradual solution. For him that meant freeing slaves when they had paid off their sale price, providing oversight for freed slaves and education for their children, and allowing freedmen to cultivate land or work for whites. Like antebellum abolitionists, he asked, "Can we be innocent and yet [be] silent spectators of this mighty infringement of every humane and sacred right?" Also like the abolitionists, Benezet argued for the equality of blacks asserting that "the notion . . . that the blacks are inferior to the Whites in their capacities, is a vulgar prejudice, founded on the Pride or Ignorance of their lordly Masters, who have kept their Slaves at such a distance, as to be unable to form a right judgment of them." As did most opponents of slavery, he also found that the institution harmed whites. It produced "Idelness, discourage[d] Marriages, corrupt[ed] the youth, and ruin[ed] and debauche[d] Morals."[26]

Benezet and Woolman had an impact on their church, if no other defined group in colonial society. New York Quakers in 1771 denounced the selling of slaves and in 1777 disowned slaveholders (a year after Philadelphia did the same), while the New England Yearly Meeting in 1773 ordered the freeing of all slaves and the disowning of Quakers who did not emancipate their slaves. In 1781 Virginia Quakers disowned those who held slaves. By 1782 all slaves in New England belonging to Quakers were to be free, and the next year former slaves began to receive compensation and support for their moral and religious training. Although emancipation was slower in New York and New Jersey where there were more slaves and where slavery was thus more a part of life, by 1787, no Quaker north of Virginia owned slaves.

Revolution and Independence

As Quakers debated the place of slavery in their lives, American colonials in general debated their relationship with Great Britain. In doing so, slavery inevitably worked its way into their arguments setting the stage for what many mistakenly believed would be not only the quick end to the slave trade but the demise of slavery itself in the new United States.

In 1774 almost one in every five Americans was a slave. Slaves were a major part of the population of Maryland (80,000), Virginia (165,000), North and South Carolina (15,000 and 110,000), Georgia (16,000), and even New York (15,000) and Rhode Island (4300). Most colonials were indifferent or unconcerned about slavery, but those who supported it saw it as a "necessary evil" that provided the foundation for much of the colonial economy and social structure. Even in colonies where large numbers of unskilled labor was not needed, slaves provided an alternate choice for domestic servant, factory worker, seaman, farmhand, and skilled worker.

While Philip S. Foner has argued that "the question of Negro slavery never became the central issue of the American Revolution, and . . . many Americans refused to see any connection between their assertion of their natural rights to life and liberty and the enslavement of black people,"[27] Enlightenment concepts of equality and man's control over his life affected how some colonials viewed their problems with Britain, and once revolutionary thinking began to spread, it became difficult to ignore the conflict between ideals and reality, just as it did for the Quakers.

There are many explanations for the Americans' revolt against British rule, but certainly playing a part was the determination of particular colonials to protect their ability to define and maintain their property against perceived unconstitutional threats. Because Britain exerted little direct control over the colonies for most of their 160 years of existence, colonials had learned how to oversee that property on their own. Their colonial assemblies were elected by property owners and composed of property owners. Under the theory that only a man or his chosen representative could determine the fate of his property, the assemblies taxed and by the 1770s supported the argument that direct representation was the only system under which a government could tax its people. According to John Locke, government existed to protect the natural right of private property, an aspect of liberty and freedom.

The basis for much of the wealth that seemed threatened by Britain's Sugar Act and Stamp Act, among others, was slavery. Because slavery did not play the same role in the colonies north of Virginia and

Maryland—and it did not affect the lives of all southern colonials in the same way—no one argues that slavery or property-based-on-slavery was the sole or even the major spark of the War for Independence. Still, slaves were valuable property and property, along with life and liberty, was a defining issue for colonial rebels. Threats to colonials' ability to control and protect their property economically and politically required response. As a petition to the Virginia assembly from Pittsylvania County in làte 1785, two years after the revolution during which Britain had employed colonials' slaves against them, explained: "When the British Parliament usurped a Right to dispose of our property without our Consent," colonials risked "Lives and Fortunes." Despite these sacrifices, "Enemies of our Country, tools of the British Administration, and . . . certain deluded Men among us, [sought] TO WREST FROM US OUR SLAVES."[28]

The document announcing the rebels' determination to be free of British control—the Declaration of Independence—was written by the slave-owning Thomas Jefferson for a slave-owning people. It is a broad statement justifying the breaking of political bonds as a result of the conspiracy to deny colonials their rights of "life, liberty, and the pursuit of happiness [centered on property]." It speaks of the rights of "all men," but its speaks for men who meant that statement only for whites.

Despite the limited intent of the Continental Congress that signed the declaration, both white and black Americans spoke out against slavery during the revolutionary decades. Among whites was a writer for the *Virginia Gazette* in 1767 who noted Africans' "birthright" to freedom and who called slavery "a constant violation of that right, and therefore of justice." In 1769 a minister from Massachusetts, Samuel Webster, seconded this view in *An Earnest Address to My Country on Slavery*. He appealed to readers to "break every yoke and let these oppressed ones go free without delay," an early call for immediate abolition. In 1773 a debater at Harvard noted that supporting slavery, which violated "natural and civil Liberty," contradicted the actions of those who "urge principles of natural equality in defence of their own liberties."[29]

The American rebels' support for liberty while tolerating, if not supporting, slavery was noted on both sides of the Atlantic. British author Samuel Johnson asked, "How is it that we hear the loudest *yelps* for liberty from the drivers of negroes?" Another British critic added,

"If there be an object truly ridiculous in nature, it is an American patriot, signing resolutions of independence with one hand, and with the other brandishing a whip over his frightened slaves." John Allen of New Hampshire agreed, pointing out that Americans were "fasting, praying, nonimporting, nonexporting, remonstrating, resolving and pleading" for their rights at the same time that they were engaged in "lawless, cruel, inhuman, and abominable" enslavement of their "fellow creatures."[30] Another American asked how those who oppose "paying the poor pittance of a glass, a paper, and paint tax, and [who] cry aloud on freedom and virtue" could "be at home the greatest tyrants on earth."[31] Nathaniel Niles of New England insisted, "[L]et us cease to enslave our fellow-men, or else let us cease to complain of those what would enslave us." In his will, Richard Randolph of Virginia noted how white Americans could support slavery "in contradiction of their own declaration of rights, and in violation of every sacred law of nature, of the inherent, inalienable and imprescriptible [sic] rights of man, and of every principle of moral and/ political honesty."[32]

The contradictions were apparent to both black and white. Boston blacks petitioned the Massachusetts General Court in 1773, asserting that "great things" should come from those who took "such a noble stand against the designs of their *fellow-men* to enslave them."[33] In 1774 blacks who were "held in a State of Slavery within the bowels of a free and Christian country" asserted their natural right to freedom and the need for emancipating slaves when they reached the age of twenty-one. That same year, a black wrote in the *Massachusetts Spy* that slavery was "a cloud" over the colony's liberty.[34] Blacks in Connecticut, Massachusetts, and New Hampshire petitioned their colonial/state legislatures for gradual emancipation. Acting individually, they cited the principles of liberty in their suits for freedom. Also, blacks seeking (and often promised) freedom served on both sides of the Revolution. In time, perhaps as many as 8000 blacks served in the Continental Army, some taking such new surnames as Liberty and Freedom, while close to 100,000 may have fought under the King's banner.

Colonials who led the Revolution frequently expressed views in opposition to slavery, proof that anti-slavery ideals were spreading beyond the Quakers. In his 1764 *The Rights of the British Colonies Asserted and Proved*, James Otis asked, "Does it follow that tis right to enslave a man because he is black? Will short curl'd hair like wool, in-

stead of Christian hair . . . , help the argument? Can any logical infer-
ence in favour of slavery be drawn from a flat nose, a long or a short
face?" He concluded that those who would "barter away other men's
liberty" would "care little for their own."[35]

Dr. Benjamin Rush, himself the owner of a slave, wrote anonymously against slavery and the slave trade in a pamphlet, *Address to the
Inhabitants of the British Settlements in America upon Slave-Keeping*
(1773), a work for which he credited Anthony Benezet and which contributed to Pennsylvania's 1773 heavy tax on slave imports. In it, the
physician sought to counter the view that the African was subhuman
and innately unequal and unqualified for civilized life. Slavery was responsible for their vices, such as idleness and thievery, and for their
limited abilities. In 1774, Rush helped form the Pennsylvania Society
for Promoting the Abolition of Slavery and the Relief of Free Negroes
Unlawfully Held in Bondage. As the revolution approached its end,
Rush pointed out the illogic of a fight for liberty ending in the importation and enslavement of Africans; slaves needed to be treated well
and prepared for eventual freedom.

Thomas Paine, who arrived in America only in 1774 but who already knew Benezet's and Rush's writings, argued that Africans had
done nothing to warrant the loss of their liberty; they still had "a natural, perfect" right to freedom. After attacking the legitimacy of slavery and the horrors of the slave trade, the author of *Common Sense*
argued that being born free was "the natural, perfect right of all mankind." For him, supporting slavery was no different than supporting
"murder, robbery, lewdness, and barbarity." He also attacked "the most
horrid of all traffics, that of human flesh" and called for "continental
legislation" against slave importation, for better treatment of slaves,
"and in time . . . their freedom."[36]

Patrick Henry, who argued for liberty or death, thought of slavery
as a "lamentable evil," but nevertheless did not free his slaves because
of "the general inconvenience of living without them." Like another
Virginian, James Madison, he hoped that future generations would find
a way to end the institution; in the meantime, he urged slave owners
to treat their slaves leniently. Madison, whose father-in-law was a
Quaker who freed his slaves, referred to slavery as "the most oppressive dominion ever exercised by man over man."[37] The future president
retained ownership of his human property but focused on being an ex-

emplary owner. He was willing to live with the institution rather than see society harmed by the presence of thousands of poor, propertyless, racially different, angry people. There was a chance that future generations would find a solution to slavery's impact on the nation.

Thomas Jefferson coauthored a 1776 bill to emancipate slaves born after the bill's passage; he also wrote a draft of a Virginia state constitution which prohibited further slave imports. A slave owner, he believed both that slavery was evil and that the black was intellectually, physically, and emotionally inferior to whites. Henry Laurens, a leading planter and merchant in South Carolina, traded slaves as late as the early 1770s. His views changed to judgmental uncertainty and then to opposition. By the Revolution, he was writing, "I abhor slavery" and asserting that slaves were "well entitled to freedom."[38] He looked forward to a time when "gratitude as well as justice" would prompt compliance with "the golden rule." Working on manumitting his own slaves, he feared "trust[ing] in Providence for defence and security" while he enslaved those who deserved freedom.[39]

Alexander Hamilton, aid and adviser to George Washington, believed that "the contempt [whites] have been taught to entertain for the blacks" led to many incorrect ideas. Hamilton, who became a charter member of the New York Manumission Society, believed that slavery was wrong and, unlike most Americans of his time, that blacks were not inferior to whites; in fact, he argued that "their natural faculties are as good as ours."[40] His beliefs, however, did not lead him to free his own slaves.

Unlike Hamilton, Benjamin Franklin, who printed Sandiford's and Lay's anti-slavery attacks and in 1758 helped found a school for blacks in Philadelphia, believed that blacks were inherently inferior to whites. While arguing that blacks required white supervision and thus did not make colonials inconsistent in their demands for liberty, Franklin also saw the slave trade in 1772 as "a detestable commerce." He encouraged the anti-slavery efforts of Anthony Benezet and expressed pleasure that "the disposition against keeping negroes grows more general in North America."[41] By 1787 he was president of the Pennsylvania Abolition Society.

These and other anti-slavery views of colonials were indirectly supported by a 1772 court case in England, *Somerset v. Stewart*. James Somerset, a Virginia slave, was sold to Charles Stewart, a Bostonian who transported him to London in late 1769 for a temporary sojourn and who planned to ship him to the West Indies in 1771. Granville Sharp, a well-known Quaker, supported Somerset's case in order to obtain a court ruling on whether a person could be legally held as a slave in Britain. The possible repercussions of a decision prompted planters from the West Indies to pay for the legal team opposing Somerset's freedom.

Lord Mansfield, the chief justice of Britain's highest common-law court, ruled that Somerset was free: a person could not be held as a slave in Britain because that nation did not have laws creating slave status. His broader argument affected slaves in the 1770s, as well as guided abolitionist arguments decades in the future: slavery did not exist naturally; it required positive law. "It is so odious," he explained, "that nothing can be suffered to support it, but positive law."[42] For those who opposed slavery, it meant that government could prevent the existence of slavery simply by failing to enact laws creating it. As for slaves, some who learned of the decision ran away and tried to reach Britain. Advertisements for runaway slaves included references to the case, with one noting that slaves thought that they would find freedom in Britain, "a Notion now too prevalent among the Negroes, greatly to the Vexation and Prejudice of their Masters."[43]

Not surprisingly, neither the Quakers nor the ideals of the revolution brought an end to slavery. Slavery and the slave trade had existed in the former British colonies for over 160 years; slaves were a major economic investment before the War for Independence, and colonial liberty showed few signs of expanding sufficiently to include black liberty. Some legislatures struck at the slave trade, as did the First and Second Continental Congresses, and numerous antislavery societies, dominated by Quakers, were formed, including the first secular abolition society in the United States: the Society for the Relief of Free Negroes Held in Bondage in (Philadelphia, 1775). Still, antebellum abolitionists would face a system even more entrenched than that faced by the Quakers of the 1700s or the revolutionaries of the 1770s.

Notes

1. Thomas E. Drake, *Quakers and Slavery in America* (New Haven, CT: Yale University Press, 1950), 4.

2. Montesquieu, *The Spirit of the Laws*, vol. 1 (Littleton, CO: Fred B. Rothman, 1991), 255–259.

3. Quoted in Arthur Zilversmit, *The First Emancipation: The Abolition of Slavery in the North* (Chicago: University of Chicago Press, [1967]), 59.

4. John Saffin, quoted in Philip S. Foner, *Blacks in the American Revolution* (Westport, CT: Greenwood, 1976), 12–13.

5. Quoted in Edwin H. Cady, *John Woolman: The Mind of the Quaker Saint* (New York: Washington Square Press, 1966), 70.

6. Fox, quoted in Drake, *Quakers and Slavery*, 6; Edmundson, quoted in Arthur J. Worrall, *Quakers in the Colonial Northeast* (Hanover, NH: University Press of New England, 1980), 153.

7. Quoted in Zilversmit, *The First Emancipation*, 55.

8. Quoted in Michael L. Conniff and Thomas J. Davis, *Africans in the Americas: A History of the Black Diaspora* (New York: St. Martin's Press, 1994), 190.

9. Quoted in Zilversmit, *The First Emancipation*, 56.

10. Quoted in ibid., 57.

11. Quoted in Drake, *Quakers and Slavery*, 34.

12. Cady, *John Woolman*, 71.

13. Elihu Coleman, quoted in Mary S. Locke, *Anti-Slavery in America from the Introduction of African Slaves to the Prohibition of the Slave Trade (1619–1808)* (1901; reprint, New York: Johnson Reprint Company, 1968), 24.

14. Drake, *Quakers and Slavery*, 40, 43.

15. Zilversmit, *The First Emancipation*, 68.

16. Quoted in Locke, *Anti-Slavery in America*, 27.

17. Quoted in Foner, *Blacks in the American Revolution*, 17.

18. Quoted in Locke, *Anti-Slavery in America*, 25, 31.

19. Drake, *Quakers and Slavery*, 47.

20. Zilversmit, *The First Emancipation*, 72.

21. Quoted in Zilversmit, *The First Emancipation*, 70–71; Drake, *Quakers and Slavery*, 57; Locke, *Anti-Slavery in America*, 29.

22. Quoted in Drake, *Quakers and Slavery*, 58–59.

23. Quoted in Cady, *John Woolman*, 97, 100.

24. Ibid., 112.

25. Quoted in Zilversmit, *The First Emancipation*, 85, 86.

26. Quoted in Foner, *Blacks in the American Revolution*, 18.

27. Ibid., 51.

28. Quoted in John P. Kaminski, ed., *A Necessary Evil? Slavery and the Debate over the Constitution* (Madison, WI: Madison House, 1995), 35.

29. Quoted in Foner, *Blacks in the American Revolution*, 26–27.

30. Quoted in James Oliver Horton and Lois E. Horton, *In Hope of Liberty: Culture, Community, and Protest among Northern Free Blacks, 1700–1860* (New York: Oxford University Press, 1997), 58, and Gerald Sorin, *Abolitionism: A New Perspective* (New York: Praeger, 1972), 30–31.

31. "Anti-slavetrader," quoted in Zilversmit, *The First Emancipation*, 94.

32. Quoted in Gary B. Nash, *Race and Revolution* (Madison, WI: Madison House, 1990), 10, and Willie Lee Rose, "The Impact of the American Revolution on the Black Population," in Paul E. Finkelman, ed., *Articles on American Slavery*, vol. 4, *Slavery, Revolutionary America, and the New Nation* (New York: Garland, 1989), 417–418.

33. Quoted in Zilversmit, *The First Emancipation*, 101.

34. Both quoted in Foner, *Blacks in the American Revolution*, 29.

35. Quoted in Nash, *Race and Revolution*, 8, and James B. Stewart, *Holy Warriors: The Abolitionists and American Slavery* (New York: Hill and Wang, 1976), 20.

36. Quoted in Philip S. Foner, comp. and ed., *The Complete Writings of Thomas Paine*, vol. 2 (New York: Citadel Press, 1945), 18, 20.

37. Quoted in Richard R. Beeman, *Patrick Henry: A Biography* (New York: McGraw-Hill, 1974), 96, and Jack N. Rakove, *James Madison: The Creation of the American Republic*, 2d ed. (New York: Longman, 2002), 144.

38. Quoted in Matthew T. Mellon, *Early American Views on Negro Slavery: From the Letters and Papers of the Founders of the Republic* (Boston: Meador Publishing, 1934), 59, and Foner, *Blacks in the American Revolution*, 61.

39. Quoted in Locke, *Anti-Slavery in America*, 52.

40. Quoted in Mellon, *Early American Views*, 60, 61.

41. Quoted in ibid., 23.

42. Quoted in A. Leon Higginbotham Jr., *In the Matter of Color: Race & the American Legal Process: The Colonial Period* (Oxford: Oxford University Press, 1980), 11.

43. Quoted in Foner, *Blacks in the American Revolution*, 27.

CHAPTER 3

"Justice Is in One Scale, and Self-Preservation in the Other": Slavery and Anti-Slavery in the New Nation

The end of the Revolution and the beginning of the new nation brought hope for slavery's opponents, but they did not bring a change in the social order, freedom for all slaves, or equal treatment for blacks in general. They "dealt a heavy, though not mortal, blow to slavery."[1] The "spirit of freedom," as George Washington referred to it, had ebbed, and the perception of the black as inferior continued, as did Americans' reverence for all types of property.[2] Still, the immediate postwar years brought some progress with the gradual ending of slavery north of Delaware, the prohibition of slavery in the Northwest Territory, the easing of manumission restrictions in some southern states, and the abolition of the foreign slave trade. For those supporting the total abolition of slavery, it was a hopeful time despite the acceptance of slavery in the new Constitution of 1787, the doubling of the southern slave population from 1770 to 1810, and the growing belief in black inferiority and threats to white security. By the early 1830s, when abolitionism took shape, opponents of slavery knew that the earlier optimism had achieved little.

Northern Abolition

After the Revolution, some slaves were freed as a result of their military service; some were manumitted by masters who had decided that cries of liberty and chains of slavery could not coexist. More broadly, through statute and judicial decision, northern states moved against slavery for a variety of reasons. These included an economic orientation away from large-scale, cash-crop products farmed by large numbers of unskilled workers; a preference for workers who would in time contribute as tax-paying, frontier-settling farmers, merchants, and soldiers; the impact of a depressed economy in the 1780s; and the fear of the twin evils of slave uprisings and miscegenation. The more important that slavery was in a state's economy and the greater the number of slaves present in a state, the more difficult the road to emancipation and the loss of valuable property. Liberty involved the protection, maintenance, and use of property—not the *loss* of property, particularly at the hands of government. Also affecting property-minded owners was the prospect of being held financially responsible for freed slaves; however, countering that was the demand by white laborers to eliminate the competition of unfree blacks.

Abolition began as early as 1777, much of it following petitions and appeals from northern slaves and free blacks who appealed to Revolutionary and Enlightenment principles. For example, slaves in Vermont petitioned by calling attention to the need to guarantee "that the name of slave may not be heard in a land gloriously contending for the sweets of freedom."[3] In Massachusetts, blacks cited Christian principles and man's inherent liberty as they called for gradual emancipation, beginning with slave children who reached the age of twenty-one. Such a policy was a controversial one for abolitionists, some of whom felt that it was also necessary to end the slave trade and others who believed that such a step was better than no progress.

Vermont (constitution), New Hampshire (bill of rights), Connecticut (statute), Rhode Island (statutes), and Massachusetts (constitutional Declaration of Rights and judicial decisions) acted in the 1770s and 1780s. In Pennsylvania, the declining number of slaves and the determined effort of both Quakers and some Scotch-Irish Presbyterians led to slavery's abolition in 1780. As in New England, the state provided for gradual emancipation, a policy that was not satisfactory to the Quakers and that left Pennsylvania with slaves as late as 1840.

Manumission

While northern states were taking steps to eliminate slavery, however slowly, states of the upper South were giving hope to anti-slavery advocates that abolition was in the foreseeable future throughout the nation. They did so through their easing of manumission restrictions—first Virginia (1782) and then Delaware (1787), Maryland (1790), and Kentucky (1792). Masters could act through will or deed. Some did so under the influence of Christian and Enlightenment principles; other masters found manumission a useful way to reduce an unprofitably large workforce or to end their responsibility for unproductive dependents.

Regardless of their reasons, slave owners freed thousands of slaves in the twenty years after 1790: Maryland's free black population quadrupled, reaching almost 34,000 in 1810; Virginia's more than doubled, hitting over 30,000 in 1810. By that year, the Upper South states of Delaware, Maryland, Virginia, Kentucky, North Carolina, and Tennessee, as well as the District of Columbia, had more free blacks than did the states of the North (94,000 to 78,000).

Then, responding to fears prompted by the slave uprising in St. Domingue (Haiti) and to the growing numbers of free blacks, Virginia repealed its manumission law in 1806 and barred newly freed slaves from staying in the state for more than a year. If they stayed longer, they risked reenslavement. States of the lower South required legislative approval of private manumissions. Their number of free blacks remained tiny.

The Northwest Ordinance

The new nation's first constitution, the Articles of Confederation, which went into effect in 1781, said nothing about slavery, the slave trade, or fugitive slaves. In response to concerns about repeating the tyranny of Parliament, states retained most of their sovereignty, including the power to define and protect property and deal with slavery. Despite its limited powers, however, the single-house Congress made at least one important step on the road to slavery's abolition. On July 13, 1787, it enacted the Northwest Ordinance. Providing a system of government for the territory north of the Ohio River—territory that was rapidly filling with settlers and that would soon become the states of Ohio (1803), Indiana (1816), Illinois (1819), Michigan (1837), and Wisconsin (1848)—its sixth article also prohibited slavery in that area:

> There shall be neither slavery nor involuntary servitude in the said territory, otherwise than in the punishment of crimes . . . : provided always, that any person escaping into the same, from whom labour or service is lawfully claimed in any one of the original states, such fugitive may be lawfully reclaimed.[4]

The Congress, in effect, was, while respecting slave property, asserting the power to prohibit slavery in the territories belonging to the United States. This assertion of power would be used by abolitionists and anti-expansionists to support bans on slavery by the Congress under the new constitution written in 1787. However, limiting the territory covered suggested that territory south of the Ohio River was to have slavery; in other words, the national government was both prohibiting slavery where it barely existed and accepting it where it already existed. Plus, like the gradual emancipation measures of the northern states, the Northwest Territory did not see the immediate disappearance of slaves. Men and women enslaved before 1787 remained slaves, and most of the region turned to a slavery-like indentured servitude. In addition, the law's fugitive slave clause respected slave owners' property rights anywhere in the area.

The Constitution and Slavery

Concerns about the protection of property rights, the security of the social order, and the national government's inability to tax, regulate trade, and maintain a military grew through the 1780s. In response, a new constitution, which was written in 1787, had not only a significant effect on the power and structure of the national government but also a critical and divisive impact on the future of slavery and on the hopes and strategies of future abolitionists.

While the framers of the new document did not use the words

slavery or slave or Negro and used such neutral terms as "citizens," "persons," "other persons," and "person held to Service or Labour," they frequently dealt with the institution as they faced the reality that some states would not abandon their labor system regardless of economic, political, moral, and Enlightenment ideas against it. The result was, according to South Carolina's Charles Cotesworth Pinckney in 1788, "the best [possible] terms for the security of this species of property."[5]

What they created or accepted in the Constitution of 1787 assured eventual conflict over the power of the national government over slavery. It spawned an unwinnable debate about the Constitution's pro- or anti-slavery nature that divided the nation and even the abolitionists of the mid-1800s. Because the Constitution seemed to make clear that slavery was a state issue, it gave some abolitionists of the 1830s–1850s reasons for seeing it as a creation of sin that required no respect, but because it suggested national power over a couple of areas, other abolitionists saw it as an anti-slavery weapon.

The strengthened national government gained the power to prohibit the foreign slave trade, although not for twenty years, a reprieve which slave importers exploited. In addition, the Constitution required the return of slaves who escaped from one state to another, thus authorizing the passage of the Fugitive Slave Law in 1793. Other provisions were less direct but still reflected a desire to protect a slave-based society; for example, Congress gained the power to handle "insurrections" and "domestic violence" but was unable to tax exports (including crops produced by slave labor). In addition, the acceptance of slavery was reflected in the so-called Three-Fifths Compromise. Having decided that the House of Representatives would be based on population and that Congress could tax on the basis of a state's population, the Constitution's framers had to decide *what* population would be used: total or white only. Southerners preferred that white population be used when their states faced taxes but total population when determining representation. Northerners opposed giving the South additional votes when not all Southerners were free to act politically, but they supported taxing southern states on the basis of their total population. The solution was a compromise where slaves were counted, just not in their full numbers: 60 percent of slave numbers would be added to a state's white population figure. Even if this compromise did not totally satisfy Southerners, it gave them significant political clout beyond the actual weight of white votes. That clout would frequently determine presidential elections and the balance of power in Congress for three-quarters of a century.

Working against slavery and in favor of future slavery opponents, particularly those who focused on its expansion into new territories, was Article IV, Section 3 which empowered Congress to make "all necessary rules and regulations" for the territories.

Abolition of Slave Trade

The slave trade was an important issue for abolitionists who believed that banning the trade was an essential step to the final demise of slavery. By the time the new Constitution of 1787 gave Congress the ability to end the slave trade in 1808, Quakers had resumed their opposition to the trade and most states had already taken action for a variety of reasons. State prohibitions, however, did little good. With less competition there were more profits as slave traders found new ports and, when necessary, smuggled their product. The states had few enforcement mechanisms and smuggling had long been an accepted business practice. A broader ban by the nation was supported by states such as Virginia and Maryland whose economic shifts had reduced the need for slave labor.

Between 1787 and when a national ban when into effect in 1808 on the recommendation of President Thomas Jefferson, thousands of slaves entered the country. In fact, those two decades were the peak years for American importation. Despite—or because of—that surge in importations, anti-slavery advocates were hopeful that ending the trade would inevitably lead to slavery's demise as the source of African slaves ended. Further efforts against slavery were unnecessary, argued such men as Jedidiah Morse, an anti-slavery Congregationalist minister from Connecticut. Ending the slave trade, according to English abolitionist Thomas Clarkson, would be "laying the axe at the very root" of slavery.[6]

With its ban also beginning in 1808, Britain took the lead in enforcing the new prohibitions against the slave trade. Its navy gave it the ability to take effective action and its diplomatic strength allowed it to affect national policies. The United States' efforts were minimal, with southern votes preventing British searches of American ships suspected of involvement in the slave trade. Britain's industrial revolution and Eli Whitney's cotton gin stimulated illegal importations by increasing the demand for cotton.

Discrimination against Free Blacks

Many of the free blacks in Virginia and the states to its north lived in urban settings, such as Philadelphia, Boston, New York, Baltimore, and Richmond. There they found the opportunity to develop communities which provided them with leadership, psychological support, schools, and institutions supporting black equality, abolition, and their African heritage. They formed insurance companies, benevolent societies, and churches.

Such communities were needed because slavery was not disappearing, racial stereotypes and pseudoscientific studies were supporting white racism, and discrimination against blacks was increasing. With the Revolution's end, most white Americans remained uninterested in heeding the exhortations of a handful of emancipationists to help the black American help himself. Africans were suitable for slave labor and undeserving of equal treatment because, as the scientific racism of the time argued, blacks were a separate species inferior to whites in "both mind and body."[7] Exceptions such as poet Phillis Wheatley and mathematician/scientist Benjamin Banneker were just that. The increasingly popular concept of the Great Chain of Being organized all things, inanimate, animate, and divine, into a hierarchy that put man in the middle. Humans, like others on the chain, fell into ranks based on physiognomy and anatomical traits. Judged by color, facial angle, savagery, and frequency of enslavement, Africans were at the bottom of the human chain. Calls for equal treatment of freed blacks seemed silly if not suicidal. Science said that Africans were inferior to Europeans; environment (enslavement) was replaced by heredity as the scientific explanation for the black's condition, thus the need to treat them differently than whites. Slavery demonstrated, not created, black inferiority.

Countering claims of such inferiority was difficult for free blacks in the North because of the large numbers of slaves and the discrimination facing the few free blacks. For example, churches with both black and white members increasingly excluded blacks from leadership roles and from communion; they segregated them in church and in cemeteries. (Even the Quakers did not admit blacks as members until 1790.) As a result, blacks formed separate congregations and even new denominations, including the African Methodist Episcopal (AME) Church. In education, whites often barred black children from their schools or refused to support separate black schools. In response, blacks set up their own schools which they struggled to support financially. Many black parents saw little point in such institutions because educated blacks had little luck finding employment. Plus, whites saw the schools as threatening: educated blacks could lead slaves in revolt and could compete with whites for jobs.

Whites were correct. The schools did help provide blacks with educated leaders, such as Richard Allen, a founder of the AME Church. But these leaders did not agree about the situation of black Americans, free and slave, or about how to make it better. Like many whites, some blacks believed that slavery was wrong and that it would end one day; others, Allen included, asserted that blacks needed to fight, although not physically, for their liberty and equality. Blacks must petition, protest, and organize. They needed to do so because they had little political voice, as they were barred from voting in most states, including Connecticut (1814), New York (1821), Rhode Island (1832), and Pennsylvania (1838).

Colonization

Much of the early effort of abolitionists who appeared in the 1830s was directed against the strategy of removing blacks from the country; however, in the early 1800s, colonization offered opponents of slavery a conservative solution.

Colonizationists had mixed reasons for supporting the removal of blacks from the United States. Many were simply seeking a way of ridding the country of unwanted African Americans. Personal profits and national economic growth were, in the eyes of many colonizers, dependent on the continuation of slavery but not the presence of free blacks. Removing free blacks who, according to Virginian John Randolph, spread "mischief" and "discontent" among slaves would help secure slave property. Kentuckian Henry Clay believed that colonization would "rid our country of a useless and pernicious, if not dangerous portion of its population" while perhaps lifting Africa "from ignorance and barbarism."[8] Owners eager to manumit their slaves but hesitant to do so because they feared the presence of a growing "class of very dangerous people" would be encouraged to act if colonization removed the threat.[9] Colonizationists who believed that white perceptions of blacks and not any inherent black inferiority was the basis of racial tensions were nevertheless faced with the fact that, as Clay explained, "No talents however great, no piety however pure and devoted, no patriotism, however ardent" could shake whites' negative perception.[10] Thus, regardless of the legitimacy of the perceptions of black inferiority, whites and blacks were never going to be able to live together peacefully and productively. Colonization was the answer, especially if states and individuals insisted on freeing slaves.

For those supporting gradual emancipation, colonization offered the uplift of blacks as masters prepared slaves for freedom. For those who sought the Christianizing of Africa, American blacks seemed suitable missionaries. Among the pro-black, anti-slavery colonizationists, at least until the 1830s, were future abolitionists Benjamin Lundy, William Lloyd Garrison, James G. Birney, Arthur and Lewis Tappan, and Theodore Dwight Weld. For them colonization would prove to be a transition to abolitionism; supporters of emancipation and the black, these men found colonization to be a way to help both.

The formal colonization solution in the United States began in December 1816 in the Capitol building in Washington, D.C., with the founding of the American Colonization Society (ACS). It was dominated by southerners, including Virginians James Monroe, John Marshall, John Randolph, and by slave owners. Following the British model in Sierra Leone, the ACS sought to encourage slave owners to free their slaves and to relocate the freed slaves to Africa. Such a venture necessitated organization and money, both of which colonizationists sought from the national government and through their insider contacts. Both, however, were in short supply and, all in all, the plan to remove blacks from the country and to use them as missionaries was impractical.

It was more than impractical for American blacks. For them, Africa was not home; the United States was. As one black Philadelphian asserted, "We are *natives* of this country."[11] Black opponents of colonization sought to counter the charge that assimilation was hopeless, asserting that flaws noted among blacks were the result of slavery, not an inherent inferiority. They realized that colonization would not lead to either emancipation or equal rights for blacks remaining in the United States. By the late 1820s blacks were able, through both their example and their arguments, to convince a handful of white men and women to reject removal as a substitute for abolition *and* to support a new perception of blacks as deserving of both freedom and equality. The more vocal they were in their opposition to colonization, the more future abolitionists listened. Thus, even though colonization had little if any chance of removing significant numbers of American blacks—fewer than 4000 were relocated by 1860—it did provide a push for some white and black Americans to become abolitionists tackling both slavery and racism/prejudice.

However, for blacks born in Africa and for those who saw their situation in the United States as oppressive and, most importantly, hopeless, colonization offered an answer. Most support came from the upper South in such places as Baltimore and Richmond, towns that offered free blacks few opportunities. For Paul Cuffe, migration to Africa during the early 1800s would provide black Americans with an escape from discrimination. Other American blacks, including Richard Allen of the AME Church and his son John, who emigrated, found colonization to the Caribbean appealing. Haiti's struggle for independence had made it a symbol of freedom and a lure for those seeking peace away from white discrimination. Blacks in Richmond, Virginia, rejected removal to Africa and suggested a separate black colony within the United States.

Despite the formation of the ACS, most northern whites were unconcerned with either slavery or colonization in the 1810s and 1820s. Exceptions included John Kendrick of Massachusetts who, years of ahead of those usually linked with the goal, advocated immediate abolition. In 1817 in *Horrors of Slavery*, he mocked the notion of a gradual end to slavery, asking how such an "impolitic, antirepublican, unchristian, and highly criminal" institution could be ended in any other way than in one stroke.[12] Even in the South, critics were not entirely absent. Virginian George Bourne, a Presbyterian minister whose views strongly influenced the young William Lloyd Garrison, advocated immediate abolition a year before Kendrick did. His attacks on slavery and on the churches and ministers that failed to act against it led his church to condemn him for heresy and for Virginians to push him out of their state. Quaker Benjamin Lundy, who also had a significant influence on Garrison, was organizing anti-slavery societies in Ohio and Tennessee from the late 1810s; in 1821 he began publishing the anti-slavery *Genius of Universal Emancipation* in the slave state of Tennessee.

Haiti, Prosser, and Vesey

The slave revolt in Haiti that began in 1791 and unsuccessful slave uprisings in Virginia and South Carolina in the early 1800s forced slavery advocates to consider reasons both to end the institution and to continue it. On the one hand, if slaves, rather than being contented, were so unhappy with their condition that they were willing (and able) to organize, rebel, and kill whites, perhaps the institution was too dangerous to keep. Slavery should end, and freed slaves be removed from the country. As Virginia Governor James Monroe explained in 1800 after the unsuccessful Gabriel revolt near Richmond, "Unhappily while this class of people exists among us we can never count with certainty on its tranquil submission."[13] On the other hand, if Africans were so deceitful, duplicitous, and dangerous, perhaps slavery was the only way to control them. If so, ending the importation of dangerous foreign slaves, controlling and removing free blacks, discouraging manumission, and restricting the lives of slaves were all necessary and appropriate steps.

Beginning in 1789 the French Revolution caused many Americans to fear the influence of radicalism on their society's social order. Then in 1791 civil war broke out in St. Domingue. Slaves rose up in mass. In 1801 Toussaint L'Ouverture unified the island of Santo Domingo and outlawed slavery. After his capture and with yellow fever and the islanders' guerrilla warfare wearing down French forces, former slave Jean Jacques Dessalines proclaimed Haitian independence when the French pulled out in 1803. He became emperor of the independent island country, the first black nation in the New World, the next year. His assassination in 1806 was followed by civil war between blacks and mulattoes.

The horrors that nearby Haiti faced for over twenty years were warning enough for American slave owners. They threatened southerners' security and their surface complacency about slavery's naturalness and rightness. Also dangerous, if unsuccessful, was Gabriel Prosser's effort to organize Richmond-area slaves. A literate blacksmith who was familiar with the ideology of the Revolution, he sought to lead slaves and poor whites on August 30, 1800, in killing pro-slavery Virginians and gaining control of the central region of their state. Although no whites were harmed and Gabriel and over two dozen other blacks were hanged, the conspiracy proved to whites that slaves could desire freedom, could organize, and could threaten white lives and control.

Two decades later, another planned rebellion sent a similar message. It occurred in South Carolina, the site of the 1739 Stono Rebellion. Twenty miles from Charleston, the Stono rebels, recent arrivals from Angola, had killed over thirty whites and plundered plantations before they were stopped—all in a single day. But it was the 1822 plot of Denmark Vesey that, according to historian Richard C. Wade, "cut into the conscience of Dixie's town dwellers" because "since the slaves lived in the same yard, it was not even possible to lock out the intruder."[14] A literate, skilled, freed slave who was influenced by the recent revolutions in the United States, France, and Haiti as well as by Christianity and by anti-slavery arguments, Vesey's apparent goal was to escape from South Carolina and sail to the West Indies. He was stopped before the revolt began. No black violence against whites had occurred, yet Vesey and thirty-four others were hanged.

Because both Gabriel and Vesey had some white support, southern fears were wide-ranging, encompassing slaves, free blacks, anti-slavery whites, and potentially any white Northerner, particularly those visiting the South. The unsuccessful slave uprisings proved that greater vigilance, repression, and protection were necessary. Maryland's, Virginia's, and North Carolina's prospects of ending slavery disappeared; the presence of uncontrolled and uncontrollable blacks offered too great of a threat. Now, slave owners could argue that they would like to emancipate their slaves but that, because colonization was impractical, the prospect of a large population of deceitful and dangerous free blacks prevented them from doing so. With declining support for environmental explanations of black inferiority, southern whites asserted that only slavery, like it or not, kept blacks under control and prevented race war.

Expansion and the Missouri Compromise

Spurred by the rise of the British textile industry, the invention of the cotton gin in 1793, and the War of 1812, cotton dominated American production and exports. Challenging the labor system behind it thus would mean affecting more than the lives of African Americans who worked the plantations as slaves. From less than 10 percent of all American exports at the turn of the century, cotton rose to be almost a third by 1820. Such numbers meant that cotton and its production were crucial to the American economy from the farms of the South to the emerging cotton factories in the North to the shipping businesses that transported and traded cotton.

With cotton's growing production came a growing demand for more land on which to produce it. As a result, Kentucky (1792) and Tennessee (1796) were soon followed into the Union by Mississippi (1817) and Alabama (1819). The purchase of the Louisiana Territory from France in 1803 opened up the possibility of even more western lands devoted to what was quickly becoming King Cotton. The increase in acreage planted in cotton meant an increase in the number of slaves. By 1820, Alabama had over 40,000 slaves, Louisiana almost 70,000, and Mississippi almost 33,000. These numbers were well short of South Carolina's 258,000 and Virginia's 425,000, but they spoke to the trend. Over half of the slaves in the South worked on cotton plantations.

Slave numbers increased most quickly in the areas newest to slavery, and slaves no longer needed in the Old South were being sold to plantations in the new states. In 1790 the area that later became the Deep South states held 20 percent of American slaves; by 1860, over half of all slaves would live there. The domestic slave trade, replacing the foreign trade as the source of many horrors, was taking on a growing economic importance as it provided the needed labor.

The controversy over slavery's expansion west of the Mississippi into Missouri was thus not a simple matter of whether that labor system should spread. It was already doing so. The question had to do with where, and how, and by whom. Because it involved constitutional and political questions, the Missouri controversy and resulting compromise marked the beginning rather than the end of the debate over slavery's expansion and, ultimately, its life and death. The death of slavery that the abolition of the slave trade was supposed to bring about was not coming. As a result, anti-slavery advocates were coming to the conclusion that stronger and more direct action was necessary.

Missouri, part of the territory acquired in 1803 from France, sought admission as a slave state in 1819. By that year, Congress had been debating for two years modifications in the Fugitive Slave Act of 1793—modifications that either threatened the recovery of slaveholders' human property or undermined the rights of blacks accused of being runaway slaves—and the nation had eleven states without slavery and eleven states with it, thus balancing, to an extent, regional influences on such issues as tariffs and internal improvements. Missouri, a state whose population was about 15 percent slave, would "unbalance" the nation.

In February, Representative James Tallmadge of New York proposed an amendment to the statehood bill. The so-called Tallmadge Amendment prohibited slavery in the state and required emancipation of existing slaves at age fifteen. It also incited southerners, but after much debate, the resulting compromise allowed Missouri to enter as a slave state and Maine as a free one. The balance was maintained. In addition, in order to avoid regular outbreaks of further debate, the Missouri Compromise stipulated that the region of the Louisiana Purchase north of 36° 30' would be free of slavery. Below 36° 30' the new Arkansas Territory was open to slavery.

The compromise seemed to one observer, Thomas Jefferson, to offer no real solution. As he prophetically explained in April 1820, "A geographical line, coinciding with a marked principle, moral and political, once conceived and held up to the angry passions of men, will never be obliterated; and every new irritation will mark it deeper and deeper. . . . [W]e have the wolf by the ears, and we can neither hold him, nor safely let him go."[15] The crusade of the abolitionists in the 1830s–1850 and the battle over expanding or limiting slavery in the Mexican Cession would prove the anti-slavery slaveholder correct.

David Walker and Nat Turner

In 1829 and 1831, Southerners' fears had reasons to grow. In 1829, a young black Boston businessman called on blacks to resist slavery, and in 1831 a Virginia slave organized a bloody uprising.

Born free in South Carolina in the late 1790s, the literate and well-traveled David Walker also may have been personally involved in

Vesey's plans while in Charleston. In Boston he published *Appeal . . . to the Colored Citizens of the World*, a twenty-six-page pamphlet. In it Walker denounced slavery and colonization and urged free blacks to consider how they were treated and to evaluate their freedom, which he referred to as "the very lowest kind— . . . the very *dregs*!" He told whites that "you may do your best to keep us in wretchedness and misery, to enrich you and your children; but . . . wo, wo, will be to you if we have to obtain our freedom by fighting."[16] Southern whites were disturbed both by the ideas in the publication and by Walker's efforts to circulate it among slaves. Some allegedly offered a reward for Walker's capture. Walker died in 1830, but the likelihood that free blacks were influencing slaves was a growing worry for white Southerners.

The ultimately unsuccessful slave rebellion led by Nat Turner, a literate slave preacher, combined with events in the North to invigorate both the defense of slavery and the attack on it. In August 1831, near the Virginia-North Carolina border, Turner's visions about God's desire to end slavery led him and several dozen other slaves on a murderous spree, their ultimate objective unclear. Approximately five dozen white men, women, and children died at their hands as they moved through fifteen plantations. Less than thirty-six hours after the rebellion had started, most of the rebels had been captured or killed. In the meantime, as many as 120 innocent blacks were killed as a result of Virginians' fears and desire for revenge. Over two dozen blacks, including Turner, were hanged.

Occurring only nine years after Denmark Vesey's planned uprising and within two years of Walker's *Appeal*, Turner's slaughter prompted obvious questions. When and where would the next outbreak of murderous violence occur? How could it be prevented? The South's answer to the second question made it less rather than more receptive to the pleas and demands of those who were beginning their campaign to promote a simple answer: end slavery—now.

The Virginia legislature's postrebellion debate over slavery was the South's last public questioning of slavery. The dozens of dead whites and the hundreds of dead blacks seemed to argue for the elimination of slavery, but pro-slavery advocates asserted that the uprising required the continuation of slavery and that slave *property* had to be respected and protected. Because there were insufficient funds to support the colonization of Virginia's freed slaves and because white Virginians could not tolerate the idea of large numbers of free blacks in their state, emancipation had little, if any, appeal as a means of preventing slave uprisings.

From the 1830s on, to equivocate about slavery or to accept any anti-slavery argument was to be unsouthern. As Peter Kolchin has written, "Southern politics during the antebellum period often re-volved around who could prove himself to be a better defender of Southern interests—by being more pro-slavery than his opponent."[17] Thanks in part to the federal arrangement of the American nation, the result was a comprehensive, unapologetic, assertive defense that saw any attack on slavery as an attack on the South and its way of life, even though only about a third of Southerners owned slaves. It was no longer possible to speak of slavery as a moral wrong that was, unfortunately, economically necessary. For those who had doubts about or were opposed to slavery, silence and caution were the usual path, especially given that there was no viable, acceptable alternative to slavery. Southern anti-slavery voices did not disappear, but their numbers were few: Robert J. Breckenridge of Kentucky wrote in 1830 that slavery was "an ulcer eating its way into the very heart of the state"; a North Carolina minister argued that even inferior blacks had "as good a right to the free use of whatever power the creator has given them" as whites; a Fredericksburg, Virginia, woman concluded that slavery "hardens the feelings."[18]

As in the past, the Bible, science, history, first-person evidence, and socioeconomic realities were all called upon to support slavery. The Bible demonstrated that God's chosen people, the Hebrews, owned slaves; that God condemned certain people to be slaves (the curse of Ham); that God ordained slavery in the books of the Old Testament; and that slavery was part of God's plan to bring Christianity to hea-thens. Slavery was God's will.

Often contradicting the scriptural explanations was the new sci-ence of the nineteenth century. Scientists argued that blacks were the result of a separate creation, and some, such as Dr. Josiah Nott, that blacks were a separate species. Anthropologists proved blacks' physi-cal and intellectual inferiority to whites, their inability to survive as free people, and their suitability for slavery. Pro-slavery arguments also referred to the existence of slavery in advanced societies. Pointing to ancient Greece and Rome, as well as to the United States of the slave-owning Founding Fathers, they noted how a slave class allowed the elite to devote themselves to public service and to culture. Related to this argument was the political one that slavery was part of the compromise that helped create the Union and that maintained an orderly society; slavery's destruction would lead to the destruction of the United States. The principles in the Declaration of Independence either did not apply to blacks or were false.

More convincing and comfortable for many Southerners was the evidence they saw on a daily basis: blacks were temperamentally and intellectually incapable of independent lives. Southern defenders of slavery noted the value of slavery to slave, master, South, nation, and world. Slaves lived protected, valued, and contented lives (while wage laborers in the North did not); slavery guaranteed an orderly and conservative society (while wage labor in the North led to selfishness and dangerous isms); and slavery produced a large number of products on which northern industry and society depended and which the United States traded to other parts of the world. Every region of the country traded with the South and used southern products, and thus every region had something to lose if the South lost its labor system.

Virginia—and the other slave states—responded to threats not by ending slavery but by making slavery even more restrictive. Teaching slaves to read and write and allowing their own ministers to preach to them were prohibited by law. More slave patrols and restrictions on free blacks entering the states sought to eliminate troublemakers. Over time and varying by place, the restrictions were eased or left unenforced, but no longer did most Southerners apologize for slavery. Now, they defended it as, in the words of South Carolinian John C. Calhoun, "a positive good."[19]

In 1820, Thomas Jefferson noted that "justice is in one scale, and self-preservation in the other."[20] The impact of that reality on abolitionism would soon become clear. The entrenchment of slavery into American life, its acceptance in the nation's Constitution, the southern determination to defend it, the confidence that blacks were inferior and undesirable, and Northerners' perception of slavery as a natural part of their world if not their states all meant that over the next thirty years those who sought the institution's end would be fighting a formidable, if not unbeatable, foe.

Notes

1. Darlene Clark Hine, William C. Hine, and Stanley Harrold, *The African-American Odyssey*, vol. 2, 2d ed. (Upper Saddle River, NJ: Prentice Hall, 2003), 86.

2. Matthew T. Mellon, *Early American Views on Negro Slavery: From the Letters and Papers of the Founders of the Republic* (Boston: Meador Publishing, 1934), 63.

3. Quoted in Philip S. Foner, *Blacks in the American Revolution* (Westport, CT: Greenwood, 1976), 77.

4. Paul E. Finkelman, *Slavery and the Founders: Race and Liberty in the Age of Jefferson*, 2d ed. (London: M. E. Sharpe, 2001), 40–41.

5. Ibid.,10.

6. Judith Jennings, *The Business of Abolishing the British Slave Trade, 1783–1807* (London: Frank Cass, 1997), 36.

7. Thomas Jefferson, quoted in Hine, Hine, and Harrold, *The African-American Odyssey*, 104.

8. Both quoted in P. J. Staudenraus, *The African Colonization Movement, 1816–1865* (New York: Columbia University Press, 1961), 28.

9. James Monroe, quoted in ibid., 51.

10. Quoted in Paul Goodman, *Of One Blood: Abolitionism and the Origins of Racial Equality* (Berkeley: University of California Press, 1998), 2.

11. Benjamin Quarles, *Black Abolitionists* (1969; reprint, New York: Oxford University Press, 1977), 7.

12. Merton L. Dillon, *Benjamin Lundy and the Struggle for Negro Freedom* (Urbana: University of Illinois Press, 1966), 14.

13. Winthrop D. Jordan, *White over Black: American Attitudes toward the Negro, 1550–1812* (1968; reprint, New York: W. W. Norton, 1977), 394.

14. Richard C. Wade, *Slavery in the Cities: The South, 1820–1860* (New York: Oxford University Press, 1964), 228, 230.

15. *Thomas Jefferson: Writings* (New York: Library Classics of the United States, 1984), 1434.

16. Peter P. Hinks, ed., *David Walker's Appeal to the Coloured Citizens of the World* (University Park: Pennsylvania State University Press, 2000), 31, 73.

17. Peter Kolchin, *American Slavery, 1619–1877* (New York: Hill and Wang, 1993), 198.

18. All quoted in Carl N. Degler, *The Other South: Southern Dissenters in the Nineteenth Century* (New York: Harper & Row, 1974), 20, 31, 34.

19. Quoted in Stephen B. Oates, *The Fires of Jubilee: Nat Turner's Fierce Rebellion* (New York: Harper & Row, 1975), 143.

20. Thomas Jefferson to John Holmes, April 22, 1820, in *Thomas Jefferson: Writings*, 1434.

CHAPTER 4

"THOUGH THE HEAVENS SHOULD FALL": ABOLITIONISM TAKES SHAPE—THE 1830s

In the 1830s, abolitionists demanded not the gradual and eventual destruction of slavery which emancipationists of the past sought, but an immediate end. For them, slavery was a part of a complex system supported by a belief in blacks' racial inferiority and the rightness of racial discrimination; therefore, ending slavery, even if the nation did so immediately, would fix only part of the country's "slavery" problem. Slavery built on and supported discrimination; the country had to eliminate both. At stake were not only the lives of millions of enslaved Americans but also the treatment of hundreds of thousands of free blacks. At stake were also the principles that underlie the Revolution, the Declaration of Independence, the Constitution, and the American political/social system as a whole. Could the country live with slavery and be true to its principles of freedom and liberty? Could it live without slavery and honor its faith in individual rights and the sanctity of property? Could slavery be destroyed without destroying the nation? Was the nation worth saving if it allowed slavery and discrimination?

Reform Movements

The abolitionists who appeared in the 1830s to threaten the nation's racial order were part of a broad reform period. In the 1820s–

1840s, Americans, particularly in the northern states, concluded that moral standards were falling. They saw a decline in spirituality, purity, and adherence to traditional civic ideals. The nation was in crisis, but a reform zeal sparked by the revivalism and evangelicalism of the 1820s—as well as by the theories of natural rights in the Declaration of Independence and the Enlightenment's theories of man's equality and capabilities—spurred men and women to search for a new moral vision, a new sense of community, and a greater self-control. The Second Great Awakening of the first half of the 1800s transformed many religious groups and thousands of individuals as it emphasized individual will, conversion, good works, and salvation. For many Americans the result was a belief in their ability to change themselves and their communities. A few went so far as perfectionism, believing that a life totally without sin was possible.

By the end of the first half of the nineteenth century, reformers were targeting education, women's rights, capital punishment and prisons, the legal and medical professions, alcohol, Catholicism, labor, debt imprisonment, the mentally ill, voting and office holding, prostitution, postal deliveries on Sunday, poverty, and slavery. For a tiny number of reformers, slavery was the central sin of the nation, and its immediate elimination would best begin the task of national salvation. Failure to act would open the United States to the wrath of God; therefore, the social and economic disruptions that could ensue with uncompensated, immediate emancipation were of minor concern. As Benjamin Lundy, editor of *Genius of Universal Emancipation*, proclaimed on the paper's masthead, "Let Justice Be Done Though the Heavens Should Fall."[1]

In a century when Americans were used to local and state regulations for "the people's welfare,"[2] even if such restrictions limited their right to property, many of the reformers and their organizations pressed state legislatures to mandate and, frequently, to finance and administer reforms. But in the South the rights of the slave owner and those hoping to achieve elite status through one day owning slaves trumped state power. Challenges to slavery, to the deference of women to men, and of the masses to civil authority and elite rule were rejected as interfering with the southern way and as disrupting the overall social order. Henry W. Ravenel, a planter in South Carolina, bragged in 1852 that the South was "the conservator of law and order—the enemy of innovation and change" and that it was prepared to "stay that furious tide of social and political heresies now setting towards us."[3] Mocked as demonstrations of the dangers of too much individualism and too much freedom, the various reforms were seen as weakening the traditions and order of the South and as the fanatical ideological siblings of abolitionism, the most hated of the reforms.

In the North, reform was much more popular, if not universal. Less convinced of the need to conserve the old order and more open to revivalism's suggestion of improvement, Northerners responded to the sermons of Charles Grandison Finney and Lyman Beecher. With the biracial appeal of the revival, the stage was set for interracial cooperation against what some saw as society's greatest ill.

The British Abolitionist Model

The appearance of a new revival-inspired anti-slavery effort came at much the same time as the abolitionist movement in Britain was reaching its goal, thus providing a small group of American reformers with hope and inspiration. Begun as a campaign to end the slave trade, the British anti-slavery effort ended with the abolition of slavery in the empire.

Highlighted by the efforts of Granville Sharpe to publicize the injustices of slavery and to use the law against slavery—including the *Somerset* case of 1772—England's anti-slavery campaign took firm shape in the late 1700s. Sharpe pushed for and purchased land in Sierra Leone to establish a colony of freed slaves; fellow abolitionist William Wilberforce, an Evangelical, became an anti-slavery member of the House of Commons. Both men were among the founders in 1787 of the Society for Effecting the Abolition of the Slave Trade which refused, despite Sharpe's efforts, to make abolition of slavery itself a goal. Members believed that Parliament had power to end the trade but that abolition of slavery in the empire involved colonial rights and must "be a work of gradual and slow consummation."[4]

While Wilberforce continued his efforts in Parliament, even introducing an anti-slavery proposal in 1791, war with France essentially brought British abolitionist efforts to a standstill for over a decade, and the uprising in Haiti raised doubts and worries. Then, British abolitionists found support in the Coalition Ministry formed in 1806 by a prime minister and a foreign secretary who had long opposed the slave trade. In 1807 Parliament passed Lord Grenville's bill abolishing the slave trade. As the United States would do a decade later, although with none of the same seriousness of enforcement, Britain declared in 1811 that a British subject participating in the slave trade was guilty of piracy and subject to the death penalty. British pressures helped push the Dutch (1814), French (1815), and Portuguese (1815–1830) to abolish the trade. The British navy blockaded the West African coast seizing 1600 ships and freeing 150,000 slaves from 1820 to 1870.

Supporting a new campaign for emancipation of slaves and influencing a shift to immediate emancipation both in Britain and the United States was an 1824 pamphlet, *Immediate Not Gradual Abolition*, written by Elizabeth Heyrick, a Quaker. Supported by various women's abolitionist groups, she attacked the policy and the male members of the Society for the Mitigation and Gradual Abolition of Slavery throughout the British Dominions. By 1830 the organization adopted her position on immediatism and became the Society for the Abolition of Slavery throughout the British Dominions; nonetheless, abolitionist women kept pressuring for immediate abolition, even threatening to withhold their significant financial support.

Barraged by anti-slavery petitions and with many of its members reelected on pledges of supporting abolition, a reformed Parliament voted in 1833 to end slavery in the empire. An interested young Boston publisher, William Lloyd Garrison, was visiting Britain for the first time, meeting with abolitionist leaders and studying their strategies and organization, when Parliament made its decision. While owners would be compensated, slaves over age six would undergo a six-year apprenticeship before receiving full freedom. Those under six were freed on August 1, 1834, and Antigua and Bermuda freed their slaves immediately. Opposition to the brutality and exploitation of the apprenticeship system led to its abolition in 1838.

Following their successes, British abolitionists, including George Thompson, Charles Stuart, and Harriet Martineau visited the United States. They offered criticisms of slavery and sometimes support, money, plans, and promises to put pressure on American churches. In return, they were met by grateful American abolitionists and angry anti-abolitionist mobs. Members of American anti-slavery societies sent members to Britain for emotional, political, and financial support; American anti-slavery newspaper articles, pamphlets, and books, including Angelina Grimké's *Appeal to the Christian Women of the South*, were published in Britain. British abolitionists organized a Free-Produce Movement in order to end British use of slave-produced products and thus indirect British support of American slavery. They were in large part inspired by the logic of black American abolitionist Henry Highland Garnet: "the cotton which we used, the sugar with which we sweetened our tea, and the rice which we ate, were actually spread with the sweat of the slaves, sprinkled with their tears . . . until an early grave relieved them from their misery."[5]

William Lloyd Garrison and Immediate Abolitionism

Two years before he was present in Britain when Parliament abolished slavery, William Lloyd Garrison published the first issue of the *Liberator* in Boston, Massachusetts. No longer seeking the gradual or eventual end of slavery, the twenty-five-year-old former colonizationist was demanding the immediate end of a sinful institution that denied men and women their natural rights. For abolitionists such as he, slavery was a moral wrong—not just an imperfect economic and social system—that clashed with both the ideals underlying the Declaration of Independence and the precepts of Christianity. It made "angels weep."[6] Those who enslaved others were sinners. In fact, slavery was a national sin and not acting against slavery made one "the consentor to & the abettor of the mansteler's sin."[7] Calamity and doom—sent by God and initiated by slaves—awaited the South if slave owners refused to act, although Garrison and other like thinkers opposed violence and frequently said so, urging abolition as a way to prevent violence and criticizing abolitionists who used force even, as in the case of Elijah P. Lovejoy, who was killed by an anti-abolitionist mob, in their own defense. This view of slavery meant one significant change from British abolition efforts: the Americans would not accept compensated emancipation. To do so would be to reward sin.

For Garrison, and even those with whom he would soon split over a variety of disagreements, colonization had once "seemed the only way out," but, thanks to black opposition to emigration, the antebellum abolitionists determined "that the bedrock issue was racial equality,"[8] thus negating a solution which removed the allegedly inferior black from the country. Thus, while Benjamin Lundy, Quaker editor of the

Genius of Universal Emancipation for whom Garrison had worked, supported gradual emancipation and colonization (at least for certain purposes), Garrison announced in the first edition of the *Liberator* that "I will not equivocate . . . I will not retreat a single inch—AND I WILL BE HEARD" on immediate abolition.[9]

The *Liberator* was not the first, only, or last anti-slavery publication. But due to its timing, its militancy, its demands, and the availability of abolitionist ideas through cheap postal rates, the growing number of newspapers linked it after August 1831 to the most devastating slave uprising in American history: Nat Turner's. Despite the fact that Garrison and abolitionists in general expected the end of slavery to come with changed public opinion—not with violence or through national laws—and that they believed a modified moral view would lead Southerners to end slavery without colonization or compensation, abolitionists and their writings drew the concerned attention of those fearful of and expecting the next slaughter. And for good reason. The immediate emancipation which they demanded did not necessarily, at least in the early years, mean that their practical goal was abolition overnight, but it certainly stood for what should be done, in their eyes, in response to the sin of slavery. It was a statement of determination to accept no compromise with evil, to take immediate steps to end white oppression of blacks.

Until Southerners pointed a collective finger at Garrison, he had garnered little attention or interest, much less support, in the North. This was true even though slavery's opponents, with increasingly little room to operate in the South, were concentrating their writings, speeches, and petitioning in the nonslave states of the North. He was one of many reformers, and his target of reform was one in which few Northerners took an interest. Even in their hometown of Boston, the *Liberator* and its editor were generally unknown until he began his attack on the American Colonization Society. Historian Aileen Kraditor has called abolitionism in the period after 1831 "a tiny and despised movement."[10] Reasons were obvious. Abolitionists of the 1830s, unlike those who preceded them, were uncompromising, tenacious, fervent, and provocative. Gone were moderation and gentility. They challenged the American order.

For most northern whites, slavery was a norm in their country. So too was black inferiority, which was ordained by God; whites knew blacks to be "an inferior and degraded class, who never could be made good and useful citizens."[11] For anti-blacks—that is, for most northern whites—abolitionism meant black assimilation, and assimilation meant amalgamation. Because those enslaved were inferiors whose freedom would threaten white society, abolition was a dangerous cause advocated by radicals, not a moral crusade advanced by forward-thinking moderates. Plus, linking abolitionist societies with the British abolitionist movement suggested foreign interference with domestic institutions. In addition, many northern businesses and jobs were tied to the slave economy of the South, particularly in such port cities as New York, and white workers feared that abolition would prompt black movement north and lead to job competition. Working-class whites feared that black progress would come at the white man's expense, especially given the economic panics and depressions that marked the antebellum years. Opposing slavery meant opposing the economic success—as well as the social stability—of the nation; opponents of slavery, therefore, were easily seen as dangerous and destructive.

Whether immediatists believed in true immediate abolition or supported immediate steps to eventual abolition, according to their critics, their goal and their approach to it threatened to make calm discussion and coexistence impossible. The New York *Commercial Advertiser* castigated the abolitionists in 1835 for "having distracted churches, destroyed the peace of families and communities, embarrassed the literary and religious institutions, menaced the property and even the existence of the union, involved the officers of our government in dangerous perils, and created the most appalling apprehensions of a civil and servile war."[12] As the president of Brown University wrote Garrison, "The tendency of your remarks is to prejudice [slave-owners'] minds against a cool discussion of the subject."[13] Southerners were not going to permit interference with their labor/social institution; thus, demands that slavery be abolished were tantamount to supporting the destruction of the Union. In addition, because slavery was a constitutionally and legally supported labor and social system, arguments for its abolition were arguments against the Constitution and the Union.

Because of these northern views, historian Benjamin Quarles has described the life of an abolitionist as one of "economic reprisals, a freezing of one's credit, a loss of employment, or a blacklisting of one's name."[14] By advocating black rights and acting on their principles—es-

corting blacks to meetings, attending black weddings and parties—
abolitionists were disowned by their families, faced demands for the
immediate repayment of loans, and endured physical attacks on themselves and their property.

Goals and Strategies

With the publication of the first edition of the *Liberator* came the
formation in 1832 of the New England Anti-Slavery Society by a dozen
white men, including Garrison and New York businessmen Arthur and
Lewis Tappan, in a schoolroom below a black church in Boston. "Fruit
of white-black collaboration,"[15] the organization differed from previous
groups in the direction that it pushed and in its inclusion of black members. The society broke from the thinking that slavery's end could come
gradually and with the removal of blacks from the country. That step
was marked by Garrison's publication of *Thoughts on African Colonization* (1832). Attacking the idea that blacks were "of inferior capacity,"
he prophesied great accomplishments for blacks once "the mists of
prejudice" disappeared.[16] He also attacked colonization and the American Colonization Society despite his early support of both. In fact, in
1831 Garrison gave only one-tenth the space in the *Liberator* to supporting abolition that he gave to attacking colonization, part of the reason why Northerners found his cause so threatening: for them,
colonization provided an anti-slavery and a racial answer. With blacks'
opposition to colonization highlighted in part two of *Thoughts on
African Colonization*, the publication undermined much of the support
for the ACS.

In December 1833 various anti-slavery societies met in Philadelphia to form the American Anti-Slavery Society (AASS), a step inspired
in part by the organizations which Garrison had witnessed in 1831 during his British visit. Sixty-three delegates, including three blacks, met
to take a stand against slavery and for the equality of blacks. The
founders, a third of whom were Quakers (including four women),
agreed upon a Declaration of Sentiments and named a board of man-
agers that included six blacks. Their initial task was to educate the public. Their strategy was conversion through "moral suasion." Petitions,
speakers, publications, and special agents would spread the word of

slavery's sin. In its first years, the AASS was the glue uniting various state and local societies and auxiliaries.

Developing in abolitionists' writings and early organizations was a commitment to the belief that racial prejudice and slavery were complementary ills. As the AASS's constitution of 1832 stated, these abolitionists aimed not just to end slavery or to end the problem of a biracial nation, as colonizationists sought to do, but to eliminate white prejudice against blacks and, as a result of doing so, to "obtain for [blacks] equal civil and political rights and privileges with the whites."[17] They believed that the irrationality of prejudice could be defeated, particularly by Christian faith in man's goodness and his equality before God.

Nevertheless, abolitionists generally did see racial differences between whites and blacks, most often citing an environmental explanation. In tune with their times, they tended to see white men as the personification of maleness—intellectual, aggressive, assertive—and black men as having feminine traits—emotional, submissive, peaceful. It was a time, however, which admired sentimentality, and the blacks' alleged docility, patience, and passivity (even to the point of not rising up against slavery) were seen as praiseworthy. According to abolitionists, the races were different, but God made them all, and he made each with its own rights. In addition, all men shared an innate moral sense, a conscience about right and wrong, regardless of their intellectual differences; this meant that everyone had the potential to control his own life regardless of his intellect. Environmental influences such as slavery itself, not God-ordained inferiority, made blacks prone to disreputable behavior, such as thievery and laziness (just as slavery turned whites into proud, arbitrary, cruel, adulterous murderers). Worried, however, that this explanation would absolve individuals from responsibility for their actions, most abolitionists discounted it for slave owners while explaining slaves' behavior as being a result of their enslavement. They argued that blacks were capable of improvement and progress and that slavery, not innate inferiority, limited them. As Lydia Maria Child, a noted author and abolitionist, explained the abolitionists' hopes in 1839, "I would not select an ignorant man, of any complexion, for my companion; but when you ask me whether that [poor, uneducated, black] man's children shall have as fair a chance as my own, to obtain an education, and rise in the world, I should be ashamed of myself, both as a Christian and a republican, if I did not say, yes, with all my heart."[18]

Perceived racial differences did not stop abolitionists from making their movement an interracial one. Garrison, for example, employed blacks, presented lectures to them, traveled with them, stayed at their homes, and welcomed them to his. The *Liberator* ran notices of blacks' lectures, including those of Maria W. Stewart, usually hailed as the first American-born woman to lecture publicly. Abolitionist papers published black speeches, essays, and poems, ran advertisements for black stores, and editorially encouraged white patronage of these businesses. The publications carried notices of black civic affairs and even marriages. In addition, abolitionists fought to end segregation in churches, schools, and travel. But their belief in racial differences did undermine many of their efforts. Often patronizing, paternalistic, and condescending (as was typical of the upper class in the nineteenth century), they were comfortable only with educated, successful free blacks (and only with educated, successful men in general) such as Philadelphia businessman James Forten and, in time, the former slave Frederick Douglass. Broader northern racism was responsible for much of the problem. As New York abolitionist Arthur Tappan explained the complex racial and social situation facing abolitionists, "though I would willingly . . . have publicly associated with a well educated and refined colored person, male or female, I felt that their best good would be promoted by refraining from doing so till the public mind and conscience were more enlightened on the subject."[19] Theodore Dwight Weld explained to Tappan's brother Lewis that he would not walk publicly with a black woman "because to do it would bring down a storm of vengeance upon the defenceless people of Color, throw them out of employ, drive them out homeless, and surrender them up victims to popular fury."[20] Defiance of white social taboos also risked undermining the goal of abolition; abolition would be linked with amalgamation and social equality.

Regardless of racial realities, abolitionists saw slavery as the worst of all sins, with support or even acceptance of it violating Christian principles. Their advocacy of Christian egalitarian values required that they attack as sinners anyone who did not condemn slavery. According to Garrison, "Pennsylvania is as really a slave-holding State as Georgia" because nonslave states were "agents" for slave ones.[21] Acclaimed abolitionist orator Wendell Phillips noted that "our fate is bound up with that of the South, so that they cannot be corrupt and we sound; they cannot fall, and we stand."[22] As abolitionists who sold and bought "free" products—items not produced in any way by slave labor—argued, those who did not own slaves could nevertheless act in ways that supported slavery.

While some supporters of slavery argued that true freedom meant the ownership of productive property, abolitionists found freedom in the ability to contract one's labor. For them, wage labor was not, as many believed at the time, the virtual equivalent of slavery—with both wage laborer and slave being coerced into involuntary labor—but was the manifestation of true freedom. (Perhaps this was why the abolitionists generally concerned themselves little with the exploitation of the white working man, or perhaps their lack of interest was because they were not fundamentally opposed to the developing commercial, capitalist society.) Self-ownership made contracting one's labor (a type of property) possible. Northerners and Southerners agreed that "contract marked the line between freedom and bondage."[23] By law, slaves could not contract; they did not own themselves—they were not free. Escaped slave Frederick Douglass asserted that freedom to him meant "appropriating my own body to my use."[24]

Abolitionists also noted how slavery violated the marriage contract and violated female purity. It denied black men their job as masters of their homes and protectors (and, essentially, owners) of their wives. Abolitionist speaker and writer Angelina Grimké noted in 1836 that slavery *"robs the slave of all his rights as a man,"* including "wages, wives, children." It also involved "fornication, adultery, [and] concubinage" and the exposure and handling of women's bodies.[25] Slave women were, in an argument new with some abolitionists, denied property in themselves and thus denied their status as free people; abolition would bring self-ownership to women as well as men.

All of this meant that abolitionists had many reasons for wanting to convince whites to accept the sin of slavery and reject the crime of denying blacks their inherent rights and their coverage by the principles of the Declaration of Independence. Through reasoned critiques, emotional polemics, and factual treatises, each reformer was a teacher and a preacher of morality and rights. Armed with confidence, sincerity, and an unbending faith in their inevitable success, they were determined to "[bring] heaven and earth together."[26]

In the abolitionist's mind, whites did not understand either why they discriminated or the impact of their actions. The abolitionists, therefore, saw their job as educating both blacks for freedom and whites for equal treatment of blacks. Whites, who had limited familiarity with slavery or free blacks, needed to learn of the impact of the "moral pestilence" of slavery and of the accomplishments of free blacks. Whites would then see what blacks were capable of and would realize that "color phobia was irrational, antirepublican, and blasphemous."[27]

Churches and Abolitionism

Such would not be an easy task, even by calling on Christian principles. Although Southerners argued that abolitionism "derive[d] its whole strength from the religious influence of the North,"[28] most northern whites and most northern churches did not share the abolitionists' view that the holding of blacks as slaves was a sin and that churches must act against it as they would against other sins. Despite a brief post-Revolutionary move to natural rights and equality, most denominations whether liturgical or evangelical saw the need for no more than supporting colonization and missionary work among slaves. For many churches, the goal was generally to reform slavery, not to end it. Some supported slavery as based in Scripture, some saw it as a strictly secular matter, some asserted the need to accommodate the views and practices of southern churchgoers, and some focused on a holiness that came from within and not from reforming others. Most northern churches rejected abolition's argument that slave owners were sinners, seeing holding slaves as a neutral fact that had to be evaluated on a case-by-case basis or as an imperfection in imperfect men. Connecticut Congregationalist Horace Bushnell lamented in 1839, "If there was ever a people on earth involved in crime, yet who deserved sympathy and gentleness at the hand of the good, it is the slaveholding portion of our country" who inherited the institution.[29] Even abolitionist publications of the 1830s labeled slave owners as victims as well as sinners.

Charles Grandison Finney, the famed revivalist who worried "that we are in our present course going fast into civil war," urged abolitionists to make the end of slavery part of a "general revival of religion" so that "the public mind can be engrossed with the subject of salvation." Failure to change people's moral beliefs would lead to "a wave of blood over the land."[30] The Reverend Lyman Beecher's daughter Catherine also saw the abolitionists as pushing too hard when they "trie[d] to coerce rather than persuade public opinion."[31] A St. Louis judge agreed that the abolitionists had a religious motivation but needed to modify their ways: "They seem to consider themselves as special agents . . . [with] their eyes fixed on some mystic vision—some Zion . . . within whose holy walls they would impound us all, or condemn us to perish on the outside."[32]

Tied in the southern mind to a perverted, unorthodox, false, heretical northern religion, abolitionism as presented by Garrison and others in the 1830s was a clear threat, however much it was and remained the view of a tiny number of Americans. Abolitionists were the Antichrist. Abolitionists, not slave owners, were the sinners; anti-slavery, not slavery, was immoral. Slavery and black inferiority were God's way; therefore, abolitionists "were in effect anti-God and anti-Bible."[33] According to South Carolina minister James Henley Thornwell in 1850, "the world is the battleground—Christianity and Atheism the combatants."[34] For him and many other Southerners, their Bible provided sanction for slavery and support for racial inequality, not for abolition.

The abolitionists, however, far from being anti-God or antireligion were based in a religious tradition. Inspired by the revivalism of the early 1800s, they went beyond standard Biblical references of Protestantism, and they argued that in failing to respond to slavery the churches were failing in their Christian duty. Both moderate and radical abolitionists charged that churches were the protectors of slavery. By 1840 many abolitionists were so frustrated by the use of religion to support slavery, by the churches' refusal to stand against slavery, by the focus of revivals on building membership rather than reforming society, and by sectarian partisanship that they doubted that religion and a general conversion from sin would play (or was necessary to play) a defining role in the institution's demise. Garrison was extreme in his argument that the clergy were part of a slavery plot, but he was simply on the far end of a common position. As Weld and his wife Angelina Grimké saw it, the clergy was guilty of "truckling subserviency to power" and "clinging with mendicant sycophancy to the skirts of wealth and influence."[35]

Lewis Tappan, a Unitarian who returned to his original Congregationalism, was one of the abolitionist critics of denominational and interdenominational benevolent organizations. Such groups upset abolitionists because they accepted donations from slave owners and allowed these men to serve as officers and agents. Plus, the groups did not speak or act against slavery. The abolitionists were particularly upset with the American Board of Commissioners for Foreign Missions (ABCFM) and the American Home Missionary Society, both of which stepped carefully to avoid affecting southern donations. In response, abolitionists formed anti-slavery missionary groups, including, in 1846, the American Missionary Association (AMA), which refused contributions from and association with slave owners.

In similar fashion, abolitionists found fault with the American Tract Society (ATS) and the American Bible Society (ABS). The ATS failed to publish tracts against slavery and even to allude to anti-slavery in its publications. According to former slave and abolitionist William Wells Brown, the ATS gave a prize "for the best essay against the 'vice' of dancing" but "never published a word against the system of slavery."[36] The result was the American Reform Tract and Book Society, formed in 1851. The new organization published religious literature that related to the moral questions involved with slavery. The ABS, for its part, refused to distribute Bibles to slaves even though its goal was a Bible in every family. In response, abolitionist members began a "Bibles for Slaves" drive but little change came about.[37]

By the mid-1840s some abolitionists were refusing to receive communion with slaveholders and withdrawing from churches whose members included slave owners or those who refused to take a stand against slavery and slave owners; Parker Pillsbury and Stephen S. Foster found it necessary to interrupt services with anti-slavery pronouncements. Churches argued that ejecting slave owners would free them from the church's enlightening influence. Still, Baptists, Methodists, and Presbyterians sometimes expelled slave-owning church members, and disagreements over abolitionism contributed to the splits within the Baptist and the Methodist churches in the mid-1840s.

State versus National Power

To most Americans, there was a clear line separating the jurisdiction, responsibilities, and powers of the national and state governments. Few, if any, questioned that slavery was in the state sphere and could not be touched by national power (except for the international slave trade, probably slavery in the territories, and implicitly putting down slave insurrections); only the southern states could end their slavery, and Northerners had no reason to share the guilt of slavery in a far-off place over which they had no power. Although the Declaration of Sentiments of the AASS acknowledged that the national government had no authority over slavery in the states, abolitionist views on the Constitution and slavery would change and vary over the years, particularly in the 1840s–1860s.

In the 1830s, while accepting the "federal consensus" of state power over slavery,[38] some abolitionists concluded that the Constitution did not put slavery totally outside the power of the national government and thus did not, yet again, absolve Northerners of guilt. Under the Constitution, Congress passed and enforced the Fugitive Slave Act of 1793, allowed slavery in the District of Columbia which it controlled, and permitted slavery in the area below the 36° 30' line of the Missouri Compromise. In fact, abolitionists' linkage of slavery to Congress through the District of Columbia was the motivation behind many of the petitions sent to Congress in the mid- and late-1830s, petitions that prompted the passage of the Gag Rule in 1836. Organized for the AASS by Theodore Dwight Weld, John Greenleaf Whittier, and Henry B. Stanton, the campaign distressed Southerners and Northerners although it hardly made abolitionists out of the two million who signed petitions in 1838–1839 or out of those concerned about restricting white civil liberties.

Anti-Abolitionism

Throughout the antebellum period, northern whites saw the abolitionists as disruptive and divisive. In fact, the North led the South in the production of anti-abolitionist materials in the 1830s. While abolitionists disclaimed violence, those who opposed them used any and every means of attack. As historian Paul Goodman argues, "Abolitionism grew . . . in the teeth of elite hostility, intense popular prejudice, and physical violence."[39] Anti-abolitionist mobs, generally planned by and including "gentlemen of property and standing,"[40] were frequent in the North. In violence's peak year of 1835, almost four dozen riots

occurred against abolitionists or related to black status, about half of
them in the North.

Anti-abolitionist mobs roamed through many northern towns attacking black property and supporters, often inspired by fears of miscegenation. Garrison himself was attacked by a mob in Boston in 1835
and dragged through the streets until jailed overnight for his own protection. In New York, the home of Lewis Tappan was attacked, as were
numerous black churches and schools, homes and businesses. The
AASS's postal campaign in the South prompted death threats against
both Lewis and Arthur Tappan and other AASS officials. Aimed at the
southern slave owner, not the slave, the campaign was not unlike other
reform campaigns of the period; however, Southerners saw the attack
on slavery as equivalent to an attack on the Union and thus in need of
northern response, which included mobbing.

When Prudence Crandall insisted in 1833–1834 on operating a
school for black girls in Canterbury, Connecticut, she was harassed and
her schoolhouse and her home attacked. Philadelphia's Pennsylvania
Hall was burned to the ground three days after it opened in May 1838,
the destruction prompted by the interracial meeting ("social amalgamation") there of the Anti-Slavery Convention of American Women.[41]
The mayor and the fire companies did nothing to stop the mob or save
the building. Anti-abolitionist violence culminated in the shooting
death of Elijah P. Lovejoy, a Presbyterian minister and abolitionist editor. In late 1837 a mob attacked his anti-slavery newspaper, the
Observer, in Alton, Illinois, a town which had seen itself as progressive,
even admitting black and white children equally into its schools. It had
welcomed Lovejoy in 1836 before he became openly anti-slavery and
pro-AASS and before he helped organize a local abolition society.

For many observers, the abolitionists were responsible for the violence directed at them: their aberrant views on race and slavery threatened the South and thus the nation. Violent response was logical. The
Cincinnati *Republican* announced that "the reckless and unprincipled
fanatics" deserved the attacks on them for challenging "popular sentiment."[42] In 1835 James Gordon Bennett, editor of the New York *Herald*,
explained that "a few thousand crazy-headed blockheads" so frightened
the nation "that the ordinary operation of laws against evil doers [in
general] are thrown aside."[43] Less concerned with slavery than with the
state of American society, Northerners were seeking to maintain a bal-

anced and conservative order. Abolitionism was fanaticism, not a legitimate reform movement. It threatened society and "the bonds of union."[44] It was "a sedition against religion, republicanism, harmony, deference, and benevolence."[45] Abolitionism "menaced the union, tottering on the verge of dissolution."[46]

Pressure for modification—or, better yet, silence—came not just from violence. Even as they acknowledged slavery to be evil, city meetings throughout the North sought to restrict abolitionist "fanatics" and "madmen."[47] In 1836, the House of Representatives, despite the First Amendment's provision on the right to petition the government, imposed the "Gag Rule" requiring that "all petitions, memorials, resolutions propositions, or papers, relating in any way, or to any extent whatever, to the subject of slavery, or the abolition of slavery" be tabled.[48] It made the restriction permanent in 1840 despite the determined opposition of Representative and former president John Quincy Adams, who was not an abolitionist. Also on the national level, Postmaster General Amos Kendall called the destruction of abolitionist mail "a palpable self-defense" and "patriotism" because it protected "community" from "perverted" higher law.[49] President Andrew Jackson asked Congress in 1835 to deny mailing privileges to "incendiary publications intended to instigate the slaves to insurrection," even though abolitionist literature (along with kerchiefs, medals, and emblems) was addressed to whites, not illiterate slaves.[50]

Abolitionism was thus clearly intense and unpopular work; however, while its numbers stayed small, it had some successes in the 1830s for at least a couple of reasons. Reaching thousands of Northerners were a varied group of abolitionist publications, as well as speeches. Some explained the sin of slavery; some focused on the economic and psychological harm the institution created. Lydia Maria Child's *An Appeal in Favor of That Class of Americans Called Africans* (1833) centered its attack on the denial of human dignity and potential and on the environmental circumstances that led whites to be racist. Angelina Grimké's *Appeal to the Christian Women of the South* (1836) challenged Biblical arguments in support of slavery and sought to clarify the beliefs, methods, and goals of abolitionists. Theodore Dwight Weld's *American Slavery as It Is* (1839) used Southerners' own words to prove the brutality and inhumanity of slavery, providing tales of whipping and branding, slave catching and selling, and destruction of families.

In similar fashion, James G. Birney's *The American Churches: The Bulwarks of American Slavery* (1840) allowed Presbyterian, Methodist, and Baptist ministers to speak in support of slavery and attempt to explain how Christianity permitted slavery. Dozens of narratives by escaped and former slaves revealed slavery's inhumanity, its harmful effects on whites, and the potential of black Americans.

In large part because of these writings and such skilled speakers and organizers as Theodore Dwight Weld and Parker Pillsbury, abolitionism drew members from the middle class despite the opposition it received from this class. Its "moral suasion" of speeches and pamphlets won over perhaps as many as 140,000 by the late 1830s. Through local societies, supporters paid dues, sought to discover the best candidates for office, circulated petitions, and organized abolitionist lectures. Attacks on abolitionists' rights of speech, press, assembly, and petition also raised concern, if not among AASS membership, among some non-abolitionist Northerners about how far the nation should go and who would pay the price for protecting and placating southern slave owners.

Black Abolitionists

As long as slavery existed, the freedom and rights of black Americans would be limited and transient. As the Reverend Joshua Easton explained to the white members of the Massachusetts Anti-Slavery Society in 1837, if slavery and "the spirit which makes color a mark of degradation" were not both attacked, "the spirit of slavery will survive, in the form of prejudice, after the system is overturned."[51] In similar fashion, Theodore S. Wright told the New England Anti-Slavery Society in 1836 that "prejudice is slavery"; it "must be killed or slavery will never be abolished."[52]

Thus, in the 1820s free blacks—frequently ministers and well educated—formed organizations aimed at abolition and in 1830 began a decades-long convention movement supporting equal rights. Delegates sought national coordination and unity. They discussed emigration, temperance, and education. Blacks also formed the broad-ranging American Moral Reform Society. More concrete in their goals than white abolitionists, they were tackling practices that made them "slaves to the community":[53] segregated schools and transportation, limits on their rights to testify, restrictions on their right to serve on juries and in state militias, discriminatory practices by employers and white churches, and disfranchisement. Suffrage, according to some blacks, would define their freedom and equality.

The abolitionist demand for immediate emancipation and racial equality grew in large part out of African Americans' largely ignored efforts to challenge the inconsistencies between white practices and white ideals, especially those associated with the Revolution. In addition, blacks' words in *Thoughts on African Colonization* forced readers to confront what blacks thought about their treatment. As English observer Harriet Martineau argued in 1839, colonization efforts "originated abolitionism" when it stirred free blacks to respond.[54]

These men and women were the inspiration for the white abolitionists, and they provided significant support in the 1830s for the widely unpopular abolitionist societies. Blacks were the majority of the subscribers to the *Liberator* (75 percent in 1834). They were also agents for the paper, as well as financial backers individually and as groups. Some blacks served as unofficial body guards for threatened white colleagues; several named their sons after Garrison. By the 1840s, blacks who had escaped southern slavery, most notably Frederick Douglass and William Wells Brown, were major figures on the abolitionist lecture circuit. Through their speeches and their written narratives, they were proof of the humanity and potential of those enslaved; they conveyed the brutality of slavery and made compelling arguments for the debt that white America owed slaves for the latter's labor.

Particularly in the 1830s, white abolitionists encouraged blacks to improve themselves in order to counter claims of inferiority. As Garrison explained, "Till they are equal to other people in knowledge and cultivation, they will not and cannot rank as equals."[55] Blacks agreed with the need for evidence of black achievement. As Richard Allen of the African Methodist Episcopal church argued, "If we are lazy and idle, the enemies of freedom plead it as a cause why we ought not to be free."[56] Sharing a view of white society and culture as superior, black abolitionist leaders, such as Douglass, believed in black uplift and encouraged continuation of self-help organizations aiming at temperance, education, care of widows and children, and jobs.

Blacks, however, also believed that they should play an activist abolitionist role. A convention in Hartford, Connecticut, in 1840 unanimously adopted a resolution stating that "we cannot delegate the protection of our rights to others in any such sense as to relieve us of the measure." In Boston in 1840 another resolution announced that while blacks "fully approve of the course pursued by our [white] friends, we nevertheless feel it a duty incumbent upon us to labor unceasingly for ourselves."[57] The *Colored American* of 1839 added a different perspective: "As long as we let [white abolitionists] think and act for us, . . . so long they will outwardly treat us as men, while in their hearts they still hold us as slaves."[58]

Their concerns led blacks to both integrated abolition societies and all-black auxiliaries. Because many white Americans viewed membership in benevolent societies as limited to the elite and by invitation only and because racial equality did not necessitate integration, white abolitionists faced criticism from blacks for not doing more to help, including hiring blacks for work in abolitionist societies. Black members of the AASS served on committees and offered resolutions, but some blacks' demands for more led to the formation of their own groups. Although all-black societies were targeted as encouraging prejudice and discrimination, such organizations appeared from Massachusetts to Michigan. Some invited white members, some were limited to women, and some were for children and adolescents. Their goal was to support white efforts or, in response to limits on their decision making roles in white organizations and to the impractical methods and abstract goals of whites, to push for more aggressive strategies and more practical steps.

Black abolitionists in white-led organizations tended to oppose distractions such as women's rights and to oppose the factionalism that developed by the end of the 1830s. As the divisions within white abolitionism became greater, blacks were often caught in the middle. Failure to adhere to the "party line" of Garrison's supporters or of the more moderate Tappanite abolitionists made blacks vulnerable to accusations that they were unfit for policy making, that they did not understand the complexities of more abstract issues, that their goals were too narrow or too self-interested, or that they were disloyal—all explanations with racist undertones.

Regardless of these problems, black abolitionists joined whites in celebrating British achievements in abolishing slavery. They also took advantage of a receptive British audience, traveling to Britain to meet, plan, build support, raise funds, and lecture, sometimes to crowds of thousands. Despite difficulties in obtaining passports, black abolitionists crossed the Atlantic and, with rare exception, impressed their hosts who treated them cordially and with respect. One British newspaper commented in 1854 that "if these are not men, where shall they be found?"[59] The British, facing no economic or social threat from the temporary visitors, demonstrated strong anti-slavery views. They gave American blacks a taste of life without, or with a minimum of, racial prejudice.

Women and Abolitionism

Women boldly attended the AASS organizational meeting and abolitionist and feminist Lucretia Mott had spoken there, but no woman signed the Declaration of Sentiments, and until 1840 they played limited roles in organized and male-dominated anti-slavery. Still, welcomed into abolitionism by William Lloyd Garrison, they formed auxiliary organizations even before the AASS's 1833 founding, a major step for a segment of the population traditionally excluded from such serious public work. In 1832 the first women's anti-slavery society was formed in Massachusetts: the Female Anti-Slavery Society of Salem. It was also the first organized by free black women. The next year saw the formation of the first anti-slavery society by black and white women: the Philadelphia Female Anti-Slavery Society.

By the 1830s women from well-to-do families had gained greater access to education, but women's participation in public activities was considered to be unfeminine and inappropriate, a threat to society, to the family, and to men. Men and women were seen as inherently different, with women less aggressive, physically weaker, and less intelligent but superior in terms of piety, intuition, sexual purity, submissiveness, and child-rearing ability. Their place was the private, domestic sphere. Despite societal pressures, some women did become involved in reform activities relating to the family and home; however, even these activities sometimes provoked opposition and violence.

Women who moved into men's political sphere, including public speaking, and who threatened the social order by opposing slavery faced "social ostracism, persecution, slander, [and] insult."[60] Fighting against slavery put women in a position "to overthrow government, civil and domestic, the Sabbath and the church and ministry."[61] Abolitionism was seen as unacceptable for women, although women pointed to the slave home, the enslavement of African women, and the slave woman's chastity (the last a topic that raised questions about a speaker's own sexual purity); women had to act when other "women are brutalized, scourged, and sold."[62] A lecturer in Sangerville, Maine, urged women in New England to "arise . . . [and] call for the freedom and protection of their sisters in bonds."[63] Also important were the broader issues "of justice, of humanity, of morality, of religion."[64] As Maria Weston Chapman of Boston explained, "We deem there is nothing unfeminine in aiding our husbands, brothers, and sons, to support the principles they have adopted." She added that abolitionism was women's work because it meant being "a minister of Christian love," a clear reference to the religious base of many women's anti-slavery motivations.[65]

In the patriarchal society of the antebellum decades, women—white or black—who spoke before audiences, particularly those composed of both men and women, were being authoritative and demonstrating the masculine traits of virility and endurance. They were threatening the balance within the family. As one woman commented, "[I]f I was a man, how I would lecture. But I am a woman, and so I sit in the corner and knit socks."[66] Angelina Grimké, who became one of abolitionism's most effective speakers, explained in 1837 that she "used to say 'I wish I was a man, that I might go out and lecture' " but "the idea never crossed my mind that *as a woman* such work could possibly be assigned to me."[67] Women who spoke, with the exception of those who preached as a result of the revivalism of the Second Great Awakening and not because of any assertion of a new social order, were radical and disruptive.

Because of these gender barriers, abolitionist publications and speakers addressed women's issues and arguments against women's involvement in the crusade against slavery. In 1838 Sarah Grimké's *Letters on the Equality of the Sexes* called for men to "take their feet from off our necks"[68] as she responded to criticism of her public speaking as "a scandalous offense against propriety and decency."[69] Despite Grimké's demands, verbal abuse, ostracism, disgrace, and even violence met the abolitionist woman. In the city which housed the *Liberator*, the press referred to Boston's women abolitionists as "petticoat politicians," and a mob of white men menaced the members of the Boston Female Anti-

Slavery Society.[70] The overall antiwoman behavior led Angelina Grimké to decide that "it is not the cause of the slave only which we plead but the cause of Woman as a responsible & moral being. . . . What an untrodden path we have entered upon!"[71]

A growing sense of that path led some women to focus on their virtual slave status, as seen through three events, two tied directly to abolitionism. First, when the American women delegates to the World Anti-Slavery Convention meeting in London in 1840 were denied recognition and required to sit in the gallery as observers, male delegates, including Garrison, joined the women in the gallery in protest. Second, the women's treatment in London led to a women's rights convention in New York in 1848. Three hundred men, including Frederick Douglass, and women (all white) met in Seneca Falls and issued their own declaration of sentiments, including a radical demand for suffrage. Third, and occurring almost simultaneously with the 1840 London convention, male abolitionists' disagreement on the role of women in abolitionism and the emphasis which women's rights should be given in the campaign against slavery contributed to a schism in the abolitionist ranks.

For most black women, the abolitionist campaign was more direct and racially tied. They had long protested against discrimination and slavery, raised money for the support of black institutions such as schools and orphanages, and signed petitions. Slave women had run away and had filed freedom suits. Some had bought their freedom and that of family members. While no black woman (and no white) had been a member of revolutionary era anti-slavery societies, they formed the first women's anti-slavery society in 1832 in Salem, Massachusetts. Unlike white abolitionist women whose central concern was slavery, black women emphasized both slavery and equal rights for blacks.

Black women's participation in abolitionist societies threatened the American social order in two ways: it challenged standards for "respectable" women, particularly if they engaged in public speaking, and it challenged expectations of black deference to whites. Many black men shared white America's gender standards, including a disdain for women speakers, especially when they criticized black men. Those who exhibited such feminine traits as a "gentle and easy manner," according to the Washington *Times*, were more acceptable.[72] In the *North Star*, Frederick Douglass explained that women were expected to exhibit "the highest tone of purity and strictest observance of duties pertaining to woman's sphere." Philip A. Bell, another black abolitionist, argued that women who used "slang phrases and low personalities . . . must not expect to be treated with that courtesy which is universally paid to ladies."[73] These expectations were problems for women who often had to use physical force to protect themselves and other blacks.

The work of black and white women abolitionists continued into the 1840s and the 1850s. Their fundraising, distribution of propaganda, circulation of petitions, and pressuring of government leaders continued even as men moved from moral suasion to political action through the Liberty, Free Soil, and Republican parties. While formulating policy or strategy was seen as a man's role, women were involved in all aspects of the organization and propaganda of abolitionism, including support and operation of free produce stores, but they mainly circulated petitions and devised ways to raise money to be used by the male-only societies.

For the abolitionists, therefore, the 1830s was a decade of organization and hope, of commitment in the face of opposition. Men and women, blacks and whites were righteous crusaders against sin and failed republicanism. Moral suasion would convert churches and slave owners, northerners and businesses. They would quickly learn differently.

Notes

1. Merton L. Dillon, *The Abolitionists: The Growth of a Dissenting Minority* (DeKalb: Northern Illinois University Press, 1974), 30.

2. Peter J. Novak, *The People's Welfare: Law and Regulation in Nineteenth-Century America* (Chapel Hill: University of North Carolina Press, 1996), 2.

3. Quoted in Peter Kolchin, *American Slavery, 1619–1877* (New York: Hill and Wang, 1993), 188.

4. Joseph Woods, quoted in Judith Jennings, *The Business of Abolishing the British Slave Trade, 1783–1807* (London: Frank Cass, 1997), 37.

5. *The Anti-Slavery Reporter*, quoted in Joel Schor, *Henry Highland Garnet: A Voice of Black Radicalism in the Nineteenth Century* (Westport, CT: Greenwood, 1977), 117.

6. "Mr. Thome," quoted in Eliza Wigham, *The Anti-Slavery Cause in America and Its Martyrs* (London: A. W. Bennett, 1863), iv.

7. Amos A. Phelps, quoted in James B. Stewart, *Holy Warriors: The Abolitionists and American Slavery* (New York: Hill and Wang, 1976), 44.

8. Paul Goodman, *Of One Blood: Abolitionism and the Origins of Racial Equality* (Berkeley: University of California Press, 1998), xv.

9. Quoted in Russel B. Nye, *William Lloyd Garrison and the Humanitarian Reformers* (Boston: Little, Brown, 1955), 48.

10. Aileen S. Kraditor, *Means and Ends in American Abolitionism: Garrison and His Critics on Strategy and Tactics, 1834–1850* (1967; reprint, New York: Random House, 1969), 10.

11. Lydia Maria Child, quoted in John L. Thomas, ed., *Slavery Attacked: The Abolitionist Crusade* (Englewood Cliffs, NJ: Prentice-Hall, 1965), 68.

12. Quoted in Lorman Ratnor, *Powder Keg: Northern Opposition to the Antislavery Movement, 1831–1840* (New York: Basic Books, 1968), 71.

13. Quoted in Nye, *William Lloyd Garrison*, 51.

14. Benjamin Quarles, *Black Abolitionists* (1969; reprint, New York: Oxford University Press, 1977), 37.

15. Goodman, *Of One Blood*, 35.

16. Quoted in ibid., 55.

17. Quoted in ibid., 58.

18. Quoted in Thomas, *Slavery Attacked*, 67.

19. Quoted in Bertram Wyatt-Brown, *Lewis Tappan and the Evangelical War against Slavery* (Cleveland, OH: Press of Case Western Reserve University, 1969), 176.

20. Quoted in Robert C. Dick, *Black Protest: Issues and Tactics* (Westport, CT: Greenwood, 1974), 200.

21. Quoted in Lawrence J. Friedman, *Gregarious Saints: Self and Community in American Abolitionism, 1830–1870* (New York: Cambridge University Press, 1982), 27.

22. David F. Ericson, *The Debate over Slavery: Antislavery and Proslavery Liberalism in Antebellum America* (New York: New York University Press, 2000), 62.

23. Amy Dru Stanley, *From Bondage to Contract: Wage Labor, Marriage, and the Market in the Age of Emancipation* (Cambridge: Cambridge University Press, 1998), 19.

24. Quoted in ibid., 23.

25. Both quoted in ibid., 24, 29.

26. James Thome, quoted in Thomas, *Slavery Attacked*, 29.

27. Quoted in ibid., 69; Goodman, *Of One Blood*, 61.

28. John R. McKivigan and Mitchell Snay, eds., *Religion and the Antebellum Debate over Slavery* (Athens: University of Georgia Press, 1998), 1.

29. Quoted in Ratnor, *Powder Keg*, 103.

30. Quoted in ibid., 94–95, 101.

31. Quoted in David Grimsted, *American Mobbing, 1828–1865: Toward Civil War* (New York: Oxford University Press, 1998), 66.

32. Luke E. Lawless, quoted in Dillon, *The Abolitionists*, 75.

33. David B. Chesebrough, *Clergy Dissent in the Old South, 1830–1865* (Carbondale: Southern Illinois University Press, 1996), 12.

34. Quoted in ibid., 13.

35. Quoted in Ronald G. Walters, *The Antislavery Appeal: American Abolitionism after 1830* (Baltimore: Johns Hopkins University Press, 1976), 43.

36. Quoted in R.J.M. Blackett, *Building an Antislavery Wall: Black Americans in the Atlantic Antislavery Movement, 1830–1860* (Baton Rouge: Louisiana State University Press, 1983), 148.

37. Quoted in John R. McKivigan, *The War against Proslavery Religion: Abolitionism and the Northern Churches, 1830–1865* (Ithaca, NY: Cornell University Press, 1984), 124.

38. William M. Wiecek, *The Sources of Antislavery Constitutionalism in America, 1760–1848* (Ithaca, NY: Cornell University Press, 1977), 16.

39. Goodman, *Of One Blood*, 66.

40. Leonard L. Richards, *"Gentlemen of Property and Standing": Anti-Abolitionist Mobs in Jacksonian America* (New York: Oxford University Press, 1970).

41. Quoted in Margaret Hope Bacon, "By Moral Force Alone: The Antislavery Women and Nonresistance," in Jean Fagan Yellin and John C. Van Horn, eds., *The Abolitionist Sisterhood: Women's Political Cultures in Antebellum America* (Ithaca, NY: Cornell University Press, 1994), 286.

42. Quoted in Grimsted, *American Mobbing*, 60.

43. Quoted in Richards, *"Gentlemen of Property,"* 10.

44. Quoted in Larry E. Tise, *Proslavery: A History of the Defense of Slavery in America, 1701–1840* (Athens: University of Georgia Press, 1987), 277.

45. Ibid.

46. Letter in Cincinnati *Whig*, in Grimsted, *American Mobbing*, 60.

47. Ibid., 19.

48. Dwight Lowell Dumond, *Antislavery: The Crusade for Freedom in America* (1961; reprint, New York: Norton, 1979), 237.

49. Ibid., 23.

50. Kraditor, *Means and Ends*, 6.

51. Quoted in Dillon, *The Abolitionists*, 106.

52. Quoted in Dick, *Black Protest*, 202, 204.

53. David Ruggles, quoted in Gerald Sorin, *Abolitionism: A New Perspective* (New York: Praeger, 1972), 112.

54. Harriet Martineau, *The Martyr Age of the United States* (1839; reprint, New York: Arno Press and New York Times, 1969), 5.

55. Quoted in Friedman, *Gregarious Saints*, 166–167.

56. Quoted in Quarles, *Black Abolitionists*, 91–92.

57. Both quoted in Dick, *Black Protest*, 171, 172.

58. Quoted in Leon F. Litwack, "The Emancipation of the Negro Abolitionist," in Martin Duberman, ed., *The Antislavery Vanguard: New Essays on the Abolitionists* (Princeton, NJ: Princeton University Press, 1965), 144.

59. Quarles, *Black Abolitionists*, 129.

60. Elizabeth Chase, quoted in Julie Roy Jeffrey, *The Great Silent Army of Abolitionists: Ordinary Women in the Antislavery Movement* (Chapel Hill: University of North Carolina Press, 1998), 3.

61. Quoted in Debra Gold Hansen, "The Boston Female Anti-Slavery Society and the Limits of Gender Politics," in Yellin and Van Horne, *The Abolitionist Sisterhood*, 54.

62. Ruth Bogin and Jean Fagan Yellin, "Introduction," in Yellin and Van Horne, *The Abolitionist Sisterhood*, 8.

63. Quoted in Jeffrey, *The Great Silent Army*, 30.

64. Bogin and Yellin, "Introduction," 6.

65. Quoted in ibid., 7, 8.

66. Child, quoted in Jeffrey, *The Great Silent Army*, 34.

67. Quoted in Kathryn Kish Sklar, *Women's Rights Emerges within the Antislavery Movement, 1830–1870: A Brief History with Documents* (Boston: Bedford/St. Martin's, 2000), 93.

68. Quoted in Hansen, "The Boston Female Anti-Slavery Society," in Yellin and Van Horne, *The Abolitionist Sisterhood*, 52.

69. Massachusetts Association of Congregational Ministers, quoted in ibid., 53.

70. Quoted in ibid., 49.

71. Bogin and Yellin, "Introduction," 1.

72. Quoted in Shirley J. Yee, *Black Women Abolitionists: A Study in Activism, 1828–1860* (Knoxville: University of Tennessee Press, 1992), 119.

73. Quoted in ibid., 45.

CHAPTER 5

"CONTRARY TO THE LAWS OF GOD AND THE RIGHTS OF MAN": POLITICS VERSUS SPIRITUALITY— THE 1840s

The struggle over slavery was not just between abolitionists and those who owned slaves, supported slavery, or supported a (white) man's right to own human property. It was also among the abolitionists themselves as they fought over goals and methods.

The nation's expansion westward kept the argument over slavery and its related critical issues uppermost in the national debate. It also made slavery's supporters aggressive in their defense of the enslavement of blacks, in their promotion of slavery's expansion, and in their assertion of the nation's responsibility to protect and even promote slavery. While anti-expansionists fought to keep slavery from expanding and to keep southern Slave Power from greater control of the country, abolitionists continued their struggle to end both slavery and racial distinctions. For many in both groups, pamphlets, preaching, and prayer would be second in importance to politics in the 1840s, particularly on the national level, but that decision and others related to reform of the country were the source of nonending disagreement, bickering, name-calling, innuendoes, charges, and countercharges within abolitionism.

Internal Dissension

Almost from the beginning of and certainly by the late 1830s, disagreements existed within the American Anti-Slavery Society (AASS). The issues separating antebellum abolitionists were few but significant; they disagreed on the essential nature of American society and government and on the reform they sought, as well as on the best strategy for achieving it. The result was that abolitionists had what John L. Thomas has called "a civil war of their own."[1] A simplistic division would break abolitionists into the radical, anticlerical, perfectionist Garrisonians generally of New England and the moderate, church-oriented, evangelical Tappanites centered in New York. Abolitionists did not always fit neatly into one of the groups, and historians continue to debate the exact nature of abolitionists' disputes and whether their disagreements—over the status of American society, political action, women's roles and rights, the Constitution, the church, and even government in general—were more important and influential than their agreements.

The militant or radical group included William Lloyd Garrison and Wendell Phillips. Most Americans of the antebellum period might have defined abolitionism by their views, but they did not represent all abolitionists, and their beliefs played the key role in dividing the abolitionists. Social radicals, Garrisonians found fault in more than slavery and sought answers away from the political system and in the moral purification of the country. While slavery was a sin, it was not the only one, although it was the worst. These men (and women) were upset by Christian churches' acceptance of slavery (but not of the Christian religion itself) and thus their complicity in its continued existence; they supported breaking all ties with such institutions.

Garrisonians opposed the government, and they saw the political process as corrupt. They rejected office seeking and holding and would not themselves vote, even if they could cast ballots for anti-slavery candidates. They stood behind moral suasion, using propaganda to "abolitionize the consciences and hearts of the people."[2] As the Tennessee Society for Promoting the Manumission of Slaves (founded in 1814) and the Union Humane Society (founded in 1815) had concluded years earlier, casting votes for anyone other than a clear opponent of slavery was sharing in the guilt of slavery. Thus, because the Garrisonians op-

posed "the hostile origin and progress of the existing political organization" (part of their eventual policy of nonresistance), as well as "the
unworthy character of its leading influences," they opposed the Liberty
Party of 1840. They believed that "the scattering of votes" would "more
effectually influence the existing parties to act for our cause" than
would a third party.[3] By 1848, however, Garrison found the Free Soil
Party to have potential use.

The Garrisonians of the late 1830s and beyond concluded that
their nation's constitution, not just its political parties, made slavery
possible and even supported and promoted it, and, therefore, they
sometimes called for separation from the South (disunion). However
much the position might have been leverage for forcing the South to
end slavery itself by denying it federal power to handle slave uprisings,
it cost the Garrisonians support in the 1840s–1860s. Other abolitionists feared that the Union would split and slavery would continue; nonabolitionists simply feared for the Union itself. Aided in his ideas by
the publication of James Madison's notes on the constitutional convention, published in 1840, Garrison came to see the Constitution as
"a covenant with the devil and an agreement with hell."[4] As the Massachusetts Anti-Slavery Society proclaimed in 1840, the Constitution
required the forcible return of fugitive slaves, thus creating "the menial
and degrading duty of guarding the plantations of Southern slave-
masters." The Constitution also gave the slave South disproportionate
political power by allowing slave property to count toward the southern states' representation in Congress and by allowing slavery and the
slave trade in Washington, D.C. In addition, it permitted states to deny
blacks citizenship and to deny abolitionists "protection for our persons
or property." For Garrisonian abolitionists, the only response was to
"ABJURE OUR ALLEGIANCE TO THE CONSTITUTION OF THE
UNITED STATES AND THE UNION" because of its "unnatural and
unholy alliance between Liberty and Slavery." The professed goal of the
Massachusetts Anti-Slavery Society was to "break up this iniquitous alliance." According to Garrison, slavery foes had "to withdraw their allegiance from this compact [the Union], and by a moral and peaceful
revolution . . . effect its overthrow."[5] Non-Garrisonians were unhappy
that these extreme views were often seen as those of all abolitionists.

By the late 1830s a moderate group that included James G. Birney, a former Alabama slave owner, Joshua Leavitt, editor of the *Eman-*

cipator (published by the AASS), and Lewis Tappan, a wealthy New York businessman and reformer, had come to the conclusion that moral suasion was not sufficient and that a church-led reform attacking slavery was not going to occur, although neither approach should be abandoned. Unlike the Garrisonians, they desired a political strategy because politics offered a viable means of attacking slavery. For them, the Constitution and the government were tools against slavery and American society was essentially sound; only slavery truly stood in the way of a stronger, more moral nation. Churches, businessmen, and political parties simply needed reform when they put other obligations ahead of acting against slavery.

These abolitionists sought to work within the governmental system and to use political parties—the Democrats and the Whigs and, then, in 1840, the anti-slavery Liberty Party—to find a compromise anti-slavery platform that would attract both candidates and voters. Through political involvement, abolitionists could affect northern political thinking. Such was the view espoused by the *Abolitionist*, a weekly founded in 1839 in Massachusetts to counter the various "isms" that had infiltrated and allegedly corrupted the abolitionist message of Garrison's *Liberator*. William Goodell, editor of New York's abolitionist *Friend of Man*, asserted that "to talk of being an *abolitionist*, and not in favor of *political action* against slavery, is a contradiction in terms."[6] Birney was willing to accept the presidential nomination of the Liberty Party in 1840, arguing that abolitionists should vote against "any one . . . who is but the pliant minister of the Slave Power" in order to "rescue of the country from the domination of the Slave Power, and for the emancipation of the slaves."[7]

Political abolitionists sought to end the South's disproportionate political power in Congress, in the Electoral College, and in the appointment of Supreme Court justices. The result was the South's "hold[ing] the Union . . . as a conquered province."[8] Such an argument would become convincing to Northerners by the 1850s. Until then, Joshua Leavitt was clear on what must be done: because supporters of slavery were dishonest men who could not be persuaded to change their position, "WE MUST VOTE THEM DOWN." For the Maryland abolitionist, "the ONLY means . . . by which slavery can be annihilated without commotion, rapine, and indescribable woe" was the political process.[9]

Contributing to the debate over politics and strategy and compli-
cating the public's perception of abolitionism was Garrison's move to
nonresistance, what moderate abolitionist Henry B. Stanton in 1839
called "the crazy banner of the non-government heresy."[10] Garrisonian
nonresistants, who were a minority even in pro-Garrison abolitionist societies, held that political, governmental, and church systems created by
men were evil and impure, that they were based in and maintained by
coercion and violence. Only God was the source of law; neither human
government nor slave masters could rule human beings. Nonresistants
saw cooperation with the political system as contributing to the corrupt
status quo, and Garrisonian nonresistants opposed armies, conscription,
capital punishment, and jails, although Garrison never recommended
civil disobedience. They must not respond to violence with more violence. Most abolitionists and Americans in general disagreed with nonresistance, seeing licentiousness and anarchy as its logical results.

Also dividing the abolitionists was women's rights. Garrison stated
his position, and that of the AASS, clearly: "As our object is universal
emancipation,—to redeem woman as well as man from a servile to an
equal condition,—we shall go for the RIGHTS OF WOMAN to their
utmost extent."[11] The activities of abolitionist women, including sisters
Sarah and Angelina Grimké, and the response to them as behaving in-
appropriately and dangerously prompted the Garrisonians to place sexual inequality alongside racial inequality. Facing backlash from
churches and voters, they also had to worry about opposition from
within abolitionist ranks. For many non-Garrisonians, the goal of abolition was too important to risk by taking on the women's rights issue
or any of Garrison's other perfectionist goals. Abolitionism was radical
enough; adding Garrison's other issues caused "more mischief than
[Garrison's] neck is worth," according to Elizur Wright Jr. in 1837.[12]
The problem was much the same then as today: Garrison and abolitionism were so linked together in the public mind that the views of
the former were assumed to be the views of the latter.

Schism

Divisions within the AASS were clear by 1839 at the meeting of
the Massachusetts Anti-Slavery Society. Disputes over the role of political action, churches, women, nonresistance, and the *Liberator*'s edito-

rial direction inevitably surfaced in New York in May 1840 at the meeting of the American Anti-Slavery Society. Both sides were well-
represented as they sought to settle on a platform and the place of
political activity. Garrison used women delegates to block a resolution
critical of those who did not use voting as an abolitionist weapon and
to elect Abby Kelley, a Quaker teacher from Massachusetts and an AASS
lecturer, to the Executive Committee. The votes provoked the exodus
of Lewis Tappan and 400 moderate (male) delegates. In a nearby building they formed the purist, religious, political American and Foreign
Anti-Slavery Society (AFASS).

Tappan asserted that it was Garrison, not the women, who
prompted his action, a view that fit with Henry B. Stanton's belief that
Garrison had decided to "rule or ruin the antislavery cause" and Amos
A. Phelps's assertion that Garrison's "overgrown self-conceit had
wrought him into the belief that his mighty self was abolition incar-
nate."[13] The women's issue from their perspective was the spark, not
the cause, of the schism; Tappan accused Garrison, whom a majority
of women abolitionists supported, of "foist[ing] . . . the woman question." He interpreted the AASS constitution as allowing women members but as limiting "the *business*" to men. As Tappan clarified, "Women
have equal rights with men, and therefore they have a right to form societies of women only. Men have the same right. *Men* formed the Amer.
Anti S. Society [*sic*]."[14]

Abolitionists knew that the role of women in abolitionism was not
the single divisive issue. Garrison's antagonism to the clergy because of
their acceptance of slave owners and nonaction on slavery, his support
for a variety of radical reforms that diverted attention from abolitionism, and his general opposition to political action other than petitioning were as divisive. Amos Phelps spoke for many abolitionists when he
concluded that the AASS was "no longer an antislavery society, but in
its principles and modes of action a women's rights, non-government,
antislavery society" that required members to support "non-resistance,
women's rights, perfectionism, etc., too."[15] Upon breaking with Garrison, former slave Frederick Douglass defined Garrisonianism as "an
'ism' which comprehends opposition to the church, the ministry, the
Sabbath, and the Government as Institutions in themselves considered
and viewed apart from the question of Slavery."[16]

Now the nation had two opposing national abolitionist organizations (and soon three with the formation of the Liberty Party in 1840). Neither organization truly functioned nationally, organizations in the West operated fairly independently, local societies and individuals dominated, and each group and virtually each individual marched to a different drum. Although Lewis Tappan opposed the "sad sight" of "the friends of human rights contending angrily among themselves,"[17] that was in many ways the natural fate of abolitionism. The heyday of abolitionist organization was over, but the battle continued because abolitionists were, as Tappan indicated, bound together by a belief in human rights. All agreed that slavery must end. For a growing number of them during the 1840s, if moral suasion was not working and if the political system was, the choice was clear. Law had made slavery, and law would unmake it. Political power was in the hands of the slave South; thus, the original goal of changing southern morals became the goal of ending southern political power. With it would go slavery.

Churches and Come-Outers

The growing political focus of many abolitionists in the 1840s and 1850s did not eliminate the role of moral suasion or efforts to work with and through churches. Toward the former, both the AASS and the AFASS wrote articles, produced pamphlets, sent out speakers, and collected petitions. They continued to send agents to Britain to keep attention on and isolate American slavery; through their lectures, former slaves "diffuse[d] strange ideas of the peculiar institution."[18] Garrisonians also broadened their attack against the government and Constitution of the United States. The Tappan brothers, despite economic setbacks, provided support for social and educational efforts on behalf of fugitive and free blacks, as well as for nonslave communities in the South. As for the churches, Christian abolitionists held interdenominational anti-slavery conventions in an effort to turn mildly anti-slavery Christians into abolitionists and to spur anti-slavery politicians. In addition, abolitionists of all types seceded from established churches: the "come-outers."

Reasons for secession were obvious, if not convincing for all abolitionists. Because churches feared that discussion of slavery would be divisive, they ignored the efforts of abolitionist members to tackle the topic. The Methodists and the Baptists, however, divided regionally in the mid-1840s as a result of pro-slavery agitation. Some historians have

argued that anti-slavery also played a role in the division of the Presbyterians in 1837. Regardless of the reasons for the schisms, northern
branches generally varied little from their prebreak positions, even if
northern Methodists, who did not declare slave owning to be a sin and
did not bar slave owners from membership, refused to appoint slave
owners as missionaries and bishops.

Some church-going abolitionists, reflecting the views of the
AFASS, believed that churches could yet be converted to a key role in
the fight against slavery; others, anti-institutional abolitionists, saw no
hope in any church. The latter were part of a diverse group of abolitionists who believed that the established churches were unable to reform themselves and end their accommodation of slavery. In general,
both types of come-outers sought to save their own souls and to take
a stand against their church's failure to oppose slavery, although many
acted for reasons unrelated to slavery. They had perfectionist and abolitionist goals and sought to break from corrupt, coercive institutions.
Increasingly in the 1840s, the abolitionist come-outers created denominational anti-slavery organizations, such as the American Baptist
Anti-Slavery Convention, as well as interdenominational ones, including the American Missionary Association. The Wesleyan Methodist
Connection, which had close links to the latter, claimed as many as
15,000 members in the mid-1840s, many of them non-Methodist. Abolitionists James Birney, who published *The American Churches: The Bulwarks of American Slavery* in 1840, and Gerrit Smith were among those
who left the Presbyterian church, but others also left the Methodist and
Baptist churches.

Such groups as the Free Presbyterian Church and the American
Baptist Free Mission Society were traditional churches minus policies
and actions that tolerated slavery and racial prejudice. The former man-
dated that "no person holding slaves, or advocating the rightfulness of
slaveholding, can be a member of this body"; the latter's constitution
limited membership to those "who are not slaveholders, but who believe that involuntary slavery, under all circumstances, is sin, and treat
it accordingly."[19] Even Quakers, finding their church no longer interested in abolition and ready to punish members who were, formed
come-outer churches. Non-Garrisonian "come-outers" opposed nonresistance and disunion and advocated political action as part of a religious duty to oppose slavery. Garrisonians, in response, criticized

come-outers who did not make complete breaks with those still associating with or accepting slave owners.

The Liberty Party

Prior to 1838, abolitionist political action centered on effective voting. Abolitionists sent questionnaires to candidates to obtain their views on slavery-related issues. If no candidate responded appropriately, they scattered their votes randomly or they refrained from voting for any candidate. Whatever step they took, they would not be aiding abolition's opponents. In general, candidates could answer vaguely, ignore questions, or lie; plus, support pledged was not necessarily support given, especially because candidates and office holders had other issues to consider. In addition, few voting districts had sufficient abolitionists to wield decisive electoral power, and when the choice was not obvious, abolitionist voters often resorted to party loyalties at a time noted for its "unflinching adherence to party."[20] For some abolitionists, the Whigs seemed to offer an acceptable hope as their numbers included such slavery foes as John Quincy Adams of Massachusetts and Joshua Giddings of Ohio.

By the late 1830s both black and white abolitionists were discussing the need for an independent party that would allow them to vote only for slavery's opponents. (At the same time, Garrisonian abolitionists continued their opposition to political action and their preference for moral suasion. Garrison himself asserted that, at least for him, voting was a sin.) Both black and white opponents of a third party worried that such immersion in the political system would corrupt the pure, religious, moral ideals of abolitionism; the clergy would abandon a movement that associated with the corruption and self-interest of spoilsmen. Others argued that the step, while revealing abolitionism's small numbers and weaknesses, would antagonize the Whigs and Democrats. Anti-slavery Whigs, in fact, complained that the new party was likely to draw support away from them and give elections to the Democrats. To yet others, including Gamaliel Bailey, editor of the Cincinnati *Philanthropist*, a national party based on abolitionist goals was illogical and impossible: slavery was a state matter. In addition, such a party would soon fill with unprincipled and dishonorable men interested only in votes and whose provocative positions would push slaves to violence. Countering this argument was the one that saw an independent party avoiding corruption because of its temporary nature—slavery's end would mean the party's end; in fact, it would help purify American politics because of its "humane and holy object."[21]

The Liberty Party was created both as a (temporary) political party and as a religious crusade by men whom Douglas M. Strong labels "political eccentrics who practiced radical spirituality."[22] Its members criticized Christian abolitionists who continued voting for Whigs or Democrats as both were controlled by southern Slave Power; they argued that Christians who would not allow slave owners in their churches must "vote as they pray."[23] The Liberty Party of the 1840s focused its attack on slavery, but it broadly asserted why slavery needed to end. For example, the party stated that slavery impoverished the South, degraded working men in general by making labor undignified, and limited workers' opportunities. The party accepted that slavery in the states was constitutional, but it argued that the Constitution restricted the national government from supporting the institution. The Fifth Amendment, which barred Congress from denying life, liberty or property without due process, meant that the national government could not support slavery in the District of Columbia or in the territories and that it could not support the domestic slave trade. Liberty Party speakers explained slavery's limits much as Lord Mansfield had in *Somerset*: slavery ended its control of men and women when they left the state whose laws enslaved them. The party condemned both slavery and racial prejudice as against God's laws, calling slavery "a great question of public morality."[24] In addition, it urged churches to exclude slave-owning worshippers and pro-slavery ministers.

The party focused on the status and treatment of free blacks. Eager to undermine northern racism, it made two arguments: intelligent and capable blacks, including the former slave and abolitionist Frederick Douglass, disproved allegations of black inferiority, and slavery itself, not inherent racial differences, explained differences between whites and blacks. The party's position was that discriminatory state laws should end and that opportunities for black equality and rights—including suffrage and education—should be assured. Because they feared allegations of miscegenation, they avoided issues of social equality although they charged slavery with being the source of race mixing. Like other abolitionists, they opposed colonization.

The party's presidential candidate in 1840, former slave-owner

James G. Birney, garnered only 7000 votes—out of the almost two and a half million cast—for a party that as yet had no formal name. (The name "Liberty" would come in 1841 to emphasize the contrast with slavery.) Outmatched in money, organization, political experience, and range of issues, it had little chance, especially as many anti-slavery Whigs stuck with their party's nominee, William Henry Harrison, despite his running mate's slave holding. Birney's vote total was strikingly less than the two million signatures on abolition petitions to Congress only two years earlier, proof that signing a petition hardly made one a committed political abolitionist. While many black abolitionists, including Henry Highland Garnet and James McCune Smith, supported the party, as did come-outers, most white abolitionists were opposed or indifferent to the independent party; Whigs and, particularly, Democrats barely gave it notice. Many anti-slavery Whigs put party and practical issues such as the tariff and banking—and the defeat of Democratic President Martin Van Buren—ahead of principle, even when abolitionists argued that slavery's impact on the nation contributed to the economic hard times of the Panic of 1837. They also simply continued to vote for the lesser of two evils, that is, the candidate with the least objectionable stance on slavery.

Asserting that his party was anti-slavery, not abolitionist, Liberty Party speaker and writer Salmon P. Chase sought to adjust the party's political orientation and to clarify its position on the national government's authority over and involvement in slavery. As he saw it, the party sought to end the national government's control by southern Slave Power and to end its link to and support of slavery. Unlike Garrison, who was reaching the conclusion that the Constitution deserved no better than a public burning, Chase argued that the Constitution was anti-slavery. As he would soon clarify in the spirit of *Somerset*, "Freedom is national; slavery only local and sectional," an explanation that by the late 1850s Southerners were reversing into slavery national and freedom local.[25] Following the same reasoning, Henry B. Stanton sought adequate constitutional power to end slavery congressionally, and other abolitionists advanced steadily to the idea that the Constitution was an anti-slavery document. The key was political action that would give abolition the political influence to use Congress's alleged anti-slavery powers; however, some Liberty supporters, such as Lewis Tappan, disliked Chase's move to political arguments and away from the moral duty of ending slavery. Some, such as Joshua Leavitt, refused to give up the abolitionist label or to abandon their demand for immediate abolition.

Adhering to its original moral position, the Liberty Party attracted few converts as Chase's political position became more attractive to and used by anti-slavery advocates in both major parties—the Conscience Whigs and the Barnburner Democrats. Political and economic appeals, not support for black rights, were turning more Northerners against slavery. The target was the South's power, and the concern was slavery's social and political impact on the rest of the nation.

Within weeks of his inauguration, Harrison, whose inaugural address chastised those who were "harbingers of disunion, violence and civil war,"[26] was dead, and his slave-owning vice president, John Tyler of Virginia, was in the White House. Tyler, who relied on southern advisers, was proof to the Liberty Party that, even with their disappointing start, their existence was justified. The almost equal support for Whiggism and Democracy in many states supported the Liberty Party's argument that it could have a determining impact. The key was dedication and determination as it continued to limit itself to slavery-related issues. It took no position on such questions as internal improvements and trade. No other issue could be tackled, the party explained, until the corrupting influence of slavery was eliminated.

Because it achieved few electoral success in 1841 and 1842, debate over the party's future continued. Even in the 1844 presidential election which pitted two slave-owning candidates, James Knox Polk of Tennessee and Henry Clay of Kentucky, Birney drew less than 3 percent of the total vote. The continuing depression, the increasing number of fugitive slaves reaching the North, and white concerns over civil liberties as a result of the Gag Rule did little for the Liberty Party except take critical votes from Clay in New York, thus giving the election to Polk. One group wanted to continue as started; another wished to expand the party into a broader reform group; and a third, including Chase, Bailey, and Stanton, argued for uniting all anti-slavery advocates, regardless of party and regardless of a dilution of Liberty Party principles, into an anti-slavery alliance.

Texas and the Mexican War

After asserting their independence from Mexico in 1836, the Americans who had settled in the Mexican state of Coahuila y Texas hoped not for nationhood but for annexation to the United States. They had no success until a joint congressional resolution was passed in 1845 during the fading months of President John Tyler's administration. During the late 1830s and early 1840s, until the forces of Manifest Destiny propelled the nation to further expansion, both major political parties feared the impact of a debate over Texas annexation. The Whigs and the Democrats knew that the prospect of adding proslavery Texas to the Union would resurrect the tensions of the Missouri debate, and those of both parties who opposed the South's disproportionate political power were reluctant to add to it and hurt northern tariff and banking goals. Because each party included both Northerners and Southerners and did not wish to alienate and perhaps even lose a significant part of its membership, it was impossible to get the necessary two-thirds vote of the Senate to approve an annexation treaty with the Republic of Texas. Plus, annexation of an area whose independence Mexico did not recognize meant the possibility of war with the United States' southern neighbor.

Immediately before the Texans revolted, Quaker abolitionist Benjamin Lundy had sought land and settlement rights from the Mexican government in order to create an asylum for blacks outside the United States. For Lundy, the plan would provide respite from white discrimination and would provide blacks with an opportunity to demonstrate their abilities and potential. They could also produce cotton and other products in competition with slave labor, thus offering an option for those who refused to purchase anything created by slave labor and thus demonstrating to slave owners that freeing their slaves and working them as wage laborers was a viable option. After the revolution, Lundy wrote a series of essays on Texas which was published in the Philadelphia *National Gazette* and which argued that the revolution was part of a slaveholders' conspiracy. Reprinted as *The Origin and True Causes of the Texas Revolution Commenced in the Year 1835* and under various other titles, Lundy's explanation of the revolt was used by Congressman John Quincy Adams to delay, if not permanently prevent, Texas's annexation.

James Polk's election to the White House in 1844 encouraged renewed action, even though southern efforts to annex the area and to stop anti-Texas petitions to Congress returned civil liberties to the national front. Because Polk was a proponent of western expansion, his election suggested a national mandate for adding territory; therefore, before turning over the presidency to Polk, Tyler guided through Congress a joint resolution requiring only a majority vote of each house. The Texas bill was a major setback for abolitionists. John Quincy Adams called it "the heaviest calamity that ever befell myself and my country."[27] In December 1845 it made Texas the twenty-eighth state. With Florida's addition earlier that year, Texas gave the country fifteen slave states; Iowa (1846) and Wisconsin (1848) quickly restored the slave/free balance.

Texas's annexation led a small number of abolitionists to propose the dissolution of the Union and to demand "no union with slaveholders."[28] For those who opposed that goal, the slogan was useful in symbolizing their frustration and anger. For disunionists, including Garrison, Texas's annexation demonstrated the immorality and corruption of a government that allowed and even encouraged slave owning. Disunion would end association with a great evil. For other abolitionists and for nonabolitionists, however, disunion meant abandoning slaves and treason, respectively.

The Mexican War and the Wilmot Proviso

Texas's annexation led not just to calls for disunion but to war with Mexico, which had never accepted Texas's independence. The war was supported by pro-slavery Southerners and by expansionists in general and was opposed by anti-slavery Whigs and abolitionists. For the latter, "Polk's War" proved the accusation that the government—and thus the nation—had been corrupted by slavery and was in the hands of the southern slaveocracy. Joshua Leavitt "challenge[d] [anyone to name] an instance, in forty-years, where a change has been made in the general policy of the government, except at the dictation of the slaveholders."[29] For Owen Lovejoy, brother of the murdered Elijah J. Lovejoy, the question was simply, "Is it not the great business of this country to take care of slavery,—to pay its bills, to fight its battles, and generally to do its scavenger work?"[30] The overall pro-slavery expansionism of the war was sufficient to convince Lewis Tappan in 1847 to found a new anti-slavery newspaper in Washington, the *National Era*, edited by Gamaliel Bailey. By 1853 it had 25,000 subscribers (versus 3000 combined for Garrison's *Liberator* and the AASS's *National Anti-Slavery Standard*).

Because, as historian Anne Marie Serio states, "the issue was the annexation of Texas, but the prize was California,"[31] the war immediately raised questions about what the United States would do with the new territory that seemed to be in its future. A proposal from a Democratic Pennsylvania Congressman, David Wilmot, guaranteed that Thomas Jefferson's concerns about "irritation[s]" in 1820 were accurate.[32] In an amendment to an 1846 appropriations bill, Wilmot echoed the Northwest Ordinance when he proposed that "neither slavery nor involuntary servitude shall exist in any part of said territory" acquired by the war.[33] Typical of anti-slavery Northerners of the period, Wilmot did not share the abolitionists' concern for the immorality of slavery. As he explained his motivations, "the negro race already occupy enough of this fair continent; let us keep what remains for ourselves, and our children . . . for the free white laborer."[34] Thus, the proviso received support from those who saw it as a step in the eventual destruction of an inhumane institution and from others who frequently saw the institution as immoral and evil but who supported the proposal as a method for "keeping the territory clean of negroes."[35]

During the House and Senate battles over the proviso, which was never approved, Southerners, initially little concerned by the proposal, called for united action to stop a conspiracy that insulted the South and threatened to make the region "like a caged debtor."[36] While some opponents of the measure were arguing that the territory's soil and climate made it unsuited for slavery, Senator John C. Calhoun of South Carolina explained that national territory belonged to all of the states, that Congress could not limit the rights of states or individuals within the territory, and that the South would not accept "acknowledged inferiority." The South, he asserted in an argument that confirmed the views of the Garrisonians, had the Constitution on its side.[37]

Whether Calhoun's analysis was acceptable to the rest of the nation would become clear sooner than most Americans expected when the 1850s ushered in yet another crisis related to slavery. It would also begin with one of the most dangerous pieces of legislation ever passed by Congress—at least in the eyes of abolitionists. Moral suasion had yet to change Southern hearts; political action had failed to affect the nation's stand on slavery; disunion carried little appeal. The 1850s would offer more constitutional solutions, more political creations, and more calls for violence.

Notes

1. John L. Thomas, ed., *Slavery Attacked: The Abolitionist Crusade* (Englewood Cliffs, NJ: Prentice-Hall, 1965), 3.

2. Quoted in Ronald G. Walters, *The Antislavery Appeal: American Abolitionism after 1830* (Baltimore: Johns Hopkins University Press, 1976), 14.

3. Massachusetts Anti-Slavery Society, quoted in Thomas, *Slavery Attacked*, 88.

4. Quoted in Louis S. Gerteis, *Morality & Utility in American Antislavery Reform* (Chapel Hill: University of North Carolina Press, 1987), 44.

5. All quoted in Thomas, *Slavery Attacked*, 87–93.

6. Quoted in Hugh Davis, *Joshua Leavitt: Evangelical Abolitionist* (Baton Rouge: Louisiana State University Press, 1990), 148.

7. Quoted in Thomas, *Slavery Attacked*, 84.

8. Joshua Leavitt, quoted in ibid., 74.

9. Quoted in Richard H. Sewell, *Ballots for Freedom: Antislavery Politics in the United States, 1837–1860* (New York: Oxford University Press, 1976), 5–6.

10. Quoted in ibid., 33.

11. Quoted in Thomas, *Slavery Attacked*, 79.

12. Quoted in Sewell, *Ballots for Freedom*, 27.

13. Quoted in Russel B. Nye, *William Lloyd Garrison and the Humanitarian Reformers* (Boston: Little, Brown, 1955), 118, and Benjamin P. Thomas, *Theodore Weld: Crusade for Freedom* (New Brunswick, NJ: Rutgers University Press, 1950), 182.

14. Quoted in Thomas, *Slavery Attacked*, 85–86.

15. Quoted in Nye, *William Lloyd Garrison*, 116.

16. Quoted in R.J.M. Blackett, *Building an Antislavery Wall: Black Americans in the Atlantic Antislavery Movement, 1830–1860* (Baton Rouge: Louisiana State University Press, 1983), 116–117.

17. Quoted in Thomas, *Theodore Weld*, 186.

18. Richard Webb, quoted in Blackett, *Building an Antislavery Wall*, 197.

19. Quoted in John R. McKivigan, *The War against Proslavery Religion: Abolitionism and the Northern Churches, 1830–1865* (Ithaca, NY: Cornell University Press, 1984), 100, 103.

20. Cornelius Cole, quoted in William Gienapp, *The Origins of the Republican Party, 1852–1856* (New York: Oxford University Press, 1987), 6.

21. Gerrit Smith, quoted in Sewell, *Ballots for Freedom*, 83.

22. Douglas M. Strong, *Perfectionist Politics: Abolitionism and the Religious Tensions of American Democracy* (Syracuse, NY: Syracuse University Press, 1999), 6.

23. Quoted in John R. McKivigan, "Church-Oriented Abolitionism and Antislavery Politics," in Alan M. Kraut, ed., *Crusaders and Compromisers: Es-*

says on the Relationship of the Antislavery Struggle to the Antebellum Party Sys-tem (Westport, CT: Greenwood, 1983), 183.

24. Quoted in ibid., 182.

25. Eric Foner, *Free Soil, Free Labor, Free Men: The Ideology of the Re-publican Party before the Civil War* (New York: Oxford University Press, 1970), 3.

26. Quoted in Sewell, *Ballots for Freedom,* 80.

27. Quoted in Richard H. Sewell, *A House Divided: Sectionalism and the Civil War, 1848–1865* (Baltimore: Johns Hopkins University Press, 1988), 21.

28. Quoted in Merton L. Dillon, *The Abolitionists: The Growth of a Dis-senting Minority* (DeKalb: Northern Illinois University Press, 1974), 150.

29. Quoted in Thomas, *Slavery Attacked,* 74.

30. Quoted in Dillon, *The Abolitionists,* 164.

31. Anne Marie Serio, *Political Cartoons in the 1848 Election Campaign* (Washington, DC: Smithsonian Institution Press, 1972), 3.

32. *Thomas Jefferson: Writings* (New York: Library Classics of the United States, 1984), 1434.

33. John H. Schroeder, *Mr. Polk's War: American Opposition and Dissent, 1846–1848* (Madison, WI: Madison House, 1971), 46.

34. Quoted in Sewell, *Ballots for Freedom,* 173.

35. Thomas H. Benton, quoted in ibid., 172.

36. Charleston *Mercury,* quoted in Joseph G. Rayback, *Free Soil: The Election of 1848* (Lexington: University Press of Kentucky, 1970), 27.

37. Ibid., 28.

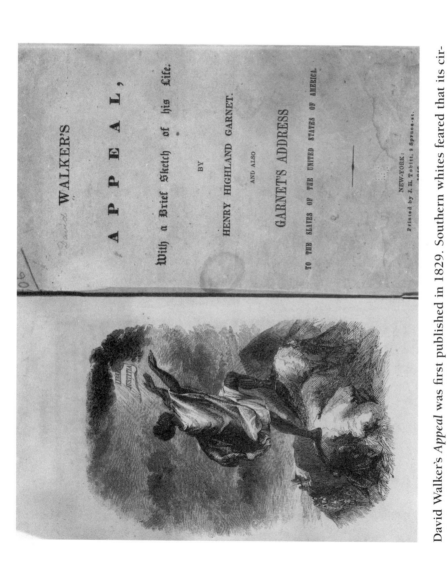

WALKER'S

APPEAL,

With a Brief Sketch of his Life.

BY

HENRY HIGHLAND GARNET.

AND ALSO

GARNET'S ADDRESS

TO THE SLAVES OF THE UNITED STATES OF AMERICA.

NEW-YORK:
Printed by J. H. Tobitt, 9 Spruce-st.

David Walker's *Appeal* was first published in 1829. Southern whites feared that its circulation in their states would lead to slave uprisings. This title page and frontispiece are from an 1848 printing. (Library of Congress)

In 1831, only months after the first issue of the *Liberator*, Nat Turner led an uprising of slaves in Virginia. Linked in southern minds to the abolitionist paper, it prompted bloody retaliation, stricter laws against slaves and free blacks, and a stronger defense of slavery. (Library of Congress)

The supplicant male slave with the slogan, "Am I not a man and a brother?" were on the seal of the Society for the Abolition of Slavery in England. They were also widely used by American abolitionists, in this case by John Greenleaf Whittier, for his anti-slavery poem, "Our Countrymen in Chains." (Library of Congress)

In December 1833, the American Anti-Slavery Convention met in Philadelphia. This manifesto was published as a broadside to present the group's arguments against the evils of slavery. (Library of Congress)

Opposition to abolitionism in the South prompted a variety of efforts to prevent the spreading of anti-slavery ideals. This depiction of a raid in July 1835 on the Charleston, South Carolina, post office shows Southerners' opposition to Arthur Tappan, president of the American Anti-Slavery Society, and the burning of the *Liberator* and other abolitionist publications. (Library of Congress)

Violence against abolitionists was frequent through all parts of the country. General anti-abolitionism and fear of amalgamation and social equality led a Philadelphia mob to burn down the newly built Pennsylvania Hall in May 1838, the day after Angelina Grimké gave her last public address there. (Library of Congress)

ABOLITION FROWNED DOWN.

Former president John Quincy Adams of Massachusetts led the fight in the House of Representatives against the "Gag Rule" which prohibited consideration of anti-slavery petitions. This cartoon shows South Carolina representative Waddy Thompson Jr. defending the restriction. (Library of Congress)

Expansion of slavery became an increasingly important issue to anti-slavery Northerners. With the election of Democrat James K. Polk in 1844, demands increased for the annexation of Texas despite the debate over its coming in as a slave state and Mexico's insistence that the area still belonged to it. (Library of Congress)

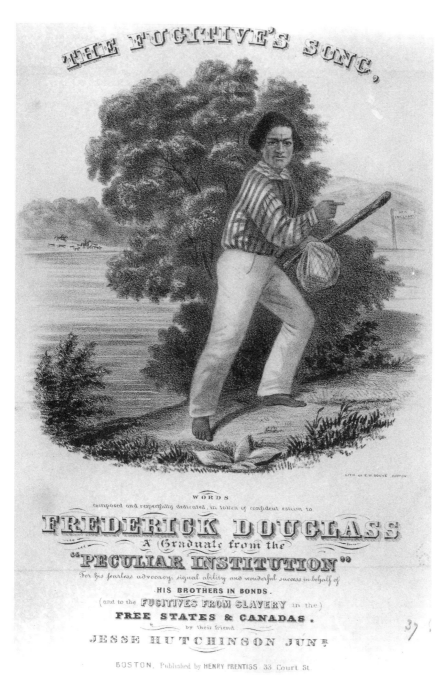

Frederick Douglass, who escaped from slavery in Maryland in 1838, became one of the leading abolitionist speakers. In 1845 his *Narrative of the Life of Frederick Douglass* appeared, as did this cover for sheet music for "The Fugitive's Song." (Library of Congress)

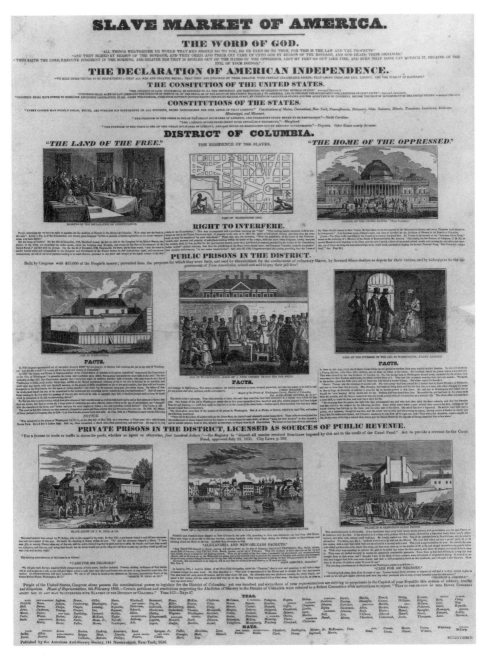

Even abolitionists who denied that Congress had power to end slavery in the states believed that the Constitution gave Congress power to end both slavery and the slave trade in Washington, D.C. Their campaign included this 1836 broadside. Not until 1859, however, did Congress end the slave trade in the federal district; slavery ended there in 1862. (Library of Congress)

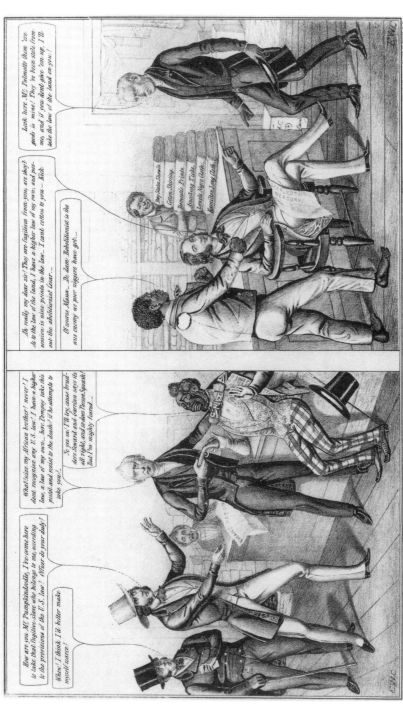

WHAT'S SAUCE FOR THE GOOSE IS SAUCE FOR THE GANDER.

Many Northerners swore to resist enforcement of the Fugitive Slave Act of 1850. Southerners saw the law as protecting their property just as the law, according to this 1851 cartoon, protected northern products. (Library of Congress)

MARRIAGE OF THE FREE SOIL AND LIBERTY PARTIES.

This 1848 depiction of the formation of the Free Soil Party indicates the difficulties of uniting abolitionists and blacks with elements of the Democratic and Whig parties. (Library of Congress)

Abolitionists long argued that more than a formal end of slavery was necessary to provide blacks with true freedom. This 1866 depiction of life under slavery (being sold) and after slavery (being whipped) supports their insistence that more was needed than the Thirteenth Amendment. (Library of Congress)

Recognition of the contributions of the abolitionists came with the Thirteenth Amendment and the end of the Civil War, even though the abolitionists heatedly argued among themselves about if and when they had accomplished their goals. This 1866 print includes a wide range of the men who fought against slavery and racial inequality. (Library of Congress)

CHAPTER 6

"THE STORM, THE WHIRLWIND, AND THE EARTHQUAKE": FROM POLITICS AND VIOLENCE TO FREEDOM—THE 1850s–1860s

While abolitionists were unable to compromise with evil and sin, Southerners consistently matched their inflexibility. Both had long seen the other as a threat to the nation, but in the 1850s events almost on a yearly basis kept southern fears high and made abolitionist dreams of a reformed nation seem impossible to reach. Abolitionists who opposed violence found themselves circuitously accepting and even supporting it. As Frederick Douglass explained, "For it is not light that is needed, but fire; it is not the gentle shower, but thunder. We need the storm, the whirlwind, and the earthquake."[1] They also supported a new political party centered on preserving white rights. Because of southern reactions to the revised strategy, slavery ended in bloodshed, not repentance and reform, and left critical questions about the nature of black freedom.

The Free Soil Party and the 1848 Election

Fueled by the debate over Texas and the land to be acquired from Mexico, Conscience or Free-Soil Whigs, such as Charles Sumner of

Massachusetts, were calling for "one grand Northern party of Free-dom."[2] They believed that slavery harmed the entire country morally, politically, and economically and that Mexican War hero and slave owner Zachary Taylor would be the presidential nominee of their party in 1848. Even the anti-abolitionist Democrats were divided over Texas's admission, the Wilmot Proviso's prohibition of slavery in territory ac-quired from Mexico, and the 1846 Walker Tariff's reduced rates that benefited the southern economy. Radical members were challenging the degree of southern and pro-slave influence in the party, especially in New York where young radical "Barnburners" worried about the "so-cial and political degradation of the white laborer."[3]

Even though some elements in the Liberty Party opposed a fusion that meant "the *nonextension* of slavery where it is *not*, and the *maint-enance* of slavery where it is,"[4] others viewed the nonexpansion of slav-ery as they had once viewed the abolition of the international slave trade: as a critical step in the eventual, inevitable destruction of slav-ery. As a result, fusion came in 1848 when Liberty men Salmon Chase, Joshua Leavitt, and Henry Stanton joined representatives from the Whigs and the Barnburner Democrats in Buffalo, New York, to design a platform and nominate a presidential ticket for the Free Soil Party. The "motley assembly"[5] that included black abolitionists Henry High-land Garnet, Frederick Douglass, and Charles Lenox Remond agreed on a platform that reflected a concern not for whether blacks became free, "but, whether 'white men' were 'to *remain* free.'"[6] The party op-posed slavery's expansion and advocated federal government action against slavery within its constitutional jurisdiction, including the ter-ritories, but it also supported such nonslave issues as free land, inter-nal improvements, and tariff reform. The delegates "propose[d] no interference by Congress with slavery within the limits of any State"; they asserted that "Congress has . . . no . . . power to institute or esta-blish slavery." With a motto of "Free Soil, Free Speech, Free Labor, and Free Men"[7] and a platform silent on abolition, the Free Soilers nomi-nated Martin Van Buren for president. One of the nation's leading Dem-ocrats, Van Buren's anti-abolition stands had been followed by opposition to Texas's annexation and to the expansion of slavery into western lands.

Reaction was mixed. While the anti-political, anti-institutional William Lloyd Garrison found the new party, despite its weak commitment to abolition and black rights, commendable and deserving of support, some members of the lingering Liberty Party, including James Birney and Gerrit Smith, opposed the new coalition and formed the Liberty League, asserting that slavery was so sinful that no human law could legalize it and that Congress had constitutional power to abolish slavery throughout the nation. Blacks seemed unsure about the Free Soil Party, but Garrisonian Charles Lenox Remond of Massachusetts argued that "we cannot wait the advent of a pure government; we must act under the present one, corrupt as it is."[8] Frederick Douglass agreed on this policy of practicality, but he, Martin R. Delany, and other blacks would soon decide that the party's concerns were too much the white man and too little the black. The answer for Douglass was the narrow-based Liberty Party, which he continued to support intermittently until the 1860s.

Despite enthusiastic campaigning, the Free Soilers were disappointed by the 1848 election results. Van Buren drew well in Massachusetts and New York, but he still received only 10 percent (291,804) of the national popular vote (versus 2500 for Liberty League candidate Gerrit Smith) and none of the electoral votes as Taylor won the presidency. Democratic and Whig stands against the expansion of slavery in order to preempt the new party and the strength of party loyalty defeated the Free Soilers; nevertheless, a dozen of their candidates won seats in the new Congress. Salmon P. Chase was also elected to the Senate.

The political future of the Free Soil Party was not bright, but its impact on American history was already obvious in terms of the fate of the Democratic and Whig parties, both of which "were approaching, if they were not already in, a state of crisis" because of the slavery issue.[9] Charles Sumner concluded that, as a result of the 1848 campaign and election, "the public mind has been stirred on the subject of slavery to depths never reached before."[10] If so, the American political scene was taking abolition out of the hands of the abolitionists. The major parties, with self- and national preservation in mind, had to find a solution to the slavery question; moral reform was not the goal.

The 1850s and Rising Tensions

Within months of the acquisition of California as part of the land acquired through the Mexican War, the area began to fill with "forty-niners" seeking quick wealth through gold. Californians, skipping the territorial phase because of their rapidly increasing population, drafted and sent to Congress a constitution prohibiting slavery. Because of southern opposition, another compromise was needed, but the 1850s was a very different decade from the 1820s when Southerners accepted the prohibition of slavery in the territory above 36° 30'. Logically, a slave-based economy might not be able to exist in the mountains and deserts of the lands west of Texas or in the forests of the Oregon Territory acquired diplomatically in 1846. Southerners, however, were increasingly insistent on the *principle* of property rights, on their right to own slaves anywhere in the Union, and on that right's protection and promotion by the national government.

The abolitionists' continuing demand that the slave trade and slavery be ended in the District of Columbia also upset Southerners, as did northern opposition to slavery's movement into the other lands of the Mexican Cession. Texas's boundary claims and its national debt, as well as southern frustration with northern states' personal liberty laws, added to tensions. In 1842 in *Prigg v. Pennsylvania*, the Supreme Court had ruled that the fugitive slave clause of the Constitution required enforcement by the national government, not by the states. State laws dealing with the return of fugitives were unconstitutional. In response to the ruling, Connecticut, Massachusetts, New Hampshire, Pennsylvania, Rhode Island, and Vermont had passed "personal liberty" laws that prohibited state aid to the enforcers of the national law of 1793. Southern demands for greater protection of their valuable property grew as aid to fugitives increased.

The political solution was the Compromise of 1850 or, in the words of its creator Kentuckian Henry Clay, "an amicable arrangement of all questions in controversy between the free and slave states, growing out of the subject of Slavery" that at least temporarily healed the "five gaping wounds" of the nation.[11] Among those who spoke against the compromise's five bills was William Henry Seward. As did other abolitionists, he argued that slavery was a sin and could not be supported by the Constitution or by higher law, but supporters of compromise—for economic and political, if not moral, reasons—prevailed, especially after the death of obstructionist John C. Calhoun in March 1850. The South Carolinian had argued that limiting Southerners' access to the territories was destroying the Union. Also dead was President Taylor who had opposed Clay's proposal and who was succeeded by compromiser Millard Fillmore. With Southerners pulling back from their talk of northern domination and the need for secession, the compromise was law by September.

The compromise provided that California was admitted as a free state. The other land acquired from Mexico, now divided into the New Mexico and Utah territories, was to be organized without reference to slavery; the people would decide on the existence of slavery when their area applied for statehood, an application of "popular sovereignty," the view that "the people of the territory . . . settl[e] the matter for themselves."[12] Texas's borders were scaled back; in return, the national government assumed its debts. The slave trade in the District of Columbia (but not slavery itself) was ended, and a stronger fugitive slave law was enacted. Most Americans were relieved, finding the compromise acceptable and the best that the times permitted.

Most controversial for abolitionists, Free Soilers, and Northerners in general, and greatest in its potential to reopen and redefine rather than close the slavery debate, was the Fugitive Slave Act. Its opponents' hope was that the bill was unenforceable, even as some Southerners threatened secession if it was. The statute's opponents concentrated on the fact that the law did not allow accused runaways the protection of habeas corpus or a jury trial and that it did not allow a hearing before a judge. A federal commissioner was sufficient. Making matters worse was the fact that a commissioner would be paid five dollars if he released a man or woman and ten dollars if he ruled that a captive must be returned to the South. Enforcement—or kidnapping, according to the law's opponents—was encouraged by the provision that federal officials responsible for the capture of an alleged runaway faced a fine of $1000 for failing to act. These men could require the aid of citizens, and persons who aided a runaway faced six months in prison and a $1000 fine for each slave not returned.

Many white Northerners believed that the statute limited the freedom of northern whites and, by requiring aid in capturing fugitives, made the North pro-slavery. Frederick Douglass asserted that the law made the North "a hunting ground."[13] For blacks, the issue was their lives; for whites, their civil liberties. Worried that even a free-born northern black had no security in his freedom, many blacks left northern states for Canada; black supporters of colonization and even some long-term opponents of colonization saw emigration, including to now independent Liberia, as the black American's only solution to white oppression. James Birney advised free blacks to leave the country to save themselves. Others were prepared to fight for their freedom. Douglass wrote, "The only way to make the Fugitive Slave Law a dead letter, is to make half a dozen or more dead kidnappers."[14] He warned that the streets "would be running with blood" if efforts were made to enforce the law.[15] It was a statement that reflected black abolitionists' more militant tone in the 1850s, a shift responding to the apparent failure of moral suasion and political action. Henry C. Wright, a nonresistant, announced, "Every man, who believes resistance to tyrants to be obedience to God, is bound by his own principles (not by mine) to arm himself with a pistol or a dirk, a bowie-knife, a rifle, or any deadly weapon, and inflict death with his own hand, on each and every man who shall attempt to execute the recent law of Congress."[16]

Although most captured fugitives were returned to the South, many Northerners defied the law, rescuing and hiding alleged fugitives, with some even working on the stations of the so-called Underground Railroad that took escaped slaves as far north as Canada. Garrison, continuing his opposition to the pro-slavery Constitution, burned copies of the document in 1854. The emotional opposition to a bill that seemed to make a mockery of freedom and liberty, even if it had a constitutional base, also led Northerners to make a national best seller out of Harriet Beecher Stowe's melodramatic and damning picture of slavery, *Uncle Tom's Cabin*, first published in serial form in the *National Era* in 1851. Appearing as a book in 1852, it sold two million copies over the next five years. Stowe explained that she "must speak for those who cannot speak for themselves."[17] In 1855 Solomon Northup's memoir of his story as a free black kidnapped into slavery, *Twelve Years a Slave*, sold widely as it confirmed fears raised by the Fugitive Slave Act and emotions raised by Beecher's novel. In many ways, the law—which Stowe's brother, the Reverend Charles Beecher, called "an unexampled climax of sin"[18]—and the books did what the abolitionists had failed to do: they turned slavery into something real and personal, even for whites who shared all of the racial prejudice of their day and who found the life of the southern slave to be too distant to provoke action.

Southerners tended to see the slave rescues, the popularity of antislavery stories, and the calls for violence against those defending slave property as confirmation that abolitionism had taken over the North. Such a conclusion reduced confidence that the national government would protect southern rights—a far cry from the southern acceptance of sin desired by abolitionists.

The Republican Party

In 1852, with the Whigs and Democrats running on pro-Compromise platforms, the Free Soilers once more took an anti-slavery stand. Now under the name "Free Democratic" party, they did so in a platform that supported diplomatic recognition of Haiti, attacked provisions of the Compromise of 1850, and called slavery "a sin against God and a crime against man."[19] The party's continued failure to take a stand in favor of equal rights challenged the support of blacks, and the party drew only half as many popular votes in the presidential race as it did four years earlier. Still, with the developing demise of the Whig Party over economic, nativist, and slavery pressures, some Free Democrats hoped that their party would replace it as the second major party in the nation.

Instead, the final blow for both the Free Soilers and the Whigs, losers in the 1852 presidential race to yet another slave owner, was also the next demonstration of slavery's power: Democratic Illinois Senator Stephen A. Douglas's 1854 plan to organize the Nebraska Territory. The area above 36° 30' made free by the Missouri Compromise over thirty years earlier, Nebraska would be divided into two territories, Nebraska to the north and Kansas to the south, with the implication that one would end up open to slavery and one closed, a step that Salmon P. Chase and Joshua Giddings called "an atrocious plot to . . . convert [the region] into a dreary region of despotism, inhabited by masters and slaves."[20] Even though Douglas believed that weather, climate, and the "necessary pursuits of people"[21] made it unlikely that slavery would enter the area and even though he opposed an outright repeal of the Missouri Compromise line, he bowed to southern demands. The bill, with repeal of the earlier compromise, passed easily in the Senate, 37–14, and had strong southern support in the House's final 113–100 vote.

As predicted, many northern opponents of the measure were upset by its revocation of the 36° 30' line—Abraham Lincoln reported that his and Douglas's state of Illinois was "thunderstruck and . . . reeled and fell in utter confusion"[22]—and by the economic threat that the measure posed to free whites. Those upset over slavery's expansion were concerned by the renewed aggressiveness of pro-slavery interests. The Slave Power, a conspiracy to spread slavery and insure the permanence of slaveholders' influence in the national government, appeared a clear threat even to many nonabolitionists. Yet again, in other words, northern whites focused on slavery in terms of the economic opportunities and political rights of *whites* with pro- and anti-slavery forces battling politically and physically in "Bleeding Kansas" over the fate of slavery in the new territory. Whites saw slavery as an institution that survived by limiting the rights of whites, that turned the white laboring man into "white niggers." Just as the Fugitive Slave Act raised concerns about the rights and liberties of free men, the fight over Kansas's future led white Northerners to conclude—once again—that slavery sacrificed the political rights and civil liberties of whites to protect slave property and the power of slave owners. As Lincoln warned, "In our greedy chase to make profit of the negro, let us beware, lest we cancel and tear to pieces even the white man's charter of freedom."[23]

The stage and issues were thus set for a new anti-slavery coalition. For some, that was the Know-Nothing or American Party, a group that opposed immigrants, Catholics, blacks, and sometimes slavery. Despite much criticism for its nativism, the Know-Nothings drew many reformers seeking coalition, including men who supported black rights but questioned the Irishman's capacity for being a useful worker and citizen. For William Lloyd Garrison, "the sooner the Union goes to pieces, the better,"[24] but for most political abolitionists the answer was what some were already calling the Republican Party. Presenting that party as the party of abolition, however, is to misrepresent its origins, ideology, and goals. As anti-slavery publisher Horace Greeley wrote, "Never on earth did the Republican Party propose to abolish slavery."[25] With abolitionism continuing through the American Anti-Slavery Society (AASS), the American and Foreign Anti-Slavery Society (AFASS), come-outers, and the Liberty League, the Republicans were less radical, judgmental, and demanding. Slavery could continue, just not expand; slavery could exist, but the disproportionate power of slaveholders had to end if the free white workingman was to live in a country that rewarded his labors, gave him the opportunity for improvement, and protected his liberty. Slavery was not a step toward a free-labor capitalist system; it was a deterrent and impediment to it. Free labor helped make northern society dynamic, mobile, progressive, competitive, full of opportunities, and undoubtedly superior to that of the South; it offered economic independence, a fluid social order, equal opportunity, and middle-class status for everyone who worked hard. In other words, it made the (free-labor) North everything that the (slave) South was not. The fate of the West rested on the question of slavery's expansion there. As the *Pennsylvania Weekly Telegraph* told Southerners, "You must not carry your blighting institution of Slavery into the public Territories to compete with, degrade and impoverish our White Labor. . . . Keep your negroes at home, gentlemen, and if you choose to go into the Territories [do so without slavery]."[26]

Supporting "free soil, free labor, free men," Republican platforms in 1856 and 1860—called "sneaking, lily livered, pharisaical, humbug" by abolitionist Elizur Wright Jr.[27]—opposed expansion into the territories. Because of perceived constitutional restraints, a moderate focus, and concern for northern public opinion, they did not urge abolition in states where slavery existed. Republicans believed that the Constitution limited their line of attack but that the nonextension of slavery was a necessary and effective first step toward slavery's eventual destruction. Most, but not all, Republicans by the late 1850s believed that the Constitution limited the national government's relationship to slavery, that slavery was a state institution and could not exist without legislation enabling it (an application of *Somerset*), and that Congress should end the domestic slave trade and its support of slavery in the District of Columbia and the territories. As Lincoln warned in 1859, "Never forget that we have before us this whole matter of the right or wrong of slavery in this Union, though the immediate question is as to its spreading out into the new Territories and States."[28]

Among the radical members of the party who wanted slavery's end nationally were Salmon P. Chase and Charles Sumner. Sumner called slavery "barbarous" and slave owners "Barbarians."[29] Such denunciations led to Sumner's caning by Representative Preston Brooks of South Carolina in 1856, an attack which made the senator abolition's newest martyr. For other radicals, including Benjamin Franklin Wade, the destruction of slavery was a necessity, even if the price was the Union. Charles Francis Adams, Henry Wilson, Thaddeus Stevens, Thurlow

Weed, James M. Ashley, Zachariah Chandler, and John P. Hale had for years taken stands in favor of the rights of free blacks and runaways, focusing on such issues as black suffrage, exclusion of blacks from various states, aid for fugitive slaves, and legal discrimination.

Many Republicans, particularly in the western states, added a decided racist note unsurprising for the period, referring to "Niggers," vehemently denying any interest in social equality, advocating colonization, and opposing political rights such as voting and jury duty. A congressman from Iowa asserted that because the Republican Party hoped to bar slaves from the western territories it was "the only white man's party in the country."[30] Still, for Southerners and Democrats, the party was the "Nigger Party" and its members were "Black Republicans."[31]

Despite their general nonabolitionism, Republicans frequently countered charges that the Negro was inferior to the white and undeserving of citizenship; they frequently advocated economic and basic political rights and the need for educational opportunities for blacks. In general, inferiority meant neither the right to enslave nor the right to oppress. For politically oriented northern blacks, the party was the newest best option, and radical anti-slavery Republicans found that the party's platform allowed them to "stand upon it and preach from it the whole anti-slavery gospel."[32] Garrisonians worried that Republicans would not seek the country's moral reformation in the form of the equal treatment of blacks; moderate Arthur Tappan wrote it off as "a white man's party united for selfish purposes."[33] The radical abolitionists of the Liberty League, which absorbed the American and Foreign Anti-Slavery Society in 1855 to become the American Abolition Society, also found no answers in the new party. Proclaiming slavery to be "sinful, illegal, and unconstitutional," it ran Gerrit Smith for president in 1856 under its Radical Abolitionist Party banner. Smith, who drew support from Frederick Douglass and Lewis Tappan, argued that the Republicans did not "oppose slavery where it is, and oppose[d] it only where it is not."[34]

With the Democrats' platforms from 1844 to 1856 labeling abolitionists threats to "the happiness of the people,"[35] even some Garrisonians supported the Republicans' 1856 nominee, John C. Fremont, who won all but five northern states, and Garrison refused to join those who saw Republicans as more dangerous than slave owners to abolition.

Frederick Douglass's Paper supported Fremont (although Douglass would return to the Liberty Party fold in 1860). Come-outers found the party flawed but acceptable as they hoped to influence it through cooperation with abolitionist members. By 1860, the party was clearly abolitionists' most accepted and best practical political hope.

The appearance of the Republicans did more than give political hope. It revitalized the moral battle, and it encouraged further constitutional discussion. Christian abolitionist revivals marked the 1850s, with the focus once more on the person of the slave and the moral necessity to end both slavery and discrimination against blacks. Congregationalists and, by 1857, Presbyterians took anti-slavery positions. Individual Methodists acted outside of their churches. Long-standing state and women's organizations continued their publications, lectures, petitioning, and fundraising, while other groups were formed. On the constitutional side, while slavery's opponents had long accepted that the Constitution gave the states power over slavery, some abolitionists, including William Goodell, moved to the position that, instead, it gave Congress the power to destroy slavery. Goodell, along with Gerrit Smith, Frederick Douglass, and the Tappans, asserted the general unconstitutionality of slavery through the Liberty League and the American Abolition Society in 1855.

The Black Response

For black abolitionists the frustrations were growing. For obvious reasons, Martin Delany lamented in 1852 that "I have no hopes in this country—no confidence in the American people."[36] Even white abolitionists seemed at times to offer more problems than aid. A continued emphasis on slavery versus black rights, their domination of leadership and policy positions in abolitionist organizations, and their tendency to dictate proper thought and behavior rankled. Garrisonians opposed Frederick Douglass's decision in 1847 to draw readership and funds away from the *Liberator* by establishing his own newspaper, the *North Star*. They later opposed his rejection of Garrisonian positions on the Constitution, political action, and nonresistance. Their press charged the former slave with a variety of offenses, from marital infidelity to dishonesty to desertion from abolitionism, and it raised questions about his racial limitations.

While some blacks rejuvenated the convention movement, emphasizing racial solidarity, collective action, abolition, and equality before the law, local and state societies were active. In addition, although uncertain about the correct political method for ending slavery and taking varied and inconsistent positions on the various anti-slavery parties, they continued their interest in political action—despite being denied suffrage in all but a handful of states—and leading the resistance to the Fugitive Slave Act.

The white-controlled legal system offered little support. In 1854 in *Dred Scott v. Sandford*, Chief Justice Roger Taney argued for the majority of the U.S. Supreme Court that the Constitution protected property from Congressional or territorial threat and that slaves were property. Congress, therefore, had overstepped its authority in the now repealed Missouri Compromise and, significantly for those who feared Slave Power's expanding influence, Congress could not prohibit slavery in the territories. Many blacks and whites feared that the logic would be applied to the state and local level, barring all prohibitions of slavery. Distressingly for abolitionists and blacks if not for other Northerners, Taney also announced that blacks were not and could not be American citizens and, in chilling words, had "no rights which the white man was bound to respect."[37] For some blacks, the ruling was final proof that the United States offered no hope for equality or even safety and fair treatment. Robert Purvis declared that he had nothing but "contempt, loathing, and unutterable abhorrence!" for the government that gave blacks so little.[38]

With the decade thus seeming to give them little choice, black abolitionists were coming to accept both violence and emigration. From the veiled support of Nat Turner's Rebellion in 1831, they moved to a much more open support of slave revolt by the 1850s. By the end of the decade, slaves who took action were seen as "noble and heroic." Going beyond David Walker in 1829 and Henry Highland Garnet in 1843—"*Rather die freemen than live to be slaves*"—militant blacks after the Fugitive Slave Act publicly called on slaves to "cut their masters' throats" and to take other necessary violent action.[39] Charles Lenox Remond believed that "American slavery will go down in blood. . . . [A] retribution that the American people deserve."[40]

Some former opponents of colonization—a minority of black leaders expressing their views—shifted to support emigration because, as a bishop of the African Methodist Episcopal Church lamented, "we are whipped, we are whipped and we might as well retreat in order."[41] Martin Delany, who confessed to William Lloyd Garrison "that I have no hopes in this country," began looking for a site to which American blacks could emigrate, generally focusing on Central and South America and the Caribbean.[42] Others looked to Canada; some merely turned to the western United States; many targeted Haiti. The former anti-colonizationist Henry Highland Garnet looked to "Mexico, California, the West Indies, or wherever it promises freedom and enfranchisement." Garnet, who "would rather see a man free in Liberia, than a slave in the United States," saw limited emigration as a way of developing the African economy, bringing Christianity to Africa, and, much as Benjamin Lundy had years before, demonstrating the potential of free black labor and challenging southern agricultural production.[43] Opponents of the various plans, however, found little in them to help the condition of slaves or to ease discrimination for free blacks who remained in the United States. For most American blacks the answer to slavery and inequality was self-defense and continued efforts through moral suasion; violence was not the answer, not even against slave catchers.

More Tension

The late 1850s were filled with increasing tensions, from Sumner's caning and continued conflict in Kansas to the publication of another attack on the South and the threat of an abolitionist-led slave rebellion. In 1857 twenty-seven-year-old North Carolinian Hinton Rowan Helper published *The Impending Crisis of the South: How to Meet It*. A believer in black inferiority and colonization, he presented a statistical argument against slavery as "an unmitigated despotism."[44] He used fifty-eight tables to prove that every aspect of northern society was stronger and more prosperous; the South would never develop equal commercial or literary success or full civil liberties, and it would never end its exploitation of the white nonslave owning masses as long as it retained slavery. These arguments were generally quite different from those of the abolitionists, but Helper's book won praise from the *Liberator* and other abolitionist publications and it soon became a major tool of the new Republican Party, which advocated it as the best path to abolition.

Two years later, white abolitionist John Brown was cited as a "noble hero-martyr" in the AASS's Annual Report, and his raid in Harpers Ferry, Virginia, was called "an act of humanity and heroism" by the Michigan Anti-Slavery Convention.[45] Blacks in Providence, Rhode Island, hailed Brown as a "hero, philanthropist and unflinching champion of liberty";[46] a black anti-slavery organization in Ohio referred to him and his men as "heaven appointed Heralds and Prophets."[47] An opponent of moral suasion as a failed strategy, Brown had spent the 1850s recruiting support from black leaders, including Douglass, Delany, and Garnet, none of whom joined his small group of conspirators. Although Brown's ultimate goal was unclear when he, thirteen whites, and five blacks attacked the federal arsenal, and although Brown was executed for his actions, he (as did the Fugitive Slave Act and *Uncle Tom's Cabin*) influenced Northerners against slavery. On December 2, 1859, the day of his execution in Virginia, black businesses closed, prayer meetings were held, resolutions of veneration were passed, and donations were made to John Brown relief organizations. In the South, violence against abolitionists and even nonabolitionist Northerners increased, with whippings and tar-and-featherings common and with nineteen killed.

Even nonviolent abolitionists were compelled by their failures and their cause to praise Brown, with black abolitionist Robert Purvis labeling him "the Jesus Christ of the 19th century" and Lewis Tappan arguing that Brown responded to "the prompting of a disinterested and noble heart, in a cause he honestly believed was the cause of God and humanity."[48] Acceptance of, if not support for, the inevitability of violence had been building. By 1857 the pacifist Massachusetts Anti-Slavery Society was pledging support for slaves seeking freedom "whether by flight or insurrection."[49] Garrisonian Abby Kelley concluded that same year that slavery was maintained by violence and thus was a war that required a response in kind. Abolitionist orator Wendell Phillips agreed, asserting that he "want[ed] to accustom Massachusetts to the ideas of insurrection; to the idea that every slave has a right to seize his liberty on the spot."[50] Thomas Wentworth Higginson, a Unitarian minister, argued for the slave's right to use whatever weapon available to overthrow slavery. Garrison and Parker Pillsbury argued that slaves could not consent to being slaves and had the duty to resist their enslavement; for Pillsbury, slavery would end not with moral reform but with blood. While Garrison supported "peace," he wished for "success to every slave insurrection" because he supported the oppressed over the oppressor once insurrections began. "Rather than see men wear their chains in a cowardly and servile spirit, I would, as an advocate of peace, much rather see them breaking the head of the tyrant with their chains."[51] ("Timely repentance" by slave owners would prevent the broken heads.) Elizur Wright announced that "the sin of this nation . . . is to be taken away, not by Christ, but by John Brown," in other words, by slave insurrections.[52]

One year later, upon Whig-turned-Republican Abraham Lincoln's victory in the presidential election of 1860, abolitionist veteran Joshua Leavitt celebrated that "it is a joy to have lived to this day"[53]—just the reaction that convinced Southerners that slavery's end was near if they did not act. Lincoln during the 1840s and early 1850s had seen slavery only as a "distracting question,"[54] but after the 1860 election, Wendell Phillips noted that the new Republican president, while "not an abolitionist, [and] hardly an antislavery man," stood for "an antislavery idea." He concluded that "for the first time in our history, the *slave* has chosen a President of the United States."[55] That was enough for the South, which reacted as Gerrit Smith predicted that it would: "[Lincoln's] victory will be regarded by the South as an Abolition victory."[56] The Richmond *Enquirer* lamented "that the Northern people, by a sectional vote, have elected a president for the avowed purpose of aggressions on Southern rights"; northern voters were "contaminated with abolitionism and hostility to the South." Such contamination, concluded the New Orleans *Bee*, meant "further and more atrocious aggressions." *De Bow's Review* predicted that "within the next four or five years" the abolitionist Republicans would control the national government.[57]

Southerners were not to be convinced otherwise; congressional passage and presidential endorsement of a thirteenth amendment to the Constitution guaranteeing slavery where it already existed was insufficient. So too was repeal of personal liberty laws in three northern states and Republican promises to enforce the Fugitive Slave Law. The "facts" of the previous thirty years spoke for themselves. Plus, Lincoln's prediction in his House Divided speech of 1858 that the Union would not continue both slave and free but would become all of one or the other confirmed their fears that abolitionism would guide the new president.

Lincoln's election, they concluded, would encourage slave uprisings and abolitionist fanatics like John Brown. The Republican president would use his power of patronage to build Republicanism in the South, thus "abolitioniz[ing]" it.[58]

Abolitionists saw a different problem than did Southerners. They were concerned by the placating steps taken in Washington in response to southern threats of secession and, therefore, relying on decades of experience with self-interested politicians and voters, they worked to avoid a compromise that would ensure the continuation of both slavery and southern political strength. Unlike some Northerners who sought to avoid secession at all costs, the abolitionists accepted it. Garrison, for example, saw southern secession as an opportunity to end the union with slavery, "reliev[ing] us from all responsibility for [the South's] evil course."[59] Wendell Phillips argued in January 1861 that "the best way to get rid of this evil is . . . to let all connection with it be severed immediately and it will die for lack of Northern support"— with slavery "drop[ping] to pieces" soon after.[60] After the secession of the first seven southern states in late 1860 and early 1861, the response of fearful Northerners to such arguments was a new wave of anti-abolitionist violence.

War

After the Confederate attack on Fort Sumter, South Carolina, in April 1861, most abolitionists no longer accepted secession. Even advocates of nonresistance and disunion supported the new president's determination to preserve the Union. Although anti-slavery writer George William Curtis lamented in 1861 that "there is very little moral mixture in the 'anti-slavery' feeling of this country,"[61] for Garrison "the North [was] rushing like a tornado in the right direction."[62] Abolitionist opposition to government power in *defense* of slavery was not, in other words, matched by abolitionist opposition to government power for the *destruction* of the institution. According to Phillips, "the war is not aggressive, but defensive"; the war was "Freedom against Slavery."[63]

The chief of police in Cincinnati disagreed, noting that the war was a "white man's fight, with which niggers had nothing to do."[64] According to Congress it was a war "to preserve the union, with all the dignity, equality and rights of the several states unimpaired."[65] These were undoubtedly discouraging perspectives. Also discouraging were Lincoln's pledges to save the Union either with or without slavery—a reflection of the president's wartime political, military, and diplomatic priorities and strategies, his understanding of his and Congress's constitutional powers, and his expectation that slavery would die an eventual natural death. Lincoln also cancelled orders issued by his field generals freeing slaves, leading Stephen Foster, Abby Kelley's husband, to call him "a greater slavecatcher than Jefferson Davis," president of the Confederacy.[66] Garrison, who supported Lincoln but nevertheless was critical of much of what he did, complained that the president was without "a drop of antislavery blood in his veins" and that he was "unnecessarily timid."[67] He privately accused the president of being as responsible for slavery as those who originally enslaved the Africans. A generally pro-Lincoln abolitionist, Samuel J. May, lamented that "Lincoln is the criminal."[68] Phillips, Garrison's rival for wartime leadership of abolitionism, compared Lincoln to Benedict Arnold and Aaron Burr and charged that the only success of the Union army was in "catch[ing] negroes and find[ing] owners for them."[69]

Despite these discouraging events in 1861–1862, abolitionists did not lose hope. In Congress they found anti-slavery—even abolitionist—spokesmen who challenged the president. Through the Joint Committee on the Conduct of the War, through such men as Ohioan Benjamin Wade, Pennsylvanian Thaddeus Stevens, Indianan George W. Julian, and Charles Sumner and George Boutwell of Massachusetts, and through such legislative steps as the Confiscation Acts of 1861 and 1862 and the abolition of slavery in the District of Columbia and the territories in 1862, abolitionists saw progress. Finally, even in Lincoln they found an anti-slavery leader. His 1863 Emancipation Proclamation ending slavery in southern-held areas marked for Garrison "the bright noon of day."[70]

All abolitionists, however, did not react positively because the sin of slavery ended coercively only in rebel areas. Slavery as an American institution continued. Under the presidential order, abolition was beginning not as a result of changed hearts and a sense of justice but of "military necessity";[71] it was not the changed "*moral sentiment*" sought by Kelley, Lydia Maria Child, and the other abolitionists.[72] As Frederick Douglass elaborated, "Liberty came to the freedmen . . . not in mercy, but in wrath, not by moral choice, but by military necessity, not by the generous action

of the people among whom they were to live, . . . but by strangers, foreigners, invaders, trespassers, aliens and enemies."[73] Theodore Dwight
Weld, however, recognized that the war was necessary to end slavery:
without southern victories, Northerners would allow slavery to continue.
"So every [Northern] reverse is a victory [for abolition]."[74]

According to historian James Brewer Stewart, the proclamation ordering that all slaves in rebel-held areas be free on January 1, 1863,
"made Union troops into true armies of emancipation."[75] Perhaps they
were in the eyes of Southerners and some abolitionists, but they were
hardly so in the view of most white Northerners whose reaction to a
war of abolition fought in part by black soldiers—a step approved by
Lincoln—prompted vocal opposition and even the famous Draft Riots
in New York City.

Emancipation and Reconstruction

In 1865, two years after Lincoln's partial wartime ban, slavery
ended permanently and nationwide through a constitutional amendment, the first in over sixty years. It was a major step taken hesitantly
by many Americans and a step that once again had little of the abolitionists' moral concerns behind it. Lincoln had asked in 1862 whether,
even under his constitutional power as commander in chief, "*my word*
[could] free the slaves."[76] A change in the Constitution would be the
nation's word. Supported by Lincoln, the Thirteenth Amendment
worked its way through the Senate and House by early 1865, was rat-
ified by the necessary twenty-seven states by the end of the year, and
was in effect in December 1865.

Not moral reform or racial egalitarianism but political and military necessity, as well as the anti-South feelings of Northerners, had
ended slavery. Northerners were not going to endure hundreds of thousands of deaths and leave Slave Power intact. The moderation and
vagueness of the Thirteenth Amendment—it simply stated that slavery
could not exist in the United States—achieved the abolitionist goal of
abolition, but it left unclear whether it also achieved the goal of racial
equality. So-called Radical Republicans had wanted the latter explicitly
stated but knew that neither the American public nor the Congress
would accept such a provision. Some supporters of the amendment argued that the elimination of slavery meant that everyone was *equally*

free, at least in terms of civil (economic) rights, a view confirmed by the passage of the Civil Rights Act of 1866 on the authorization of the amendment. Others, mainly Democrats and men from the border states, saw the amendment as ending only the chattel aspect of slavery; black inferiority and discriminatory treatment would continue.

With Congress's adoption in early 1865 of the constitutional amendment, Garrison felt that his crusade was won, agreeing with Lincoln who noted in February 1865 that "it winds the whole thing up."[77] Garrison also believed that the AASS should dissolve; the "other work" of political decisions regarding "equal political privileges" would be handled by new broader coalitions. Upon ratification by the states, the *Liberator* announced, "[T]he *anti-slavery work is done*. The Nation, by a vast majority, has confessed the principles of the movement to be just, and has overthrown slavery."[78] Disagreeing were those who saw slaves still on southern plantations and racial inequality still present and those who like Phillips saw "justice and absolute equality before the law" depending on the continued efforts of abolitionists.[79]

Phillips, with the support of most black and female abolitionists, argued that the former slave was owed land, education, and the vote, as well as the protection of national legislation. Such steps, practiced in Front Royal, South Carolina, during the war, would come for all freedmen only if the abolitionists continued to pressure for them and the national government used its power against a South that was, as Garrison acknowledged, "still demonized by her old slave system."[80] To reach Phillips's goal of "effectual freedom, real freedom, something that can maintain and vindicate itself,"[81] abolitionist organizations needed to continue, not disband.

Garrison might have been cheered by delegates at the 1864 Republican (National Union) convention—welcomed vindication for a man long attacked as a fanatic and irrational—but he steadily found himself on the losing end of votes on Phillips's AASS resolutions as the abolitionists continued the bickering that had long divided them. Phillips's resolution opposing Lincoln's reelection led insurgent Republicans, supported by most black abolitionists, to nominate John C. Fremont while the main party stayed with Lincoln. For the abolitionists, it was a demonstration of the abolitionists' continuing difficulty in achieving unanimity—a dangerous situation. Plus, Fremont was likely to draw votes away from Lincoln, making victory more likely for his Democratic challenger, George McClellan. Lincoln was reelected, but the division between Garrison and Phillips grew larger as they disagreed over another issue, enfranchisement of freedmen. Both the Massachusetts Anti-Slavery Society and the AASS sided with Phillips, who believed that the vote would allow blacks to assert their demands and pressure political leaders. Garrison argued that the national government had no power over suffrage in the states and that northern states which denied blacks the vote had no moral weight to force southern enfranchisement.

Along with Maria Chapman and several other first-generation immediatists, Garrison left the AASS in 1865 just as the war ended and just after an assassin ended Lincoln's life and presidency. He had been repeatedly defeated by Phillips who was now president of the organization that voted in favor of "absolute equality before the law—absolute civil equality for the freedman."[82] Garrison's last edition of 1800 issues of the *Liberator* appeared on December 29, 1865; it announced the ratification of the Thirteenth Amendment which he viewed as "the complete triumph as well as utter termination of the Anti-Slavery struggle."[83] "[T]he old 'covenant with death' is annulled," he wrote.[84] Abolitionists now needed to join other Americans in freedmen's aid societies or else, in the words of Garrisonian Oliver Johnson, be "swallowed up in victory."[85]

Battles still needed to be fought, but new generations of abolitionists would have to fight them.

Notes

1. Frederick Douglass, *The Frederick Douglass Papers*, series 1, *Speeches, Debates, and Interviews*, vol. 2, ed. John Blassingame (New Haven, CT: Yale University Press, 1979), 371.

2. Quoted in Richard H. Sewell, *Ballots for Freedom: Antislavery Politics in the United States, 1837–1860* (New York: Oxford University Press, 1976), 132.

3. Joseph G. Rayback, *Free Soil: The Election of 1848* (Lexington: University Press of Kentucky, 1970), 77.

4. *American Freeman*, quoted in Sewell, *Ballots for Freedom*, 152.

5. Henry B. Stanton, quoted in Anne Marie Serio, *Political Cartoons in the 1848 Election Campaign* (Washington, DC: Smithsonian Institution Press, 1972), 12.

6. Quoted in Rayback, *Free Soil*, 211.

7. Quoted in Serio, *Political Cartoons*, 12.

8. Robert C. Dick, *Black Protest: Issues and Tactics* (Westport, CT: Greenwood, 1974), 112.

9. Rayback, *Free Soil*, 303.

10. Quoted in ibid., 309.

11. Quoted in Craven, "The Crisis," in Edwin C. Rozwenc, ed., *The Compromise of 1850* (Boston: D. C. Heath, 1957), 7, and Richard H. Sewell, *A House Divided: Sectionalism and the Civil War, 1848–1865* (Baltimore: Johns Hopkins University Press, 1988), 34.

12. George M. Dallas, quoted in Rayback, *Free Soil*, 116.

13. Quoted in Gerald Sorin, *Abolitionism: A New Perspective* (New York: Praeger, 1972), 115.

14. Quoted in Clara Merritt DeBoar, *Be Jubilant My Feet: African-American Abolitionists in the American Missionary Movement* (New York: Garland, 1994), 69.

15. Quoted in James Oliver Horton and Lois E. Horton, *In Hope of Liberty: Culture, Community, and Protest among Northern Free Blacks, 1700–1860* (New York: Oxford University Press, 1997), 253.

16. Quoted in Lewis Perry, *Radical Abolitionism: Anarchy and the Government of God in Antislavery Thought* (Ithaca, NY: Cornell University Press, 1973), 237–238.

17. Quoted in Eliza Wigham, *The Anti-Slavery Cause in America and Its Martyrs* (London: A. W. Bennett, 1863), 99.

18. Quoted in Sewell, *A House Divided*, 38.

19. Quoted in Sewell, *Ballots for Freedom*, 244.

20. Quoted in ibid., 255.

21. Quoted in Robert W. Johannsen, *Lincoln, the South, and Slavery* (Baton Rouge: Louisiana State University Press, 1991), 23.

22. Quoted in ibid., 24.

23. Quoted in Nicole Etcheson, *Bleeding Kansas: Contested Liberty in the Civil War Era* (Lawrence: University Press of Kansas, 2004), 24, 25.

24. Quoted in Russel B. Nye, *William Lloyd Garrison and the Humanitarian Reformers* (Boston: Little, Brown, 1955), 164.

25. Quoted in Sorin, *Abolitionism*, 143.

26. Quoted in Sewell, *Ballots for Freedom*, 306.

27. Quoted in Bertram Wyatt-Brown, *Yankee Saints and Southern Sinners* (Baton Rouge: Louisiana State University Press, 1985), 337.

28. Quoted in Eric Foner, *Free Soil, Free Labor, Free Men: The Ideology of the Republican Party before the Civil War* (New York: Oxford University Press, 1970), 311.

29. Quoted in David Donald, *Charles Sumner and the Coming of the Civil War* (New York: Alfred A. Knopf, 1960), 354.

30. Quoted in Foner, *Free Soil*, 265.

31. Quoted in ibid., 263, 265, and Benjamin Quarles, *Black Abolitionists* (1969; reprint, New York: Oxford University Press, 1977), 189.

32. George Julian, quoted in Sewell, *Ballots for Freedom*, 285.

33. Quoted in Merton L. Dillon, *The Abolitionists: The Growth of a Dissenting Minority* (DeKalb: Northern Illinois University Press, 1974), 211.

34. Quoted in John R. McKivigan, *The War against Proslavery Religion: Abolitionism and the Northern Churches, 1830–1865* (Ithaca, NY: Cornell University Press, 1984), 157, and in Foner, *Free Soil*, 302.

35. Quoted in Joel H. Silbey, "'There Are Other Questions Beside That of Slavery Merely': The Democratic Party and Antislavery Politics," in Alan M. Kraut, ed., *Crusaders and Compromisers: Essays on the Relationship of the Antislavery Struggle to the Antebellum Party System* (Westport, CT: Greenwood, 1983), 146.

36. Quoted in Leon F. Litwack, "The Emancipation of the Negro Abolitionist," in Martin Duberman, ed., *The Antislavery Vanguard: New Essays on the Abolitionists* (Princeton, NJ: Princeton University Press, 1965), 152.

37. *Dred Scott v. Sandford*, 19 Howard 393 (1857).

38. Quoted in Jane H. Pease and William H. Pease, *They Who Would Be Free: Blacks' Search for Freedom, 1830–1861* (New York: Athenaeum, 1974), 242.

39. Quoted in ibid., 237, 238, 240.

40. Quoted in Dick, *Black Protest*, 150.

41. Bishop Daniel A. Payne, quoted in ibid., 28.

42. Quoted in Pease and Pease, *They Who Would Be Free*, 261.

43. Quoted in Dick, *Black Protest*, 28, and Pease and Pease, *They Who Would Be Free*, 268.

44. Hugh C. Bailey, *Hinton Rowan Helper: Abolitionist-Racist* (University: University of Alabama Press, 1967), 17.

45. Quoted in Ronald G. Walters, *The Antislavery Appeal: American Abolitionism after 1830* (Baltimore: Johns Hopkins University Press, 1976), 31, and Dillon, *The Abolitionists*, 242.

46. Quoted in Dick, *Black Protest*, 149.

47. Quoted in Pease and Pease, *They Who Would Be Free*, 248.

48. Quoted in Carlton Mabee, *Black Freedom: The Nonviolent Abolitionists from 1830 through the Civil War* (London: Macmillan, 1970), 321, and DeBoar, *Be Jubilant My Feet*, 67.

49. Quoted in Walters, *The Antislavery Appeal*, 30.

50. Quoted in ibid., 227.

51. Quoted in George M. Fredrickson, ed., *William Lloyd Garrison* (Englewood Cliffs, NJ: Prentice-Hall, 1968), 61–62.

52. William Lloyd Garrison and Elizur Wright Jr., quoted in Perry, *Radical Abolitionism*, 258, 259.

53. Quoted in Sewell, *Ballots for Freedom*, 3.

54. Quoted in Johannsen, *Lincoln*, 19.

55. Quoted in Irving H. Bartlett, *Wendell Phillips: Brahmin Radical* (Boston: Beacon Press, 1961), 223.

56. Quoted in Ralph Volney Harlow, *Gerrit Smith: Philanthropist and Reformer* (New York: Henry Holt, 1939), 427.

57. All quoted in Johannsen, *Lincoln*, 123.

58. Michael F. Holt, *The Political Crisis of the 1850s* (New York: John Wiley & Sons, 1978), 225.

59. Quoted in Nye, *William Lloyd Garrison*, 169.

60. Lorenzo Sears, *Wendell Phillips: Orator and Agitator* (New York: Doubleday, Page, 1909), 217.

61. Louis S. Gerteis, *Morality & Utility in American Antislavery Reform* (Chapel Hill: University of North Carolina Press, 1987), 170.

62. Quoted in Nye, *William Lloyd Garrison*, 170.

63. Quoted in ibid., 25.

64. Quoted in Horton and Horton, *In Hope of Liberty*, 269.

65. Quoted in James B. Stewart, *Wendell Phillips, Liberty's Hero* (Baton Rouge: Louisiana State University Press, 1986), 225.

66. Quoted in Dorothy Sterling, *Ahead of Her Times: Abby Kelley and the Politics of Antislavery* (New York: Norton, 1992), 333.

67. Quoted in Nye, *William Lloyd Garrison*, 172, 175.

68. Quoted in Stewart, *Wendell Phillips*, 239.

69. Ibid., 230.

70. Henry Mayer, *All on Fire: William Lloyd Garrison and the Abolition of Slavery* (New York: St. Martin's Press, 1999), 547.

71. Abraham Lincoln, quoted in ibid., 547.

72. Lydia Maria Child, quoted in James M. McPherson, *The Struggle for Equality: Abolitionists and the Negro in the Civil War and Reconstruction* (1964; reprint, Princeton, NJ: Princeton University Press, 1992), 43.

73. Quoted in ibid., 202–203.

74. Quoted in Benjamin P. Thomas, *Theodore Weld: Crusader for Freedom* (New Brunswick, NJ: Rutgers University Press, 1950), 240.

75. Stewart, *Wendell Phillips*, 241.

76. Quoted in Sewell, *A House Divided*, 168.

77. Quoted in ibid., 185.

78. Quoted in ibid., 259.

79. Quoted in Sears, *Wendell Phillips*, 254.

80. Quoted in Gerteis, *Morality & Utility*, 192.

81. Quoted in Lawrence J. Friedman, *Gregarious Saints: Self and Community in American Abolitionism, 1830–1870* (New York: Cambridge University Press, 1982), 268.

82. Quoted in Stewart, *Wendell Phillips*, 265.

83. Quoted in Friedman, *Gregarious Saints*, 265.

84. Quoted in Mayer, *All on Fire*, 598.

85. Quoted in Friedman, *Gregarious Saints*, 267.

CHAPTER 7

CONCLUDING
INTERPRETIVE ESSAY

Succinctly, realistically, and accurately, Wendell Phillips predicted the fate of the abolitionists' goal:

> For a hundred years, at least, our history will probably be a record of the struggles of a proud and selfish race to do justice to one that circumstances had thrown into its power. The effects of slavery will not vanish in one generation, or even in two. It were a very slight evil if they could be done away with more quickly.[1]

As the NAACP, the National Urban League, the Congress on Racial Equality, and many other twentieth-century civil rights organizations knew, and as Booker T. Washington, W.E.B. Du Bois, A. Phillip Randolph, Thurgood Marshall, and thousands of white and black Americans who worked within their communities understood, ending slavery by itself would not end racism in the United States.

Not until the post–World War II years would national and international developments, using the base provided by the abolitionists and their twentieth-century heirs, force a revisiting of the goals of the abolitionist movement. The result was both a revised interpretation of the abolitionists as sincere and heroic reformers and much of the justice that Phillips— as well as William Lloyd Garrison, Abby Kelley, Benjamin Lundy, Frederick Douglass, Lydia Maria Child, and thousands of others—sought a hundred years before. The abolitionists had wanted better Americans and a better America, and they had wanted to achieve this goal through an acceptance of sin and of the need for moral reform, not through government mandates. But in the 1860s, their nation's government ended the legal institution that held human beings as lifetime, inherited property. The nation's government, not its soul, had acted, and as a result real freedom was still a distant goal for black Americans in a white nation.

The Radical Republicans of Reconstruction had attempted to use national power to define and protect real freedom. Through compromises, a hallmark of the nation's handling of slavery, they were able to add two additional amendments to the Constitution in 1868 and 1870. These were to clarify both the freedom of blacks and the status of all Americans. The Fourteenth Amendment defined citizenship to include blacks; it also prohibited denial of due process and required equal protection under the laws; the Fifteenth prohibited restrictions on black male suffrage. In both constitutional additions, because the former slave South was already defining black freedom to mean continued black subjugation, Congress was given the power to enforce the amendments' provisions, a power which Congress used, with presidential support, in the early 1870s.

Ratification of the Fifteenth Amendment and Congress's efforts to protect black voters apparently contributed to Wendell Phillips's (but not all other abolitionists') conclusion that "our long work is sealed at last."[2] Suffrage would allow blacks, like whites, to pursue their own interests and in doing so expand the liberty and opportunities of everyone. It would also relieve fears that the national government would use its powers, increased by wartime necessities, to override states and provide special favors for the inferior black while whites had to rely on their own resources. For those who disagreed with Phillips, the ballot without land and with white planter opposition meant little.

Abolitionist hopes and northern fears related to race and federalism also appeared when Congress sought to end much of the nation's racial discrimination through the Civil Rights Act of 1875. Advocated by Senator Charles Sumner, it defined the Fourteenth Amendment's prohibitions as applying to individuals as well as states, thus truly threatening a reordering of American society. Fighting against what appeared to be forced social equality, whites were rescued by the Supreme Court in 1883. The *Civil Rights Cases* assured them that changes in the Constitution did not limit how individuals could treat each other; blacks would not be "the special favorites of the law."[3] Considering the widespread disinterest in blacks and that the abolitionists had long urged that blacks simply enjoy the same status and rights as whites, it was an ironic analysis at best.

As this ruling by the nation's highest court indicated, a variety of political, cultural, economic, and racial realities quickly undermined Reconstruction efforts to ensure the end of slavery and blacks' equal rights under the law, that is, something more than the pseudofreedom experienced by free blacks before emancipation. The same barriers that blocked the antebellum abolitionists blocked the Reconstruction ones. Even after approving three new constitutional amendments and numerous enforcement statutes, the nation demonstrated that "so much of the holy and grand work has been accomplished" but "the spirit of American Slavery still lives."[4] Abolitionist Abby Kelley was blunt: because of the treatment of the freedmen in the South, "I contend that we have not freedom."[5] Slavery's replacement was not freedom but discrimination and inequality. By the end of the century, slavery's "badges and incidents"[6]—harassment, segregation, debt peonage, lynching, disfranchisement—dominated the southern scene, and the nation virtually apologized in *Plessy v. Ferguson* (1896) for its earlier efforts, however feeble, to follow the abolitionists to equality. The "equal" in the Fourteenth Amendment, the Court said, did not mean equal; the heirs of the antebellum colonizationists argued that it could not because the law could not change reality: blacks and whites were not the same and could not live together without distinctions.

The abolitionists faded into history, kept alive in memory by occasional praise and by frequent allegations that they were overrated troublemakers. Future president Theodore Roosevelt, writing in the late 1800s, a period noted for its racism and its efforts to heal the rifts of the Civil War by understanding the southern position, explained:

> [T]he Abolitionists have received an immense amount of hysterical praise which they do not deserve, and have been credited with deeds done by other men whom, in reality, they hampered and opposed rather than aided. After 1840, the professed Abolitionists formed a small and comparatively unimportant portion of the forces that were working towards the restriction and ultimate destruction of slavery; and much of what they did was positively harmful to the cause for which they were fighting.[7]

In other words, slavery would have died a natural death without the anti-slavery provocateurs, both whites and blacks would have had time (generations?) to adapt to a new relationship between superior white and inferior black, the nation would have avoided a costly civil war, and blacks would not have had to endure the difficulties of handling too much freedom. For a nation that comfortably assigned blacks second-class citizenship and that ignored and even justified racially based deprivations and violence, the abolitionists and their subversive crusade were part of American history's mistakes.

More important to most Americans after the Civil War than the application of American ideals to a group that did not deserve them was the impact of urbanization, industrialization, and imperialism. As Americans became less rural and agrarian, as railroads and telephones connected people across thousands of miles, as women broadened their sphere into the workplace and office, and as the United States played a bigger role on the world scene, concepts of black inferiority deepened and the equal freedom sought by the abolitionists became a life of poverty, exploitation, physical danger, ignorance, and alienation.

Colleagues and children of the abolitionists, as well as black leaders on all levels of society, struggled against white indifference and antagonism to rejuvenate the abolitionist crusade in some form. Oswald Garrison Villard (grandson of abolitionism's most famous crusader), Francis and Archibald Grimké (nephews of abolitionism's most famous sisters), and Moorfield Storey (secretary of Senator Charles Sumner) did what they could through writings, legal action, and organization. Booker T. Washington, who came to national prominence the same year that Frederick Douglass died, 1895, accommodated publicly and challenged privately; W.E.B. Du Bois sought a black leadership class and organizations to demand full equality. The National Association for the Advancement of Colored People (NAACP), founded in 1909, was a creation of whites and blacks, men and women, and for almost half a century it would be the most public and notorious heir of the abolitionists as it challenged the country, most frequently in the courts, to live up to its promises of equality.

Another Try

If the Civil Rights Movement of the 1950s–1970s was the Second Reconstruction, as many have called it, it was also the second abolitionist movement. As in the 1830s–1860s, it involved internal dissension, moral suasion, political action, and violence, with most of the violence, once again, directed against the reformers. Just like a hundred years earlier, it included men and women, blacks and whites, groups and individuals. Just like before, it involved civil liberties, religious values, individual commitment, national reform, constitutional interpretations, and a renewed vision of republican ideals, but little leadership from white churches. Just like before, it required commitment and change in the North as well as the South; just like before, the reformers needed help from the national government.

While the reformers of the mid-twentieth century failed to overcome and change an entire nation's thinking, unlike the abolitionists they achieved not a narrow battlefield victory but a broader rejuvenation and transformation of the nation's soul. Could liberty and slavery exist together? The abolitionists had said no, but the rest of the nation was either indifferent or hostile to their goal. Could equality and inequality exist together? The civil rights reformers of the 1950s–1960s said no, but this time much of the nation, including its presidents and Supreme Court, agreed.

What each reform movement ultimately achieved continues to be a subject of perspective and debate, but each challenged the country to live up to its ideals, ideals stated in the Declaration of Independence and then in the Reconstruction amendments. And each did so accepting, as Frederick Douglass explained in 1857, that one could not have "the ocean without the awful roar of its many waters."[8]

Notes

1. Quoted in Herbert Aptheker, *Abolitionism: A Revolutionary Movement* (Boston: Twayne Publishers, 1989), xv.

2. Quoted in Lawrence J. Friedman, *Gregarious Saints: Self and Community in American Abolitionism, 1830–1870* (New York: Cambridge University Press, 1982), 274.

3. *Civil Rights Cases*, 109 U.S. 3 (1883).

4. Sallie Holly, quoted in Louis S. Gerteis, *Morality & Utility in American Antislavery Reform* (Chapel Hill: University of North Carolina Press, 1987), 210.

5. Quoted in Dorothy Sterling, *Ahead of Her Times: Abby Kelley and the Politics of Antislavery* (New York: Norton, 1992), 345.

6.   *Civil Rights Cases,* 109 U.S. 3 (1883).

7.   Quoted in John F. Hume, *The Abolitionists, Together with Personal Memories of the Struggle for Human Rights, 1830–1864* (1905; reprint, New York: Negro Universities Press, 1969), 1.

8.   Quoted in ibid., 17.

BIOGRAPHIES: PERSONALITIES OF THE ABOLITIONIST MOVEMENT

Anthony Benezet (1713–1784)

The man whom many have called the leading anti-slavery propagandist of the mid- and late 1700s was born in northern France in 1713, the child of a Huguenot (Protestant) merchant. Because of increasing religious persecution, his family moved to London when he was two; they then settled in Philadelphia when he was seventeen (1731). In Pennsylvania Benezet joined the Society of Friends (Quakers). Failing at manufacturing, he turned to teaching, first in Germantown and then in 1842 in Philadelphia at the Friends' English School.

Although an opponent of many social ills, including war, mistreatment of Native Americans, and alcohol, most of Benezet's adult life revolved around teaching and opposing slavery. He was successful in both endeavors despite frequent ill health. While teaching at the English School, he began an evening school in his home for slave children. In 1770 he established the Negro School of Philadelphia. He taught at both this school and the English School.

Having turned against slavery in the 1750s, Benezet sought to convince other Quakers that the labor system was not consistent with Christian principles. He argued that slavery was a sin that degraded both master and slave. Those who tolerated slavery were hardly different from those who bought and sold slaves. He published numerous anti-slavery pamphlets, some of which were highly influential in Britain's anti-slavery efforts, inspiring some of Britain's most noted abolitionists. Among his writings was *A Short Account of that Part of Africa Inhabited by Negroes* (1762), which he hoped would convince Parliament to abolish the slave trade. Most important of his many works was

Some Historical Account of Guinea (1772). Upon reading one of Benezet's works, slave-owning American Patrick Henry concluded that slavery was "repugnant to humanity . . . inconsistent with the Bible."[1] American physician Benjamin Rush, who was motivated by Benezet to write *Address to the Inhabitants of the British Settlements in America upon Slave-Keeping*, noted in 1774 that the Quaker's "name is held in veneration in these parts and deserves to be spread throughout the world."[2] In addition, Benezet corresponded broadly, writing even the monarchs of Britain, France, and Portugal. He also issued the call for the first meeting of the Pennsylvania abolition society (1775).

He died in 1784 and was buried in the Friends' Burial Ground in Philadelphia, mourned by hundreds of black Philadelphians.

James Gillespie Birney (1792–1857)

Born on February 4, 1792, in Danville, Kentucky, James G. Birney was the son of one of the wealthiest men in the state. He became the owner of his first slave, Michael, on his sixth birthday. At age eleven, he was sent to Transylvania University in Lexington where he received a classical education. Both his father and his aunt argued against slavery—his father having played a leading role in attempting to make Kentucky a free state in the early 1790s—and he was surrounded by the slavery debate in college at Transylvania and then at the College of New Jersey (now Princeton), where he moved in 1805. In Philadelphia, where he studied law, he met and became friends with successful black sail maker James Forten and with anti-slavery Quakers. He was admitted to the bar in 1814.

Returning to Kentucky, Birney resumed his life as a slave owner. A practicing lawyer in Danville, Birney was elected to the town council. He moved into state politics backing Henry Clay's reelection to the House of Representatives and being elected to the state legislature in 1816. While in the legislature, he opposed a bill requesting that neighboring states penalize those who aided fugitive slaves. Birney asked, "Shall the State of Kentucky do what no gentleman would do—turn slavecatcher?"[3] He also married into one of the state's leading families, the McDowells, in 1816. Among the couple's wedding gifts were several household slaves.

In 1818 Birney settled near Huntsville in the Alabama territory. His goal was to farm cotton and to practice law. Birney owned forty-three slaves but saw slavery as evil and awaited the system's gradual demise. He played a role in framing a state constitution that provided for the humane treatment of slaves, for jury trials of slaves charged with serious crimes, and for punishment of anyone who killed a slave.

Elected to the state legislature in 1819, Birney played an active role in state politics. Facing economic difficulties because of market conditions, personal extravagances, gambling, poor land investments, and the death of an infant daughter, his drinking and gambling increased. In 1823 the Birney family, having sold all of the family slaves (except two house servants), moved to Huntsville so that Birney could return to the practice of law.

A revival conversion prompted Birney to turn to reform. In 1826 he began his support of colonization. His efforts to return to public office met continued failure because of his growing anti-slavery views; however, he was elected alderman in 1828 and mayor in 1829.

The strong anti-black, pro-slavery reaction to Nat Turner's rebellion was the final incentive for Birney to leave Alabama, but before he did so he became an agent for the American Colonization Society. He moved his family to Kentucky to continue his work for the ACS. With them went the house slaves, who had refused to be freed.

In Kentucky Birney began to see slavery as a sin. As a result, he broke his ties with the American Colonization Society and held a ceremony to manumit his slaves. He also wrote *Letter to the Churches; to the Ministers and Elders of the Presbyterian Churches in Kentucky* (1834) attacking slavery on religious grounds. He also began working as an agent for the American Anti-Slavery Society.

Birney moved his anti-slavery newspaper, *The Philanthropist*, to Cincinnati in 1836 where it became the voice of the Ohio Anti-Slavery Society. He wrote numerous anti-slavery articles and delivered many lectures advocating abolition. Opposing William Lloyd Garrison on a variety of issues, he was among those who broke with the AASS in 1840. In that year he also became the presidential candidate for the newly formed anti-slavery Liberty Party and published *The American Churches: The Bulwarks of American Slavery*. The party renominated him in 1844.

Soon thereafter Birney was paralyzed and suffered a series of strokes and heart attacks; he also suffered through years of despondency and religious disillusionment. The Compromise of 1850 convinced him of the futility of his abolitionist efforts. In 1853, because of successful land investments, Birney was able to join fellow abolitionists Theodore Dwight Weld and Angelina Grimké in the Raritan Bay Union community in New Jersey. There he returned to study and writing, mostly on religious issues. He died in November 1857.

Lydia Maria Child (1802–1880)

The famous abolitionist, publicist, and author Lydia Maria Child was born Lydia Francis in Medford, Massachusetts, the youngest of the five children of a baker. Her parents preached hard work, thriftiness, and industriousness. They also apparently taught her about the evils of slavery.

Sent to live with her married sister in Norridgewock, Maine (then a part of Massachusetts), Child learned the domestic arts that would fit her for a married life. She also had contact with local Indians, spending time in their camps and learning of whites' brutal treatment of them.

After six years preparing to be a teacher and then teaching, Child—who by then had renamed herself Lydia Maria—moved to Watertown, Massachusetts, where she opened a girls' school and turned to writing, producing *Hobomok, a Tale of the Times* (1824), an historical novel with hints of intermarriage and miscegenation. Child next wrote a children's book, *Evenings in New England* (1824), and another historical novel, *The Rebels, or Boston before the Revolution* (1825). In 1824 she met her future husband, David Lee Child, editor of the *Massachusetts Journal*, a Whig newspaper. They married in 1828. Child continued writing and was the founder and editor of *The Juvenile Miscellany* (1826–1834), a bimonthly magazine for children, the first in the nation. Her husband's financial problems led Child to follow the success of *The Frugal Housewife* (1829), which would go through thirty-three editions, with other domestic advice manuals.

The Childs turned their political and humanitarian interests toward Native Americans and black Americans. They worked to stop the removal of the Cherokees from the Southeast in 1828–1831, and they supported the abolitionist efforts of William Lloyd Garrison, who worked briefly for David Child in 1828. Lydia later explained that her association with Garrison redirected her life: "old dreams vanished, old associates departed, and all things became new."[4] In 1833 she published *Appeal in Favor of That Class of Americans Called Africans* (1833), the first anti-slavery book produced in the United States, and one which influenced the turn to abolitionism of such notables as Charles Sumner, William Ellery Channing, and Wendell Phillips.

Lydia Child's *Appeal* undermined her career as a writer: *The Juvenile Miscellany* folded and sales of her books dropped. She was barred from the Boston Athenaeum, the library where she had done most of the research for *Appeal*. Although Child also lost many friends, she was determined to continue the fight against slavery. She did so in additional publications and in legal research for abolitionist cases. In 1840 she became one of the first female members of the American Anti-Slavery Society. Her commitment also was revealed in two years as a farm wife in support of her husband's sugar beet farm in Massachusetts, an effort to provide a free-labor alternative to slave-produced sugar cane. After two years as editor of the abolitionist *National Anti-Slavery Standard* in New York, Child quit to return to writing. Numerous articles, short stories, and books followed, and Child resumed her place as one of the most respected authors of her time. Among her writings were two bestselling volumes of *Letters from New York* (1843, 1845).

Reconciling after a lengthy separation, the Childs returned to Massachusetts in 1850. Lydia Child soon also returned to writing against slavery, particularly spurred by the caning of Senator Charles Sumner in 1856. After working to provide relief shipments to anti-slavery Kansans, Child responded to John Brown's raid with *Correspondence between Lydia Maria Child and Gov. Wise and Mrs. Mason, of Virginia* in 1860. Child also collected money to aid the families of Brown's men.

Before the Civil War, Child produced three more abolitionist works and edited the fictionalized memoir of Harriet Jacobs, *Incidents in the Life of a Slave Girl* (1861). During the conflict, she worked for black suffrage and education and for the redistribution of land to the freedmen. In addition, with the war's end she produced *The Freedmen's Book* (1865), a reader, and *A Romance of the Republic* (1867), a novel on intermarriage. By the 1870s she was focusing on women's suffrage, Indian rights, and religious tolerance.

Childs died in 1880, six years after her husband.

Frederick Douglass (1818–1895)

Frederick Douglass was born Augustus Washington Bailey in 1818 in Talbot County, Maryland, the property of Aaron Anthony and the child of Harriet Bailey, a slave. Douglass never knew the identity of his father but was told that he was a white man. Raised by his grandparents, his life was relatively safe and secure. At age seven, he was sent to Baltimore in 1825 to live with Hugh and Sophia Auld as the companion of their son Tommy.

Sophia Auld oversaw Douglass's early lessons in reading until stopped by her husband. Douglass continued his education through the aid of white boyhood friends and by studying a book of speeches. He also learned more about slavery and abolition from talk on the street and from newspapers.

Douglass returned to the Talbot County plantation at age thirteen, now the property of Aaron Anthony's daughter. She allowed him to return to Baltimore and the Aulds, but her death within the year made Douglass the property of her husband Thomas. When Douglass was fifteen, Thomas Auld hired him out to Edward Covey. Beaten daily, Douglass soon fought back.

Douglass was then hired out for two years to William Freeland who treated him well but who returned him to Baltimore when he suspected him of conspiring to escape. Promised his freedom when he turned twenty-one and if he caused no trouble, Douglass learned caulking and hired out his labor. In 1838 Douglass dressed as a sailor and escaped to New York. He thereupon married Anna Murray, a free black who had encouraged him to escape. Seeking a safer location, they moved to New Bedford, Massachusetts. It was then that Frederick Augustus Washington Bailey became Frederick Douglass.

Douglass read the *Liberator* and attended abolitionist meetings, first speaking at a meeting in 1841. Greatly influenced by William Lloyd Garrison, with whom he allied, he began touring, a dangerous step because he was a fugitive slave. His speaking also raised issues because over time he sounded less and less like a slave, raising concerns that audiences would not believe that he had once been a slave.

Narrative of the Life of Frederick Douglass appeared in 1845, the first of three autobiographies Douglass wrote. His growing fame as an abolitionist speaker and writer took him to Britain where he toured. He returned to the United States after British supporters arranged to buy his freedom, a step opposed by abolitionists who believed that this act acknowledged the legality of slavery. Despite opposition from the Garrisonians, Douglass then launched the *North Star*. This abolitionist newspaper, begun in 1847, became *Frederick Douglass's Paper* in 1851 and was published until 1860.

An advocate of black self-help, Douglass attended black national conventions in the 1840s and 1850s. By the late 1840s he began to accept slave rebellion and black political action, attending the convention of the Liberty League in 1848. He also changed his view on the Constitution, seeing it as anti-slavery by the 1850s.

He was a member of the American Abolition Society, founded in 1854 in response to the reopening of territory to slavery through the Kansas-Nebraska Act. His support switched from the Liberty Party to the new Republican Party and back. During the Civil War he also supported the administration of Abraham Lincoln, who sought his advice, although he criticized it for not moving fast enough toward abolition. Douglass played only a minor role in Reconstruction and post-Reconstruction racial policy, turning down an offer in July 1867 from President Andrew Johnson to serve as head of the Freedman's Bureau but actively working for black suffrage and for the election of Ulysses S. Grant as president in 1868 and 1872. Douglass's support for the Republican Party led to his later appointments as U.S. marshal (1877), recorder of deeds for the District of Columbia (1880), and minister to Haiti (1889). In 1870 he served as editor of the Washington-based *New National Era* writing in support of black achievements; he also lectured. In 1877 he was president of the Freedman's Savings and Trust Company; its collapse returned him to the lecture circuit.

In 1884 Douglass married Helen Pitts, a white woman twenty years his junior. He died of a heart attack in Washington, D.C., on February 20, 1895.

Henry Highland Garnet (1815–1882)

Henry Highland Garnet was born in 1815 in Kent County, Maryland, the property of William Spencer. He escaped slavery in 1824 with his parents. He attended the African Free School of New York in the mid-1820s. After working as a cabin boy, ship's cook, and steward in 1828, Garnet returned to New York in 1829. During a two-year indentureship as a farmworker, Garnet injured his knee so severely that he used a crutch for thirteen years; in December 1840 the leg was amputated at the hip.

Garnet returned to school, studying Greek and Latin at a new high school for blacks. In 1834 he was among the founders of a youth group dedicated to moral and intellectual advancement, the Garrison Literary and Benevolent Association. Converted and encouraged by the minister of his church to join the Presbyterian ministry, he went to the Noyes Academy in New Hampshire in 1835. After Noyes was destroyed by a mob, he moved to Oneida Institute in 1836, graduating with honors in 1840. Already an experienced abolitionist speaker, in1840 Garnet made his first major address to the American Anti-Slavery Society, although he soon supported the seceding American and Foreign Anti-Slavery Society.

Moving to Troy, New York, Garnet taught school, studied theology, and married a former student of Prudence Crandall, the white woman who had unsuccessfully sought to establish a school for black girls in Connecticut. Publisher of the *Clarion*, Garnet also became pastor of the Liberty Street (black) Presbyterian Church in 1840; in 1842, he was ordained. He taught at the church's day school. Garnet also began his support of the anti-slavery Liberty Party. In 1844 he argued before the New York legislature for black suffrage; he was a member of the New York Colored Suffrage Convention.

Garnet's skills as an orator were soon well known. Drawing the most early attention was his speech before the National Negro Convention in 1843. In "Address to Slaves of the United States of America," he told his Buffalo, New York, audience, "You cannot suffer greater cruelties than you have already. *Rather die freemen than live to be slaves.*"[5] The address, which was not published until 1848, was not endorsed by the convention and was attacked by Garrisonians, but Lewis Tappan asked Garnet to be the New England agent for the Union Missionary Society. He also worked in support of temperance.

Garnet aided New Yorker Gerrit Smith when the wealthy white abolitionist decided to give land to poor whites and blacks in the mid-1840s. Garnet helped select the land recipients.

In 1848 he was invited to lecture by the British Free Produce Association. After traveling and lecturing in Britain, Garnet, whose leadership of black abolitionists declined after the 1840s, served as a Presbyterian missionary in Jamaica in the mid-1850s. While there, he and his wife focused on establishing schools. Ill health forced his return to the United States where he served as pastor of the Shiloh Presbyterian Church in New York City. An opponent of colonization in the 1840s, Garnet increasingly saw emigration as a solution for some American blacks.

A target of the mobs of the New York Draft Riots of 1863, Garnet worked to help former slaves during the Civil War. Moving to Washington, D.C., he became pastor of the Fifteenth Street Presbyterian Church of Washington, D.C. In February 1865, he was the first black to deliver a sermon in the chamber of the House of Representatives. As the editor of the Southern Department of the *Anglo-African*, Garnet undertook a four-month tour of the South after the war. For two years (1868–1870) he served as president of Avery College in Pittsburgh.

Garnet's wife died in 1870, and in 1879 he married a New York educator sixteen years his junior. In 1881, he was appointed minister to Liberia. He died two months after arriving in Monrovia.

William Lloyd Garrison (1805–1879)

The most famous of all immediate abolitionists, William Lloyd Garrison was born in 1805 in Newburyport, Massachusetts. Descended from Puritan loyalists and Irish immigrants, Garrison was raised by his mother, a Baptist, after his father, a sea captain with a weakness for alcohol, abandoned the family. They moved to Baltimore, Maryland, where she worked as a nurse and where Garrison, who had little formal schooling, was apprenticed for seven years. Returning to Baltimore, he apprenticed as a printer. He moved from local papers to the Vermont *Journal of the Times* and then to Nathaniel White's temperance paper, the *National Philanthropist* (1828).

An early supporter of colonization, Garrison in 1829 coedited Benjamin Lundy's abolitionist *Genius of Universal Emancipation*. In 1830 he was sued for libel after he accused a Newburyport shipowner of involvement in the domestic slave trade, calling him a murderer and a robber. Unable to pay the $100 fine, he was jailed for almost two months until Arthur Tappan, the New York businessman and abolitionist, provided the money.

In addition to lecturing against both slavery and colonization to black and white audiences in Boston, Philadelphia, and New York, Garrison began his own paper. In January 1831 at the age of twenty-five and without capital, Garrison began publication of the weekly antislavery *Liberator*. He would publish it without interruption until 1865, the year that the Thirteenth Amendment ended slavery in the United States. Supported by northern black subscribers in its initial years and by lecture fees and contributions from Tappan, the paper was commonly viewed as presenting the opinions of all abolitionists. Although nonthreatening in appearance—slim, prematurely bald, and funereal in dress—Garrison's approach was direct and challenging.

In 1832 Garrison helped organize the Massachusetts Anti-Slavery Society and in 1833 the American Anti-Slavery Society. In 1832 he published *Thoughts on African Colonization*, the leading critique of the American Colonization Society and of the idea of colonization in general. An advocate of moral suasion, he sought to convince Americans to reject the sin of slavery. In 1833, he visited Britain, meeting with its abolitionists there.

Garrison's reform interests were both broad and radical, and, as a result, he alienated many other abolitionists during the 1830s, leading to a split in the American Anti-Slavery Society at the end of the decade. Garrison's views on women (they should be equal participants in the abolitionist movement and its organizations), religion (churches contributed to slavery both through direct support and through neutrality and apathy), nonresistance (governments should not have power over people; only God should), the political system (political parties were pro-slavery and the system was corrupt), voting (it was sinful for him to vote), the Constitution (it was a pro-slavery document), the anti-slavery Liberty Party (it was sidetracking abolitionism and being corrupted), and violence (armed rescue of slaves and slave uprisings were wrong) led to conflicts with other abolitionists throughout the 1830s–1850s.

While Garrison opposed political abolitionism, he found the new Republican Party to be worthy of general support by the late 1850s. During the Civil War, despite his nonresistance, he supported the efforts of the Lincoln administration.

With slavery's end, Garrison focused on other reforms, including women's suffrage, Native American rights, and temperance. He died on May 24, 1879, in New York.

Sarah Moore Grimké (1792–1873) and Angelina Emily Grimké (1805–1879)

Sarah and Angelina Grimké were among the fourteen children born into a South Carolina slave-owning family. Their father, John Faucheraud Grimké, the Oxford-educated chief justice of the state's highest court, owned a plantation about 200 miles from where the family lived in Charleston. Because the family home was served by slaves, the sisters became familiar with the treatment of slaves. Sarah Grimké later remarked that "slavery was a millstone around my neck, and marred my comfort from the time I can remember myself."[6]

In the 1820s, the self-educated sisters rejected their Episcopalian faith, slavery, and the South and moved north. Both became Quakers and, although living comfortably on the inheritance from their father, became itinerant ministers.

After joining the Philadelphia Female Anti-Slavery Society in 1835, Angelina Grimké endorsed the abolitionists' petition movement. She also published an anti-slavery pamphlet, *Appeal to the Christian Women of the South* (1836) urging action against slavery. When the pamphlet was sent to Charleston by the American Anti-Slavery Society (AASS), it was publicly burned, and she was warned to stay away from the city or risk physical harm. At age thirty-two she also became a paid agent (speaker) for the AASS.

After a break with the Quakers over her public speaking, older sister Sarah also turned to abolitionism, publishing an anti-slavery work in 1836, *Epistle to the Clergy of the Southern States*. In December 1836 she joined her sister as an agent of the AASS. Their strong views on the proper roles of women led each to write on women's rights as well as slavery.

In May 1837 Angelina Grimké joined about 200 black and white women abolitionists in a national convention of anti-slavery women. Sarah Grimké presented her *Appeal to the Women of the Nominally Free States*. Then, starting out in Boston, the sisters went on a speaking tour during which they attacked slavery and defended women as "responsible moral being[s]."[7] Thousands came to hear the sisters, particularly Angelina whose oratory impressed even Wendell Phillips, abolitionism's most acclaimed speaker. In late 1837, Sarah Grimké wrote the letters that would be published the following year as *Letters on the Equality of the Sexes and the Condition of Woman*; Angelina's correspondence appeared as *Letters to Catherine E. Beecher, in Reply to an Essay on Slavery and Abolitionism*.

In February 1838, Angelina Grimké became the first woman to address the state legislature of Massachusetts. She and her sister followed that appearance with a lecture series. Then, in May 1838 Angelina Grimké married fellow abolitionist Theodore Dwight Weld. She was thereupon excommunicated by the Quakers for marrying a Presbyterian, her sister suffering the same fate for attending the marriage ceremony. Angelina's last public address was just two days after her wedding; she spoke to a crowd in Pennsylvania Hall in Philadelphia the day before a mob burned it down. In 1839 she and her husband left the public attack on slavery to others and, with Sarah joining them (nineteenth-century Americans did not approve of unmarried women living on their own), retired to a farm in New Jersey. Determined to show that her public role had not made her unfit for domestic life, Angelina bore two sons and a daughter. With Sarah the Welds established a school in New Jersey and, in 1863, in Massachusetts.

After several weeks of illness, Sarah Grimké died on December 23, 1873. William Lloyd Garrison spoke at her funeral. Angelina, paralyzed by strokes, died six years later on October 26, 1879, with Elizur Wright Jr. and Wendell Phillips speaking at her services.

Benjamin Lundy (1789–1839)

Born in January 1789 in Greensville, New Jersey, Benjamin Lundy was the only child of Joseph and Elizabeth Lundy, Quakers and farmers. Work on his father's farm harmed his health and permanently damaged his hearing.

Moving to Wheeling, Virginia (now West Virginia), in 1809, Lundy, despite his small stature and partial deafness, became an apprentice saddler and experienced the freer life of a non-Quaker community; however, he soon decided to adhere to traditional Quaker dress, speech, behavior, and beliefs. He was horrified by the internal slave trade which he witnessed and, as a result, dedicated his life to opposing slavery. Moving to the nearby Quaker community of Mount Pleasant, Ohio, and working as a saddle maker, Lundy was surrounded by strong anti-slavery voices. In 1815 he married a Quaker girl from the town, Esther Lewis, and they moved to a nearby town where he established a successful business.

Lundy formed the Union Humane Society in 1816. The organization, which supported gradual emancipation, opposed racial prejudice and legal restrictions on black rights. In 1817 Lundy became his town's agent for *The Philanthropist*, a paper that targeted many reforms, including slavery, and that was published by Charles Osborn, a gradual emancipationist. Lundy also joined the ranks of colonizationists, although in time he came to oppose the American Colonization Society.

Opposed to the expansion of slavery, Lundy became more familiar with its impact on slaves and their owners during a brief stay in Missouri in 1818. In 1819 he returned to help the anti-slavery forces there, writing and organizing. Believing that the anti-slavery papers of his day were inadequate in their anti-slavery focus, in 1821 Lundy began publication in Ohio of the *Genius of Universal Emancipation.* Moving to the slave state of Tennessee the next year, he continued his paper. In 1824, Lundy moved his paper to Baltimore where he worked to support the emigration of American blacks to black-ruled Haiti. He also devised a plan to establish a cooperative farm worked by free blacks in the deep South. When his wife died in Tennessee, Lundy placed his five children, including a newborn, with family and friends so he could continue to focus on abolition.

Soon after publishing a plea for Congress to abolish slavery in the District of Columbia in 1827, he was assaulted and charged with libel for publishing attacks on the slave trade and on a "soul seller."[8] He determined to redirect his efforts to the Northeast, a task which brought mixed results for the unprepossessing Lundy who traveled through New England and then New York. Returning to Baltimore, he escorted a dozen freed slaves to Haiti in order to ensure their freedom.

After William Lloyd Garrison briefly edited the *Genius* (1828), Lundy published the paper on his own and for a short time ran a free-produce store. Moving to Washington, D.C., he became subscription agent there for Garrison's new paper, the *Liberator.* He also shifted his emphasis to aiding free blacks, supporting a plan for a refuge for them in Canada where he traveled in 1831. Lundy also considered Mexico as a site for a black asylum, visiting Texas three times in the early 1830s to negotiate for land and the right of Americans to settle there. The trips left him exhausted and ill, as well as out of sync with abolitionism. His plan was mere colonization to most abolitionists, but he won the support of David Lee and Lydia Maria Child. Texas's successful revolt from Mexican rule ended their plans. Former president and representative John Quincy Adams used Lundy's essays on the slave South's role in the Texas revolution, first printed in the Philadelphia *National Gazette*, to oppose the area's annexation.

In 1836 Lundy returned to publishing with the *National Enquirer and Constitutional Advocate of Universal Liberty* as a weekly and the *Genius of Universal Emancipation* as a quarterly. With these publications and his collection of writings on Texas annexation, *The War in Texas*, he continued his crusade to prevent enlargement of slave territory. He also advocated political action against slavery and worked in Pennsylvania for a law that would guarantee trial by jury for fugitive slaves. By the late 1830s Lundy had become an opponent of Garrisonianism.

Ill and outside of most abolitionist efforts, Lundy retired from abolitionist work in 1838. Before he could join his family in Illinois, most of his possessions were destroyed when a mob burned the new Pennsylvania Hall in Philadelphia. In Illinois he returned to abolitionist work, even renewing publication of the *Genius* in 1839. His abolitionist efforts, as well as plans for a second marriage and a farm, ended in August 1839 with his death from a fever.

Arthur Tappan (1786–1865) and Lewis Tappan (1788–1873)

Brothers Arthur and Lewis Tappan were both born in Northampton, Massachusetts, the two youngest sons in a family of farmers and storekeepers.

Lewis made a fortune during the War of 1812. Aided by a loan from his brother, Arthur began a silk-importing business in New York; by the late 1820s, it was the largest in the nation. Lewis joined Arthur's mercantile house and in 1841 founded the first agency in the country to rate commercial credit (the firm later became Dun & Bradstreet). He retired from the firm in 1840, leaving his financially struggling brother a copartner.

Lewis Tappan's interest in philanthropic work began early in Boston as he sought to aid the poor in various ways. He was a sabbatarian (an opponent of Sunday stagecoach service and mail delivery) and a founder of the General Union for Promoting the Observance of the Christian Sabbath. Derisively called Saint Arthur by his critics, Arthur Tappan, who gave no public speeches and kept his writings brief, made an impact through monetary contributions. In 1825 he founded the American Tract Society which distributed inspirational religious booklets. He was an officer in numerous benevolent organizations, and both brothers worked against prostitution and alcohol. Both brothers were also influenced by revivalist Charles Grandison Finney and founded the *New York Evangelist* to spread his revivalist views. They formed the Association of Gentlemen to promote good works.

The Tappans became famous for their activities as immediate emancipationists. In the early 1830s, Arthur's influence dominated, particularly financially; in the 1840s–1850s, his brother was one of the leaders of abolitionism in terms of organization, policy making, and publishing. Arthur was a member of the American Colonization Society until late 1833. He paid William Lloyd Garrison's fine for libel and helped Garrison begin publication of the *Liberator* in 1831. Arthur Tappan also helped pay Prudence Crandall's costs when she fought to maintain her school for black girls in Connecticut. In 1833, he was a founder and the first president of the New York Anti-Slavery Society, and both he and his brother were founding members of the American Anti-Slavery Society (AASS), Arthur serving as the first president and Lewis as a member of the Executive Committee. In addition, Arthur Tappan was a critical force in the establishment of Oberlin College in Ohio, providing a large endowment to support the abolitionists who gathered there after leaving Lane Seminary in Cincinnati. The school drew much of his time, interest, and money until 1836 when he and his brother worried about its anti-slavery emphasis.

He converted to abolitionism after his brother Lewis, who had a talent for office responsibilities and for writing and editing, became close friends with abolitionist speaker and organizer Theodore Dwight Weld when Tappan's sons were attending Oneida Academy in New York. Inspired by Weld's efforts in Cincinnati, he launched projects to help impoverished and uneducated New York blacks. Under his direction, the AASS in 1835 prepared over a million items for mailing, spurring southern and northern, state and national efforts to restrict mailing privileges. In New York, both brothers were subjected to threats and harassment and even to violence and rioting.

As a result of southern refusals to continue trade with the Tappan firm, as well as a destructive fire, in May 1837 Arthur Tappan announced debts of over one million dollars, a situation which undermined his anti-slavery influence and limited the time that he could devote to the cause. The rest of his life was filled with limited financial recoveries aided by his brother Lewis.

The Tappans' disagreement with Garrison on a wide variety of issues led to their secession from the AASS in 1840. Arthur Tappan was elected president of the new American and Foreign Anti-Slavery Society. At the same time, Lewis Tappan's attention was drawn to the case of the fifty-four Africans who mutinied onboard and seized the *Amistad* in 1836. For two years he was responsible for their obtaining spiritual guidance, an interpreter, and legal counsel; he worked with the case until the final decision by the Supreme Court in 1841 that freed the Africans. A supporter of the Liberty Party during the 1840s, he also founded, organized, and raised funds for the American Missionary Association (1846). In response to the Kansas-Nebraska Act's reopening of territory to slavery in 1854, he helped found the American Abolition Society to replace the American and Foreign Anti-Slavery Society. He hesitantly voted for the Republicans in 1856.

Lewis Tappan made his last public appearance in the January 1863 celebration of the Emancipation Proclamation. His brother Arthur died in July 1865, and Lewis's biography of him appeared in 1870. Lewis Tappan died in 1873 at the age of eighty-five.

David Walker (1796?–1830)

David Walker was born in Wilmington, South Carolina, to a free black woman. His father, a slave, died before his birth. A free man because of his mother's status, Walker saw the brutality and pain of slavery through his travels. He moved to Charleston sometime in the 1810s and likely knew or was familiar with Denmark Vesey and his planned revolt of 1822. He was also likely influenced by the African Methodist Episcopal church.

By 1825 Walker had moved to Boston and opened a business selling second-hand clothes, a popular enterprise at the time for local blacks. In Boston he became familiar with African history, became a Prince Hall (African) Mason, joined a black Methodist church, and helped establish the anti-colonizationist Massachusetts General Colored Association. The last aimed to unite blacks to promote abolition and intellectual and moral improvement. A speech he delivered to the organization was published in *Freedom's Journal*, the nation's first black newspaper. An advocate of black education, self-help, equality, and anti-slavery, Walker was also an agent for the newspaper.

David Walker's 1828 speech provided the foundation for the first of three editions of *David Walker's Appeal, in Four Articles; Together with a Preamble to the Coloured Citizens of the World, But in Particular, and Very Expressly, to Those of the United States of America* (1829). Direct and eloquent, the *Appeal* sought peace and equality but made clear the ramifications of white resistance to these goals and the brutal, un-christian treatment of American blacks. It urged blacks to defend themselves, arguing that death was preferable to enslavement. Walker expected his *Appeal* to be read by literate blacks to the illiterate and urged pride in black history and awareness of black potential.

Walker's publication scared white Southerners into greater fear of a race war. In large part, they were concerned by Walker's efforts to distribute his *Appeal* throughout the South. In addition, unlike anti-slavery writings which were aimed at white readers, the *Appeal* targeted black ones. Southerners demanded the repression of the pamphlet, as well as Walker's death or extradition south.

Walker died from unknown causes in August 1830, a few days after his infant daughter's death and shortly before his son's birth. Rumors suggested poisoning; evidence suggests consumption, the same illness that took his daughter's life.

Black abolitionist Henry Highland Garnet argued in 1848 that while "Mr. Walker is know principally for his 'Appeal,' . . . it was . . . by his unceasing labors in the cause of freedom, that he has made his memory sacred."[9]

Theodore Dwight Weld (1803–1895)

The son of a Presbyterian minister, Theodore Dwight Weld was born in Hampton, Connecticut, in 1803. At age twenty-two he and his family moved to upstate New York. At Hamilton College, he was converted by and became a follower of Charles Grandison Finney, the leading evangelist of the 1820s–1830s. He enrolled at reform-oriented Oneida Academy in New York in the early 1830s. Weld enjoyed the school's emphasis on manual labor and reform issues, including colonization. While at Oneida, he met Lewis Tappan, the New York merchant and abolitionist whose sons attended the school. Moving to Lane Seminary in Cincinnati, Ohio, with two dozen other Oneidans, Weld, who had become an immediate abolitionist, helped organize a series of debates on slavery that led to the students' support of immediatism. In 1834 he supported a group of thirty-nine students (the Lane Rebels) who left the seminary for Oberlin College in northern Ohio when Lane's board of directors attempted to thwart their support of abolitionism and their work and close association with blacks.

Declining a professorship at Oberlin, Weld began a short career as an anti-slavery agent. A successful traveling abolitionist speaker in Ohio and New York in 1835–1837, he focused on the denial of liberty. He argued for abolitionist support of northern blacks. He was responsible for increasing the number of abolitionists in upstate New York and the Midwest. This phase of Weld's life ended when he lost his voice, whether to physical or psychological problems, it is not clear. By then he had become well known, revered by some and hated (and mobbed) by others.

Weld recruited and trained anti-slavery agents (the Seventy) in Ohio, New York, and New England. In New York, Weld shifted to writing for anti-slavery publications. Taking on the job of training new abolitionist speakers, he met Angelina and Sarah Grimké, two of the leading female abolitionists of the period, in 1837–1838 at New York training sessions. In May 1838 he married Angelina Grimké, their wedding attended by such abolitionist luminaries as William Lloyd Garrison, James G. Birney, Gerrit Smith, Maria Weston Chapman, John Greenleaf Whittier, Lewis Tappan, and Abby Kelley.

Weld turned down many speaking and service offers but edited the *Antislavery Almanacs* for 1839–1841. In 1839 Weld, with the aid of his wife and sister-in-law, anonymously published *American Slavery as It Is: Testimony of a Thousand Witnesses*. Weld wrote widely about slavery and abolition, which he usually did under pen names, but this pamphlet was his most influential abolitionist work, even more so than *The Bible against Slavery* (1837). *American Slavery as It Is*, which sold over 100,000 copies in its first year, was probably the most important anti-slavery publication until *Uncle Tom's Cabin* in 1852, which drew upon its descriptions for much of its details about slavery.

Weld and his family moved to a farm in New Jersey in 1840, financed in part by a loan from Lewis Tappan. Frustrated by the unbending support for slavery and the divisions among his fellow abolitionists, Weld focused on teaching and various community projects. Not until 1862 did he once again publicly (and briefly) lecture against slavery.

He died in 1895 in Hyde Park, Massachusetts.

John Woolman (1720–1772)

Born in 1720 near Mount Holly, New Jersey, John Woolman was the eldest child of Quakers and farmers. After leaving home at age twenty to work in a village shop as a conveyancer (one who prepares legal documents transferring title to property), he learned tailoring and in 1747 bought the shop and eleven acres of land. He was successful as Mount Holly's surveyor, conveyancer, and business agent. Married in 1749 to Sarah Ellis, he became upset over the success of his business and believed that "Truth required me to live more free from outward cumbers."[10] Prayer led him to cut back on his business and soon to sell the shop. He supported his family by working as a tailor, farmer, and scribe.

Woolman's maternal grandfather had owned slaves, but his father opposed the practice. His own opposition to slavery grew when the shop owner for whom he worked had him write up a bill of sale for the shop slave. He completed the task but "was so afflicted in my mind"; he concluded, "slave keeping to be a practice inconsistent with the Christian religion."[11] He lost income when he refused to write up slave sales. His interest in slavery grew, and in 1746 he spent three months in Virginia as a traveling minister.

In 1753 he published *Considerations on the Keeping of Negroes*. The Quakers' Philadelphia Yearly Meeting approved it for publication. The Meeting also approved its circulation to all Yearly Meetings. In *Considerations*, which was the most widely circulated anti-slavery tract to that point, Woolman challenged Quakers to acknowledge their inconsistency in supporting "the Gospel of universal love and peace among mankind" and in owning slaves.[12]

Largely because of John Woolman's efforts and arguments about God's displeasure and likely punishments, the Philadelphia Yearly Meeting of 1758 expressed concern with importing, buying, selling, and owning slaves. Woolman and three others were appointed to meet with slave owners. With fellow Quakers Anthony Benezet and John Churchman, he was a leader of the Quaker radicals. They inspired the London Yearly Meeting to condemn the slave trade.

In 1757 Woolman made a two-month tour of Maryland, Virginia, and North Carolina. Rather than stay at the homes of slave owners for free, thus accepting the labor of slaves, he gave money to the slaves or to slave owners to pass on to them. He also gave up sugar and rum, products produced largely by slave labor, and refused to accept travel expenses provided by slave-owning Quakers.

During the 1760s Woolman traveled by foot in the South. His

simple means of travel was meant to win the attention and play on the conscience of Quaker slave owners and to show his identification with slaves. Part two of *Considerations on the Keeping of Negroes*, which argued against the biblical base of slavery and against racial discrimination, appeared in 1762.

John Woolman died of smallpox in Britain in 1772 while on a religious visit.

Notes

1. Quoted in Benjamin Quarles, *The Negro in the American Revolution* (Chapel Hill: University of North Carolina Press, 1961), 35.

2. Quoted in Carl Binger, *Revolutionary Doctor: Benjamin Rush, 1746–1813* (New York: W. W. Norton, 1966), 96.

3. Quoted in Betty Fladeland, *James Gillespie Birney: Slaveholder to Abolitionist* (Ithaca, NY: Cornell University Press, 1955), 17.

4. Quoted in Blanche Glassman Hersh, *The Slavery of Sex: Feminist-Abolitionists in America* (Urbana: University of Illinois Press, 1978), 12–13.

5. Quoted in Robert C. Dick, *Black Protest: Issues and Tactics* (Westport, CT: Greenwood, 1974), 137.

6. Quoted in Catherine H. Birney, *Sarah and Angelina Grimké: The First American Women Advocates of Abolition and Woman's Rights* (Boston: Lee and Shepard, 1885), 10.

7. Quoted in Kathryn Kish Sklar, *Women's Rights Emerges within the Antislavery Movement, 1830–1870: A Brief History with Documents* (Boston: Bedford/St. Martin's, 2000), 28.

8. Quoted in Merton L. Dillon, *Benjamin Lundy and the Struggle for Negro Freedom* (Urbana: University of Illinois Press, 1966), 119.

9. Quoted in Peter P. Hinks, ed., *David Walker's Appeal to the Coloured Citizens of the World* (University Park: Pennsylvania State University Press, 2000), xlii.

10. Quoted in Edwin H. Cady, *John Woolman: The Mind of the Quaker Saint* (New York: Washington Square Press, 1966), 77.

11. Quoted in Thomas E. Drake, *Quakers and Slavery in America* (New Haven, CT: Yale University Press, 1950), 52.

12. Quoted in ibid., 59.

PRIMARY DOCUMENTS OF ABOLITIONISM

Anthony Benezet on Slavery

Anthony Benezet, a Quaker teacher, was one of the 1700s' most influential opponents of the slave trade and slavery. Through his writings, published in the American colonies and Britain, he influenced both Americans, including Dr. Benjamin Rush, and Britons. In them he attacked the horrors of the slave trade and the harmful effect of slavery on both slaves and masters. As did many other critics of slavery, he called attention to the unchristian nature of slavery.

Some who have only seen negroes in an abject state of slavery, broken-spirited and dejected, knowing nothing of their situation in their native country, may apprehend that they are naturally insensible of the benefits of liberty, being destitute and miserable in every respect, and that our suffering them to live amongst us . . . is to them a favor; but these are certainly erroneous opinions with respect to far the greatest part of them. . . .

. . . [I]t may well be concluded that [the Africans'] acquaintance with the Europeans would have been a happiness to them had those last not only bore the name, but been influenced by the spirit, of Christianity. But, alas, how hath the conduct of the whites contradicted the precepts and example of Christ! Instead of promoting the end of his coming by preaching the gospel of peace and good-will to man, they have, by their practices, contributed to inflame every noxious passion of corrupt nature in the negroes . . . which must necessarily beget in their minds such a general detestation and scorn of the Christian name as may deeply affect, if not wholly preclude, their belief of the great truths of our holy religion. . . .

Those who are acquainted with the [slave] trade agree that many negroes on the [African] sea-coast . . . have learned to stick to no act of cruelty for gain. . . . When the poor slaves . . . come to the sea-shore, they are stripped naked and strictly examined by the European sur- geons, both men and women, without the least distinction or mod- esty. . . . Reader, bring the matter home, and consider whether any situation in life can be more completely miserable than that of those distressed captives. When we reflect that each individual of this num- ber had some tender attachment, which was broken by the cruel sepa- ration; some parent or wife, who had not an opportunity of mingling tears in a parting embrace; perhaps some infant, or aged parent, whom his labor was to feed and vigilance to protect; themselves under the dreadful apprehension of an unknown, perpetual slavery, pent up within the narrow confines of a vessel, sometimes six or seven hundred to- gether, where they lie as close as possible. Under these complicated dis- tresses, they are often reduced to a state of desperation, wherein many have leaped into the sea and kept themselves under water till they were drowned; others have starved themselves to death. . . .

When the vessels arrive at their destined port in the Colonies, the poor negroes are to be disposed of to the planters; and here they are again exposed, naked, without any distinction of sex, to the brutal ex- amination of their purchasers; and this, as it may be judged, is to many of them another occasion of deep distress, especially to the females; add to this, that near connections must now again be separated, to go with their several purchasers. In this melancholy scene, mothers are seen hanging over their daughters, . . . and daughters clinging to their parents, not knowing what new stage of distress must follow their sep- aration, or if ever they shall meet again. . . .

Can any human heart that retains a fellow-feeling for the suffer- ings of mankind be unconcerned at relations of such grievous afflic- tion, to which this oppressed part of our species are subjected? God gave to man dominion over the fish of the sea, and over the fowls of the air, and over the cattle, &c., but imposed no involuntary subjec- tion of one man to another. . . .

[Quoting from "An Essay in Vindication of the Continental Colonies of America":] "Shall a civilized, a Christian nation encourage slavery because the barbarous, savage, lawless African hath done it? Mon- strous thought! To what end do we profess a religion whose dictates we so flagrantly violate? Wherefore have we that pattern of goodness and humanity if we refuse to follow it? How long shall we continue a practice which policy rejects, justice condemns, and piety dissuades? Shall the Americans persist in a conduct which cannot be justified, or persevere in a conduct from which their hearts must recoil?"

Source: Anthony Benezet, "Caution and Warning to Great Britain and Her Colonies on the Calamitous State of the Enslaved Negroes in the British Dominions," in *Views of American Slavery, Taken a Century Ago* (Philadelphia: Association of Friends for the Diffusion of Religious and Useful Knowledge, 1858), 34–39, 43.

John Woolman

The Quaker John Woolman turned against slavery early in life. The defining event came at his job as a conveyancer. Afterward, he dedicated much of his life to convincing others to oppose slavery. In this description from his *Journal*, his gentleness and caring spirit are obvious.

My employer, having a negro woman, sold her and desired me to write a bill of sale, the man being waiting who bought her. The thing was sudden; and though I felt uneasy at the thoughts of writing an instrument of slavery for one of my fellow-creatures, yet I remembered that I was hired by the year, that it was my master who directed me to do it, and that it was an elderly man, a member of our Society, who bought her; so through weakness I gave way, and wrote it; but at the executing of it I was so afflicted in my mind, that I said before my master and the Friend that I believed slave-keeping to be a practice inconsistent with the Christian religion. This, in some degree, abated my uneasiness; yet as often as I reflected seriously upon it I thought I should have been clearer if I had desired to be excused from it, as a thing against my conscience; for such it was. Some time after this a young man of our Society spoke to me to write a conveyance of a slave to him, he having lately taken a negro into his house. I told him I was not easy to write it; for, though many of our meeting and in other places kept slaves, I still believed the practice was not right, and desired to be excused from writing it. I spoke to him in good-will; and he told me that keeping slaves was not altogether agreeable to his mind. . . .

Source: The Journal of John Woolman (Boston: Houghton Mifflin, 1909), 64–65.

Benjamin Rush and Slavery (1773)

Benjamin Rush was a physician, revolutionary, and abolitionist. In 1773, when many white colonials were questioning their treatment by Britain, he published "On Slave-Keeping." In it he questioned assertions of black inferiority, suggesting an environmental explanation for racial differences, and the biblical support of slavery. Like many other American opponents of slavery, he finds the institution harmful to both blacks and whites.

. . . Slavery is so foreign to the human mind, that the moral faculties, as well as those of the understanding are debased, and rendered torpid by it. All the vices which are charged upon the Negroes in the southern colonies and the West-Indies, such as Idleness, Treachery, Theft, and the like, are the genuine offspring of slavery, and serve as an argument to prove that they are not intended by Providence for it.

. . . The vulgar notion of their being descended from Cain, who was supposed to have been marked with this [black] color, is too absurd to need a refutation.—[Their color] subjects the Negroes to no inconveniences, but, on the contrary, qualifies them for that part of the Globe in which Providence has placed them. . . .

It has been urged by the inhabitants of the Sugar Islands and South Carolina, that it would be impossible to carry on the manufactories of sugar, rice, and indigo, without Negro slaves. No manufactory can ever be of consequence enough to society, to admit the least violation of the laws of justice or humanity. . . .

But there are some who have gone so far as to say, that slavery is not repugnant to the genius of Christianity, and that it is not forbidden in any part of the Scriptures. . . . If it could be proved that no testimony was to be found in the Bible against a practice so pregnant with evils of the most destructive tendency to society, it would be sufficient to overthrow its divine original. . . . Christ commands us to look upon all mankind, even our enemies, as our neighbours and brethren, and "in all things, to do unto them whatever we would wish they should do unto us." . . . [A]ltho' he does not call upon masters to emancipate their slaves, or upon slaves to assert that liberty wherewith God and nature had made them free, yet there is scarcely a parable or a sermon in the whole history of his life, but what contains the strongest arguments against slavery. . . .

[Supporting enslavement of Africans because they are introduced to Christianity] . . . is like justifying a highway robbery, because part of the money acquired in this manner was appropriated to some religious use. . . . A Christian slave is a contradiction in terms. . . . [Plus] every attempt to instruct or convert them, has been constantly opposed by their masters. Nor has the example of their Christian masters any tendency to prejudice them in favor of our religion. . . . I say nothing of the dissolution of marriage vows, or the entire abolition of matrimony. . . . Would to heaven I could here conceal the shocking violations of chastity, which some of them are obliged to undergo without daring to complain. Husbands have been forced to prostitute their wives, and mothers their daughters, to gratify the brutal lust of a master[,] . . . by men who call themselves Christians! . . .

[I]s not keeping a slave, after you are convinced of the unlawfulness of it, a crime of the same nature? All the money you save, or acquire by their labour is stolen from them; and however plausible the excuse may be, that you form to reconcile it to your consciences, yet be assured, that your crime stands registered in the court of Heaven as a breach of the eighth commandment.

The first step to be taken to put a stop to slavery in this country, is to leave off importing slaves. . . . As for the Negroes among us, who, from having acquired all the low vices of slavery, or who, from age or infirmities are unfit to be set at liberty, I would propose, for the good of society, that they should continue the property of those with whom they grew old, or from whom they contracted those vices and infirmities. But let the young Negroes be educated in the principles of virtue and religion—let them be taught to read and write—and afterwards instructed in some business, whereby they may be able to maintain themselves. Let laws be made to limit the time of their servitude, and to entitle them to all the privileges of free-born British subjects. . . .

Source: Benjamin Rush, "An Address to the Inhabitants of the British Settlements in America upon Slave-Keeping" (New York: Hodge and Shober, 1773), 4–6, 10–11, 14–16, 18, 21–23.

Thomas Jefferson's Views of Blacks and Slavery (178?)

Just a few years after writing the Declaration of Independence, Thomas Jefferson, a slave owner who freed his slaves, wrote on various aspects of life in his new state of Virginia. Amidst discussion of rivers, climate, colleges, and revenue sources were analyses of the differences between blacks and whites, the reasons for and impact of black inferiority, and the need to end slavery.

It will probably be asked, Why not retain and incorporate the blacks into the State [rather than try to deport them], and thus save the expense of supplying, by importation of white settlers, the vacancies they will leave? Deep-rooted prejudices entertained by the whites; ten thousand recollections, by the blacks, of the injuries they have sustained; new provocations; the real distinctions which nature has made; and many other circumstances, will divide us into parties, and produce convulsions, which will probably never end but in the extermination of the one or the other race. . . . The first difference which strikes us is that of color. [Whatever its cause] . . . the difference is fixed in nature, and is as real as if its seat and cause were better known to us. . . . Add to these, flowing hair, a more elegant symmetry of form, their own judgment in favor of the whites, declared by their preference of them, as uniformly as is the preference of the Oran-ûtan for the black woman over those of his species. The circumstances of superior beauty, is thought worthy attention in the propagation of our horses, dogs, and other domestic animals; why not in that of man? . . . [T]here are other physical distinctions proving a difference of race. They have less hair on the face and body. They secrete less by the kidneys, and more by the glands of the skin, which gives them a very strong and disagreeable odour. This greater degree of transpiration renders them more tolerant of heat, and less so of cold than the whites. . . . They seem to require less sleep. . . . They are at least as brave, and more adventuresome. But this may perhaps proceed from a want of forethought, which prevents their seeing a danger till it be present. . . . They are more ardent after their female; but love seems with them to be more an eager desire, than a tender delicate mixture of sentiment and sensation. Their griefs are transient. . . . In general, their existence appears to participate more of sensation than reflection. . . . [I]n memory they are equal to the whites; in reason much inferior . . . ; and that in imagination they are dull, tasteless, and anomalous. . . . It will be right to make great allowances for the difference of condition, of education, of conversation, of the sphere in which they move [when looking at them in the United

States]. . . . But never yet could I find that a black had uttered a thought above the level of plain narration; never see even an elementary trait of painting or sculpture. In music they are more generally gifted than the whites with accurate ears for tune and time. . . . Among the blacks is misery enough, God Knows, but no poetry [growing out of it]. . . . Religion indeed has produced a Phyllis Whately [*sic*]; but it could not produce a poet. The compositions published under her name are below the dignity of criticism. . . . [The black's] . . . imagination is wild and extravagant, . . . and, in the course of its vagaries, leaves a tract of thought as incoherent and eccentric, as is the course of a meteor through the sky. . . . The improvement of the blacks in body and mind, in the first instance of their mixture with the whites, has been observed by every one, and proves that their inferiority is not the effect merely of their condition of life. . . . I advance it therefore as a suspicion only [since there has been little study of the general situation], that the blacks, whether originally a distinct race, or made distinct by time and circumstances, are inferior to the whites in the endowments both of body and mind. . . . This unfortunate difference of color, and perhaps of faculty, is a powerful obstacle to the emancipation of these people. . . . Among the Romans emancipation required but one effort. The slave, when made free, might mix with, without staining the blood of his master. But with us a second is necessary, unknown to history. When freed, he is to be removed beyond the reach of mixture. . . .

. . . I tremble for my country when I reflect that God is just; that his justice cannot sleep for-ever; that considering numbers, nature and natural means only, a revolution of the wheel of fortune, an exchange of situation is among possible events. . . . The Almighty has no attribute which can take side with us in such a contest. . . . I think a change already perceptible, since the origin of the present revolution. The spirit of the master is abating, that of the slave rising from the dust, his condition mollifying, the way I hope preparing, under the auspices of heaven, for a total emancipation, and that this is disposed, in the order of events, to be with the consent of the masters, rather than by their extirpation.

Source: Thomas Jefferson, *The Writings of Thomas Jefferson*, vol. 2 (Washington, DC: Issued under the auspices of the Jefferson Memorial Association, 1907), 192–201, 227–228.

The United States Constitution on Slavery

Three provisions in the new Constitution of 1787 dealt specifically with slavery and slaves, even though those two words never appear in the Constitution. To a large extent, the provisions reflect the delegates' willingness to compromise. Other parts of the Constitution dealing with Congress's power in the territories, its power to regulate trade and impose tariffs on imports, and its power to suppress insurrections would play a part in the debate between pro- and anti-slavery forces in later years. The First Amendment added to the Constitution would also play a role when slavery's defense threatened white civil liberties.

Article I, section 2, paragraph 3. Representation and direct Taxes shall be apportioned among the several States which may be included within this Union, according to their respective Numbers, which shall be determined by adding to the whole Number of free Persons, including those bound to Service for a Term of Years, and excluding Indians not taxed, three fifths of all other persons.

Article I, section 9, paragraph 1. The Migration or Importation of such Persons as any of the States now existing shall think proper to admit, shall not be prohibited by the Congress prior to the year one thousand eight hundred and eight, but a Tax or duty may be imposed on such Importation, not exceeding ten dollars for each Person.

Article IV, section 2, paragraph 3. No Person held to Service or Labour in one State, under the Laws thereof, escaping into another, shall, in Consequence of any Law or Regulation therein, be discharged from such Service or Labour, but shall be delivered up on Claim of the Party to whom such Service or Labour may be done.

Indirectly:

Article I, section 8, paragraph 3. [The Congress shall have Power] To regulate Commerce with foreign Nations, and among the several States. . . .

Article I, section 8, paragraph 15. [The Congress shall have Power] To provide for calling forth the Militia to execute the Laws of the Union, suppress Insurrections and repel Invasions.

Article IV, Section 3, paragraph 2. The Congress shall have Power to dispose of and make all needful Rules and Regulations respecting the Territory or other Property belonging to the United States. . . .

Amendment 1. Congress shall make no law . . . abridging the freedom of speech, or of the press; or the right of the people peaceably to assemble, and to petition the Government for a redress of grievances.

Congressional Abolition of International Slave Trade

The Constitution permitted Congress to ban the Atlantic slave trade as early as 1808. In anticipation of this date, President Thomas Jefferson proposed a prohibition in December 1806. Congress passed it in March 1807. The law abolishing the foreign slave trade set a fine of up to ten years and a prison sentence of five to ten years for those convicted of smuggling slaves into the country. The prohibition was not enforceable in areas that sympathized with the trade—over 10,000 slaves were imported illegally during the law's first five years in effect.

An Act to prohibit the importation of slaves into any port or place within the jurisdiction of the United States, from and after the first day of January, in the year of our Lord one thousand eight hundred and eight.

Be it enacted, etc. That, from and after the first day of January, one thousand eight hundred and eight, it shall not be lawful to import or bring into the United States or the territories thereof, from any foreign kingdom, place, or country, any negro, mulatto, or person of color, with intent to hold, sell, or dispose of such negro, mulatto, or person of color, as a slave, or to be held to service or labor. . . .

David Walker's Appeal, in Four Articles (1829)

Born free in North Carolina in 1797, David Walker moved to Boston in the 1820s. There he published his *Appeal . . . to the Coloured Citizens of the World*. Unlike many other later abolitionist works which were aimed at white readers, the *Appeal* targeted literate blacks with the hope that they would read it to illiterate slaves and free blacks. While he urged black violence only in response to white actions, Walker and his book were seen as threats to the legal institution of slavery.

The whites want slaves, and want us for their slaves, but some of them will curse the day they ever saw us. As true as the sun ever shone in its meridian splendor, my colour will root some of them out of the very face of the earth. They shall have enough of making slaves of, and butchering, and murdering us in the manner which they have. . . . Whether I write with a bad or a good spirit, I say if these things do not occur in their proper time, it is because the world in which we live does not exist, and we are deceived with regard to its existence.—It is immaterial however to me, who believe, or who refuse—though I should like to see the whites repent peradventure God may have mercy on them, some however, have gone so far that their cup must be filled.

. . . if you commence, make sure work—do not trifle, for they will not trifle with you—they want us for their slaves, and think nothing of murdering us in order to subject us to that wretched condition— therefore, if there is an *attempt* made by us, kill or be killed. Now, I ask you, had you not rather be killed than to be a slave to a tyrant, who takes the life of your mother, wife, and dear little children? Look upon your mother, wife and children, and answer God Almighty; and believe this, that it is no more harm for you to kill a man, who is trying to kill you, than it is for you to take a drink of water when thirsty. . . .

Men of colour, who are also of sense, for you particularly is my APPEAL designed. . . . I call upon you . . . to cast your eyes upon the wretchedness of your brethren, and to do your utmost to enlighten them—*go to work and enlighten your brethren!* . . . Look into our free- dom and happiness, and see of what kind they are composed!! They are of the very lowest kind—they are the very *dregs!*—they are the most servile and abject kind, that ever a people was in possession of! . . . And yet some of you have the hardihood to say you are free and happy! . . . Your full glory and happiness, as well as all other coloured people under Heaven, shall never be fully consummated, but with the *entire emancipation of your enslaved brethren all over the world.*

Source: Peter P. Hinks, ed., *David Walker's Appeal to the Coloured Citizens of the World* (University Park: Pennsylvania State University Press, 2000), 22–23, 28, 30–31.

Colonization versus Immediate Emancipation

Abolitionist publications of the 1830s spent considerable time la- beling colonization as anti-black and pro-slavery. They also sought to clarify the meaning of immediate abolition. Elizur Wright, a for- mer colonizationist, explains the problems of colonization and the benefits of immediate abolition.

... [T]here pervades the whole community [American Colonization Society], a strong prejudice against the colored race.... The Society not only acknowledges the existence of such a prejudice, but it pronounces it unconquerable. It asserts, without reserve, that this prejudice is sufficient for ever to prevent the blacks from rising to an equality with the whites, in this the native land of both.... Therefore the Colonization Society, in applying its remedy for slavery, *humors its own wicked prejudice*. In what light is a remedy to be regarded, which, while it has no chance of curing the evil for which it was intended, absolutely poisons the person who administers it? ...

... A majority of the Society, at its establishment, consisted of slave-holders—of slave-holders who took special care to have it understood that they did not renounce the sin—that they considered the *right* of the master *sacred*! ... No scheme arising out of that miscalled morality, which apologizes for slavery, can either be right of itself, or made so by the patronage of all the saints on earth, or the angels in heaven. It is manifest from the *conduct* of the members, that the *motive* of the Society ... can be nothing better than to escape the righteous curse of God, in some other way than by a direct repentance, confession, and reparation of injury—the only way which he has appointed....

The doctrine [of immediate abolition] may be thus briefly stated. It is the duty of the holders of slaves immediately to restore to them their liberty, and to extend to them the full protection of law, as well as its control. It is their duty equitably to restore to them those profits of their labor, which have been wickedly wrested away, especially by giving them that moral and mental instruction—that education, which alone can render any considerable accumulation of property a blessing. It is their duty to employ them as voluntary laborers, on equitable wages. Also, it is the duty of all men to proclaim this doctrine—to urge upon slaveholders *immediate emancipation*, so long as there is a slave— to agitate the consciences of tyrants, as long as there is a tyrant on the globe.

... So long as the slaves are left entirely to the control of individual masters, some kind and lenient, freeing now and then a slave, and promising freedom to others, and exercising a sort of patriarchal authority, while others are, each in his own way, more harsh and severe, the unity of the slaves, as a body, is broken. They have no common cause. . . . Go on, then, refuse to emancipate, add insult to injury—add stings to desperation—make death easier than bondage—for, in so doing, you assuredly hasten the day, when the American bill of rights shall mean what it says.

But if you recoil at the prospect—if sanity has not yet bid adieu to your heads, and the milk of human kindness is not quite dried up from your breasts—look at the other side. Immediate emancipation would reverse the picture. It would place a motive to love you in the room of every one which now urges the slaves to hate you. They would then become, for you well know how grateful they are for even the slightest favors, your defenders instead of your murderers. . . .

. . . We plead for no *turning loose, no exile, no kicking out of house and home, but for complete and hearty* JUSTICE. . . . A wise and vigorous system of free labor and or primary instruction, should be immediately erected on the dark pile of oppression, which we urge them instantly to demolish. . . . We hold the masters bound, individually and in the aggregate, first to LIBERATE and then to ENLIGHTEN the IMMORTAL MINDS that have been abused and debased by their avarice and lust! . . .

. . . [Y]our sole object is to rid yourselves of colored freedom, lest your slaves should be provoked to think themselves men, and discover that they too have rights. Shame on you too, benevolent colonizers! Do not add to your unchristian prejudice the gratuitous sycophancy of doing their foulest deeds for manstealers! . . .

When we say that slave-holders ought to emancipate their slaves immediately, we state a *doctrine* which is *true*. We do not propose a *plan*. Our *plan*, and it has been explained often enough not to be misunderstood, is simply this: To promulgate the true *doctrine* of human rights in high places and low places, and all places where there are human beings. . . .

We expect to see the free colored American so educated and elevated in our own land, that it shall be notorious that the slave is BROTHER TO A MAN! In the meantime we expect to see the great body of slave-holders exasperated, foaming with rage and gnashing their teeth, threatening loudly to secede from the Union! Madly prating about the invasion of sacred rights, the disturbance of their domestic quiet, and the violation of solemn compacts. . . . Nevertheless, we expect to see some tyrants, conscience-stricken, loosen their grasp; we expect, with God's good help, to hear the trumpet of the world's jubilee announcing that the *last fetter* has been knocked off from the heel of the *last slave. . . .*

Source: John L. Thomas, ed., *Slavery Attacked: The Abolitionist Crusade* (Englewood Cliffs, NJ: Prentice-Hall, 1965), 11–17.

William Lloyd Garrison's Domination of Abolitionism

In the eyes of many Americans, in the antebellum period and even today, abolitionism was defined by the views and actions of William Lloyd Garrison. In this August 28, 1837, letter to James T. Woodbury, Garrison deals with this perception. He also recounts the early struggles of himself and fellow abolitionists as they fought not only against slavery and racial discrimination but also against anti-abolitionist attitudes.

. . . From the commencement of the campaign up to the present time, every man, who has joined the anti-slavery ranks, has had to endure the opprobrium of being stigmatized as "a Garrison man," or "a Garrisonite," or, in your choice phraseology, as "swallowing Garrison." This is personal experience and historical fact. When my friend Arthur Tappan espoused my abolition sentiments, he became, in popular language, "a Garrisonite"—and so did James G. Birney. The rod which was held *in terrorem* over the heads of people, by the rulers in church and state, to prevent their joining the abolition ranks, was, that by such a procedure they must be branded as "Garrison men." That rod is still held up, and it has frightened many a man from the performance of a high and solemn duty, because he has loved the praise of men more than the favor of God. . . .

. . . I was a poor, self-educated mechanic—without important family connexions, without influence, without wealth, without station—patronized by nobody, laughed at by all, reprimanded by the prudent, contemned by the wise, and avoided for a time even by the benevolent. I stood alone, an object of wonder, pity, scorn and malevolence. . . . The pressure upon me was like an avalanche, and nothing but the power of God sustained me. The clergy were against me—the rulers of the people were against me—the nation was against me. But God and his truth, and the rights of man, and the promises of the Holy

Scriptures, were with me. From the very first moment that I buckled on my armor, I was assured that I could not maintain my ground; that I should retard, instead of aiding the cause of emancipation; that my language was not to be tolerated; and that no person of sane mind would rally under my standard. Now, sir, if I possess any influence, it has been obtained by being utterly regardless of the opinions of mankind. . . . I have flattered no man, feared no man, bribed no man. . . .

Your assertions that I am laboring, as editor of the Liberator, "to overthrow the Christian Sabbath, and the Christian ministry, and the Christian ordinances, and the visible church, and all human and family governments," and that with the cause of abolition I am "determined to carry forward and propagate and enforce my peculiar theology," are utterly destitute of truth.

Source: Reprinted with permission of the publishers from *Letters of William Lloyd Garrison: Volume II, 1836–1840*, edited by Louis Ruchames, pp. 293–297, Cambridge, Mass.: Harvard University Press, Copyright © 1971 by the President and Fellows of Harvard College. The Letters of William Lloyd Garrison are held by Boston Public Library, Boston, Massachusetts.

The American Anti-Slavery Society

The American Anti-Slavery Society was founded in 1833 as a vehicle to promote immediate, uncompensated emancipation. Its goal was to convince slave owners through moral suasion to abolish the institution and to convince Americans in general that blacks and whites were equal. The society's Declaration of Sentiments presented its basic principles on race and slavery and its commitment to attack sinners who owned and traded slaves and those who allowed the institution of slavery to continue.

[T]hose, for whose emancipation we are striving,—constituting at the present time at least one-sixth part of our countrymen,—are recognized by the laws, and treated by their fellow beings, as marketable commodities—as goods and chattels—as brute beasts;—are plundered daily of the fruits of their toil without redress;—really enjoy no constitutional nor legal protection from licentious and murderous outrages upon their persons;—are ruthlessly torn asunder—the tender babe from the arms of its frantic mother—the heart-broken wife from her weeping husband—at the caprice or pleasure of irresponsible tyrants;—and, for the crime of having a dark complexion, suffer the pangs of hunger, the infliction of stripes, and the ignominy of brutal servitude. They are kept in heathenish darkness by laws expressly enacted to make their instruction a criminal offense.

These are the prominent circumstances in the condition of more than TWO MILLIONS of our people. . . .

Hence we maintain—

That in view of the civil and religious privileges of this nation, the guilt of its oppression is unequalled by any other on the face of the earth. . . .

We further maintain—

That no man has a right to enslave or imbrute his brother—to hold or acknowledge him, for one moment, as a piece of merchandise . . . —or to brutalize his mind by denying him the means of intellectual, social and moral improvement.

The right to enjoy liberty is inalienable. . . . Every man has a right to his own body—to the products of his own labor—to the protection of law—and to the common advantages of society. It is piracy to buy or steal a native African, and subject him to servitude. . . .

Therefore we believe and affirm—

That there is no difference, *in principle*, between the African slave trade and American slavery;

That every American citizen, who retains a human being in involuntary bondage, is [according to Scripture] a *man-stealer*;

That the slaves ought instantly to be set free, and brought under the protection of law; . . .

That all those laws which are now in force, admitting the right of slavery, are therefore before God utterly null and void. . . .

We further believe and affirm—

That all persons of color who possess the qualifications which are demanded of others, ought to be admitted forthwith to the enjoyment of the same privileges . . . ; and that the paths of preferment, of wealth, and of intelligence, shall be opened as widely to them as to persons of a white complexion.

We maintain that no compensation should be given to the planters emancipating their slaves—

Because it would be a surrender of the great fundamental principle that man cannot hold property in man;

Because Slavery is a crime, and therefore it is not an article to be sold;

Because the holders of slaves are not the just proprietors of what they claim. . . .

Because if compensation is to be given at all, it should be given to the outraged and guiltless slaves. . . .

We regard, as delusive, cruel and dangerous, any scheme of expatriation which pretends to aid, either directly or indirectly, in the emancipation of the slaves, or to be a substitute for the immediate and total abolition of slavery.

We fully and unanimously recognize the sovereignty of each State, to legislate on the subject of the slavery which is tolerated within its limits. . . .

But we maintain that Congress has a right, and is solemnly bound, to suppress the domestic slave trade between the several States, and to abolish slavery in those portions of our territory which the Constitution has placed under its exclusive jurisdiction.

We also maintain that there are, at the present time, the highest obligations resting upon the people of the free States, to remove slavery by moral and political action, as prescribed in the Constitution of the United States. . . .

We shall send forth Agents to lift up the voice of remonstrance, of warning, of entreaty and rebuke.

We shall circulate, unsparingly and extensively, antislavery tracts and periodicals.

We shall enlist the *pulpit* and the *press* in the cause of the suffering and dumb.

We shall aim at a purification of the churches from all participation in the guilt of slavery. . . .

We shall spare no exertions nor means to bring the whole nation to speedy repentance.

Our trust for victory is solely in GOD. We may be personally defeated, but our principles never. *Truth, Justice,* and *Humanity,* must and will gloriously triumph. . . .

[W]e will do all that in us lies . . . to overthrow the most execrable system of slavery that has ever been witnessed upon earth . . . and to secure to the colored population of the United States all the rights and privileges which belong to them as men and as Americans—come what may to our persons, our interests, or our reputations—whether we live to witness the triumph of justice, liberty and humanity, or perish untimely as martyrs in this great, benevolent and holy cause.

Source: Hugh Hawkins, ed., *The Abolitionists: Immediatism and the Question of Means* (Boston: D. C. Heath, 1964), 52–56. © 1964 by D.C. Heath & Company. Reprinted by permission of Houghton Mifflin Company.

Angelina Grimké Explains Abolitionist Goals and Methods

Angelina Grimké and her sister Sarah were two of abolitionism's most outspoken lecturers and writers during the 1830s. Angelina replied to the much more moderate Catherine Beecher, daughter of the Reverend Lyman Beecher, in two letters published in 1837, just a year before she married and withdrew from the abolitionist crusade. In them she explains why abolitionists opposed slavery and why they sought its immediate end.

Brookline, Mass. 6 *month*, 12*th*, 1837

My Dear Friend: . . .

. . . Thou thinkest I have not been 'sufficiently informed in regard to the feelings and opinions of Christian females at the North' on the subject of slavery; for that in fact they hold the same *principles* with Abolitionists, although they condemn their measures. . . . Let us examine them, to see how far they correspond with the principles held by Abolitionists.

The great fundamental principle of Abolitionists is, that man cannot rightfully hold his fellow man as property. Therefore, we affirm, that *every slaveholder is a man-stealer.* We do so, for the following reasons: to steal a man is to rob him of himself. It matters not whether this be done in Guinea, or Carolina; a man is a *man*, and *as* a man he has *inalienable* rights, among which is the right to personal *liberty*. Now if every man has an *inalienable* right to personal liberty, it follows, that he cannot rightfully be reduced to slavery. But I find in these United States, 2,250,000 men, women and children, robbed of that to which they have an *inalienable* right. How comes this to pass? Where millions are plundered, are there no *plunderers*? If, then, the slaves have been robbed of their liberty, *who* has robbed them? Not the man who stole their forefathers from Africa, but he who now holds them in bondage; no matter *how* they came into his possession. . . . The only difference

I can see between the original man-stealer, who caught the African in his native country, and the American slaveholder, is, that the former committed *one* act of robbery, while the other perpetrates the same crime *continually*. . . .

. . . Now, our *measures* are simply the carrying out of our *principles*. . . . [A]ll who really and heartily approve our *principles*, will also approve our *measures*. . . .

But there is another peculiarity in the views of Abolitionists. We hold that the North is guilty of the crime of slaveholding—we assert that it is a *national* sin. . . . If Abolition principles are generally adopted at the North, how comes it to pass, that there is no abolition action here, except what is put forth by a few despised fanatics, as they are called? Is there any living faith without works? . . .

. . . Our principle is, that *no circumstances can ever justify* a man holding his fellow man as *property*; it matters not what *motive* he may give for such a monstrous violation of the laws of God. The claim to him as *property* is an annihilation of this right to himself, which is the foundation upon which all his other rights are built. It is high-handed robbery of Jehovah; for He has declared, "All souls are *mine*." . . .

Brookline, Mass. *6th month, 17th*, 1837

Dear Friend: Where didst thou get thy statement of what Abolitionists mean by immediate emancipation? I assure thee, it is a novelty. I never heard any abolitionist say that slaveholders 'were physically unable to emancipate their slaves, and of course are not bound to do it,' because in some States there are laws which forbid emancipation. This is truly what our opponents affirm; but *we* say that all the laws which sustain the system of slavery are unjust and oppressive—contrary to the fundamental principles of morality, and, therefore, null and void.

We hold, that all the slaveholding laws violate the fundamental principles of the Constitution of the United States. . . .

Now, thou will perceive, that, so far from thinking that a slaveholder is bound by the *immoral* and *unconstitutional* laws of the Southern States, *we* hold that he is solemnly bound as a man, as an American, to *break* them, and that *immediately* and openly. . . .

. . . When Jehovah commanded Pharaoh to 'let the people go,' he meant that they should be *immediately emancipated.* . . . And so also with Paul, when he exhorted masters to render unto their servants that which is just and equal. Obedience to this command would *immediately* overturn the whole system of American Slavery; for liberty is justly *due* to every American citizen, according to the laws of God and the Constitution of our country; and a fair recompence for his labor is the right of every man. . . .

If our fundamental principle is right, that no man can rightfully hold his fellow man as *property*, then it follows, of course, that he is bound *immediately* to cease holding him as such, and that, too, in *violation of the immoral and unconstitutional laws.* . . . Every slaveholder is bound to cease to do evil *now*, to emancipate his slaves *now*.

Dost thou ask what I mean by emancipation? . . . 1. It is "to reject with indignation, the wild and guilty phantasy, that man can hold *property* in man." 2. To pay the laborer his hire, for he is worthy of it. 3. No longer to deny him the right of marriage. . . . 4. To let parents have their own children. . . . 5. No longer to withhold the advantages of education and the privilege of reading the Bible. 6. To put the slave under the protection of equitable laws.

. . . Which of these things is to be done next year, and which the year after? and so on. *Our* immediate emancipation means, doing justice and loving mercy *to-day*—and this is what we call upon every slaveholder to do.

I have seen too much of slavery to be a gradualist. . . . Oh, my very soul is grieved to find a northern woman . . . framing and fitting soft excuses for the slaveholder's conscience, whilst with the same pen she is *professing* to regard slavery as a sin. . . .

Thine *out* of the bonds of Christian Abolitionism,

A. E. GRIMKÉ

Source: A. E. Grimké, Letters to Catherine E. Beecher in Reply to An Essay on Slavery and Abolitionism (Boston: Isaac Knapp, 1838), 3–13.

Wendell Phillips

At an open meeting in Faneuil Hall in Boston, October 30, 1842, a wealthy resident of the city, abolitionist Wendell Phillips, responded to the capture of George Latimer, a fugitive slave from Virginia. In addressing the Boston audience, the acclaimed orator raised three controversial issues related to abolitionism: the responsibility of Northerners for slavery, the pro-slavery nature of the Constitution, and the evils of the fugitive slave clause.

I know that I am addressing the white slaves of the North. [Hisses and shouts.] Shake your chains; you have not the courage to break them. This old hall cannot rock as it used to wit the spirit of liberty. It is chained down by the iron links of the United States Constitution. [Hisses and uproar.] Many of you, I doubt not, regret to have this man given up, but you cannot help it. There stands the bloody clause in the Constitution—you cannot fret the seal off the bond. The fault is in allowing such a Constitution to live an hour. . . . When I look upon these crowded thousands, and see them trample on their consciences and the rights of their fellow-men at the bidding of a piece of parchment, I say my *curse* be on the Constitution of these United States. [Hisses and shouts.] . . . Shall our taxes pay men to hunt slaves? Shall we build jails to keep them? [uproar.] If a Southern comes here to get his lost horse, he must prove title before a jury of twelve men. If he comes to catch a slave, he need only to prove title to any Justice of the Peace whom he can make his accomplice. I record here my testimony against this pollution of our native city. Then in the free state who helps hunt slaves is no better than a bloodhound. The attorney is baser still. But any judge who should grant a certificate would be the basest of all. . . .

Source: Lorenzo Sears, *Wendell Phillips: Orator and Agitator* (New York: Doubleday, Page, 1909), 101–102.

"Massachusetts to Virginia" (1843)

John Greenleaf Whittier, a Quaker and an abolitionist, wrote numerous poems attacking slavery, including "The Slave-Ships" about the slave trade, "The Hunters of Men" about runaway slaves, and "A Sabbath Scene" about churches' aid to slavery. In 1843, he critiqued the lost status of the state of Virginia as it continued to hold and support slaves into the middle of the nineteenth century. In the following verses from this lengthy poem, he links Virginia to its revolutionary ideals, reminds readers of the fate of fugitive slaves, and calls attention to the treatment of slaves as property.

What asks the Old Dominion? If now her sons have proved
False to their fathers' memory, false to the faith they loved;
If she can scoff at Freedom, and its great charter spurn,
Must we of Massachusetts from truth and duty turn?

We hunt your bondmen, flying from Slavery's hateful hell;
Our voices, at your bidding, take up the blood-hound's yell;
We gather, at your summons, above our fathers' graves,
From Freedom's holy altar-horns to tear your wretched slaves!

Thank God! Not yet so vilely can Massachusetts vow;
The spirit of her early time is even with her now;
Cream not because her Pilgrim blood moves slow and calm and cool,
She thus can stoop her chainless neck, a sister's slave and tool!

All that a sister State should do, all that a free State may,
Heart, hand, and purse we proffer, as in our early day;
But that one dark loathsome burden ye must stagger with alone,
And reap the bitter harvest which ye yourselves have sown!

Hold while ye may, your struggling slaves, and burden God's free air
With woman's shriek beneath the lash, and manhood's wild despair;
Cling closer to the "cleaving curse" that writes upon your plains
The blasting of Almighty wrath against a land of chains.

Still shame your gallant ancestry, the cavaliers of old,
By watching round the shambles where human flesh is sold;
Gloat o'er the new-born child, and count his market value, when
The maddened mother's cry of woe shall pierce the slaver's den!

Lower than plummet soundeth, sink the Virginia name;
Plant, if ye will, your fathers' graves with rankest weeds of shame,
Be, if ye will, the scandal of God's fair universe;
We wash our hands forever of your sin and shame and curse.

Source: The Poetical Works of John Greenleaf Whittier, vol. 3 (Boston: Houghton, Mifflin, 1891), 82–84.

The Anti-Slavery Alphabet (1847)

Abolitionists used a variety of strategies for reaching Northerners in their effort to reform the nation and tie all Americans to the sin of slavery. From pictures to purses to coins, they spread their mes-

sage. This simple poem walked young readers through basic abolitionist beliefs.

A is an Abolitionist—
    A man who wants to free
The wretched slave—and give all
    An equal liberty.

B is a Brother with a skin
    Of somewhat darker hue,
But in our Heavenly Father's sight,
    He is as dear as you. . . .

H is the Hound his master trained,
    And called to scent the track
Of the unhappy fugitive,
    And bring him trembling back.

I is the Infant, from the arms
    Of its fond mother torn,
And, at a public auction, sold
    With horses, cows, and corn. . . .

M is the Merchant of the north,
    Who buys what slaves produce—
So they are stolen, whipped and worked,
    For his, and for our use. . . .

Z is a Zealous man, sincere,
    Faithful, and just, and true;
An earnest pleader for the slave—
    Will you not be so too?

Source: The Anti-Slavery Alphabet (Philadelphia: Printed for the Anti-Slavery
Fair, 1847).

Slave Power and National Power

Charles Sumner, a "Conscience Whig" from Massachusetts who
later became one of the Radical Republicans of the Reconstruction
period, described the power and reach of slavery and of the national government at Faneuil Hall in Boston on September 23,
1846. The event was the Whig State Convention of Massachusetts.

The time, I believe, has gone by, when the question is asked, *What
has the North to do with Slavery?* It might almost be answered, that, po-

litically, it has little to do with anything else,—so are all the acts of our Government connected, directly or indirectly, with this institution. Slavery is everywhere. Appealing to the Constitution, it enters the Halls of Congress, in the disproportionate representation of the Slave States. It holds its disgusting mart . . . in the shadow of the Capitol, under the legislative jurisdiction of the Nation. . . . It sends its miserable victims over the high seas, from the ports of Virginia to the ports of Louisiana, beneath the protecting flag of the Republic. It presumes to follow into the Free States those fugitives who . . . seek our Altars for safety; nay, more, with profane hands it seizes those who have never known the name of slave, freemen of the North, and dooms them to irredeemable bondage. . . . It assumes at pleasure to build up new slaveholding States; striving perpetually to widen its area, while professing to extend the area of Freedom. It has brought upon the country war with Mexico with its enormous expenditures and more enormous guilt. . . . [I]t controls the affairs of Government,—interferes with the cherished interests of the North, enforcing them and refusing protection to her manufactures,—makes and unmakes Presidents,—usurps to itself the larger portion of all offices of honor and profit, both in the army and navy, and also in the civil department,—and stamps upon our whole country the character . . . of the monstrous anomaly and mockery, a *slaveholding republic*, with the living truths of Freedom on its lips and the dark mark of Slavery on its brow. . . .

. . . It will not be questioned by any competent authority, that Congress may, by express legislation, abolish slavery: first, in the District of Columbia; secondly, in the Territories, if there should be any; thirdly, that it may abolish the slave-trade on the high seas between the States; fourthly, that it may refuse to admit new States with a constitution sanctioning slavery. Nor can it be questioned that the people of the United States may, in the manner pointed out by the Constitution, proceed to its amendment. . . .

Source: Charles Sumner, *The Works of Charles Sumner*, vol. 1 (Boston: Lee and Shepard, 1875), 307–308.

The Fugitive Slave Act

Abolitionists' opposition to the Fugitive Slave Act of 1850 and their continuing concern for the pro-slavery stand of many churchmen is apparent in abolitionist Eliza Wigham's 1858 pamphlet.

All the other clauses of this "Omnibus Bill" were servile sops to slavery; but chief in iniquity was the Fugitive Slave Law. To Henry Clay and Daniel Webster belongs the infamy of carrying out this atrocious bill. . . . Great indignation was at first expressed throughout the Northern States, but after a time politicians, and sadder still, ministers of all denominations were found boldly to defend the law, and advocate its being obeyed in defiance of the higher law of God. . . .

The Rev. Moses Stuart, D.D. . . . , reminds his readers that "many Southern slaveholders are true *Christians*." That "sending back a fugitive to them is not like restoring one to an idolatrous people." That "though we may *pity* the fugitive, yet the Mosaic law does not authorize the rejection of the claims of the slaveholders to their stolen or strayed *property*." This great theologian quite forgot Deut. Xiii. 15, 16. . . .

The Rev. Orville Dewey, D.D., of the Unitarian connection, maintains in his lectures that the safety of the Union is not to be hazarded for the sake of the African race. He declares that, for his part, he would send his own brother or child into slavery, if needed to preserve the union between the free and slaveholding states; and counsels the slave to similar magnanimity. . . .

[T]he Fugitive Slave Law gave a new stimulus to the horrid trade of man-hunting, by requiring Northern citizens, under penalty of fine at least, to assist in the crime of rendition, and many a poor man was hurried from the useful toil by which he was maintaining a free wife and children, to be tried and sentenced back to slavery. Many a poor woman who was living honourably with the husband of her choice in fancied security, suddenly found herself seized, proved to be a slave, and sent back to slavery; and with all her children, for, unless it could be proved that they were born in a free state, their condition followed hers.

Source: Eliza Wigham, *The Anti-Slavery Cause in America and Its Martyrs* (London: A. W. Bennett, 1863), 89–92.

The Shared Responsibility for Slavery

By the late 1850s abolitionists, split over the correct strategy to pursue and frequently disheartened by the nation's failure to reject slavery, heard more and more arguments for violence, emigration, and disunion. The aggressive and combative Stephen Symonds Foster, husband of fellow abolitionist Abby Kelley, asserted the national government's ties to slavery.

. . . The slaves, it must be remembered, are more than three and a half millions; their masters less than half a million, or as one to seven. We must, therefore, look elsewhere than to the plantation for the power which makes the plantation what it is—the charnel house of liberty, the grave of unnumbered hopes. The master, beyond all question, has his accomplices somewhere. . . .

. . . It is a sad mistake to suppose that the south alone is involved in the unparalleled crime of enslaving three and a half millions of the people of this republic. In this terrible holocaust she has officiated at the altar, it is true; but the north has furnished the knife and the wood, without which not a single victim would now be gasping in the agonies of a living death. . . .

. . . The support of the institution which had hitherto developed exclusively upon the States in which it existed, was . . . assumed by the Federal Government [under the new constitution], and the responsibility thereby thrown upon the whole country. In the United States Constitution are four important provisions, each of which, in its operations, makes the north a party to the continuance of the system, and is of such a nature as necessarily to involve all who acknowledge allegiance to the government in the guilt of that odious institution. . . .

. . . [W]e find three distinct classes of slaveholders, each sustaining peculiar external relations to the system. The first class are the claimants of slaves. The second are the members of those State governments which have adopted and now regulate the system. The third are the members of the general government—that government having assumed its protection from all forcible interference from within or from without. . . . The responsibility and guilt of slaveholding, therefore, rest upon the Federal government to the same extent, and in the same degree, that they do upon the State governments, or the slave claimants. . . . [T]his responsibility is not confined to any particular party, or class of parties, but it falls . . . upon every individual of society who gives his assent to that blood-stained instrument, or to the government of which it is the basis. . . .

In the Federal Union lies the grand secret of the strength of the slave power. Of itself that power is contemptibly weak. . . . But in its alliance with the free States, through the Federal government, its strength is immense. . . . It is able not only to command the services of the entire body of our militia when an insurrection is to be suppressed, an invasion to be repelled, or a slave to be recaptured, but it has seduced into its willing service, or awed into submission, nearly every prominent man throughout the entire north. It has by the same means corrupted the heart of the church. . . .

. . . All our commercial cities are threatened with the loss of southern trade unless they consent to remain true to the interests of slavery. . . . The tariff is also a most effective instrument in the hands of the slave power in controlling northern capitalists. . . . The enemy is at our own door. The entire government, from the president down to the humblest citizen in the retirement of private life, is, by the requirements of the Constitution, its protecter, and is sworn to defend it, if need be, with the heart's blood. . . .

To the enlightened vision there is for this evil but one remedy. Our strength all lies in a single force—the conscience of the nation. All else is on the side of the oppressor. . . . The Constitution requires of the general government the protection of slavery in such of the States as choose to retain it, with no power to regulate or abolish it. Hence the private citizen has no course left to him but either to aid in upholding the system, or renounce his allegiance to the government. His only choice is between slaveholding and revolution. . . .

Source: Stephen Symonds Foster, *Revolution the Only Remedy for Slavery*, Anti-Slavery Tracts, No. 7 (New York: American Anti-Slavery Society, [1857]), 4–16.

Disunion and National Guilt

Abolitionists believed that nonslave owners were as responsible for slavery as were slave owners, as explained in 1855 by Charles E. Hodges in a pamphlet distributed by the American Anti-Slavery Society.

. . . [T]he question . . . *not, Is it expedient? But, Is it right?* Have we a right, for the sake of national greatness and power, or territorial integrity, or any conceivable material prosperity, or for any purpose whatsoever, to sustain a union, which demands, *and for its preservation must secure*, from its citizens, a sacrifice of the fundamental and eternal laws of religion and morality? We firmly and sincerely believe that we have no such right. . . . We stand on the assertion of the simplest, the very elementary principles of morality and religion, that whatever is contrary to the universal, unchangeable, and very initial laws of God, cannot be made right by vote of a majority. . . .

It is on these simple principles that the abolitionist justifies, and commends to the consideration of a candid public, his opposition to the Union. It is wrong for us to support voluntarily, a government or political union, which sustains iniquity. If, then, our Union does sustain iniquity, it is wrong for us to abide by the Union. . . .

. . . [W]e assert, what a very few words will confirm, that in sustaining the Union, *we* are encouraging and upholding slavery; and even more strongly, that without the Union, as it now exists, slavery could not stand another day.

. . . We are in intimate union with these [slave] States, in partnership with them in crime. We swear to abide by a Constitution, which guarantees perpetual possession of his slaves to the slaveholder, which grants him unusual privileges, in proportion to the number of his slaves, and finally, guarantees perpetual enjoyment of those privileges. We meet with them in the national Congress, yielding them a larger representation there, than an equal number of non-slaveholders, in proportion to their iniquity. We make laws together, elect officers in common, pay taxes to a common treasury, collect a common revenue, make treaties and form alliances with other nations, as one people, united in principle and interest. We associate with them in church and in state . . . and do their bidding in all things, without noticeable or efficient protest. We have thus openly committed ourselves, in the eyes of the world, to a participation in their guilt, and in the court of conscience, to an equal responsibility for the sin. . . . The man who swears to sustain the Constitution . . . is certainly, in the sight of God, as guilty. . . . The cry, "Freedom national, slavery sectional," is an absurdity. It is impossible under the Union. Slavery existing any where in these States is the sin of the whole people.

Source: Charles E. Hodges, *Disunion Our Wisdom and Our Duty*, Anti-Slavery Tracts No. 11 (New York: American Anti-Slavery Society, [1855]), 2–6.

A Southerner Attacks Slavery (1857)

Hinton Rowan Helper was a nonslave owner from North Carolina who hated slavery but had no concern for slaves or for blacks in general. His interest was in the harm that slavery was doing to the nonslave owning white Southerner. In 1857, he published a statistical argument against slavery, *The Impending Crisis of the South*. In it he focused on the economic harm done by slavery. Applauded by abolitionists, the book became part of the Republican Party's literature.

. . . Among the thousand and one arguments that present themselves in support of our position [for abolition] . . . is the influence which slavery invariably exercises in depressing the value of real estate. . . .

The oligarchs say we cannot abolish slavery without infringing on the right of property. Again we tell them we do not recognize property in man; but even if we did . . . , impelled by a sense of duty to others, and as a matter of simple justice to ourselves, we, the non-slaveholders of the South, would be fully warranted in emancipating all the slaves at once, and that, too, without any compensation whatever to those who claim to be their absolute masters and owners. . . . We conclude, . . . and we think the conclusion is founded on principles of equity, that you, the slaveholders, are indebted to us, the non-slaveholders, in the sum of $22,73 [sic], which is the difference between $28,07 [the value per acre of land in the North] and $5,34 [the value per acre in the South], on every acre of Southern soil in our possession. This claim we bring against you, because slavery, which has inured exclusively to your benefit, if, indeed, it has been beneficial at all, has shed a blighting influence over our lands, thereby keeping them out of market, and damaging every acre to the amount specified. Sirs! are you ready to settle the account? . . .

Now, chevaliers of the lash, and worshippers of slavery, the total value of three hundred and thirty-one million nine hundred and two thousand seven hundred and twenty acres [owned by non-slaveholders], at twenty-two dollars and seventy-three cents per acre, is *seven billion five hundred and forty-four million one hundred and forty-eight thousand eight hundred and twenty-five dollars*; and this is our account against you on a single score. Considering how your villainous institution has retarded the development of our commercial and manufacturing interests, how it has stifled the aspirations of inventive genius; and,

above all, how it has barred from us the heaven-born sweets of literature and religion—concernments too sacred to be estimated in a pecu-
niary point of view—might we not, with perfect justice and propriety,
duplicate the amount, and still be accounted modest in our demands?
Though . . . you have maltreated, outraged and defrauded us in every
relation of life, civil, social, and political, yet we are willing to forgive
and forget you, if you will but do us justice on a single account. Of you,
the introducers, aiders and abettors of slavery, we demand indemnifica-
tion for the damage our lands have sustained on account there of; the
amount of that damage is $7,544,148,825. . . . How do you propose to
settle? Do you offer us your negroes in part payment? We do not want
your negroes. We would not have all of them, nor any number of them,
even as a gift. We hold ourselves above the disreputable and iniquitous
practices of buying, selling, and owning slaves. . . .

. . . Slavery has polluted and impoverished your lands; freedom
will restore them to their virgin purity, and add from twenty to thirty
dollars to the value of every acre. Correctly speaking, emancipation will
cost you nothing. . . . The present total market value of all your landed
property, at $5,34 per acre, is only $923,248,160! With the beauty and
sunlight of freedom beaming on the same estate, it would be worth, at
$28,07 per acre, $4,856,873,680. . . .

Source: Hinton Rowan Helper, *The Impending Crisis of the South: How to Meet
It* (New York: A. B. Burdick, 1860), [v], 123–130.

Abolitionists as the Threat

In a broad defense of slavery and attack on anti-slavery, William
Gannaway Brownlow, editor of *Brownlow's Knoxville Whig*, demonstrated in 1858 that the abolitionists had not only failed to reform
southern thinking but also were still seen as threats to the natural
racial order. Brownlow presented his ideas in a debate with Abram
Pryne, a minister and editor of the *Central Reformer*, an abolitionist paper published in New York. An opponent of secession,
Brownlow would oppose the Confederacy during the war. In 1865
he became governor of Tennessee; in 1869, he was chosen one of
the state's U.S. senators.

The visionary notions of piety and philanthropy entertained by
many men at the North, lead them to resist the *Fugitive Slave Law* of

this government, and even to *violate the Tenth Commandment*, by stealing our "men-servants and maid-servants" and running them into what they call free territory, upon their "under-ground railroads!" Nay, the *villainous piety* of some has led them to contribute *Sharp's rifles* and *Holy Bibles*, to send the *uncircumcised Philistines* of our New England States, into "bleeding Kansas," to shoot down the Christian owners of slaves, and then to perform religious ceremonies over their dead bodies! . . . Even females, as in the case of that model beauty, *Harriet Beecher Stowe*, unsex themselves, to aid in carrying on this horrid and slanderous warfare against the slaveholders of the South!

. . . [W]e cannot affiliate with men who fight under the dark and piratical flag of Abolitionism, and whose infernal altars smoke with the vile incense of Northern fanaticism! I have no confidence in either the *politician* or the *divine* at the North, constantly engaged in the villainous agitation of the slavery question. There are true, reliable, conservative, pious, and patriotic men in the North, and there are similar men in the South, who came from the North, but they are not among these graceless agitators. . . .

. . . Those politicians, and bad men, who are exciting the whole country, and fanning society into a livid consuming flame, particularly at the North, have no sympathies for the *black man*, and care nothing for his comfort. They seek their own—not the negro's good. . . .

The freedom of negroes in even your Free States, is, in all respects, only an empty name. Your citizen negro does not vote, and takes good care not to do so. The law does not interdict him this privilege. . . .

All the social advantages, all the respectable employments, all the honors, and even the *pleasures* of life, are denied the free negroes of the North, by pious Abolitionists full of sympathy for the downtrodden African! . . . Industry is closed to them. . . . The negroes even have their *own streets*, and their own low-down kennels, as is the case here in Philadelphia, even! In nearly all the Northern States, they have their own hospitals, their churches, their cars, upon which, in many instances, are written in large letters, "FOR COLORED PEOPLE."

Finally, as many of you well know, they are forced to have their own *grave-yards*—the *yellow* remains of the Northern Abolitionists, and pious white men, refusing to mingle with the bleaching bones of the dead negro, after death! Not so in the South. . . .

. . . Anti-Slavery men at the North resist this law [Fugitive Slave

Act], and thereby rebel against the Constitution and civil authorities of the country.

. . . [W]e of the South [are] on the *defensive* in this controversy. And against whom do we wage war? It is against the sanctimonious hypocrisy of a band that, with words of pity on the lips, with wailing in the tone, with woe upon the visage, and *bigotry* where the *heart* should have been, continue to agitate this question as they have been doing for years, both in and out of Congress. . . .

But why disturb a system that is beneficial to the physical and moral welfare of the negroes? Why remove them from the restraint of Christian and civilized life, and turn them back to savage barbarism, penury, want, and starvation, merely for the sake of saying they are free? Why take away the comfort they now enjoy, and turn them out to starve, or steal, or to be destroyed by a superior race? Why all this noise about freedom, when that boasted freedom would bring anarchy, poverty, suffering, moral and physical desolation to the negro? Is there any of the spirit of Christianity in all this agitation? . . .

Source: Ought American Slavery to Be Perpetuated? A Debate between Rev. W. G. Brownlow and Rev. A. Pryne (Philadelphia: J. B. Lippincott, 1858), 30, 41, 44–45, 248–252.

The Threat of Abolitionism

Anti-abolitionists argued that abolitionism was a radical doctrine. In an 1860 tract, Ebenezer Boyden of Hopedale, Virginia, presents slavery as a useful and benevolent institution and abolitionists as self-serving fanatics who threaten the Union.

[Abolitionism] has not only been carried into morals and religion, and falsely regarded as a purely ethical one, but taken also into party politics. . . . It kindled abroad slowly—was brought over and kindled slowly here. After awhile, it caught the attention of certain cunning craftsmen in politics, soon they set themselves earnestly to fan it into a blaze for their own ends. Succeeding in this, under false premises— the moral and religious—they have been seen for twenty years, busily employed in shaping by the light and heat of that blaze the gods they worship—Popularity, Place and Power. . . . [T]hey would sacrifice to their idols, both the public peace, and the immortal interests of truth and religion.

. . . With a heart so relieved from care and bitter anxiety, [the slave] goes forth to his labor day by day, and the master trudges on in life by his side, carrying, so to speak, that poor man's wife and children as a load upon his back. . . . God does not love slavery. It is an institution of government and guardianship, which He sometimes employs to bring back degenerated races. . . . The idea of the inherent wickedness of slavery, is becoming heated to the point of explosion. . . . Baseless in reason, this epidemic "African fever" shall infallibly pass away: not, perhaps, till it has disjoined and destroyed this otherwise sound and well compacted body of States. . . .

Source: Ebenezer Boyden, *The Epidemic of the Nineteenth Century* (Richmond, VA: Charles H. Wynne, Printer, 1860), 23–25.

The Emancipation Proclamation (1863)

Abraham Lincoln moved slowly in expanding the goals of the Civil War from preservation of the Union to elimination of slavery. His resistance to confiscation of southern slaves and, until 1863, to black military service antagonized abolitionists. Then in September 1862 he issued a preliminary emancipation proclamation followed by the official order on January 1, 1863. The document, which announced the freedom only of slaves in rebel-held areas, was seen as a positive step by some abolitionists and as a hollow statement by others.

. . . I, Abraham Lincoln, President of the United States, by virtue of the power in me vested as Commander in Chief of the army and Navy of the United States in time of actual armed rebellion against the authority and government of the United States, and as a fit and necessary war measure for suppressing said rebellion, do, on this 1st day of January A.D. 1863 . . . order and designate as the States and parts of States wherein the people thereof, respectively, are this day in rebellion against the United States the following [all seceded states except Tennessee, western counties of Virginia, and designated parishes in Louisiana under federal control].

And by virtue of the power and for the purpose aforesaid, I do order and declare that all persons held as slaves within said designated States and parts of States are and henceforward shall be free; and that the executive government of the United States, including the military and naval authorities thereof, will recognize and maintain the freedom of said persons.

And I hereby enjoin upon the people so declared to be free to abstain from all violence, unless in necessary self-defense; and I recommend to them that in all cases when allowed they labor faithfully for reasonable wages.

And I further declare and make known that such persons of suitable condition, will be received into the armed service of the United States to garrison forts, positions, stations, and other places and to man vessels of all sorts in said service. . . .

Source: James D. Richardson, *A Compilation of the Messages and Papers of the Presidents*, vol. 8 (New York: Bureau of National Literature, 1897), 3358–3360.

ANNOTATED BIBLIOGRAPHY

Books

Abzug, Robert H. *Passionate Liberator: Theodore Dwight Weld and the Dilemma of Reform*. New York: Oxford University Press, 1980. Seeks to present "a more 'human' Weld" by looking at "the odd mix of personal and philosophical motivations" that made him "a moral gadfly on the borders of the American mainstream" (x).

Aptheker, Herbert. *Abolitionism: A Revolutionary Movement*. Boston: Twayne Publishers, 1989. A classic analysis of abolitionism that defines the abolitionists as revolutionaries and defines their movement as "highly organized" (xiii).

Azevedo, Celia M. *Abolitionism in the United States and Brazil: A Comparative Perspective*. New York: Garland Publishing, 1995. A brief comparative look at abolitionist ideologies that covers both immediate abolitionists and anti-expansionists in the 1830s–1850s. Thirty pages of bibliography cover both the United States and Brazil.

Bailey, Hugh C. *Hinton Rowan Helper: Abolitionist-Racist*. University: University of Alabama Press, 1967. Argues that Helper was a racist and "a dreamer" (x) who sought, through his interest in statistics and opposition to slavery, to free the white South from the restraints of slavery.

Barbour, Hugh, and J. William Frost. *The Quakers*. Westport, CT: Greenwood, 1988. Part one provides an easy-to-read overview of the Quakers in America from 1650 (in England) to 1987; part two includes almost fifty pages of biographical essays, a brief chronology, and a bibliographic essay.

Barnes, Gilbert H. *The Anti-Slavery Impulse, 1830–1844*. London: D. Appleton-Century, 1933. Minimizes William Lloyd Garrison's importance in the abolitionist movement.

Bartlett, Irving H. *Wendell Phillips: Brahmin Radical*. Boston: Beacon Press, 1961. Looks at the contrasts in Phillips's life, including "the Brahmin world" and the "bizarre world of crackpots, fanatics, cranks and saints" (1) of abolitionism.

Beeman, Richard R. *Patrick Henry: A Biography.* New York: McGraw-Hill, 1974. Because of the scarcity of documents, Beeman focuses on Henry in context of his times to reveal Virginia society and thus the "pressures and principles" (xiii) that guided him.

Bender, Thomas, ed. *The Antislavery Debate: Capitalism and Abolitionism as a Problem in Historical Interpretation.* Berkeley: University of California Press, 1975. Ten essays reveal the debate over the relationship between anti-slavery and capitalism, showing the intellectual and cultural aspects of the debate.

Berlin, Ira. *Slaves without Masters: The Free Negro in the Antebellum South.* New York: Random House, 1974. Sixteen tables and four appendices help demonstrate the widespread presence of free blacks in the South and the varied but oppressed lives they led.

Berlin, Ira, and Ronald Hoffman, eds. *Slavery and Freedom in the Age of the American Revolution.* Charlottesville: University Press of Virginia, 1983. Ten essays on the impact of the revolutionary period on black Americans; authors include Gary B. Nash, David Brian Davis, and Benjamin Quarles.

Binger, Carl. *Revolutionary Doctor: Benjamin Rush, 1746–1813.* New York: W. W. Norton, 1966. Written by a medical doctor and based heavily on Rush's writings, this biography makes occasional reference to Rush's opposition to slavery and attitudes toward blacks.

Birney, Catherine H. *Sarah and Angelina Grimké: The First American Women Advocates of Abolition and Woman's Rights.* Boston: Lee and Shepard, 1885. A strongly positive dual biography that presents the sisters as living lives in "the service of the poor, the weak, the oppressed" (319).

Blackbourn, Robin. *The Overthrow of Colonial Slavery, 1776–1848.* New York: Verso, 1988. A lengthy, detailed study of the impact of outside pressures in the Western hemisphere; covers British, French, and Spanish colonies, as well as the United States, Brazil, Cuba, and Haiti.

Blackett, R.J.M. *Building an Antislavery Wall: Black Americans in the Atlantic Antislavery Movement, 1830–1860.* Baton Rouge: Louisiana State University Press, 1983. Tells the story of blacks who traveled to Britain to lecture and build support for American abolition; looks at British reaction.

Blue, Fredrick J. *The Free Soilers: Third-Party Politics, 1848–1854.* Urbana: University of Illinois Press, 1973. This "leadership study" (x) presents the Free Soil Party as made up of both opportunistic politicians and devoted idealists, as out of sync with Northern views, and as significant in formulating the policy of the Republican Party.

Bradley, Patricia. *Slavery, Propaganda, and the American Revolution.* Jackson: University Press of Mississippi, 1998. Argues that the use by American revolutionaries of slavery propaganda in pamphlets and newspapers helped continue slavery after independence. Includes a chapter on the *Somerset* case.

Breen, T. H., and Stephen Innes. *"Myne Owne Ground": Race and Freedom on Virginia's Eastern Shore, 1640–1676.* New York: Oxford University Press, 1980. Argues that property, not race, was the defining consideration in determining black status prior to Bacon's Rebellion.

Bruns, Roger, ed. *Am I Not a Man and a Brother: The Antislavery Crusade of Revolutionary America, 1688–1788.* New York: Chelsea House, 1977. This extensive collection of documents, with brief introductions, presents early anti-slavery efforts in five time periods; includes writings by John Woolman, Anthony Benezet, Benjamin Rush, Phyllis Wheatley, Thomas Paine, and Alexander Hamilton.

Cady, Edwin H. *John Woolman: The Mind of the Quaker Saint.* New York: Washington Square Press, 1966. A brief but thoughtful account of the beliefs of the Quaker abolitionist; laudatory and reverential in tone.

Chesebrough, David B. *Clergy Dissent in the Old South, 1830–1865.* Carbondale: Southern Illinois University Press, 1996. A clearly written brief look at the positions taken by southern ministers on issues related to slavery and the Civil War.

Conniff, Michael L., and Thomas J. Davis. *Africans in the Americas: A History of the Black Diaspora.* New York: St. Martin's Press, 1994. Provides a brief overview of slavery in North America, the Caribbean, Brazil, and Spanish America. Chapter three focuses on abolition and emancipation throughout the American slaveholding world.

Curry, Leonard P. *The Free Black in Urban America, 1800–1850: The Shadow of the Dream.* Chicago: University of Chicago Press, 1981. Covers jobs, housing, schools and churches, riots, crime and poverty, mortality, and black protest.

Curtin, Philip D. *The Atlantic Slave Trade: A Census.* Madison: University of Wisconsin Press, 1969. Twenty-six maps and illustrations and eighty-three tables help Curtin provide revisionist figures for and analysis of the sale of Africans to the New World.

Daly, John Patrick. *When Slavery Was Called Freedom: Evangelicalism, Proslavery, and the Causes of the Civil War.* Lexington: University Press of Kentucky, 2002. Surveys the role of evangelical pro-slavery in the South, including its response to abolitionism, particularly after 1831; explains its survival in the 1860s.

Davis, David B. *The Problem of Slavery in the Age of Revolution, 1770–1823.* Ithaca, NY: Cornell University Press, 1975. The sequel to *The Problem of Slavery in Western Culture*, this lengthy study looks at the handling and moral perception of slavery by the United States and Britain with some attention to France and Latin America.

————, ed. *Ante-Bellum Reform*. New York: Harper and Row, 1967. Eleven essays on abolitionism's motivations, social and religious foundations, and links to other reform movements of the antebellum decades.

Davis, Hugh. *Joshua Leavitt: Evangelical Abolitionist*. Baton Rouge: Louisiana State University Press, 1990. A well-written review of Leavitt's life that places him within the context of abolitionism's evolution and personalities.

DeBoar, Clara Merritt. *Be Jubilant My Feet: African-American Abolitionists in the American Missionary Movement*. New York: Garland, 1994. Reveals the role of the American Missionary Association in the *Amistad* case and in helping American blacks in Canada; covers the broad reach of its publication, *The American Missionary*, and the role of Lewis Tappan.

Degler, Carl N. *The Other South: Southern Dissenters in the Nineteenth Century*. New York: Harper & Row, 1974. The classic work on Southerners who opposed slavery and opposed secession and who supported the Union during the Civil War, the Republicans during Reconstruction, and the Populist Party during the 1890s.

Dick, Robert C. *Black Protest: Issues and Tactics*. Westport, CT: Greenwood, 1974. While not focusing on individuals, Dick spends considerable time on the "assumptions, values, and attitudes" (xi) of such men as Henry Highland Garnet, Frederick Douglass, Charles Lenox Remond, and James McCune Smith, as well as the Negro National Conventions.

Dillon, Merton L. *The Abolitionists: The Growth of a Dissenting Minority*. DeKalb: Northern Illinois University Press, 1974. After briefly covering the pre-Garrison years, Dillon looks in detail and respectfully at abolitionist goals and methods in 1829–1860, with a concluding paragraph on "the Civil War and after."

————. *Benjamin Lundy and the Struggle for Negro Freedom*. Urbana: University of Illinois Press, 1966. Calls attention to the important anti-slavery work and ideas of one of the earliest abolitionists and one of the movement's longest supporters of colonization.

————. *Elijah Lovejoy, Abolitionist Editor*. Urbana: University of Illinois Press, 1961. A brief look at the brief life of the murdered abolitionist in order to understand abolitionists in general, as well as to present the social influences affecting people's response to abolitionism during the 1830s.

Dixon, Chris. *African America and Haiti: Emigration and Black Nationalism in the Nineteenth Century*. Westport, CT: Greenwood, 2000. Reveals black views of and hopes for Haiti and the periodic efforts by American blacks to emigrate there.

Donald, David. *Charles Summer and the Coming of the Civil War*. New York: Alfred A. Knopf, 1960. A study of "the depths of Summer's mind" (ix) that reveals a complicated and determined man.

Douglass, Frederick. *The Frederick Douglass Papers.* Series 1, *Speeches, Debates, and Interviews.* Edited by John Blassingame. New Haven, CT: Yale University Press, 1979–1992. This five-volume set covers 1841 to 1895; it provides hundreds of Douglass's public presentations along with extensive explanatory notes.

Drake, Thomas E. *Quakers and Slavery in America.* New Haven, CT: Yale University Press, 1950. A thorough and valuable review of the Quakers' actions and nonactions involving slavery.

Drescher, Seymour, and Stanley L. Engerman, eds. *A Historical Guide to World Slavery.* New York: Oxford University Press, 1988. An encyclopedia covering the many forms that slavery has taken from ancient times to the present and from Asia to America; has entries on "abolition and anti-slavery," "anti-slavery literature," "manumission," "revolts," and "slave trade."

Duberman, Martin, ed. *The Antislavery Vanguard: New Essays on the Abolitionists.* Princeton, NJ: Princeton University Press, 1965. Seventeen essays by such noted historians as Benjamin Quarles, James M. McPherson, and Willie Lee Rose are dated but provide fascinating insight into developing historical interpretation.

Du Bois, W.E.B. *The Suppression of the African Slave-Trade to the United States of America, 1638–1870.* Baton Rouge: Louisiana State University Press, 1965. First published in 1896, this classic study finds that economic and political considerations led to the slave trade's legal abolition and that illegal trade continued because of lax interest in enforcement.

———. *The World and Africa: An Inquiry into the Part Which Africa Has Played in World History.* New York: Viking Press, 1947. Asserts the critical role of Africa by trying to explain why that role was so long ignored; covers the slave trade and "the rape of Africa" (44).

Dumond, Dwight Lowell. *Antislavery: The Crusade for Freedom in America.* 1961. Reprint, New York: Norton, 1979. An early revisionist work that is reverential in its look at abolitionists as moral crusaders "for the rescue of a noble people, [and] for the redemption of democracy"([v]); provides a thorough history and numerous illustrations.

———. *Antislavery Origins of the Civil War of the United States.* Ann Arbor: University of Michigan Press, 1939. Although preempted by more recent works, this study provides a useful review of abolitionist thinking and strategy and of the response of the South and the North.

Eltis, David. *The Rise of African Slavery in the Americas.* Cambridge: Cambridge University Press, 2000. A broad study that covers the early modern era of England, Europe, and Africa, as well as the Americas; looks at gender and ethnicity issues as well as such standard topics as the slave trade and the English plantations.

Ely, James W., Jr. *The Guardian of Every Other Right: A Constitutional History of Property Rights*. New York: Oxford University Press, 1992. A brief but thorough look at the important role that property rights have played throughout American history; chapter four covers 1791–1861.

Ericson, David F. *The Debate over Slavery: Antislavery and Proslavery Liberalism in Antebellum America*. New York: New York University Press, 2000. Focuses on abolitionists Lydia Maria Child, Frederick Douglass, and Wendell Phillips and on pro-slaverites Thomas R. Dew and George Fitzhugh; provides an overview of pro- and anti-slavery argument and an analysis of Civil War causation.

Essig, James D. *The Bonds of Wickedness: American Evangelicals against Slavery*. Philadelphia: Temple University Press, 1982. A nondenominational approach to the study of the reasons for the rise and decline of evangelical interest in abolition during and immediately after the Revolution.

Etcheson, Nicole. *Bleeding Kansas: Contested Liberty in the Civil War Era*. Lawrence: University Press of Kansas, 2004. A detailed look at events in Kansas related to the Kansas-Nebraska Act; gives special emphasis to the response of pro- and anti-slavery whites to various developments in the territory.

Filler, Louis. *The Crusade against Slavery, 1830–1860*. 1960. Reprint, New York: Harper Torchbooks, 1963. Views William Lloyd Garrison and the other abolitionists as crusaders for liberty as it relates abolitionism to the broader reform movements of the antebellum years.

Finkelman, Paul E. *Defending Slavery: Proslavery Thought in the Old South— A Brief History with Documents*. Boston: Bedford/St.Martin's, 2003. Part one provides a brief overview of slavery's North American history and a useful review of pro-slavery arguments during the antebellum decades. Part two provides seventeen primary documents dating from 1787 to 1866.

———. *An Imperfect Union: Slavery, Federalism, and Comity*. Chapel Hill: University of North Carolina Press, 1981. Demonstrates how Southerners and Northerners viewed the transportation of slaves into northern states from a constitutional perspective.

———. *Slavery and the Founders: Race and Liberty in the Age of Jefferson*. 2d ed. London: M. E. Sharpe, 2001. Looks at views of slavery from the 1780s through the first years of the 1800s; argues that "slavery permeated the debates of 1787" (x) and presents the Constitution as a pro-slavery document.

———, ed. *Articles on American Slavery*. Vol. 4, *Slavery, Revolutionary America, and the New Nation*. New York: Garland, 1989. John Hope Franklin, Ira Berlin, Willie Lee Rose, and Paul Finkelman are among the authors of twenty-two essays that look at slavery and anti-slavery in the late 1700s.

————, ed. *Articles on American Slavery*. Vol. 14, *Antislavery*. New York: Garland, 1989. Two dozen articles by such noted historians as David Brion Davis, Merton L. Dillon, James Brewer Stewart, and Bertram Wyatt-Brown dating from 1943 to 1987.

Fladeland, Betty. *James Gillespie Birney: Slaveholder to Abolitionist*. Ithaca, NY: Cornell University Press, 1955. A detailed biography that traces Birney's personal life and path from slave owner to abolitionist presidential candidate.

————. *Men and Brothers: Anglo-American Anti-Slavery Cooperation*. Urbana: University of Illinois Press, 1972. Argues that the American-British antislavery efforts were similar in terms of theories, strategies, and tactics.

Foner, Eric. *Free Soil, Free Labor, Free Men: The Ideology of the Republican Party before the Civil War*. New York: Oxford University Press, 1970. Studies factions of and issues facing the Free Soil Party in its first years of existence; considers slavery and race but also economic issues and northern perceptions of the North and the South.

————. *Tom Paine and Revolutionary America*. New York: Oxford University Press, 1976. A brief but broad overview of Paine's life and beliefs, with occasional references to Paine's views on slavery.

Foner, Philip S. *Blacks in the American Revolution*. Westport, CT: Greenwood, 1976. A useful, brief overview of colonial anti-slavery efforts and steps taken during the Revolution and immediately afterwards; includes three valuable documents in its appendix, including an 1852 speech by Frederick Douglass.

————, comp. and ed. *The Complete Writings of Thomas Paine*. 2 vols. New York: Citadel Press, 1945. Volume two contains two essays on American slavery, published in March and October 1775, as well as the preamble to a Pennsylvania law passed in March 1780.

Fredrickson, George M. *The Arrogance of Race: Historical Perspectives on Slavery, Racism, and Social Inequality*. Middletown, CT: Wesleyan University Press, 1988. Seventeen essays reveal how Americans thought about race in the nineteenth-century United States; chapter three focuses on William Lloyd Garrison, Frederick Douglass, and Lydia Maria Child.

————. *The Black Image in the White Mind: The Debate on Afro-American Character and Destiny, 1817–1914*. New York: Harper and Row, 1971. Fredrickson looks at images of race in the South and the North and how they affected each region's attitudes toward and treatment of blacks and each other.

————, ed. *William Lloyd Garrison*. Englewood Cliffs, NJ: Prentice-Hall, 1968. Includes twelve documents and speeches written by Garrison, a collection of commentaries by his contemporaries, and a sampling of historians' analysis of the abolitionist, the latter covering 1873 to 1965.

Friedman, Lawrence J. *Gregarious Saints: Self and Community in American Abo-litionism, 1830–1870.* New York: Cambridge University Press, 1982. Presents abolitionists as evangelical missionaries who represented and reflected northern middle-class benevolent reform values.

Gara, Larry. *Liberty Line: The Legend of the Underground Railroad.* Lexington: University of Kentucky Press, 1961. Looks at the origins of the Underground Railroad legend and compares it with historical facts; emphasizes the railroad's importance as abolitionist propaganda and the legend's growth after the Civil War.

Gerteis, Louis S. *Morality & Utility in American Antislavery Reform.* Chapel Hill: University of North Carolina Press, 1987. Considers the role of the middle class and of utilitarianism on the formation of abolitionist goals.

Gienapp, William. *The Origins of the Republican Party, 1852–1856.* New York: Oxford University Press, 1987. A study of the party's creation and the reasons for its rapid success; focuses on voting behavior in nine states and considers national, state, and local issues.

Goodman, Paul. *Of One Blood: Abolitionism and the Origins of Racial Equality.* Berkeley: University of California Press, 1998. A thoughtful and insightful blending of religious history, the rise of the market revolution, abolitionist thought, and the influence of black Americans that portrays the antebellum abolitionists as true racial egalitarians.

Griffith, Cyril E. *African Dream: Martin R. Delany and the Emergence of Pan-African Thought.* University Park: Pennsylvania State University Press, 1975. Although focusing on Delany's interests in Africa, this book covers his childhood in Virginia and his antebellum career as an abolitionist.

Grimsted, David. *American Mobbing, 1828–1865: Toward Civil War.* New York: Oxford University Press, 1998. A thorough and thoughtful review of antebellum violence in the North and South with particular emphasis on rioting related to abolitionism and to the status of blacks.

Hamilton, Holman. *Prologue to Conflict: The Crisis and Compromise of 1850.* [Lexington]: University of Kentucky Press, 1964. Provides a useful review of the issues at the heart of the Compromise and at the response in the South and North to each part of the multifaceted agreement.

Hamm, Thomas D. *The Quakers in America.* New York: Columbia University Press, 2003. Bolstered by short biographies, a chronology, and a glossary, this brief review of contemporary American Quakerism begins with a look at Quaker organization and beliefs and developments prior to the 1900s.

Hansen, Debra Gold. *Strained Sisterhood: Gender and Class in the Boston Female Anti-Slavery Society.* Amherst: University of Massachusetts Press, 1993. Analyzes the brief life of an organization that opposed slavery, was wracked by factionalism, and that did not support inclusion of the "woman question" (7) in abolitionism.

Harlow, Ralph Volney. *Gerrit Smith: Philanthropist and Reformer*. New York: Henry Holt, 1939. Seeks to resurrect interest in and acclaim for Smith as "an impulsive idealist" (218), a wide-ranging reformer, and a major financial contributor, orator, and propagandist for political abolitionism and nonviolent emancipation.

Harmer, Harry. *The Longman Companion to Slavery, Emancipation and Civil Rights*. Harlow, England: Pearson Education, 2001. A wide-ranging assortment of chronologies, lists, biographies, and maps, and bibliography and glossary that cover slavery, emancipation, and postemancipation struggles in the English, Spanish, and French-speaking worlds.

Harrold, Stanley. *The Abolitionists and the South, 1831–1861*. Lexington: University Press of Kentucky, 1995. Challenges the traditional view of abolitionism as abandoning the South by the late 1830s and as of limited importance in influencing sectional conflict.

———. *American Abolitionists*. Harlow, England: Longman, 2001. Follows abolitionism from the Quakers to the Civil War; provides a short section of documents, as well as a chronology, glossary, brief biographies, and a lengthy bibliography.

Hawkins, Hugh, ed. *The Abolitionists: Immediatism and the Question of Means*. Boston: D. C. Heath, 1964. A mix of primary and secondary writings covering the 1830s–1860s. Emphasis is on the differences among the abolitionists and historians' efforts to define and understand their movement.

Hersh, Blanche Glassman. *The Slavery of Sex: Feminist-Abolitionists in America*. Urbana: University of Illinois Press, 1978. Seeks to show the relationship between abolitionism and the early women's rights movement and to define what made some abolitionist women feminists.

Higginbotham, A. Leon, Jr. *In the Matter of Color: Race & the American Legal Process: The Colonial Period*. Oxford: Oxford University Press, 1980. A lengthy study of the legal status of blacks in six colonies and the *Somerset* case.

Hine, Darlene Clark, William C. Hine, and Stanley Harrold. *The African-American Odyssey*. 2 vols. 2d ed. Upper Saddle River, NJ: Prentice Hall, 2003. A thorough survey of African American history through Reconstruction with useful maps, charts, study questions, and bibliographies.

Hinks, Peter P., ed. *David Walker's Appeal to the Coloured Citizens of the World*. University Park: Pennsylvania State University Press, 2000. Sets up the *Appeal* with a valuable fifty-page introduction to Walker, his world, and the *Appeal*; also provides twenty pages of insightful explanatory notes.

Holt, Michael F. *The Political Crisis of the 1850s*. New York: John Wiley & Sons, 1978. Emphasizes the importance of politics in controlling sectional differences during the antebellum years and in increasing the nation's inability to handle the differences; gives fleeting attention to abolitionism.

Holt, Thomas C., and Elsa Barkley Brown, eds. *Major Problems in African-American History.* Vol. 1, *From Slavery to Freedom, 1619–1877.* Boston: Houghton Mifflin, 2000. A collection of scholarly articles and primary documents. Most of the book's ten chapters deal in some way with slave resistance.

Horton, James Oliver, and Lois E. Horton. *In Hope of Liberty: Culture, Community, and Protest among Northern Free Blacks, 1700–1860.* New York: Oxford University Press, 1997. Reviews how black Northerners formed social, political, economic, and religious institutions and how the black community was the foundation for activism against slavery and discrimination.

Huggins, Nathan Irvin. *Slave and Citizen: The Life of Frederick Douglass.* Edited by Oscar Handlin. Boston: Little, Brown, 1980. Follows Douglass from childhood as a slave to adulthood as a famed abolitionist speaker to postemancipation efforts for leadership, direction, and personal happiness.

Hume, John F. *The Abolitionists, Together with Personal Memories of the Struggle for Human Rights, 1830–1864.* 1905. Reprint, New York: Negro Universities Press, 1969. Argues that the abolitionists were the key ingredient in the Republican Party and in the demise of slavery; focuses on how "they alone and single-handed fought the opening battles of a great war" (19).

Hunt, Alfred N. *Haiti's Influence on Antebellum America: Slumbering Volcano in the Caribbean.* Baton Rouge: Louisiana State University Press, 1988. A unique study of white and black America's reactions to the slave uprising on St. Dominigue and the resulting black republic of Haiti.

Jacobs, Donald M., ed. *Courage and Conscience: Black and White Abolitionists in Boston.* Bloomington: University of Indiana Press, 1993. Looks at the role of Boston and the city's black and white abolitionists, including David Walker and William Lloyd Garrison, through ten essays written by such respected historians as William E. Gienapp, James Brewer Stewart, and James O. Horton.

Jeffrey, Julie Roy. *The Great Silent Army of Abolitionists: Ordinary Women in the Antislavery Movement.* Chapel Hill: University of North Carolina Press, 1998. Uses diaries, newspapers, and letters to examine the contributions of working and middle-class women in the 1830s–1850s; points out the "common convictions [that] undergirded their activities" (4) and emphasizes that women's activities continued in the 1840s–1850s.

Jennings, Judith. *The Business of Abolishing the British Slave Trade, 1783–1807.* London: Frank Cass, 1997. In an attempt to understand the growth of anti-slavery to a majority view in England, this work focuses on four members of the London Abolition Committee, their road to opposition to the slave trade, and their efforts to mobilize public opinion.

Johannsen, Robert W. *Lincoln, the South, and Slavery*. Baton Rouge: Louisiana State University Press, 1991. Thoughtful lectures-turned-essays seeking to counter myths about Lincoln's "evolving" (8) position on slavery before he became president.

Jones, Rufus Matthew. *The Quakers in the American Colonies*. London: Macmillan, 1911. An early attempt to present a study that is neither "from the Quaker point of view" nor "anti-Quaker" (v); devotes one chapter (out of twenty-six) to anti-slavery efforts until the Revolution.

Jordan, Winthrop D. *White over Black: American Attitudes toward the Negro, 1550–1812*. 1968. Reprint, New York: W. W. Norton, 1977. A lengthy, provocative look at racial attitudes affecting Americans; begins in Africa and covers changing views and their effect on both whites and blacks. Published in condensed form as *The White Man's Burden: Historical Origins of Racism in the United States*.

July, Robert W. *A History of the African People*. 5th ed. Prospect Heights, IL: Waveland Press, 1998. A broad-ranging history from the appearance of man in Africa through the 1990s; contact with Europe and the rise of the Atlantic slave trade are put in context of a lengthy and complex history.

Kaminski, John P., ed. *A Necessary Evil? Slavery and the Debate over the Constitution*. Madison, WI: Madison House, 1995. Documents and commentary from 1774 through ratification of the Constitution provide a broad range of opinion on slavery and its place in the country.

Kaplan, Sidney, and Emma Nogrady Kaplan. *The Black Presence in the Era of the American Revolution*. Rev. ed. Amherst: University of Massachusetts Press, 1989. An almost equal mix of narrative and lengthy quotations that include focused and expanded looks at twenty African Americans.

Karcher, Carolyn L., ed. *A Lydia Maria Child Reader*. Durham, NC: Duke University Press, 1997. A useful introduction to Child that provides a wide range of her writing, including eighteen pieces related to slavery, race, and Reconstruction.

Kelley, Robin D. G., and Earl Lewis, eds. *To Make Our World Anew: A History of African Americans*. Oxford: Oxford University Press, 2000. Ten chapters by eleven different historians cover the history of American blacks from 1502 to the end of the twentieth century.

Klein, Martin A. *Historical Dictionary of Slavery and Abolition*. Lanham, MA: Scarecrow Press, 2002. Includes a twelve-page chronology covering events from 3200 B.C.E. to 1993; provides a useful thirty-six-page bibliography.

Kolchin, Peter. *American Slavery, 1619–1877*. New York: Hill and Wang, 1993. A first-rate review of slavery's history; readable, thoughtful, and thorough.

Kraditor, Aileen S. *Means and Ends in American Abolitionism: Garrison and His Critics on Strategy and Tactics, 1834–1850*. 1967. Reprint, New York: Random House, 1969. Attempts to make sense of the division among abolitionists, defining one group as "radical in social philosophy" and another as "reformist" (9).

Kraut, Alan M., ed. *Crusaders and Compromisers: Essays on the Relationship of the Antislavery Struggle to the Antebellum Party System*. Westport, CT: Greenwood, 1983. Nine essays and thirteen tables present the role of abolition and anti-slavery in the major political parties and the Liberty and Free Soil parties, as well as the meaning of the petition campaign and the impact of various social factors.

Lerner, Gerda. *The Grimké Sisters from South Carolina: Rebels against Slavery*. Boston: Houghton Mifflin, 1967. A detailed biography that clarifies the context of Angelina and Sarah Grimké's abolitionism.

Litwack, Leon F. *North of Slavery: The Negro in the Free States*. Chicago: University of Chicago Press, 1961. The classic study of northern blacks, their opportunities and restrictions and their protests; gives particular attention to politics, education, and religion.

Locke, Mary S. *Anti-Slavery in America from the Introduction of African Slaves to the Prohibition of the Slave Trade (1619–1808)*. 1901. Reprint, New York: Johnson Reprint Company, 1968. A brief overview of the development of early temperate anti-slavery efforts with a focus on "the influence of religious and ethical principles and of political theories" (v).

Lowance, Mason, ed. *Against Slavery: An Abolitionist Reader*. New York: Penguin Books, 2000. A collection of dozens of documents covering 1700 to 1860 written by such abolitionists as Theodore Dwight Weld, Frederick Douglass, Sarah Moore Grimké, and Wendell Phillips.

Lumpkin, Katharine DuPre. *The Emancipation of Angelina Grimké*. Chapel Hill: University of North Carolina Press, 1974. Looks at Grimké's movement to abolitionism, her career as an abolitionist lecturer, and her "years of withdrawal" (xi) during the 1840s–1870s.

Mabee, Carlton. *Black Freedom: The Nonviolent Abolitionists from 1830 through the Civil War*. London: Macmillan, 1970. Covers a wide variety of nonviolent methods used by Garrisonians, Tappanites, and Quakers; traces shifts in thinking and strategy to include acceptance of some violence and even war.

MacLeod, Duncan J. *Slavery, Race, and the American Revolution*. New York: Cambridge University Press, 1974. Emphasizes the racial prejudices that existed before, and grew even stronger, after the revolution thus assuring that the revolution "promised more than it achieved" (184).

Marietta, Jack D. *The Reformation of American Quakerism, 1748–1783.* Philadelphia: University of Pennsylvania Press, 1984. Explains changes in the Quakers' religion that limited their involvement in late colonial society and government; includes the Quakers' movement against slavery.

Martineau, Harriet. *The Martyr Age of the United States.* 1839. Reprint, New York: Arno Press and New York Times, 1969. A British abolitionist's positive views of American abolitionism with comments about most important personalities.

Matthews, Donald G. *Slavery and Methodism: A Chapter in American Morality, 1780–1945.* Princeton, NJ: Princeton University Press, 1965. Presents the Methodists' views of blacks, slavery, colonization, and abolition while using the Methodist church to study general American attitudes about race and slavery.

Mayer, Henry. *All on Fire: William Lloyd Garrison and the Abolition of Slavery.* New York: St. Martin's Press, 1999. A lengthy revisionist study that sees Garrison as one of the most influential and courageous figures of the nineteenth century.

McInerney, Daniel J. *The Fortunate Heirs of Freedom: Abolition & Republican Thought.* Lincoln: University of Nebraska Press, 1994. Links the abolitionists to the ideals of the Revolution and the republic which it created.

McKitrick, Eric L., ed. *Slavery Defended: The Views of the Old South.* Englewood Cliffs, NJ: Prentice-Hall, 1963. Provides the words of John C. Calhoun, Edmund Ruffin, Edward A. Pollard and a dozen other southern supporters of slavery.

McKivigan, John R. *The War against Proslavery Religion: Abolitionism and the Northern Churches, 1830–1865.* Ithaca, NY: Cornell University Press, 1984. A readable and thorough analysis of the generally unsuccessful efforts of abolitionists to convert churches to anti-slavery positions.

McKivigan, John R., and Mitchell Snay, eds. *Religion and the Antebellum Debate over Slavery.* Athens: University of Georgia Press, 1998. Twelve essays probe the link between religion and slavery—and anti-slavery—in both the North and the South, covering the impact of each on the other.

McPherson, James M. *The Struggle for Equality: Abolitionists and the Negro in the Civil War and Reconstruction.* 1964. Reprint, Princeton, NJ: Princeton University Press, 1992. Focuses on both abolitionists and abolitionist political leaders as it explains differences among groups and individuals from 1860 to 1870.

Melish, Joane Pope. *Disowning Slavery: Gradual Emancipation and "Race" in New England, 1778–1860.* Ithaca, NY: Cornell University Press, 1998. Compares images of New England as a land of hope and freedom with the realities of the region's anti-black views.

Mellon, Matthew T. *Early American Views on Negro Slavery: From the Letters and Papers of the Founders of the Republic.* Boston: Meador Publishing,

1934. Essays present the views of Benjamin Franklin, George Washington, John Adams, Thomas Jefferson, and James Madison, often in their own words.

Meltzer, Milton. *Slavery: A World History*. Updated ed. New York: Da Capo Press, 1993. Combines the original volumes on slavery in the ancient and medieval worlds and on slavery in the 1500s–1900s. Little focus on anti-slavery thinking and actions, but places them in context.

Miller, Floyd J. *The Search for Black Nationality: Black Colonization and Emigration, 1778–1863*. Urbana: University of Illinois Press, 1975. Looks at black support of colonization ideas and schemes before 1830 and during the 1850s–1860s; gives particular emphasis to Martin R. Delany and to efforts in Africa and Haiti.

———. *The Wolf by the Ears: Thomas Jefferson and Slavery*. 1977. Reprint, Charlottesville: University Press of Virginia, 1991. Follows American views of blacks and slavery from the Declaration of Independence to the Missouri Compromise by presenting Jefferson's words and actions regarding both topics.

Miller, William Lee. *Arguing about Slavery: The Great Battle in the United States Congress*. New York: Vintage, 1995. Looks at the abolitionists' petition campaigns and the efforts to "gag" them in Congress; focuses on John Quincy Adams's efforts to end the gag.

Mintz, Steven. *Moralists and Modernizers: America's Pre–Civil War Reformers*. Baltimore: Johns Hopkins University Press, 1995. An overview that argues that antebellum reformers were both moral critics and cultural modernizers; chapter five provides a useful, brief overview of abolitionism.

Montesquieu. *The Spirit of the Laws*. 2 vols. Littleton, CO: Fred B. Rothman, 1991. Includes a biography and analysis of Montesquieu's ideas; writings in volume one cover slavery.

Nash, Gary B. *Forging Freedom: The Formation of Philadelphia's Black Community, 1720–1840*. Cambridge, MA: Harvard University Press, 1988. Skillfully and readably traces the development of a varied black community and the rise of white racism to violence against blacks in the 1830s.

———. *Race and Revolution*. Madison, WI: Madison House, 1990. Three chapters (originally lectures) and three sections of documents help describe the important place of race in the thinking of Americans during the revolutionary period.

Nash, Gary B., and Jean R. Soderlund. *Freedom by Degrees: Emancipation in Pennsylvania and Its Aftermath*. New York: Oxford University Press, 1991. Looks at "the tug of war" (xiv) between slavery and freedom and between humanitarianism and profits; shows the economic interests of abolition and the continuation of racism after freedom.

Nelson, Truman, ed. *Documents of Upheaval: Selections from William Lloyd Garrison's* The Liberator, *1831–1865*. New York: Hill and Wang, 1966. Four dozen excerpts from the *Liberator* discuss such topics as the death of Elijah P. Lovejoy, the annexation of Texas, *Uncle Tom's Cabin*, and John Brown.

Novak, Peter J. *The People's Welfare: Law and Regulation in Nineteenth-Century America*. Chapel Hill: University of North Carolina Press, 1996. Argues that laissez-faire did not dominate American thinking in the 1800s; provides numerous examples of state and local regulation.

Nye, Russel B. *William Lloyd Garrison and the Humanitarian Reformers*. Boston: Little, Brown, 1955. Sees Garrison as "a true revolutionary individualist" (201) who was led by his religious and moral values to oppose slavery. Makes clear why Garrison was both loved and hated and respected.

Oates, Stephen B. *The Fires of Jubilee: Nat Turner's Fierce Rebellion*. New York: Harper & Row, 1975. Dramatically tells the story of Nat Turner's bloody uprising and white response to it.

———. *To Purge This Land with Blood: A Biography of John Brown*. Amherst: University of Massachusetts Press, 1984. While trying to be "emphatic, not worship or derogatory" (viii), Oates presents Brown as "a revolutionary" (viii) and focuses on his religious views and his hatred of slavery.

Osborne, William S. *Lydia Maria Child*. Boston: Twayne, 1980. A focused study of five of Child's most famous books and some of her shorter writings as works of literature; presents her as an important, albeit minor, writer.

Painter, Nell Irvin. *Sojourner Truth: A Life, A Symbol*. New York: W. W. Norton, 1996. A look at the "Strong Black Woman" (4) who was unique in her ability to go from slavery to a career as a public speaker against racism and sexism.

Pease, Jane H., and William H. Pease. *They Who Would Be Free: Blacks' Search for Freedom, 1830–1861*. New York: Athenaeum, 1974. Studies northern blacks who were part of the abolitionist movement and who worked outside of it against slavery; includes the convention movement and responses to the changing northern view of slavery and "Slave Power."

———, eds. *The Antislavery Argument*. Indianapolis: Bobbs-Merrill, 1965. Almost 500 pages of documents dating from the 1700s to 1865; covers colonization, immediatism, religious and economic arguments, civil liberties, the Constitution, political action, and the Civil War.

Perry, Lewis. *Radical Abolitionism: Anarchy and the Government of God in Antislavery Thought*. Ithaca, NY: Cornell University Press, 1973. Presents abolitionists' views of authority by looking at the position of radicals on nonresistance, come-outerism, pacifism, race, and violence.

Perry, Lewis, and Michael Fellman, eds. *Antislavery Reconsidered: New Perspectives on the Abolitionists*. Baton Rouge: Louisiana State University Press, 1979. Fourteen essays by such noted historians as Leonard

Richards, William Wiecek, and Bertram Wyatt-Brown cover such topics as religion, politics, feminism, and labor.

Phillips, William D., Jr. *Slavery from Roman Times to the Early Transatlantic Trade*. Minneapolis: University of Minnesota Press, 1985. Reviews the history to 1650 in the Christian and Muslim worlds; provides maps.

The Poetical Works of John Greenleaf Whittier. 4 vols. Boston: Houghton, Mifflin, 1891. Volume three contains poems on slavery and on labor and reform; approximately a hundred poems deal with all aspects of slavery, including such people as William Lloyd Garrison, John Brown, and William Henry Seward.

Postma, Johannes. *The Atlantic Slave Trade*. Westport, CT: Greenwood, 2003. Follows the diaspora from the fifteenth century through the late nineteenth century; provides chronology, biographical sketches, documents, and annotated bibliography.

Quarles, Benjamin. *Allies for Freedom: Blacks and John Brown*. New York: Oxford University Press, 1970. Quarles presents Brown as a symbol to blacks and attributes much of the Brown legend to blacks; emphasizes 1858–1859 but follows the Brown legend after Harpers Ferry.

———. *Black Abolitionists*. 1969. Reprint, New York: Oxford University Press, 1977. Asserts the important role of blacks in the abolition movement; also looks at their dealings with whites and their treatment by white abolitionists.

———. *The Negro in the American Revolution*. Chapel Hill: University of North Carolina Press, 1961. A classic study of the wide-ranging role of blacks during the revolution, including British and rebel soldier, petitioner for freedom, cook, and spy.

———, ed. *Blacks on John Brown*. Urbana: University of Illinois Press, 1972. Documents offer positive views from blacks ranging from Frederick Douglass to Malcolm X; breaks down views into 1858–1861, 1870–1925, and 1925–1972.

———, ed. *Narrative of the Life of Frederick Douglass: An American Slave, Written by Himself*. Cambridge, MA: Belknap Press of Harvard University Press, 1960. Douglass powerfully presents his journey from privileged slave to almost defeated slave to free man.

Rakove, Jack N. *James Madison: The Creation of the American Republic*. 2d ed. New York: Longman, 2002. A brief, thoughtful biography that focuses on the core principles and beliefs that guided Madison.

Ratnor, Lorman. *Powder Keg: Northern Opposition to the Antislavery Movement, 1831–1840*. New York: Basic Books, 1968. A brief but telling study of anti-abolitionism in New England and the Middle Atlantic states. Sees racism, concerns for order, and fear of race war as having deep roots.

Rayback, Joseph G. *Free Soil: The Election of 1848*. Lexington: University Press of Kentucky, 1970. Gives particular attention to the Wilmot Proviso, the principle of Free Soil, and the role of anti-slavery in the Democrat, Whig, and Liberty parties prior to the formation of the Free Soil Party.

Richards, Leonard L. *"Gentlemen of Property and Standing": Anti-Abolitionist Mobs in Jacksonian America*. New York: Oxford University Press, 1970. A brief analysis of the makeup and motivation of mobs from 1812 to 1849 emphasizing the period of "increased hysteria, violence, and turbulence" (6) in the mid-1830s.

———. *The Slave Power: The Free North and Southern Domination, 1780–1860*. Baton Rouge: Louisiana State University Press, 2000. Rejuvenates the argument that the power of the slave-owning South in the national government sparked Northerners' fears.

Ripley, Peter, et al., eds. *The Black Abolitionist Papers*. 5 vols. Chapel Hill: University of North Carolina Press, 1985–1992. One volume each is devoted to the British Isles and Canada; three focus on the United States. Each volume begins with a useful and lengthy historical introduction.

Robertson, Stacey M. *Parker Pillsbury: Radical Abolitionist, Male Feminist*. Ithaca, NY: Cornell University Press, 2000. The only full-book biography of the anti-authoritarian, anti-clerical, confrontational field lecturer and strategist; presents Pillsbury as "a disruptive eccentric" and "a sensitive visionary" (2).

Robinson, Donald L. *Slavery in the Structure of American Politics, 1765–1820*. New York: Harcourt Brace Jovanovich, 1971. In order to explain the role of slavery in the revolutionary and early national periods, Robinson provides a broad look at such topics as the Articles of Confederation, demography, and foreign trade.

Rozwenc, Edwin C., ed. *The Compromise of 1850*. Boston: D. C. Heath, 1957. Four primary documents and seven essays by historians reveal the controversial issues of the compromise.

Ruchames, Louis, ed. *Racial Thought in America*. Vol. 1, *From the Puritans to Abraham Lincoln: A Documentary History*. Amherst: University of Massachusetts Press, 1969. Presents a wide variety of writings by abolitionists, political leaders, anthropologists, and Southerners.

Schor, Joel. *Henry Highland Garnet: A Voice of Black Radicalism in the Nineteenth Century*. Westport, CT: Greenwood, 1977. A look at the diversity among black abolitionists and the provocative and leadership role played by Garnet, particularly from 1840 to 1865.

Schroeder, John H. *Mr. Polk's War: American Opposition and Dissent, 1846–1848*. Madison, WI: Madison House, 1971. A short study of the wide-ranging opposition to the Mexican War by Whigs and Democrats, abolitionists, and clergy.

Schweninger, Loren, ed. The _Southern Debate over Slavery_. Vol. 1, _Petitions to Southern Legislatures, 1778–1864_. Urbana: University of Illinois Press, 2001– . Includes 160 petitions from southern whites and blacks involving such topics as the sale of slaves, sexual exploitation, education of slaves, behavior of free blacks, inheritance, and black legal rights.

Sears, Lorenzo. _Wendell Phillips: Orator and Agitator_. New York: Doubleday, Page, 1909. A political biography that relies extensively on Phillips's speeches and that ends with an analysis of Phillips's oratory.

Serio, Anne Marie. _Political Cartoons in the 1848 Election Campaign_. Washington, DC: Smithsonian Institution Press, 1972. A brief (nineteen pages) review of the 1848 election battle between the Whigs, Democrats, and Free Soil parties using nine political cartoons to illustrate campaign issues.

Sewell, Richard H. _Ballots for Freedom: Antislavery Politics in the United States, 1837–1860_. New York: Oxford University Press, 1976. A detailed study of the Liberty, Free Soil, and Republican parties and the impact of anti-slavery on Democrats and Whigs; covers involvement of radical abolitionism and anti-slavery views on a wide range.

———. _A House Divided: Sectionalism and the Civil War, 1848–1865_. Baltimore: Johns Hopkins University Press, 1988. A synthesis of economic, political, and social issues that finds slavery at the center of sectional disputes.

Sherwin, Oscar. _Prophet of Liberty: The Life and Times of Wendell Phillips_. New York: Bookman Associates, 1958. A dramatic and lengthy telling of Phillips's life as an abolitionist and reformer using numerous excerpts from his speeches.

Sidbury, James. _Ploughshares into Swords: Race, Rebellion, and Identity in Gabriel's Virginia_. New York: Cambridge University Press, 1998. A study of Gabriel and Richmond, Virginia, and the rebellion's place in memory and literature.

Simms, Henry H. _Emotion at High Tide: Abolition as a Controversial Factor, 1830–1845_. Baltimore: n.p., 1960. Presents what is now a fairly standard review of abolitionist views, arguments, and activities during abolitionism's first fifteen years.

Sklar, Kathryn Kish. _Women's Rights Emerges within the Antislavery Movement, 1830–1870: A Brief History with Documents_. Boston: Bedford/St. Martin's, 2000. Uses Angelina and Sarah Grimké to understand the changes in women's roles, beliefs, and behavior during the antebellum period.

Soderlund, Jean R. _Quakers & Slavery: A Divided Spirit_. Princeton, NJ: Princeton University Press, 1985. Focuses on anti-slavery's development within the Philadelphia Yearly Meeting and in local monthly meetings throughout the 1700s.

Sorin, Gerald. _Abolitionism: A New Perspective_. New York: Praeger, 1972. Presents the abolitionists as sincere, idealistic reformers who sought both abolition and racial equality; looks at their evolution and their similarities and differences.

———. *The New York Abolitionists: A Case Study of Political Radicalism*. Westport, CT: Greenwood, 1971. In focusing on fifteen New York abolitionists including Gerrit Smith, James G. Birney, and Lewis Tappan, Sorin concludes that the New Yorkers were not abolitionists because of personal frustrations and insecurities.

Stanley, Amy Dru. *From Bondage to Contract: Wage Labor, Marriage, and the Market in the Age of Emancipation*. Cambridge: Cambridge University Press, 1998. A challenging and thought-provoking look at the meaning of freedom and the nineteenth-century American's "world view" (x) regarding self-ownership and contract.

Staudenraus, P. J. *The African Colonization Movement, 1816–1865*. New York: Columbia University Press, 1961. Presents the American Colonization Society as "a large benevolent movement" (11) led by "sedate, honorable, judicious gentlemen" (28) who were not seeking to end slavery.

Stauffer, John. *The Black Hearts of Men: Radical Abolitionists and the Transformation of Race*. Cambridge, MA: Harvard University Press, 2002. This look at the relationship of Frederick Douglass, James McCune Smith, John Brown, and Gerrit Smith shows the interactions and divisions within abolitionism.

Sterling, Dorothy. *Ahead of Her Times: Abby Kelley and the Politics of Antislavery*. New York: Norton, 1992. Presents Kelly as a dedicated and effective abolitionist speaker, a skillful organizer, a model for women, and as "political to her fingertips" (2).

Stewart, James B. *Holy Warriors: The Abolitionists and American Slavery*. New York: Hill and Wang, 1976. An early synthesis of the revisionist interpretation of the abolitionists that notes both flaws and contributions.

———. *Wendell Phillips, Liberty's Hero*. Baton Rouge: Louisiana State University Press, 1986. A recounting of Phillips's rise to abolitionist fame and influence that relies heavily on the reformer/politician's speeches and letters.

Strong, Douglas M. *Perfectionist Politics: Abolitionism and the Religious Tensions of American Democracy*. Syracuse, NY: Syracuse University Press, 1999. A complicated but intriguing look at the neglected area of "common men and women" (7) who were guided into abolitionism and politics by evangelical perfectionism, the doctrine of entire sanctification, and the quest for holiness.

Sumner, Charles. *The Works of Charles Sumner*. 15 vols. Boston: Lee and Shepard, 1875. Text of the Massachusetts senator's speeches, most in opposition to slavery and in support of black rights.

Thomas, Benjamin P. *Theodore Weld: Crusader for Freedom*. New Brunswick, NJ: Rutgers University Press, 1950. The first published biography of

Weld and an early revisionist look at the abolitionists as dedicated moral crusaders.

Thomas, John L. *The Liberator, William Lloyd Garrison: A Biography*. Boston: Little, Brown, 1963. Explains Garrison as a product of an "endless fascination with upheaval" and a "hatred of institutions" (327).

———, ed. *Slavery Attacked: The Abolitionist Crusade*. Englewood Cliffs, NJ: Prentice-Hall, 1965. Thirty-four documents covering 1830 to 1865, the years which Thomas refers to as "the abolitionist crusade." Begins with a valuable five-page overview.

Thomas Jefferson: Writings. New York: Library Classics of the United States, 1984. In addition to Jefferson's public papers, addresses, and messages, includes almost 800 pages of letters to both the famous and the unknown.

Thompson, C. Bradley, ed. *Antislavery Political Writings, 1833–1860: A Reader*. Armonk, NY: M. E. Sharpe, 2003. Twenty documents covering goals, process, the Constitution, fugitive slaves, the Liberty and Free Soil parties, and civil war.

Thompson, Vincent Bakpetu. *The Making of the African Diaspora in the Americas, 1441–1900*. New York: Longman, 1987. Part three looks at African resistance to slavery in the Americas, with a focus on the Haitian revolution of 1791–1801; chapter twelve looks at anti-slavery efforts throughout the Americas.

Tise, Larry E. *Proslavery: A History of the Defense of Slavery in America, 1701–1840*. Athens: University of Georgia Press, 1987. A lengthy look at proslavery thinking and writing in both the North and the South; part one provides an overview while part two focuses on the period from the Revolution to the 1840s.

Trotter, Joe William, Jr. *The African American Experience*. 2 vols. Boston: Houghton Mifflin, 2001. A brief basic overview of African American history. Chapter nine in volume one is devoted to abolitionists, black and white.

Turley, David. *The Culture of English Antislavery, 1780–1860*. London: Routledge, 1991. Focuses on anti-slavery as "a cultural response" (2) as England's abolitionists sought public support and Parliamentary action; emphasizes the role of religion, evangelicalism in particular, and international economic factors.

Venet, Wendy Hammond. *Neither Ballots Nor Bullets: Women Abolitionists and Emancipation during the Civil War*. Charlottesville: University of Virginia Press, 1991. Looks at individual women's efforts and at the women who founded the Women's National Loyal League which helped petition against slavery.

Vorenberg, Michael. *Final Freedom: The Civil War, the Abolition of Slavery, and the Thirteenth Amendment*. Cambridge: Cambridge University Press,

2001. A study of 1863–1865 in terms of the origins of the emancipation amendment in ideas about emancipation, political transformations, and the Constitution; asserts that the amendment "*never* had a single, fixed meaning" (237).

Wade, Richard C. *Slavery in the Cities: The South, 1820–1860*. New York: Oxford University Press, 1964. A thorough but readable look at the life for slaves who lived and worked in the urban South.

Walters, Ronald G. *American Reformers, 1815–1860*. New York: Hill and Wang, 1978. A positive review of antebellum reformers as "believ[ing] in harmony and human unity" (19) who sought moral behavior and a sinless society; looks at a wide variety of reforms from abolitionism to phrenology.

———. *The Antislavery Appeal: American Abolitionism after 1830*. Baltimore: Johns Hopkins University Press, 1976. A short but wide-ranging study of "constants" (xiii) of abolitionism, including religion, morality, sex, family, economic issues, and the Union.

Walvin, James. *Black Ivory: A History of British Slavery*. Washington, DC: Howard University Press, 1994. A sweeping history that provides a comparative overview of British slavery and the slave trade in the British empire from the mid-1600s to the early 1800s.

Whitridge, Arnold. *No Compromise! The Story of the Fanatics Who Paved the Way to the Civil War*. New York: Farrar, Straus and Cudahy, 1960. While seeing the abolitionists as sincere and dedicated, Whitridge presents them and southern extremists as the causes of an avoidable civil war; their refusal to compromise led to slavery's bloody end but did not improve race relations.

Wiecek, William M. *The Sources of Antislavery Constitutionalism in America, 1760–1848*. Ithaca, NY: Cornell University Press, 1977. Focuses on the influence of the "federal consensus" (16) and the *Somerset* case on immediate abolitionists.

Wigham, Eliza. *The Anti-Slavery Cause in America and Its Martyrs*. London: A. W. Bennett, 1863. An abolitionist publication that surveys the history of abolitionism and the contributions of its major advocates, including William Lloyd Garrison, James G. Birney, Elijah Lovejoy, and John Brown.

Wilson, Carol. *Freedom at Risk: The Kidnapping of Free Blacks in America, 1780–1865*. Lexington: University of Kentucky Press, 1995. Reviews different types of kidnapping, including efforts carried out under cover of the Fugitive Slave Act of 1850.

Worrall, Arthur J. *Quakers in the Colonial Northeast*. Hanover, NH: University Press of New England, 1980. Covers 1656 to 1790. Most of chapter nine, "Philanthropy," is devoted to anti-slavery efforts, concisely reviewing Quaker efforts in the 1600s and 1700s.

Annotated Bibliography

Wright, Donald R. *African Americans in the Early Republic, 1789–1831*. Arlington Heights, IL: Harlan Davidson, 1993. Briefly reviews slavery, colonization, free blacks in the North and South, and the plans of Gabriel, Denmark Vesey, and Nat Turner.

Wyatt-Brown, Bertram. *Lewis Tappan and the Evangelical War against Slavery*. Cleveland, OH: Press of Case Western Reserve University, 1969. A thoughtful biography of one of the antebellum period's leading abolitionists, as well as a look at his brother Arthur and at issues confronting anti-slavery forces.

————. *Yankee Saints and Southern Sinners*. Baton Rouge: Louisiana State University Press, 1985. Analyses the differences between the North and the South; gives significant attention to Arthur and Lewis Tappan and to John Brown.

Yee, Shirley J. *Black Women Abolitionists: A Study in Activism, 1828–1860*. Knoxville: University of Tennessee Press, 1992. Studies the influence of race, sex, and class on the activities of free black activist women; looks at the impact of slavery, racist stereotypes, and of the Cult of True Womanhood.

Yellin, Jean Fagan. *Women and Sisters: The Antislavery Feminists and American Culture*. New Haven, CT: Yale University Press, 1990. Argues that "antislavery feminists created an independent and original culture" (xvii); focuses on Angelina Grimké, Lydia Maria Child, Sojourner Truth, and Harriet Jacobs.

Yellin, Jean Fagan, and John C. Van Horn, eds. *The Abolitionist Sisterhood: Women's Political Cultures in Antebellum America*. Ithaca, NY: Cornell University Press, 1994. Fifteen essays look at how both black and white women organized against slavery, how black female abolitionists fit into the reform movement of the antebellum period, and how women went about opposing slavery.

Zilversmit, Arthur. *The First Emancipation: The Abolition of Slavery in the North*. Chicago: University of Chicago Press, [1967]. Gives prominence to the role of Quakers in northern abolition and describes the road to abolition in each northern state.

Web Sources

http://docsouth.unc.edu/nell/nell.html
"The Colored Patriots of the American Revolution" provides narratives and pictures.

http://www.freedomcenter.org
Provides timeline, information on people, and resources related to the Underground Railroad.

http://jefferson.village.virginia.edu/utc/abolitn/abhp.html
Includes pictures and excerpts from anti-slavery writings.

http://lcweb.loc.gov/exhibits/african/afam002.html
This "African-American Mosaic" covers colonization; others cover abolition (afam005.html), prominent abolitionists (afam006.html), and conflict of abolition and slavery (afam007.html).

http://memory.loc.gov/ammem
Includes "African-American Perspectives," pamphlets from the Daniel A.P. Murray Collection, 1818–1907, and "From Slavery to Freedom," the African-American Pamphlet Collection, 1824–1909.

http://www.ohiohistorycentral.org/ohc/history/ocoa/eve/a.shtml
"Abolitionism" covers events, documents, and people with narratives and pictures.

http://www.pbs.org/wgbh/aia
"Africans in America: America's Journey through Slavery" includes pictures, documents, and information on people.

http://www.pbs.org/wgbh/amex/brown
"John Brown's Holy War" provides timeline and maps, as well as a teacher's guide.

http://rmc.library.cornell.edu/abolitionism
"I Will Be Heard!": Abolitionism in America" covers events and people from abolitionism's origins through the Thirteenth Amendment.

http://xroads.virginia.edu/~HYPER
Electronic texts of works by such authors as Harriet Jacobs, Sojourner Truth, and Harriet Beecher Stowe.

INDEX

Abolition of slavery: in Civil War, 103; in District of Columbia, 103; in Great Britain, xix, 43–45; impact of, 111–112; in North, xvii, 23–26; by Quakers, 14, 24; in South, xx, 104–105; in territories, 103; through Thirteenth Amendment, xx, 104–105; in Virginia, xii. *See also individual nations*

Abolitionism: aid from Great Britain, 44–45; black influence on, 59; black organizations, 60; black women's role in, 61–62; among blacks, 58–61, 97–99; blacks' concerns about, 97; blacks' role in, 50, 58–61; Christian base of, 53; in Civil War, 102–104; colonial period, xi, xii; disagreements within, xii–xiii, 69–73, 97–98, 160; and *Dred Scott* case, 98; focus of efforts, 46; general views, xii, 5, 41–42, 45, 55, 147–149, 153–155, 157–158, 162–163; goals, 5, 41, 49, 50–51, 111, 153–155; in Great Britain, 43–44, 117; Hinton Rowan Helper's contributions to,

99, 164; historians' views of, xi–xii, 111, 113; impact of *Somerset v. Stewart*, 20; and John Brown, 100; Lincoln's steps toward, 103, 168; opposition to, 5, 43, 53, 149–150; others' views of, xi–xii, 47–48, 55–57, 149–150, 165–168; and secession, 102; slave trade and, 28–29; sympathetic view of slave owners, 52; Thirteenth Amendment, 104–105; views on benevolent societies, 54; views on blacks, 41, 49–50, 59; views on colonization, 31–32, 45, 146–148; views on Constitution, 27, 55, 70, 72, 79, 98, 152, 154, 162–163; views on contract, 51; views on marriage, 51; views on North, 55, 154, 158–159, 161–162; views on religion, 53–54, 70; views on violence, 45–46, 55, 98, 100–101; views on women, 51, 63, 70, 73; violence against, 45–46, 55–56, 100, 102, 131; women's role in, 61–62. *See also* American Anti-Slavery Society; Garrisonians; *individual abolitionists*; Tappanites

Charleston, South Carolina, xvii, 34, 37, 126–127, 132

Chase, Salmon P., 79, 80, 88–89, 93, 95

Cherokees, 120

Child, David Lee, 120–121

Child, Lydia Maria, 4, 49, 57, 103, 111, 129; biography, 120–121

Christianity, 50, 167; and abolition, 52–54; and anti-slavery in general, 8; and colonial slavery, 3; colonization and, 31, 99; Denmark Vesey's use of, 34; immediate abolition, 45; and northern abolition, 24; pro-slavery arguments using, 38

Churches: criticized by Eliza Whigham, 159–160; criticized by James K. Birney, 58; and free blacks, 59; position of Liberty Party, 78; pressure from Britain, 44; slavery and, 32–33, 75–76, 152; view of abolitionists, 52–54; view of Anthony Benezet, 137–138; view of Benjamin Rush, 140–141; view of colonization, 52. *See also* Christianity; Come-outers; *individual churches*

Churchman, John, 135

Cincinnati, 102, 131

Cincinnati *Philanthropist*, 77

Cincinnati *Republican*, 56

Citizenship, 71, 96, 98, 112, 114

Civil disobedience, 73

Civil liberties, xi, 55, 58, 81, 91, 94, 99, 115, 144–145

Civil rights, 104

Civil Rights Act of 1866, 104

Civil Rights Act of 1875, 112

Civil Rights Cases, 112

Civil Rights Movement, xi, 114–115

Civil War, xiii, xx, 52, 102–104, 113–114, 121, 123, 125, 126, 168–169

Clarion, 124

Clarkson, Thomas, 28

Clay, Henry, 30–31, 80, 90–91, 118, 160

College of New Jersey, 118

Colonization, xi, 30–33, 34, 37, 128–129, 133; abolitionists' views of, 45–46, 146; black opposition to, 31–32, 48, 59; churches' views on, 52; Fugitive Slave Act of 1850, 91–92; Henry Highland Garnet's view of, 124; Hinton Rowan Helper's view of, 99; James K. Birney's support of, 119; Liberty Party's view of, 78; Thomas Jefferson's argument for, 143; Western Republicans' view of, 96; William Lloyd Garrison and, 46, 48, 125

Colored American, xx, 60

Come-outers, 75–76, 79, 97

Common Sense (Paine), 18

Compensated emancipation, xi, 44, 45, 46, 151–152

Compromise of 1850, xix, 90–91, 93, 119–120

Confiscation Acts, 103

Congregational Church, 97

Congress: actions against slavery, 55; in Civil War, 103; in District of Columbia, 55, 71, 95, 159; Free Soil Party's view of, 88; Gag Rule, xix, 57; power in the territories, 28, 83, 98, 144, 159; power over insurrections, 27; power over slavery, 55; power

About the Author

CLAUDINE L. FERRELL is Associate Professor, History and American Studies, at the University of Mary Washington, and is the author of *Reconstruction* (Greenwood, 2003).